Also by Blue Saffire

Calling on Quinn

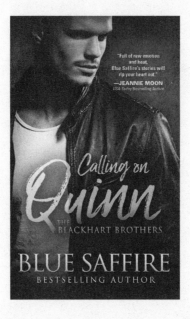

IN
DEEP

BLUE SAFFIRE

Published by Sourcebooks Casablanca, an imprint of Sourcebooks
P.O. Box 4410, Naperville, Illinois 60567-4410
(630) 961-3900
sourcebooks.com

Printed and bound in the United States of America.
SB 10 9 8 7 6 5 4 3 2 1

PROLOGUE

BREATHE

Kevin

I drag a hand through my hair. My stomach feels sour. The room has a stillness that doesn't feel right.

Looking around the basement of my home, none of the gym equipment has been able to lure me into the abyss I require. There's been no escaping my thoughts. Something is off.

I never should have pushed her so hard. Yet, I don't think this is about our fight. My gut tells me something is wrong. No matter how mad Dem gets with me, she still makes sure I know she's okay.

Replaying our fight, I try to see if our words were heated enough to warrant her ignoring my calls and not checking in. I work my jaw. From the beginning, it was clear things would be complicated between us, but we've come so far.

It's the reason I lost my cool this time. I want more. I want her in every way. I want a future.

Thinking back on it now, I feel like shit. It wasn't the time to argue with her. It was an asshole move on my behalf. Now I'm not sure if she hasn't called because of it or if something else is wrong.

"Fuck," I bellow and punch the heavy bag in front of me.

I shove both hands in my hair and throw my head back. I have to make a decision. My instincts are telling me the clock is ticking and I need to make a move.

The PI and ex-detective in me demand I go with my gut. The

sound of paws on the steps draws my attention. Sunny, Dem's pit bull, ambles down the stairs and over to me.

I squat in front of him and scratch behind his ears. Sunny whimpers and looks up at me. I get the feeling he knows something's wrong with his mommy too.

"She's not avoiding me, is she, boy? Mum's in trouble, isn't she?"

Sunny barks as if responding to me. I tug my phone from my pocket and pull up the one person I know will help me see this clearly. We need to act fast and think faster.

"Aye, Kevin. What about ye?" Quinn answers the line with a smile in his voice.

My heart sinks. He's probably proposed to Alicia by now and started the celebration. However, if I'm going to have that same future with the woman I care for, I need his help. My older brother has always been there to fix things when everyone has needed. I need him now.

"Something's not right, Quinn," I say quickly. "She hasn't called. Something's not right."

My stomach turns and tightens as I hear the words out loud. It's like they become true as they leave my lips. I should've called sooner.

"Ach, hold tight. I'm on my way."

I close my eyes as his words sink in. We're going to make this right. I'll find out what's going on, and I'll make it all right.

CHAPTER 1

HOW WE MET

Danita
Two and a half years ago…

"Moralez," one of the beat cops croons, holding up his beer.

I return the gesture. "Norton."

This bar is like a second home for most of these guys. Many avoiding real life, wanting to cling to the thrill of their last collar just a little bit longer. Others don't want to deal with the reality of their home life as a husband or father.

I come here for the secrets. Lips get loose after hours with a few beers in the system. This is where I do most of my real work.

"Good job out there," Norton says with a smile.

Good guy. This is his escape from his cheating wife. He won't divorce her because of their twins, but he's still faithful to her and holds on to hope that they can fix things. Hey, I'm not going to be the one to burst that bubble.

We tell the lies we need to survive, after all.

"Thanks," I murmur.

I wish I could be proud of what I've done today. I used to be able to relish getting the bad guys and doing what's right. Not here. The lines are blurred around this place. Good deeds are undone by those who are supposed to follow the rules but have turned to greed instead.

I look around at all the smiling faces. Some of these guys are as dirty as it gets. All cops, all wearing badges, but not all good guys.

For three years, I've been surrounded by snakes of the worst kind. The trouble is figuring out which ones are the bad guys and which ones are just assholes. It's my job to find the bad guys.

Something that hasn't been as easy as I thought it would be. I miss my family. I miss my real life. Going undercover always poses a risk of being in for longer than you expect, but this has been beyond what I ever expected.

I think I'm losing a piece of myself with each day, but that's what makes me work harder to do my job. After all, I have someone I promised myself I'd make proud. If I can wrap this case up, I can go home and finally lick these old wounds. Or should I say, *when* I get this done, I'm going home and I'm going to hug my family.

"Hey, Moralez." I turn and look up. Detective Harris hovers over me with a beer in his hand. "Nice stuff out there."

"Thanks." I nod, not missing the fact that he's staring down my shirt.

This guy is on my dirty list. Although I don't have him dead to rights yet, I know it's only a matter of time. He has given me this vibe since my first day. I don't trust him, and he's a chauvinistic pig.

"I thought that case was too big for you, but you surprised us all. Pretty and smart."

I turn away from him, ready to dismiss this conversation. If he's not saying something condescending, it's offensive in some other way. Yet he's totally oblivious to it, like the world is his to do as he pleases, and we all need to excuse him for his idiocy.

He doesn't get the clue when I don't respond to him. He continues to stand there breathing down my neck. When I turn back to him, his gaze roams all over me. My skin starts to crawl.

"Did you need something?" I say, hoping this once he'll take the hint.

"Actually, I was about to offer to get you another beer," he says and gives me a smile that I'm guessing he thinks is alluring.

Detective Harris is actually very attractive. That is, if he never opens his mouth to speak. The problem is all his good looks go out the window the moment he does.

There isn't enough beer in the world to make me ignore his arrogance. Those blue eyes and his handsome face aren't enough either. Although I have seen it work on a few others over the last three years.

That cocky grin grows as I look him over. He runs a hand through his thick dark hair. Yup, not doing a thing for me.

"I'm good. Thanks, though."

I turn away to do some more people watching. To my dismay, Detective Harris takes that as a cue to have a seat beside me. I look at the small dance floor with a few dancers on it, plotting my escape.

Thankfully, a few other officers come over and take a seat at my table. I almost laugh at the grunt of annoyance that comes from Detective Harris. He has to know he doesn't have a chance.

Not only because he rubs me all kinds of wrong ways, but I haven't slept with one cop on this force in the three years I've been here. It's not my style. I'm here for a job and I'm focused on getting it done.

I get close enough to these guys as friends, but I draw the line there. It's one of the reasons I stick to hanging out with the married guys who actually respect their marriages. They're also the most talkative because they feel their wives don't get the job or won't take the time to listen.

Nope, I'm not trading ass for secrets or for a way into the good old boys' club. My vibrator does just fine and I have batteries on auto-ship. No messy feelings and no attachments.

"*Oh*, look what the cat dragged in," Stevens, one of our new detectives, croons. "Blackhart. What the fuck are you doing here?"

I've heard that name before. The two detectives who left the force come up a lot. From what I gather, they were the good guys. Too good to stand by and watch the corruption plaguing this precinct.

I've often wondered if they're the reason I'm here. There was a whistleblower who got the attention of the FBI. That's how I got placed here. However, that person was never revealed to me.

All I know is I'm here to connect the dots. No one wanted me to have this assignment in the first place. Some because they didn't think I could pull it off, and others, I'm guessing, because they know if I do, a lot of heads are going to roll.

In the end, I think the fact that everyone doubts me is the reason I'm still here and why I get so little support. I'm forgotten because someone wants this case forgotten. At least, that's what my intuition tells me. It's also why I'm determined as hell to stick this out.

I turn to place a face to the name I've heard whispers about. However, I'm not ready for what I find. My mouth drops open, and I stare as if I've lost all brain function.

With looks like that, this man was never meant to be an officer of the law. He should be on someone's billboard. Fine isn't a strong enough word for this tall drink of water.

I place him at about six four. He's built, but not bulky. However, he's not that lean either. He falls right in between.

He sure as hell fills out the T-shirt and well-worn jeans he has on. The tats peeking from the right short sleeve have me licking my lips. I've never wanted to climb a tree more in my life, and I don't even like redheads. Yet, his neat quiff of red locks brings character to his strong, handsome face.

The smile that comes from his full lips is enough to make me groan. No, seriously. I stifle the sound just barely. When he gets to our table, his green eyes come into view.

They sparkle with humor and life, and yet they have a light of mystery and maybe a little hint of danger. What I don't see is the look of asshole that permeates most of the jerks around here.

That sense of entitlement because of authority doesn't ooze from him. I find that interesting. Male or female, it's a trait most cops have. Especially the dirty ones.

Don't get me wrong. I know plenty in law enforcement who are missing that look, but here in this precinct I've been assigned to, it's something you can't miss. It's that same arrogance that's going to allow me to take this place down.

"I heard you guys are showing off," the guy I'm assuming to be Blackhart says. He tugs Stevens in for a hug. "Congratulations, Detective, I told you it would happen."

"I got lucky. You and Quinn left, and they're scrambling to find a few good guys to replace you two," Stevens says with a big smile.

It's not lost on me that this guy is towering over Stevens as they stand side by side. I'm tickled because I actually have to look up at Stevens. My amusement is cut into by Detective Harris at my side.

He nearly growls, pulling my attention toward him. He glares at Stevens and Blackhart. It's clear he's not a fan.

"Fuck you, Stevens. We have plenty of great detectives without those two pussies," he snarls.

My brows shoot up. Now, Harris is no small guy, but that's some big talk. I turn to look at Blackhart.

All humor and lightness have left his face. However, the dark brooding look he now dons is sexy as hell. I let my gaze roll over him. My nipples tighten against my bra. It might be time for me to leave.

"Orin. I see they still haven't taken out the trash. Ya do know I have no problem breaking that jaw, *again*."

Oh, I like this guy, and where'd that sexy accent come from? I didn't pick that up at first. I think I'm drooling. It's very likely I have drool rolling down my chin.

"Let's go," Harris barks at me as he stands.

I look up at him like he's lost his mind. I'm not here with him, didn't arrive with him, and don't plan on leaving with him. He looks down at me expectantly.

"Excuse me?" I say and lift a brow.

"Come dance with me; this table is crowded now. I can't talk to you with all this garbage around."

"Nah, I'm good right here. Thank you."

His cheeks turn red and his nostrils flare. I don't know what his problem is, but he better get over it. I'm not interested.

"Ya heard the lass. Go on about ya business, *Orin*." Blackhart says his first name so hard, it drips with disdain.

"I don't need you to help me," I say to Blackhart.

That cloud that covered his handsome face lifts. His gaze homes in on me. This time, he's the one who appraises me. A small smile turns up the corner of his lips.

"Ach, love. I was only being the gentleman my mum raised me to be."

I squeeze my thighs together as that deep voice is aimed at me. His entire presence is intoxicating. There isn't a part of him that I've found lacking yet.

"Fuck this," Harris bites out and storms off.

I don't bother to turn to watch him go. I'm caught in a pair of green eyes that are amazing and intriguing. Blackhart's smile grows as he moves to get a stool and brings it over to sit at the head of the table, locking his eyes on me once he's seated.

"The name is Kevin, love. Who do I have the pleasure of meeting?"

"This is Detective Moralez," Stevens says proudly. "Serg replaced your pretty ass with hers."

Kevin leans back in his seat and crosses his big arms over his chest. "So, he's upgrading these days. Aye, grand. It's a pleasure to meet you. I've heard a lot about you on the way here. Nice work. Big win today."

I've been congratulated a hundred times today, but this is the first time that it's meant something. At least it feels that way as my chest swells and my heart blooms. I haven't felt this way in a long time.

Not even when Eric, my handler, gives me praise. I don't want to dig too deeply into why that is. I shrug it off and take a sip of my beer.

"Thanks," I say after I swallow.

Stevens launches into details about my most recent bust. His face glows as he gives me accolades. Stevens is one of the good guys for now. I haven't had a reason to add him to my list.

Maureen Reed, one of the other beat cops, comes over and starts up a conversation. As I get lost in talk with her about the new motorcycle she's thinking about getting, I can feel those green eyes on me. I do everything I can not to turn and look at him.

"I've never seen Blackhart look at anyone like that before," Maureen whispers in my ear.

"Yeah, well, he's not my type," I lie.

She snorts. "Honey, he's so hot, I'd fuck him, type or not."

I shake my head at her. "Listen, I need to go to the little girls' room. I'll be right back."

"Watch out for Harris." She chuckles after me.

Kevin

"Man, we miss having you and Quinn around here," Stevens says beside me.

I hear him, but I'm too busy following Moralez with my eyes. She's gorgeous. Smart and sexy. I love it.

Cal talked about her bust the entire ride here. You would think he had some part in her victory. I don't know what I was expecting, but the woman I'm staring at isn't it.

Her tight blue jeans hug her hips with the affection of a long-time lover. Those sexy heels on her feet have me tilting my head to the side as I study her. Damn, the sway of her hips is perfection. I noticed earlier that she has a great pair beneath that T-shirt.

Her voice hit me in my gut from her first word. That smoky rasp is seductive in its own right. Soft, yet a bit hoarse.

Her warm, deep-brown skin is a rich espresso tone. Her eyes are the color of amber whiskey, quite the contrast to her skin. Her dark hair is pulled back in a tight bun.

I can't help wondering what her locks look like down. Would they fall in her face as she looks at me beneath her? From the waves in the strands brushed from her face, I bet it's wavy when it's loose.

Her last name is Moralez, but she looks like she could be of mixed heritage. Not that I'm naive enough to think she couldn't be fully Latinx. My trips to Puerto Rico, Cuba, and the Dominican Republic alone have taught me better than to make that assumption. Which is why I want to get to know her better. I want to ask questions and find out all about her.

"You know that's not going to happen, right?"

I turn to Jennings, another of the good guys around here. "You think not?" I say with a grin.

"I know not. She's been around here for what? Two or three years. Not one guy, or girl for that matter, has been able to bag her. Forget it."

"Just because you failed doesn't mean I don't have a shot."

Stevens groans beside me. "I don't know. I'm with Jennings on this one. You don't stand a chance. At first, I thought it was a cop thing. You know, like she was against dating one of us. Then I thought it was a White, Black thing, but I've seen her turn down everyone. White, Black, Hispanic, male, female, cop, lawyer, bartender. She's a closed case."

"Are you assholes sure she's single? I didn't see a ring, but that means nothing," I think out loud.

"I thought that too," Jennings says. "We were partners for a little bit. Before I moved to the special unit. It's just her and her dog. She's single, single."

I sit back and think on that. It's not enough to deter me. I want her to tell me she's not interested. From the vibe I got from her earlier, I don't think I'm up for as big a challenge as these guys think.

"Good luck," Stevens says.

"I got twenty that says he crashes and burns," Jennings snorts, slapping a twenty on the table.

"What do you say, Kev? You think you can win me a twenty?" Stevens says to me.

"You should double the bet," I say as I watch Moralez and all her sexy curves disappear into the ladies' room.

CHAPTER 2

DANCE WITH ME

Danita

I return to a group full of laughter. Everyone around the table is in near tears. I take my seat and wave the waitress over. This will be my last beer of the night. I always drink enough to blend in, but not enough to lose myself and compromise my mission.

"I remember that," Maureen says as she wipes at tears. "It was a great fundraiser, though."

"What did I miss?" I say as I sit.

"Good times," Stevens says. "We have some great memories of the old crew that used to be around here."

"What changed?" I ask nonchalantly. "Things have shaken up a lot from what I hear."

Everyone around the table turns somber. The laughter dries up. A few start to look uncomfortable.

"People change," Stevens says. "Situations aren't the same."

The waitress arrives and a few others ask for another round. "I'll take care of this round," Kevin says. "I'll be leaving soon. It was good to see you guys."

Stevens's face lights up. "It was really good to see you. Cal says you guys are building something with that investigations firm. I'm glad you guys are still looking out for the people who need you."

"We do what we can," Kevin says.

"Speaking of Cal. Didn't you come with him?" Jennings says. "Where'd he get off to?"

Kevin chuckles. "My sister called on our way in. I think he ducked back out. Who knows? I'll probably be taking a cab home."

"I'll give you a ride if you need," Maureen says.

"I'll be fine," he replies, his eyes landing on me. "Hey, Moralez. Before I go, how about we head out on the dance floor?"

I can't help the smug grin that comes to my face. I roll my eyes over him and grin some more. He's not ready for this.

They've been playing a mix of Latin music for the last twenty minutes. My dad is 100 percent Puerto Rican and my mother is African American. I have more rhythm in my pinkie than this Irish dude has in his entire body.

"I don't think that's such a good idea," I scoff.

He narrows his eyes and a grin tilts his lips up. Leaning into the table, he lets his eyes pass over me like a caress. As he places his elbows on the table, his muscles bulge beneath his T-shirt.

"Are you profiling me?" he says with humor in his voice.

I mock his gesture, leaning in as well. "Profiling." I lift a brow. "Nope, I'm assessing the situation and I don't think you, or I, should take the risk."

"Aye, ya think that my Irish ass can't hold a beat. I see it in yer eyes. Come, love, let me teach ya a lesson," he says smoothly, slipping into that sexy accent again.

I can't help the smile that spreads across my lips. "Okay, you got me. I don't think you can bachata to save your life, *papi*. Save yourself the embarrassment. I take that shit serious. You're not ready for me."

He releases a full belly laugh and his face lights up. I didn't think he could get any more gorgeous. Damn, he's fine. Like, forget my three and a half years of celibacy fine.

"I think I might surprise you." He winks as the rest of the table snickers.

I look around. Suddenly, I get the feeling I'm missing out on something. I narrow my gaze at them all before turning back to Kevin.

His eyes sparkle as he stands to his full height. He nods toward the dance floor. "Come on. What do you have to lose?"

"Let's make a bet," I say.

Curiosity brightens his face. Those green eyes sharpen on me for the second time tonight. He nods for me to continue.

"I'll dance with you, but the first time you step on my feet or miss a step, it's over and you're clearing my entire tab for the night," I say.

My tab isn't that big at all, but why not have a night of free drinks? It will be the cherry on top. However, I think I've made a grave mistake as more snickers bounce around the table.

"You're on. And if I win, love, you and I leave after the dance. I want to get to know a little more about you."

I stiffen a little. Getting to *know me* is out of the question. I would allow him to get to know Danita Moralez, but he'll never know me.

Something tells me to back out now. I'm not into hookups and this is dangerous. I don't know his game or why he left the force. He could be one of the bad guys who has learned a better way to run the operation they have going on.

However, there's something that tells me to get to my feet and head out to the dance floor. The voice wins out as I stand. I walk to the other end of the table where he is and look up into his eyes.

The first thing to hit me is his cologne. It's subtle but really nice. I want to move closer to inhale him.

I shake that silly thought off and lock eyes with him. His eyes are more gorgeous up close. Wow, this man is sexy. His thick brows and long lashes tip him over into breathtaking.

I'm five seven, but even in my three-inch heels I have to look up at him. He holds out his hand and I place mine inside. The moment our palms touch, it's like a zap to my entire system. My skin hums from his touch. His long fingers swallow my hand as he leads me out to the dance floor.

A smile takes over my face as the record changes. Prince Royce and Chris Brown's "Just as I Am" comes on, and I want to hoot with laughter. The Latin Bachata-R&B mix is going to win me this bet fast. This is going to be good.

To show Kevin how bad he's fucked up, I lift my arms above my head and bend one knee in front of me. I then start to rock my hips and show off with a kick, ball, change that's sure to keep him from catching up with me.

He bites his lip as he gives me a heated stare. I continue to dance around him in a circle, taunting him with the seductive sway of my hips in my tight jeans. This was over before it started.

I throw my head back and laugh, and that's when he grabs my hand and spins me into him. I'm surprised. My laugh dies in my throat as he looks down into my eyes with a smug grin.

He starts to move our bodies to the music in perfect rhythm. He has the steps down like a pro. My lips part in disbelief, and he gives me a sexy pointed look. I snap out of it and take him to task.

However, he doesn't miss a beat. He reaches for my hands and positions them behind my head as he keeps eye contact. It's as if we're reaching out for each other and holding on to a newfound love. The passion is in the moves as he guides our bodies to dance in a circle. He then spins me back into him and places his hands on my hips.

I dance back two steps and rock two more. He follows before retreating two steps of his own. He's not just keeping up, he's guiding, and it's hot as fuck.

I'm thrilled that he doesn't seem to be counting his steps or mimicking the dance from lessons. He's in the music, in the moment. Then he turns it up a notch.

He drags my hips into his and places his forehead to mine. That humming passes through me times ten. His hand on the small of my back is warm and doing things to my body that shouldn't be possible from only his touch.

His breath fans my lips as he guides me around the small dance floor. Everyone else has moved out of the way. Or maybe I'm in this bubble and I think they've all gone.

"Still doubting me?" he says, and his voice vibrates through my body.

I'm the one to nearly stumble and miss a step. Only reason I don't is because he swiftly lifts me into his arms, placing me flush against his body without my feet touching the floor. He keeps that intense eye contact as he allows my body to slide down his.

Swaying me slowly to the beat of the music, he continues to look at me. Wrapping one arm around my waist and moving my other hand to place around his neck, he takes off around the floor again. It's sensual and sexy the way he moves us.

"Not bad, Blackhart," I pant when the song changes to a slower song, and he starts to slowly sway us again.

"Is your car here?"

I grin. "Eager much? I never said I was going to fuck you, so get that out of your mind."

"I never said I wanted to fuck you. I said I want to get to know you." He gives me a look, and I actually have the nerve to blush.

I. Don't. Blush.

This guy is definitely trouble. However, when I look into his eyes, I see something there that causes me to make a decision that's against everything I am. I don't know if it's because I've been lonely and missing the real world, or if it's the comfort I feel standing in his arms. Whatever it is has my mouth moving before I can stop it.

"We can walk to my place from here. I don't need a car," I say.

A smile lights his handsome face. "Grand, let's go."

I nod, and we return to the table to get my things. Signaling for the waitress, I let her know I'm ready to close my tab. When she gets to our table and hands over the bill, I take out my wallet to pay, but Kevin covers my hand and places a few bills on the waitress's tray.

"You do know you won the bet?" I say with a questioning gaze.

"Aye, sure do. Still want to treat you."

I'm not going to look a gift horse in the mouth. Free drinks are free drinks. With my bag in hand, I allow him to lead the way out as he hugs a few of the guys and says his goodbyes.

"Shit, my feet hurt," I groan as I step out of the bar.

"But you're wearing the hell out of those shoes, love," Kevin says beside me. "I can carry you if you like."

"I'd break your fucking back," I snort.

"I doubt it." He chuckles and bumps my shoulder. "I'll call a cab if you want. It will give me more time to get to know you while we wait."

"We'll be fine walking. It's enough of a walk to get to know me."

We're half a block away from the bar and headed in the direction of my place when it hits me that I'm about to take this guy home with me. Maybe I had too much to drink after all because this is so unlike me. I'm about to stop and call it a night as he brushes the back of his hand against mine.

That charge is back, causing me to look up at him. We lock eyes, and I forget everything I was going to say. It's as if he has me under his spell.

He creases his brows as if he's trying to find his thoughts or something as well. One moment, it's a simple caress of my hand; the next, his long fingers are entwined with mine. A shiver runs through me. The knot that forms in my belly is so tight, my breathing shifts between steady inhales and short, heavy pants.

"You feel that too?" he murmurs.

I nod because I'm not sure what my words are going to sound like.

He begins to rub circles on the back of my hand with his thumb. My nipples tighten in my bra. This man is dangerous in all the right ways.

Run, Dem. Run now.

He licks his lips as his gaze drops to my mouth. Suddenly, he breaks his own spell, clearing his throat. Thank God he turns forward.

We were both about to run into one of those parking meter ticket dispenser boxes.

He laughs, bringing a smile to my face. How is a laugh so sexy and masculine? My toes curl in my shoes. He flexes his fingers around mine as if he knows the effect he has on me.

"Cal says you've been with the department for about three years. How long have you been on the force?"

I pull up the memorized generic answer I have for this question. It burns like acid to tell him the lie, despite having told the same one to so many others over the years. "It's been seven years."

He releases a whistle. "So, you fast tracked it. Wasted no time, did you?"

"I'm not one to waste time. If I want something, I go after it."

I don't mean for my words to come off as they do, but even I can hear the double entendre in them. Kevin looks down at me and the heat in his eyes says a million words. He releases my hand to press his large palm to the small of my back.

Holy shit. My body quakes, and it has nothing to do with the night air. I swear I break out in a sweat. He's frying my brain cells.

He begins a light conversation, and I try my hardest to focus on his words. I'm fine until he gets to the more personal questions. That's when I turn the conversation over to him.

"You're a PI now, right?" I ask. It's all I can do to try to bring some of this tension down.

"Aye, my brothers and I have started a company."

"That's cool, but damn, that must be a big transition."

He gives me a bright smile. "I can be flexible. It's not hard to adjust and fit where I'm needed. As you said, I go after what I want and I'm always up for a challenge."

We're not talking about his job. Honestly, I don't care what we're talking about as long as he keeps talking. This thing building between us with each step has taken over all my good sense.

I'm so drawn to him; I don't realize I've been leaning into his side until we turn onto my street. When I go to pull away, he tightens his hold on me and splays his hand against my belly.

I'm in trouble. Back at the bar, I might have been able to cut this night short. Now, I can't get to my door soon enough.

When we do arrive at my front step, I turn to him. "Wait here, let me go inside and put my dog in the yard."

He looks at me with a knowing look. I reach into my bag and smile back at him. *Yeah, big boy, you're getting some.*

Kevin

I honestly planned to leave with her and get to know her. Sex wasn't in the plans at all. I'm intrigued by this gorgeous woman, and I wanted to dig deeper than a conversation at the bar would allow.

However, things changed on the charged walk to her place. I've never had chemistry with a woman like this, and I know I'm not the only one feeling it. When I linked my fingers with hers, I felt the shiver that rolled through her and I saw the desire in her eyes.

She asked me to wait outside while she placed her pup in the backyard.

I look around the neighborhood as I stand on her porch. It's nice. Quiet for the most part.

"Okay," she says as she swings the door open.

I step inside as I stare into her amber-colored eyes. She searches mine as I close the distance between us. I don't know what comes over me, but I cup the back of her neck and crush her full sexy lips with mine.

The moment her fingers lock in the top of my hair and she moans into my mouth, I groan and deepen the kiss. She tastes so fucking good. I move my free hand to palm her sexy ass.

I grow painfully hard in my jeans. When she reaches for the hem of my T-shirt, I smile and tug it off for her. She sucks her lip into her mouth as the crest on my chest comes into view.

She reaches to trace the *K* and the *B* in the center of the design. All three of my brothers have the same tat. It's our family crest, and each of us has our initials in the center.

Her touch scorches me, but I welcome it. I place my hands on her hips as she explores. As a gentleman, it's only right I return the favor of helping her out of her shirt. I reach for it and tug it off.

Her breasts come into view, and I groan. Yes, they were ample when she had on the V-neck T-shirt, but now, in nothing but her bra, they sit full and lush like her backside. Her skin looks so soft and beautiful within the black lace.

"You're gorgeous, love," I say and tug her into me for another kiss, but something dawns on me. "What's your first name?"

"De—Danita," she says.

I don't miss the slip and pause. I shrug it off as lust clouding her mind as much as it's clouding mine. I want her bad.

"Danita," I repeat.

"Oh God, your accent is sexy. It comes and goes," she says.

I smile down at her. "*Cha chuala thu dad fhathast.*"

Her lips part. I take advantage and capture her mouth. She grabs my ears and gives as good as she's getting.

"What did you just say?" she pants against my lips.

"You haven't heard anything yet," I reply.

"Okay, but what did you say?"

I chuckle into her mouth. "Aye, I just told you what I said, love."

"*Ohhh,*" she drags out and laughs.

It's the prettiest sound I've ever heard. I cup her face and devour her sweet cavern. With one hand, I reach behind her and release her bra.

She tosses the garment aside and reaches to unfasten my belt. I bend my legs and wrap my arms around her thick thighs, pulling her onto my waist. She breaks the kiss to look at me with wide eyes.

"Don't look so surprised. You're light as a feather."

"Bulls—"

I cut her off with a kiss. "Jeez, your mouth is foul."

"I'm so not the first cop you've known with a potty mouth," she scoffs.

I laugh. She's right. However, on the walk over, I realized she'd fit right in with me and my own.

"Nope, but you're the prettiest. Where's your bedroom?"

"Down the hall to the right."

I nod and start in the direction she calls out. Nuzzling her neck, I take in her sweet scent. Not only is she sexy, she smells so damn good, I want to eat her.

I start a trail of kisses down her neck. Once in the bedroom, I step out of my boots as she wiggles her heels off her feet. I love those heels.

Maybe I'll get her to put them back on after the first round. For now, I need a taste. I move over to the bed and place her down on it. I cup her breasts to give them my attention.

"Kevin." I love the way she calls my name as she squirms beneath me. While kneading her mounds, I start to kiss my way down her torso. When I reach her cute belly button, I circle it with my tongue.

I glide my hands down her sides, then reach for the button of her jeans. Once I pop it, I peel them open to reveal sexy black lace panties. Getting the pants from her legs, I settle on my knees and pull her to the edge.

"You're sexy," I murmur against her lace-covered mound and run a hand over her thigh. "You're already wet for me. Ach, I'm going to enjoy every inch of you."

"Kevin, please."

Hooking two fingers into her panties, I push them aside and place a kiss against her moistened skin. She smells even better down here. Like berries or some shit. I bite my lip and groan.

Swiftly, I peel the damp fabric from her body and toss them over my shoulder. With her pussy now bare to me, I'm salivating. I push her thighs toward her chest and start to acquaint myself with her pretty center.

"Mm," I groan as her flavor saturates my tongue.

"Yes," she hisses out.

A grin comes to my lips. I haven't gotten started yet. I tighten my hold on her thighs and get fully invested in my task, earning every orgasm I pull from this delicious body.

Her voice is hoarse by the time I let her take a breather. I'm also ready to burst through my jeans. I stand and start to free myself from them.

"Do you have a condom?" she says breathlessly.

I freeze and squeeze my eyes shut. I throw my head back and growl in frustration. I truly hadn't planned to have sex with her tonight. If I had, I would have made sure to stop and get some fucking condoms.

I fall to the bed beside her, facedown. "Please, baby. Tell me you have condoms."

"No. I don't," she says softly.

I roll onto my back and look up at the ceiling. This would only happen to me. I can hear my brothers laughing at me now.

"I've been celibate," I say. "My last few relationships were train wrecks. I'm getting too old for bullshit. I haven't had sex since my last breakup. I don't walk around with condoms for this exact reason. Although, tonight, I want to kick my own ass."

She laughs and shifts onto her side. I turn my head to look at her. She reaches to push her hand through my hair.

"I've been celibate for about three and a half years," she says and shrugs. "Same thing. No need for condoms."

I blow out a breath. "I hadn't planned to sleep with you in the first place." I reach out and bring her warm body to mine, tugging her into my side as I kiss the top of her head. "So, what's the pup's name?"

She beams at me. "His name is Sunny."

And for the rest of the night we get to know each other.

CHAPTER 3

MAYBE NEXT TIME

Danita

I STAND HOLDING MY FRONT DOOR OPEN, LOOKING UP AT KEVIN like a dreamy-eyed teenager. Sunny is propped against my leg, looking pretty much the same way. Kevin won him over last night as well.

The night was unexpected. I opened up to him in a way I know I shouldn't have. A lot of the things I told him were so close to the truth.

I mean, we're trained to tell half-truths to be able to keep them straight, but this was different. I shared things I've never shared with anyone else. I tried to keep most of the conversation on him, but he would stir it back to me.

We have so much in common. Not Danita and Kevin. Kevin has a lot in common with Demaris Mercado. The real me. I think I've reached my breaking point, because this was very stupid of me.

"I had a nice time getting to know you," he says, reaching to wrap one of my curls around his finger. He brushes my deep waves out of my face and kisses my forehead before he kisses my lips. "When can I see you again?"

My heart aches from the words I'm about to speak. "I don't think that's a good idea."

He frowns and moves to crowd my space, placing a hand on my hip. "Why not?"

"It's complicated. I have a lot of shit going on. I don't think I have room to start anything up with anyone."

He pinches my chin between his fingers and takes my lips in another searing kiss. I'm in a daze when he backs away. I get lost in his eyes, not able to find my voice.

"Does that feel like something you don't have room for?"

"Kevin—"

"You don't have to answer me now. I'll be out of town for work for a few days. I'd like to take you out to dinner when I get back."

I bite my lip. I know that's not going to be possible. I never should have brought him back here last night. While he was amazing with his mouth, I'm glad we didn't take it any further. That will make this so much easier on me.

"I'll think about it," I lie.

He plants another kiss on my lips. "I'll see you in a few days." His phone chimes, and he frowns down at it. "I have to go."

He murmurs the words and takes off as they roll out of his mouth. It's as if I lose something vital as he walks away. I shove the feeling down because I have no room for it.

Moving Sunny back into the apartment, I close the door behind Kevin. I look around my place. It feels so lonely all of a sudden. I wonder if it would be such a bad idea to start a relationship with someone, but quickly dismiss the thought.

I'd always feel like a liar. My biggest fear is falling in love with someone and having to walk away from them once this is all over. Or worse, I could fall for one of the bad guys.

Kevin Blackhart is definitely not the guy I want to experiment with. I know for a fact I could fall for him. I felt this connection with him last night that I've never felt with anyone before.

With a sigh, I go to fill Sunny's water and food bowls before I let him out for a bit. I'm headed for the back door when the bell sounds up front. Thinking that maybe Kevin forgot something, I double back. Sunny heads for the front door barking.

When I look out of the glass panel, it's the last person I expect.

I open the door quickly and let him in. From the look on his face, I don't think this is good.

"I didn't think you'd be checking in for a few days. What's going on? Is everything all right?"

"Who was that guy?" Eric says in answer.

"No one."

"It didn't look like no one. Listen, we're too close to closing this case. You have to think smarter. Why would you bring some guy here?"

He might be right, but I don't like his tone. Eric may be my handler, but he's not my father. I fold my arms over my chest.

"What's this visit about? If you saw him leaving, you were coming here for something."

He nods. "Yeah, I have orders to move you to a new location."

"What? Why? This place is right near the precinct."

"Exactly, anyone could follow you home, and they'd be right in the neighborhood. Nothing would look out of place. We're getting closer to what we need." He pauses to place his hands on his hips and gives me a glare as he purses his lips. "I told you to stop walking back and forth, by the way. You have a car."

"I hate driving. I'm a subway girl." I shrug.

"Well, you're not in the city. I need you to be more alert and focused."

I grind my teeth. I've *been* focused. Last night was the first time I let my guard down. However, I keep my mouth shut. He's right. If I'm getting as close as we believe, this might not be the best place for me anymore.

"But why move me now? Do you think I've been made?"

He turns for my kitchen and starts to make coffee. I look down at my bare legs. I forgot I walked Kevin to the door in a T-shirt and panties.

"Hold that thought. I'm going to throw something on," I call.

"So, that guy, is he from the force?"

"He used to work at the precinct. He was a detective," I reply as I start for my room.

However, Sunny blocks my way, circling my legs. This is the most company he has ever had. I squat and kiss his forehead.

"Who's a good boy? That's my good boy."

I pat his backside, and he takes off for the kitchen where his food is. I'm headed to the bedroom as I hear Sunny barking. I smile and shake my head.

"Sunny, leave Eric alone."

"That dog fucking hates me," Eric says, heading up the hall toward me at a rapid pace.

"He does not. You need to relax. He's trying to be friendly."

"Yeah, right."

I snicker as I enter my room and grab a pair of sweatpants to head into the bathroom with. I toss on the pants, use the bathroom, and pull my hair up before heading back out. Eric stands in the middle of my room, tapping at his phone feverishly.

"Everything okay?"

He looks up at me as if he didn't hear me reenter the room. "Yeah, fine. So, do we add that guy to the list? Can we get an indictment on him? What do you have for me?"

"Whoa. Slow down, killer." I laugh. "I never said I had anything on him. He seems to be on the up and up. Besides, like I said, he doesn't work for the department anymore. He's a PI or something."

I know he's a PI. It was something he told me last night, but for some reason, I play it off as if it's not something I paid attention to. I tell myself it's because I don't want to remember every detail he shared with me.

"Oh, okay. I thought you had something big since you brought him back here. What about that Detective Harris? Any more on him?"

"Ugh, that guy is an asshole. Nothing yet, but I swear he's going to slip up soon. He's so damn arrogant."

Eric smiles. "Don't worry. You're doing great. We knew this one wasn't going to be easy. They're a tight-knit operation. That collar yesterday may be the breakthrough we need. You earned a lot of respect with that one."

I groan. "I hope so. I need a break to get me out of here. You know?"

"If you think you need to pull out, say the word. Your safety is most important. Agents get sloppy when they're in too deep."

"I'm fine. I can handle this. I'm just a little homesick, you know what I mean?"

He moves closer and places a hand on my shoulder. "It's been three years. It's okay to throw in the towel. These guys you have are small fries, but the bureau will have to be satisfied with that. I'll get you out if that's what you need."

"I said, I'm fine."

"Listen, these guys are nothing to play with. This goes so much higher than these degenerates you're digging into—"

"I know this, Eric. I know why I'm here."

"Do you know the reason this has such a high clearance level? It's not safe for you to know who, but someone connected to our office is a part of this. It's so much bigger than you think."

I rock back on my heels. This, I didn't know. The entire case started with a whistleblower.

However, once a group with the ring's MO was found crossing over into New Jersey, Pennsylvania, and DC, the attention of my office was grabbed. Then two bodies of high-profile individuals turned up in Vegas with signs of the ring's dealings. Someone got sloppy. I knew it was a big deal, but hearing someone from the Bureau is dirty changes so much.

"Yeah, now you understand." Eric nods as I stand silently with my mouth open. "Listen, the last thing you want to do is get involved with someone. This case has the potential to burn anyone connected to you.

"As a matter of fact, I want you to promise me that if something happens…if you can't get in contact with me, you keep this shit tight. Always know that I have your back. Whatever's going on, I'll be doing all I can to get you out, but don't do anything. Don't talk to anyone, don't reveal yourself, especially not at the Bureau. I mean it, Demaris. You can't afford to be compromised. Not even your brothers are safe if you drag them into this. Your life, my life, and everyone connected to you depends on your silence. That's why I offered to get you out now, if you need it."

I chew on the inside of my mouth.

"You got it? I need to hear you say it," he demands.

"Yeah, I got. I'm staying in."

"This is the case of a lifetime. It's going to make your career. Trust me."

I wipe my hands on my T-shirt. "Yeah, I know. I'm all in. Come on. I'll make breakfast."

Kevin

"What's going on?" I ask as I push into the office.

Quinn sent me a text as I was leaving Danita's place this morning. As usual, Cal has gotten himself in the middle of some shit. I'm not surprised, just annoyed.

We told him that staying on the force would be a challenge. Especially with the things Quinn and I walked away knowing. Yeah, we have a lot of friends and connections, but we made a few enemies along the way as well.

"I've been asked to join their little gang. No, I've been *told*. When I move to detective, I have no choice. I get put on that squad, it's them or my family. Last night, I never made it inside because I was approached after I got off my call with Erin," Cal says.

"By who?"

"I don't know. They were wearing masks. I was told I had a decision to make. Join or they'd make my life hell."

"They're still up to their bullshit," Quinn grunts.

"You know you're going to have to make a choice," I say to Cal. "The offer still stands. You can always come work here."

"I'm so close to making detective. All my life I've wanted to be a cop. I'm not allowing them to run me off."

"You do understand that this could put your life in danger. Dugan isn't going to be able cover your ass on this. When you're out there, you're going to be unprotected. That's the way they play this dirty game. They will make sure you question everything until you're either dead or out of your mind with paranoia."

Cal blows a breath out and runs his hands through his hair. "This is bullshit. A bunch of dirty cops that bully others to fall in line. Why hasn't anyone blown the whistle? Why hasn't Dugan said anything? He knows what's going on."

"Aye, but this is bigger than him. I've told ya this before," Quinn says and sighs. "Ya have a hard head. We told ya to transfer or leave all together."

"Like a coward?"

"Ya can swallow that shit. Kevin and I be no one's cowards. We did the wise thing. Ya don't stand in a pit of snakes waiting to be bitten. We can do more good from here than in there," Quinn says heatedly.

"I wasn't calling you guys cowards," Cal says like a chastened child.

"This is something you need to figure out. We're here to support you either way. We won't get our hands dirty in anything illegal, but we'll do what we can if you decide to stay and tough it out."

"I won't be one of the bad guys. Erin needs me. My kids look up to me. I'm not going to jeopardize showing Con how to grow up and be a real man. You know my childhood. You know what my father was like. I won't become him. I've wanted to be a cop all my life. This is all bullshit. I'll find a way to keep my job and keep those fucks away from me."

I scrub a hand down my face. "Please do me a favor. Don't try to take these guys on."

"Aye, ya listen to Kev. And remember ya have no friends there anymore. Ya don't know who's who to trust a soul. Do yer job and keep yer head down," Quinn adds.

"If that's all, ladies, I need to be off. I have a flight to catch," I say as I stretch.

"Don't know who yer calling a lady. Ya might want to go home to shower and change yer clothes, by the way. Ya had that same shit on yesterday," Quinn says with a grin.

"I thought it was me," Cal says, scratching his head.

"Nope, not ya at all. Someone has been chasing a pair of kex. About time, maybe ya'll stop being a pain in my arse."

I flip my older brother the bird. "Fuck off."

He has a lot of nerve. Quinn rarely ever dates. We both have our reasons.

I think back to last night. I haven't ever had a connection with anyone like I did with Danita. I want to see her again. This trip can't go by fast enough.

CHAPTER 4

BLOWING OFF STEAM

Kevin
Two years later...

SWEAT DRIPS DOWN MY BARE BACK AS I THROW ANOTHER COMBINATION at the heavy bag before me. I hit the bag so hard, the impact vibrates up my arm. *Good.* That's just what I need.

I need to feel the pain to help with this guilt that's eating me up. Someone hurt my baby sister. I wasn't there for her. None of us were. I haven't been able to swallow that fact. It burns deep within my chest that the one thing I do best, I didn't do when it came to Erin.

"*Fuck!*" I roar into my gym.

I grab the punching bag and use it for support as I bury my face into it. My body hums with the abuse I've been putting it through every morning since this shit storm with Erin. My brain is fatigued from all of the questions I've bent and twisted and still haven't resolved.

I need answers.

It's been three weeks since Erin and Cal were shot in front of their home. Three weeks with no damn solid leads in sight. Whatever Cal got himself into, he buried it just like I'd like to do him.

Cal has always been a fuckup. He means well, but he has a hot head and he leads with his emotions. Yet, I never saw something like this coming. Cal always knew my brothers and I would follow him to hell and back if something bad were to happen to our sister or her children.

Yet Erin is lying in a hospital bed.

I shove at the heavy bag in frustration, reaching to wipe at my tears. I can fall apart here. I don't have to pretend to be tough for my brothers or in front of my nephew and the girls. I can allow myself to admit this shit hurts.

"I'm sorry, Erin. Ya just have to wake up, love. I'll get them all. I promise," I sob as if my sister were here to hear me.

I shake out my arms and go back to punishing my body. I'm taking this shit harder today than I have in the last few weeks. It's probably because I woke to an alert for the lunch Erin and I had planned together for this afternoon.

She wanted me to help with the permits and booking the bouncy house and some other things she had in mind for Kasey's birthday party. I have a few connections that would make things easier on my sister while planning my niece's dream party. I'd find a way to rent a chariot from heaven if Erin asked and Kasey wanted one.

I clench my jaw as I throw one last punch to get out as much frustration as I can. Silence fills the room as I stand with my chest soaked and heaving. My eyes are fixed on nothing at all. I can't seem to see past my rage this morning.

"This day will be just grand," I huff and drag my worn-out body upstairs to shower before the reno crew arrives for the day.

Thanks to Erin, this place will be finished soon. It won't be the same to have it done without her. I have no idea where to put all the furniture she ordered. That's her thing. I pay for it, and she makes it happen.

My mind buzzes with all the things I need to get done today. I'll make a few calls to book the things I remember Erin mentioning. We still have plenty of time, but my sister's a planner. She'll be back to us in time for Kasey's birthday.

I keep telling myself those words because they're what I need to keep me moving forward. This has to end with my sister opening her eyes to be there for her children. I can't see this any other way.

My phone rings, pulling me out of my thoughts. I walk over to the bench I placed it on. It's my little brother Shane. Hopefully he has some news on the leads I gave him.

If I had something to sink my teeth into, I could distract myself from my worry and thoughts. We need a solid thread to follow. I answer the call as I wipe sweat from my forehead.

"You have something for me?"

He releases a heavy breath. "No. All dead ends. I've double-checked everything you gave me," he replies.

"Fuck," I hiss. "The black book I found, nothing?"

"Nothing. Those were old Blackhart Security and Investigations clients that Debbie was able to match up with files over the last two years he's worked for us since he left the force. All his cases. Nothing dodgy about it."

I blow out an exasperated breath and clench my jaw. We're not getting answers from the police and our investigation has yet to grow legs. Three weeks later, and we're right where we started.

Tension knots in my shoulders. My head hurts. None of us are functioning the way we normally would. We're too close to this, and our worry for Erin might be clouding our focus. We all know it; we just haven't said it out loud.

"Okay. You stay on it. Quinn is bound to see what we're missing."

"Yeah, I'm banking on that. He'll see the missing pieces. I've never been more grateful for that brain of his. He'll give us a link soon," Shane says. "I need your approval on a few things at the office. You coming in today?"

"Aye, I'll be there. Need to head to Quinn's to pick the kids up for school. I'm trying to take the load off so he can think. The sooner he can start putting pieces together, the sooner this puzzle will fall into place for him."

"Okay, I'm going to look at these videos again. Maybe I'm missing something."

"Don't be hard on yourself, Shane. This is on all of us. We'll all work to figure it out," I say, hearing in his voice the pressure he's putting on himself.

"Aye, I miss her. I went to call her last night and realized I couldn't. This never should've happened."

"Aye, yer right. It shouldn't have. She's a strong lass, bro. We'll see her through this, and we'll find the ones that put her in that hospital bed. Erin is too stubborn to give up."

He sighs. "I'll see you when you get in. I think I'll head to the hospital to take Mum and Da lunch."

"Sounds good. Call me if anything new comes up."

"Aye, will do."

He ends the call, and I stand staring into space. There has to be something we're missing. I don't want to put all the pressure on Quinn to fit this together. We need to all do our parts.

"*I* need to do my part," I mutter to myself.

Danita

"Hey," Maureen says as she walks up beside me. I pause and hold the heavy bag to keep it from moving.

I nod. "What's up?"

"Heard you still haven't been assigned a partner. That's bullshit, you know?"

"Yeah, I know. I also know they're going to get away with it for as long as they can." I shrug.

"You're a good cop. I hate what they're trying to do to you. Keep your head up," she says and walks off.

Maureen used to be one of the good ones. However, this place has corrupted her, much like many of the others. Once she was promoted to detective, things changed. I was a bit disappointed to find out she has become a part of the ring.

I frown. I've heard whispers of its name, but nothing that's concrete. They are like ghosts that make plenty of noise, but you never see them.

Getting inside is still a wall I haven't breached. I've tried before, but I've had no luck. Besides, that hasn't seemed like a good idea since Eric has gone missing. I'm too vulnerable. I don't have a way out.

As I return to my workout, sweat drips from my face, and my muscles are starting to ache. I spin and kick the heavy bag before me. My focus is on my morning routine as I try to think my way through my next steps.

What went down with Cal Kelley was foul. There's blood in the water and the sharks are out to play. The question is: Are they going to invite me into the game? Better yet, are they even aware they should? Now that's the million-dollar question.

My guess is that my cover has yet to be blown. My blood begins to boil as I think of all the signs that Cal was getting in way over his head. I never should have agreed to his help. Especially not the part where he kept me so far out of the loop.

My gaze scans the gym as I bounce in place, my hands up to guard my face as if someone here will strike at any moment. That's the thing. It's more likely than not that they will.

Five years and nothing has changed. I still don't trust anyone here. I can't afford to. I've been waiting for someone to try to pump me full of lead since hearing about Cal. It's why I haven't gone looking for answers as of yet.

That stops today.

If they were going to come for me, they would have done it by now. Still, I plan to proceed with caution. I don't want to take any more drama to the Kelley door. I have to be careful about this.

I think I know where to get my answers. I hate to start with the kid, but he's my strongest lead. Cal got sloppy somehow, and I think the kid can shed light on a few things, whether he knows it or not.

With my plan in mind, I stop to wipe my forearm across my sweaty forehead. I roll my shoulders to release some of the tension. I'm as relaxed as I'm going to get. That is until the bane of my existence speaks from behind me.

"Fuck, Moralez. When are you going to let me take you out, sweetheart?" Detective Harris croons.

"Not interested. You know, it's time you get your ears checked. I've told you this…repeatedly," I call over my shoulder, not bothering to spare him a glance.

He steps up behind. "I'm telling you, we'd be great together." He runs his fingers down my arm.

I spin on my heels and glare at him. "Don't touch me."

He tosses his hands up in the air before him. That cocky smile is on his face. "Calm down, champ." He chuckles.

I've watched women fall at his feet, not me. His arrogance makes my skin crawl. It's not sexy; it makes him come off like a douche. Although you can't tell him that.

The fact that he thinks it's appropriate to touch me in a work environment speaks volumes about him and this place. These guys think they can say and do just about anything to us female officers, and we're just supposed to take it. Well, that's never going to happen when it comes to me.

I demand respect. I may be stuck here, but I'm not going to be harassed because of the fact. Since Eric disappeared, it has taken everything in me not to say screw it all. I should be making friends to continue to build this case, but sometimes I want to be like fuck it; I couldn't care less about connecting with anyone here.

Too bad my entire life and career have been on the line for the last two years. I can't afford to close off. I need to find an out. I was moved to the new apartment and then a month later…nothing. I haven't heard from or seen Eric since. I don't know if something happened to him because of the case or if something else went down.

Danita Moralez doesn't exist outside of this world, so I can't pop up into the Bureau claiming to be her, or Demaris Mercado. At least not after that conversation Eric and I had revealing the involvement of someone in the Bureau. I can't jeopardize everyone's life, or this case.

I'm a ghost.

This case was never supposed to exist for others to find. It was always understood that what's been happening in this precinct has a longer reach than a few beat cops and detectives on this peninsula. Oh, no, this group is tied into some heavy shit, and one wrong person getting wind of this investigation could cost me my life.

So although I don't give a crap about friendships, I've maintained my cover and involvement. However, I'm still not trying to get tangled with Harris. I ignore the bullshit and do my damn job, waiting to find the opportunity to get out.

I open my mouth to put Harris in his place, but I'm cut off by my sergeant's voice. "Moralez, my office. Now."

I glare at Harris one last time before I turn and leave. I'm sure we'll finish this little conversation another time. Harris likes to push my buttons.

"Asshole," I mutter to myself.

In the last two years, I've been waiting to get something on this dude. He's always around the usual players. Eric had been most interested in him as well. Harris is the one I think knows enough to get me the airtight case I need.

At first, I had my focus on him so I'd have everything in place when Eric returned. Once it started to become clear I might be in this alone, I figured if I could nail Harris and get a hook into the big fish back at headquarters, I'd be willing to risk a move to get the hell out of here. Then I'd have whoever the asshole is by the balls.

For two years, I've waited for Eric to get me out, but I'm starting to think that ship has sailed. I'm going to have to take the risk sooner or later on my own.

I sigh. My thoughts turn to Cal. I need to know what he found out. That's the key to this being over.

Oh well, for now, let's see what fresh hell awaits me before I can go do some real digging.

CHAPTER 5

HARDHEAD

Kevin

"Did ya get my text this morning?" Quinn asks as I walk into his kitchen.

"Aye," I grunt, still in a foul mood since my workout.

"Can ya have answers for me by the afternoon?"

"I'll see what I can dig up after dropping everyone off," I say.

"Are you guys talking about something to do with Mom and Dad?" Con asks from the kitchen island.

"Mind yer own," I say quickly, looking over at the wee lasses in the kitchen nook.

Just as I thought, Molly and Kasey are now looking in our direction expectantly. I detour from the plate Quinn set on the countertop for me. We've been doing our best to keep the wee ones distracted from what's been going on. Something Con is well aware of.

"Where's Mckenna?" I ask.

"She's still getting ready," Quinn replies, the exasperation clear in his voice.

I'll admit, it's been an adjustment to deal with two teenagers and two wee ones that are going on thirty. Mckenna spends almost two hours in the bathroom in the mornings. I've timed her. Thank God my rental apartment has more than one bathroom.

I've been staying in a rental when it's my turn to keep the kids. My house is under construction and no place to have children. All of this has been unexpected, but we're each doing what we can to make sure the kids are safe and comfortable.

"Good morning, Uncle Kevin." Kasey and Molly giggle as I tickle them both and kiss their little cheeks.

"Good morning, loves. Eat up. I'll be getting ya all to school this morning."

"I can get myself to school," Conroy says.

"That might be true, but I'll be taking ya nonetheless," I reply before moving to shove a bagel into my mouth.

"I'm sixteen, not six."

I narrow my eyes at Con, but I don't reply. Today wouldn't be the day to try me. Conroy has been stretching his boundaries more and more with each day.

My patience is too thin to deal with him and his bullshit this morning. I try to sympathize with his plight, but we're all feeling this situation in one way or another. Con is old enough to understand the tension that's surrounding the family at the moment.

The fact that he has been pushing our buttons has been getting stuck in my craw. Layin' boots to him is the last thing I want to do. I know he's down about what's going on with his parents, but he's right on the cusp of me not giving a fuck. The disrespect is going to stop, and soon.

"Ya keep testing me if ya want," I warn as he continues to stare me down.

"All I said was that I'm sixteen. Why can't I get to school on my own?"

"Because we need to look after ya for the time being," Quinn replies tightly.

"I can take care of myself," Con says, puffing his chest out.

There are birds with more meat. He wants to grow up so fast. One day he'll figure out that these are the years to enjoy instead of pissing them away being angry and trying to make everyone else angry.

"Why are we having this discussion again?" I ask.

"You guys never listen to me. If I were Mckenna, it wouldn't be a big deal. The girls can do nothing wrong, but it's always a problem when it's me. I can get to school on my own. I'll be driving myself soon," Conroy says defiantly.

"Con, this is not the time," Quinn chides.

"I'm smarter than you guys think."

"Ya sure about that? Because ya will be toothless if ya keep running yer gub," I bite out.

"See, you're still not listening to me," he huffs.

"Maybe that's because yer the same kid that's been cutting school to hang in yer parents' basement. Or how about the fights ya keep getting yerself into? Aye, ya didn't think we knew about that," I say when his cheeks turn red. "Ya keep playing us all for yer stooks. A fool, I'll be for no one. Trust me, Con. Today is not the day."

"Whatever," he grumbles.

I take a step in his direction to cobbler him, but Quinn places a hand on my shoulder to calm me. Rolling my shoulders, I take a step back. My eyes stay narrowed on my nephew with his big mouth.

"I'll take him," Quinn says.

"Aye, that might be best."

I turn to walk into the backyard. This kid is trying to do a number on me. I need to pull my shit together.

Danita

"Finally," I huff, sitting up straighter in my unmarked car when I see Quinn Blackhart pull up with the Kelley twins.

I've been sitting outside their school waiting and stewing from the talk I had in Sergeant Graves's office. That man makes my blood boil. I've been pulled from yet another case that I'm on the verge of closing, only to be assigned some BS.

It took everything in me not to blast him for it. This has become a pattern since Graves took over. He replaced Sergeant Owens about a year and a half ago.

At first, I thought Graves was onto me. Then I figured out that the fact of the matter is he doesn't like me. Or should I say, he doesn't much like having female officers on his squad. No matter that I'm one of the best on said squad.

This precinct has a lot of problems, not just dirty cops. It's one of the reasons I can't wait to get out of here. I've never seen things at this level. It's sickening.

I've been working with Cal Kelley on this big break he promised me for almost as long as Eric has been missing. We were careful. At least I was. Yet, everything has changed since Cal was shot, and everyone has started to move differently at the precinct.

I'd call it a coincidence if I weren't an agent. However, I am and I know better. They may not be onto me, but I get the feeling that Cal ruffled a lot of feathers, and they may have considered that he had inside help.

I may not know all the details of Cal's investigation, but I do know that he was onto the fact that there are more than dirty cops involved. Some downright filthy assholes with long arms, but still plenty of dirty cops from my squad. I wish I could say I'm surprised, but I'm not.

Those with the reach are the players that I want now; I need them all. According to Cal, he had the map I need to navigate who's safe and who's not. Without those answers, I'm toast.

"Where are you going?" I whisper.

I squint my eyes at Conroy Kelley. He has doubled back out of the front of the school. I had only planned to watch the school today, feel things out and see if anyone else is snooping around.

Graves's reluctance to assign me a new partner has served me well. I don't believe half of the bullshit excuses I've been getting for the delay. But I'm fine with having my own back.

I say an actual thanks for the lack of partner to answer to. Graves doesn't need to know what I'm doing. I'll get to that dead-end case he put me on soon enough. I want to follow this kid and see what he's up to. I have a feeling in my belly that says he's going to lead me to exactly what I need.

He jets across the schoolyard to meet up with another kid. The two lock heads together before they take off in the opposite direction of the school. My hackles raise as I watch them.

"You should be in school, kid. It's not safe out here," I mutter to myself.

I start my car and follow them. The other boy leads Conroy to a bicycle and the two clap hands before Conroy takes the bike and leaves. The other boy slips something into his pocket, leading me to believe Conroy slipped him payment for use of the bike.

I stay on Conroy as he pedals away from the school. The farther away from campus we get, the more concerned I become. It only takes a few miles before I realize this kid is heading into some real trouble.

Something that Cal did inform me of was the areas where the crews in the ring operate. I have no idea what this kid is up to, but this neighborhood isn't one he should be in. It's nothing like the cushy one Cal's home is in.

"Shit, kid."

I don't have a good feeling about this. My instincts tell me to stop him before he gets to his destination. With a groan, I roll my eyes and turn on the sirens.

He looks over his shoulder, revealing his fear-stricken face. His little ass looks like he's going to try to outrun me. "Oh no, you don't," I mutter and swerve my car in front of him.

He runs right into the passenger door and falls to the ground. I shake my head and step from my vehicle. The little shit gets up and straddles the bike as if he's going to try to run again.

"Freeze," I call out.

"Shit," he huffs, looking down at his warped tire. "I didn't do anything."

"Hands on the hood of the car," I order.

"I'm late for school. I was in a rush to get to class."

I chuckle as I step behind him. "Nice try. Your school is several miles in the other direction. Hands behind your back."

"What? You're arresting me?"

I slap the cuffs on his wrists to let the reality of the situation weigh in. Maybe the cuffs will loosen his lips. I don't want to take him in to the station for a number of reasons, but I will if I have to.

"I want to have a little talk with you. You talk, I'll drop you at school. If not, we're going in to the station."

"I have nothing to say," he says defiantly.

"The station it is." I open the door to place him in the back seat.

"Wait." His voice cracks and the little tough guy act tones down. "If you take me to the station, someone will have to come for me, right?"

"Yup. A guardian will be called."

He groans as I place him in the car. I look at the bike and roll my eyes.

"Miss, please. I'm already in a trouble with my uncle. If you take me in, he's going to jump down my throat."

I squat outside of the car to get to his eye level. "Answer my questions and school it is."

"What questions?"

"Do you remember me?"

He squints at me as the wheels turn. I wait for him to connect the dots. A few beats pass before recognition lights his eyes. The kid shuts down right in front of me.

"You can call my uncles," he says.

Shit.

"I'm not here to hurt you. Your dad was a friend of mine. I want to find out what happened to him. You're the only one that can help me do that."

"I'll give you their numbers. One of them will come and get me. I don't know you or what you're talking about," he says.

I sigh. "Kid."

"You have pen and paper. I'll give you those numbers now."

"Okay, have it your way."

I clench my jaw. I should have thought this through. My desperation has fucked this up.

I stand and slam the door shut. Turning my back to him, I grind my teeth and run my hands over my hair. I'm so frustrated.

"Think, Dem, think. You take the kid in, you're going to pull attention."

Yes, I'll pull attention, but no one will link me to Cal. After all, if I were working with Cal, why would I bring his kid in and expose myself? He's a teenager grieving.

The possibilities of him doing something stupid now that both of his parents are in the hospital is more than likely. Yeah, that makes sense. It will also get me closer to one of the Blackharts. I need to know what they know. Maybe they can get the kid to open his mouth.

It's not the best plan, but it's what I have for now. After all, I can't just show up on their doorstep. That's a bad idea for more than one reason.

"God, please be with me. Let anyone but Kevin Blackhart answer their phone," I murmur as I snatch up the bike and move to the trunk.

With the way things have been going, I don't think that prayer will be answered. "*Carajo*."

CHAPTER 6

SIDETRACKED

Danita

"Can I get you some water, kid?"

Nothing, no response. Conroy sits at my desk avoiding eye contact with me or anyone else. I tried to get him to talk in the car, but the kid shut down. He's smart.

I don't blame him for not talking. I honestly wish I didn't have to drag him into this. However, I need to figure this out before someone in here figures out who I am.

I rub my temples. This day is starting to suck, big time.

I tried every number the kid gave me before I finally gave in and called the one he said belonged to his uncle Kevin.

Even Conroy seemed not to want me to call that number. If I thought Kevin was pissed off when I told him I had his nephew in custody, he nearly burst my eardrum with the bitter scoff he gave when I told him my name, which I intentionally avoided at first.

"*The* Detective Danita Moralez," he said in a harsh tone.

"That's correct," I replied.

He barked a disgusted-sounding laugh, causing me to pull the phone from my ear. "Aye, I'm on my way."

That accent and his rumbling voice are still playing in my head. I can't help but remember the sound of it in the middle of the night. Raw with tiredness and open with honesty. It's a night that I shouldn't remember so clearly.

"Hey, Moralez," Detective Harris calls from behind me.

I roll my eyes and groan. This asshole is the last person I want to deal with. My nerves are already on edge.

I rotate my shoulders back and turn in my seat to look up at him. He's staring at Conroy with his eyes narrowed. When he turns his blue gaze on me, something I can't place crosses his face.

"Is that Cal Kelley's kid?"

I notice Conroy shift around in his seat uncomfortably. I sit back in my own and fold my arms over my chest. Harris follows the action, his eyes falling to the V of my shirt.

I look toward the paperwork on my desk. It's nothing that has to do with Conroy, but I make a show as if it does. I shrug and look back at Harris.

"His last name is Kelley. I picked him up cutting school in a gang-related neighborhood. He ran his bike into my car."

Conroy's nostrils flare, but I slide the kid a look to warn him to keep his mouth shut. For the first time since we arrived, he locks eyes with me. He then looks up at Harris.

"You know what your problem is, Moralez?" Harris seethes. "You think you're better than everybody. You do shit by your own rules. That doesn't fly well around here."

"I've been doing fine all this time."

"Yeah, well, that can change. Trust me," he snarls. "This can be a lonely place, sweetheart. You don't want to be on the outside. You're lucky I can't stand Cal or his brothers-in-law."

"Don't you have some work to do? When was the last time you actually solved a case?"

"You're so fucking hardheaded—"

He comes out of nowhere. Seriously, one minute Harris is snarling at me, the next Kevin Blackhart is in his face, nose to nose. I sit with wide eyes and my mouth open.

Oh God, he's hotter than he was two years ago. How is that even possible? I'm too stunned to react because I can't take my eyes off the sexy, seething giant squaring up to the guy that was just berating me.

Kevin

I was already pissed when I arrived. However, when one of the guys led me over to Moralez's desk and I heard the shit coming out of Orin's mouth, I lost it. I jumped right in his face, daring him to say another word.

"It seems no one has been putting ya in check since I left. So let me do the honors. If ya ever talk to her like that again, I'll put my foot so far up yer ass, ya'll taste it. Do you understand me?" He scowls back at me as his face turns red. "I said, do ya understand me?"

He gives a slight nod, and I shove him back out of my face. He stumbles a few steps and almost lands on my nephew. I'm quick to pull Conroy out of the chair.

Harris looks at me with a smug grin on his lips. "Someone book this fuck," he calls out.

I grin and fold my arms over my chest as all my old buddies mutter to themselves as they walk away, ignoring him. I shrug and glare. Harris looks around at all the guys that have turned their backs.

I glance at our surroundings. These are most of the good guys. Looks like I'm here on the right shift.

"Looks like if ya want that to happen, yer going to have to make it happen," I say, the dare clear in my voice.

"Moralez," he growls.

"I'm going to ignore that, like my harassment reports would be ignored," she replies. "Guess it's time for you to get to work."

Harris glares between the two of us, his face filling with rage. He curses under his breath as he rubs the back of his neck. Once he walks off, I turn my attention to my nephew. The look in his eyes gives me pause. I'm still pissed, but something is going on.

I turn to Danita. It's the first time I've looked at her. All the air is sucked out of the room. She's even more beautiful than I remember.

Her lashes fan out over her pretty amber whiskey-colored eyes as she stares back at me. Those full lips are pursed, begging for me to kiss them and reacquaint myself with her taste.

"You look well," I say.

"Why wouldn't I?"

"I don't know, love. Maybe because ya went missing for three and a half months after I last saw ya." I clamp my mouth shut when I realize how loud I've gotten.

"It's called vacation time and going undercover. I took a few weeks off, and then I was assigned a case."

"Aye, but you weren't an undercover detective when we met. Certainly not an undercover NARC."

"Wait, how do you know that?"

"I thought we had something." I lower my voice. "I came looking for ya. Ya moved from yer apartment, and ya took a case to get away from me. I guess I was wrong."

"Kevin." She moves closer to me. "It wasn't like that. It's way more complicated than that."

"Wait, you know her?" Conroy asks, relief filling his eyes.

"No," Danita says quickly.

I tilt my head. Reaching to brush her cheek the way I did the night we spent together, I search her face. "Are ya really going to tell that lie?"

"Mr. Blackhart—"

"Oh, don't do that," I chide and click my tongue. "We're well beyond that, love."

"All right, Uncle Kevin," Conroy croons. "She's hot and pretty badass."

Danita and I both turn to glare at him. He lifts his shoulders and his cheeks turn red. When I see he's still cuffed, my temper flares again.

"Can you uncuff him so we can go?"

"I haven't finished processing him," she says defiantly.

I groan and push a hand through my hair. Right as I get ready to ask to speak to Dugan, the chief, I see him hightailing it toward the door.

"The kid cut school," I say instead.

"Yes, I'm aware of that."

I grind my teeth. Stepping in, I lean into her ear. "Do you have any idea what's been going on in this kid's life? Cutting school is the least of his worries. Give him a break."

"I need—"

"Moralez." I look up to see it's Sergeant Graves barking her name. He's new, I never worked with him when I was on the force, but I know of him. "My office, now."

"I'll be right back," she says, giving myself and Conroy a warning glare.

I turn to Con. "You have a seat. Don't say a word to anyone here. I need to call Quinn."

CHAPTER 7

EXPLAIN

Danita

"What's Mommy going to do? Huh, Sunny?" I coo at my dog as we sit on the couch. Sunny looks at me as if to say, *you figure it out,* and places his head in my lap. "You're no help."

Thanks to Sergeant Graves, I never did get to talk to Kevin or pull any information from Conroy. Fifteen whole minutes. That's how long I sat in his office as he reamed me.

"Do you have any idea whose kid that is?" Serg ranted at me.

"I just found out he's Kelley's," I said.

I played stupid the entire time as if I didn't know who Conroy was or who he was related to. Lucky for me, one of my cases did require me to be on the same side of town that I picked Conroy up on. Once Serg finished dressing me down, I had no choice but to let Conroy go with his uncle. That was three days ago.

"Why me?" I groan and throw my head back against the couch.

I need to know what Cal stumbled into. He promised he had the key to getting me out. He said we were so close. He needed to take care of one more piece. I should be focused on getting information from the kid, but I can't stop thinking about Kevin and what he said.

"I don't know, love. Maybe because ya went missing for three and a half months after I last saw ya."

I've thought about him a few times over the last two years. Often wondering what would have happened between us in another life. I had taken the vacation for the move.

Once Eric disappeared, I took the undercover assignment to try to figure things out. I was the only officer in the precinct that fit the mold for the assignment, female and Afro-Latina. I jumped at the chance to get away for a bit as well as being placed on the squad I'd been trying to get on for three years. It was the big break we needed for the case. Yet, Eric was gone.

Suddenly, Sunny jumps up and runs to the door and starts to bark. I reach for my piece and follow after him. I'm almost to the door when the bell rings.

I hold my breath as my heart pounds. I never have any visitors. I haven't told anyone where I live since Eric disappeared. My name isn't even on the lease, nor on the bills.

When I peek out of one of the side panels, I find a large figure on my doorstep. I don't breathe easy until the red hair comes into view. I sigh in relief and place the safety back on my gun.

"What are you doing here? How did you find me?" I say when I open the door.

Sunny runs forward with his tail wagging as he barks. Kevin squats to pet his head. My little traitor soaks the attention up.

"Hello, boy. Remember me?" Kevin croons as Sunny rolls onto his back for a belly rub.

"To your room, Sunny." I bark the command.

Sunny whimpers, but he rolls over and heads back to the spare bedroom. Kevin stands and leans into the doorjamb, placing his head against it. He looks tired and stressed. I want to reach up and push his hair back from his forehead. His usual neat locks are now a mess.

"I remembered your dog's name was Sunny. Not that many pure breed blue pit bulls with that name. I used my skills to find a dog walker with a client that had a pit ball named Sunny," he says nonchalantly.

"Seriously?"

He moves to grab my waist and pushes me inside. Butterflies take off in my belly as soon as he touches me. I look into his eyes and my thoughts scramble. He has a little five o'clock shadow, and it's so hot on him.

"You said it was more complicated. Explain it to me."

"Kevin," I groan. "Can't we leave this in the past? What's done is done."

He searches my eyes. "If you were anyone else, I'd walk away. I'm not in the habit of chasing after women that don't want to be chased. You made it seem that way two years ago. I told myself to forget you. It's why I didn't try to find you then."

"Finding out that I was undercover was your way of not looking for me?" I snort.

"Aye."

"Hold on. How did you get confidential information about the case that I was on, anyway?"

"I'm a resourceful man." He smiles. "I also helped a little with the case. From time to time we get called in to help on a few. Shh, that's our little secret."

I narrow my eyes at him. I never got a bad vibe from him before. I'm not getting one now, but I'm curious.

"You probably already know you can't trust about half of the precinct. We help with cases that the boys aren't trustworthy enough for," he says as if reading my mind.

He brushes my cheek, and his gaze drops to my lips. I take a step back because if he kisses me, I know this is not going to end well. He follows, closing the space between us.

"Kevin."

"Tell me that night was a fluke. Tell me you felt none of what I felt."

I close my eyes as the memories come flooding back. That night was one of the best nights of my life. It wasn't the sexual part. That was fantastic. To be honest, I pull up those memories when I spend time with my vibrator.

However, the night was special to me because I felt like he saw me. For years, I didn't have that. I soaked up his attention during those few hours.

He will never know how much that meant to me or how much I needed it. The time I spent with Kevin may have been only a few hours, but it was a night that left an impression, which is why this can't happen. Especially not now.

"I can't tell you that."

Before the words are fully out of my mouth, he has his lips crushed to mine and his hand in my hair. My toes curl, and I grab his shirt because it's all I can do to keep from melting into the floor. It's better than I remember. His kiss is all-consuming.

He breaks the connection and places his forehead to mine. "Nothing has changed. You still set my blood on fire," he breathes.

"A lot has changed," I whisper.

He backs up and looks into my eyes. "Are you seeing someone?"

"No."

He takes me in from head to toe and grins. "You're still as sexy as ever, love. More gorgeous, if you ask me. Nothing has changed there."

"Your hair is a little longer," I murmur. "And you have more ink on your arm."

His smile brightens. "You checking me out?"

I return the smile. "I see you still have a sense of humor."

His smile falls, and he knits his brows. "Life is too short for regrets, lass. You're one regret I don't want to have."

Oh my God, seriously? It's like that night all over again. He kept saying things that would make me swoon.

Cal's face pops into my head. He got hurt because of me. His wife was shot because of me. She's Kevin's sister. If he knew, he would hate me for it.

I harden my resolve. "Some things are worth the regret. I'm telling you that I'm one of those things. You have no idea how bad an idea it is to get involved with me."

Kevin takes a step back. With a nod, he pulls his wallet from his pocket and plucks out a card. He holds it out toward me.

"I've never been able to get you off my mind. I stayed away because that's what it felt like you wanted." He moves closer, crowding my space once again. This time he leans into my ear. "You had secrets then, love, and I see you still have them now. I was willing to take you as you were. I'm still willing to take you as you are. If you decide this connection is worth the try, I'll be on the other end of that call."

With that, he places the card in my hand and kisses my forehead. Like that morning two years ago, when I watched him walk out of my home, I feel him take something with him as he leaves. I don't call after him like my brain screams for me to.

This is for the best.

Kevin

"Come on, Uncle Kevin. Why not?"

"Because I said so," I say to Con as he pouts. "You're on punishment, or have you forgotten?"

"No, I didn't forget," he mutters and slinks off like a mopey slug.

The nerve of this kid. Like I'd really allow him to go hang out with friends after he landed his hardheaded ass in a pair of cuffs. I'm sure he thought he was going to get away with going to his little party since it was Trenton's night to have him and his sisters.

Too bad for him, Trenton needed me to pick them up so he could cover a shift at the Golden Clover. Things still aren't back to normal yet. Mum and Da spend most of their time at the hospital.

We've been picking up the slack all around. I'm exhausted, but I'm not complaining.

"Uncle Kevin." Kasey comes running into the kitchen. "Can I sleep with you?"

I squat and run a hand over her hair. "What happened to your bed?"

I'm renting a three-bedroom. I got bunks for the little girls to share a room with Mckenna, and Con has his own room. When my place is finished, I'll have enough space for them to all spread out.

Kasey wraps her little arms around my neck and buries her face there. "I had a nightmare last night. Mommy and Daddy always let me sleep in their bed when I'm scared," she whispers.

My heart lurches. It aches for these kids. Con has been a pain in my ass, but he's usually a good kid, just cocky as hell. It's clear they each are trying to deal with this the best they know how.

I stand, lifting her up in one arm, and kiss the top of her head. "Sure, you can sleep in my room." I tickle her stomach. "That is, as long as you don't tell my mum that I eat cookies in bed before my bedtime."

"Promise." She giggles. "But you should brush your teeth before you go to bed."

"You're so smart, you know that?"

"Mommy's smart. She tells us to brush before bed," she says with pride.

I can't help but smile even as I fight back my emotions. My sister is doing a hell of a job raising these kids. They don't deserve to lose her.

"You know, I used to sneak your mommy cookies before bed all the time. That is until your grandma found out and put us both on punishment."

Kasey giggles some more, and it makes my night. On top of exhaustion, I can't stop thinking about Danita. I've known from the beginning she's had secrets.

It was in the careful way she worded things that night we spent together. I read between the lines. It's something not many people would pick up on, but in my profession, I'm always looking for what others aren't.

Danita was honest that night, but she was also closed off and guarded. At first, I attributed it to us being strangers. We were only getting to know each other. However, the more she loosened up, the more measured she became. I knew it for what it was. The lass has deep secrets.

Yet somehow, I don't care. I want to get to know her and peel back the layers. I think that's part of the allure. She's gorgeous and mysterious.

"Uncle Kevin, what are you thinking about?" Kasey pulls me from my thoughts as I stand her on the foot of my bed.

"A lot, sweetheart. A whole lot."

"You should write it down and make a list like Uncle Quinn. Then you won't have that worry line in your forehead."

I chuckle and kiss her cheek. "Not a bad idea, but I don't think one of your uncle's lists will fix things for me."

"Doesn't hurt to try, right?" She gives me a toothless smile.

I look down into her bright green eyes. She has so much hope in them. I haven't decided if I should have that much hope when it comes to Danita. Do I feel a connection to her? Yes. Do I want to explore that? Yes.

The problem is, I don't think she will open up enough for that to ever happen. I was once Danita. I've ruined my fair share of relationships because of it. As a cop, you don't want to take your work home, but sometimes it follows you, and it's hell on a relationship.

"Promise me something, love."

"What's that?" Kasey says with all the innocence of a sweet child.

In this moment, she reminds me so much of Erin when she was little. My baby sister looked up to me for any advice I would give her. I wish I would have given her the advice I'm about to give her daughter.

"Never date a cop. As a matter of fact, stay away from any law enforcement. We are hard to love and even harder to walk away from once you do fall."

"Ew. I'm never falling in love. Boys are yucky. They have cooties."

"Aye, they do. I want you to remember that until you're thirty."

"Promise," she says with a sage nod.

I tug her into a hug. She'll break that promise by the time she's sixteen, but I'll hold out hope that she'll find someone worthy of her good heart. I want that for all my nieces and my nephew.

"Uncle Kevin." I grin and turn to face the door. Molly stands there rubbing her eyes, holding her blanket.

"Come on, get over here. I better not wake up with anyone's foot in my mouth in the morning."

The giggles that fill the room as the girls jump on my bed and climb under the covers makes my heart swell. I'm thirty-four. Time is ticking. I want to find someone I can share moments like these with as we have our own lot.

Is that too much to ask?

CHAPTER 8

SUSPICIONS

Kevin

"What did you find?" I say to Shane on the other end of the phone as I walk through my house to see the progress.

"Not much of anything," he says in irritation.

I feel like we're going in circles. I had the same results yesterday and the day before. Every lead turns into a dead end.

Erin has been awake for two weeks, but we still aren't much further along than we were before she opened her eyes. She doesn't remember much that will help us.

I walk to the front of the house to look out into the yard where the kids are playing. I go from working my jaw in frustration to smiling at my nieces and nephew. They're having fun.

Smiles are on their faces for the moment. It warms my heart to see them in my front yard. Not for the first time, I think of my own children growing up and playing in the same yard.

As if knowing I'm watching the kids, Shane breaks through my thoughts. "How are they holding up? You need anything?"

"For now, they're grand. They're playing kickball outside."

Today is my turn to spend the day with them. I only needed to drop in to my place to walk through and make sure things are on track. It should be another three weeks or so before I can start to move in.

I plan to take the kids to Dave and Buster's after we're done here.

Hopefully I'll be able to keep those smiles in place. Although, knowing these four, I'll end up the ref as they argue amongst themselves.

"I'll keep at it. It's only a matter of time."

"Aye, call me if anything comes up."

"Will do."

"Later," I say.

I end the call and stare out the window. Something catches my eye. An unmarked car is parked a ways from my house. I narrow my eyes and decide to head out the back door.

I cross through my backyard and head into the neighbor's, moving through the yard of their house into the next. I'm able to hop the fence of the last house and come up the side.

Now behind the car, I move toward it. I can see the kids playing from here. Con is chasing after the little girls as Mckenna laughs and looks on.

I pull my attention away from them and note the plates on the parked car, then the driver. I'd know that sleek bun anywhere. I round the car and pop open the passenger's side door, sliding into the seat beside her.

She releases a heavy sigh. I stare at the side of her face. Neither of us saying a word at first.

"Are you going to tell me why you're watching my nephew?"

"I need to talk to him," she says, not turning to look at me.

"About?"

"He may have some information that can help me."

I scoff. "That's not going to be enough, sweetheart. This isn't you and me. This is my nephew. When it comes to those kids, I'm not willing to ignore the secrets."

This gets her attention. She turns to lock those whiskey-brown eyes on me. I look deep into her gaze, and for a split second, I see that vulnerability she allowed me to see once before.

"I'm going to trust you because I have no one else to trust. I think

I'm running out of time, and I've run out of options. I need to talk to your nephew—" She cuts off as a call comes in through the scanner. "Damn it, I need to go."

My fists are clenched. I don't like where this conversation was headed. If she's in some type of trouble… I cut the thought off. I don't want to think about her in danger.

"Listen, keep an eye on your nephew. Make sure he keeps himself out of trouble. I'll be in touch soon."

"Danita—" She holds up her hand.

When she looks into my eyes, I see the war within. She gives a nod. It's clear she's relinquishing whatever it is she's warring with.

"I said I need your help. I'll come to you. I promise. These are the last cards I have to play. I won't be able to tell you everything, but I'll do my best to be as honest as I can be. Fair?"

"Fair enough…for now."

"I'll give you a ring as soon as I can."

I bite back all the things I want to say as she starts the car. With a nod, I turn and step out. As she pulls away, I realize she knew I would see her. At least, I believe she wanted to be seen.

My curiosity goes through the roof. I shouldn't trust her, but I do. I look toward the house again where the kids are now sitting in the grass.

It's been about three weeks since Conroy ended up in Danita's cuffs. My head has been in the case to find Erin and Cal's shooters. However, as I think about it now, Con has been acting a little strange.

"What mess have ya gotten into, lad?"

Danita

"Look what the wind blew in," Detective Harris murmurs as I walk into the crime scene.

The house is huge. The type they show on TV shows like *Million Dollar Listings*. Marble floors and dripping chandeliers.

Some deep pockets, for sure. No wonder Serg insisted I take point on this one. Someone is sure to want answers for this.

"Why are you here?" I say to Harris.

He runs his gaze over me. "You know you and I could be something great. I love all that fire you have." He leans into my ear to whisper his next bitter words. "Too bad you're into that Irish perk."

"Excuse me?"

"Anyway. Serg wants me to work this one with you. Something about you not having a partner but wanting you on this case. Blah, blah, blah."

"Code for he didn't want you and Dawson fucking this one up," I scoff.

"Why do you hate me so much? You've never tried to be nice to me. Would it kill you to stop being a—"

"That's why I've never been nice to you. You think it's your right to speak to me any way you want and treat me with disrespect. I've told you no repeatedly."

"You're saying no, but I know I have ways to make you say yes. I'm trying to prevent you from making a big mistake," he says with a cocky grin.

"Unbelievable. Get to work or get out of my way."

He folds his arms over his chest. I ignore him and get cracking on the crime scene in front of us. I pull on a pair of gloves and start to move around the house, searching for clues.

Apparently, this place belongs to some high-profile rich guy. Serg wants me to open and shut this one as fast as I can. As I look around at the sloppy job, I don't think that's going to be a problem at all.

Harris follows behind me like a little puppy. I'm not surprised when his eyes are on me more than on the crime scene. I move into the bedroom of the home, where the safe was entered by the perps.

I scan the area and roll my shoulders as I process visually before making a move.

"Maybe if you were nicer to me, I'd help you release some of that stress," Harris says as he steps into the closet behind me. "You know, I didn't think that other guy was your type. I didn't think he was your boyfriend until he disappeared, and you started acting like…your attitude changed."

I freeze and turn to face him. When I look into his blue eyes, I see a mix of curiosity, jealousy, and…anger? It's as if he's fishing for answers.

"What guy?"

He gives a short laugh. "Come on, sweetheart. Don't play stupid. Big guy with the glasses. Intense, looked like he had a stick up his ass. Used to stop by your place."

I stiffen. "How do you know who used to stop by my place?"

He waves me off and turns to walk away. I grab his forearm and stop him. My heart is racing.

Was Eric right to be worried about my safety? Did something happen to him because of me? Could Harris be behind his disappearance?

After all, Harris was the last person Eric had been pushing for me to make a case against before he disappeared. He'd been adamant that I build something around Harris. I had tried, but I couldn't get anything solid, much to Eric's frustration.

Harris looks down at my hand on him, then back up at me. I don't release him. "Answer me."

He moves to get into my face. "Have you ever wondered why you were never recruited?"

I take a step back. He's all but admitting there's an inside ring. I narrow my gaze at him.

"They watch your every move before they come for you. One of these days, you'll thank me."

With that, he turns, leaving me stunned. I'm not sure what to think of what just happened, but I feel as unsafe as I ever have. One thing I know for sure, I'm going to need to find out what Cal knew and soon.

A shiver rolls through me. I can't help but wonder if I'm still being watched. And what does he mean that one of these days I'll thank him?

CHAPTER 9

FUN TIMES

Kevin

MOLLY'S GIGGLES FILL THE AIR OF DAVE AND BUSTER'S AS I HOLD HER up while she tosses the basketballs that her big sister hands her. We're trying to beat Con, who's standing next to us with Kasey at his side, cheering him on. It's quite comical.

"I got this, Uncle Kevin." Molly laughs.

"You wish," Con taunts, sinking his third basket in a row.

"Don't listen to him. Stay focused," I say to Molly. I know she's not going to beat him, but I give her hope anyway.

"*Oh*," Con crows as the buzzer sounds and he sinks his last shot.

"Oh man," Molly says.

I place her down on her feet. She pouts and folds her arms over her chest as she looks up at her brother. I purse my lips to keep from laughing.

"I'm going to be big one day, and we'll see what happens. Just you wait," she says.

Con tugs her in and messes her hair. "I'll be waiting."

"What do you guys want to do next? I want to play the Jurassic Park game again," Mckenna says.

"Yeah, let's go," Conroy says and takes off before anyone can reply.

Mckenna follows behind him, but I grab Molly and Kasey before they can run off. "Hold on, you two. That's a two-person game." Not to mention the violence, but I don't say that to them because it'll hurt their little feelings. "We'll find something else to do."

"Look, they're finally off Halo. We can go play that now," Molly says.

"Ha, you're not getting my ass kicked," I snort. That game is more violent than Jurassic Park.

"Swear jar. That's a dollar," Molly says as she pouts. "We're not babies. We can play it. Mommy lets us watch Con when he plays it."

"I'll put in my dollar," I say and refrain from rolling my eyes. I'm going to smack Trent upside the head for his swear jar idea. "How about we play that bowling game?"

"Okay," Molly murmurs. "But I want to do the motorcycles after."

I don't tell her I think she might be too little for those. Erin's kids are pretty tall for their ages. Maybe I'm wrong.

We make rounds to a few of the games before Con and Mckenna catch up to us. The little girls are having a blast, and the twins seem to be enjoying themselves too. I'll admit, this has been fun. They're all hilarious. Thank God they're not spoil sports.

"Uncle Kevin, I'm hungry again," Kasey says, giving me puppy dog eyes.

I've dropped almost three hundred dollars in food alone in here already. These kids eat like a basketball team. I look at my watch. I should probably get them home to bathe and get ready for bed soon.

"Looks like it's time to call it a night," I say to them all, earning groans from the twins.

"Kevin, is that you?"

I look up and lock eyes with my ex. She looks good. Still fit like the fitness trainer she is. Her brown skin has a glow to it. She's cut all her hair off and now has a pixie cut that's cute on her.

"Hey, Evelyn," I reply.

She looks around at the kids surrounding me. "Wow, is that your niece and nephew? They've gotten so big. Are the other two yours?" She bites her lip as she drags her eyes over me in an appreciative gaze.

"No, they're all Erin's."

"Hi, I'm Kasey," my niece sings as she waves up at Evelyn while Molly hides behind me shyly.

"Hello, cutie," Evelyn says in return, not taking her eyes off me.

I place a hand on Molly's head as she clings to my leg. Evelyn follows the gesture and her smile grows. Kasey reaches for my other hand.

"So you're single still?" she asks, and I shrug. "You look amazing. I've been watching you with these guys, and my friends and I thought you were such a good dad. Then I realized it was you."

"Yeah, I'm spending some time with my family. Listen, we're about to leave."

I have no desire to rekindle anything from our past. Our relationship was a dumpster fire waiting to happen. In the end, it was best we went our separate ways.

The great sex wasn't worth the fighting, lack of communication, or dishonesty. The woman knows how to use sex as a weapon and tool of manipulation. I was younger, my priorities sucked. I've grown up a lot since then.

Evelyn moves in, closing the distance, and places her hand on my chest. "Maybe we can trade numbers or something," she says and gives me a bright smile.

"I don't think that's such a good idea."

"Oh man, come on," Conroy groans, drawing my attention.

I turn to look at him, and he has a frown on his face. Following his gaze, I find none other than Detective Moralez walking toward us. She takes my breath away. I take her in from head to toe.

Her hair is loose; it's longer than it was two years ago. Her dark waves bounce around her shoulders and in her face. She has on a pair of black patent leather heels and tight blue jeans, along with a white T-shirt under a navy blue blazer. Her badge is around her neck.

I never thought I'd find a cop so sexy, but damn, Danita makes a badge and gun look hot as hell. I suck my lip into my mouth and smile as I remember peeling her out of a similar pair of jeans. Reminding myself where I am and who I'm with, I shove those thoughts back.

"Hey, I thought that was you." She holds up a takeout bag. "Looks like we had the same idea."

I narrow my eyes at her. This is no coincidence. However, I play right along with her.

"I guess great minds do think alike."

Moralez turns her attention to Evelyn. "And who do we have here?"

I don't even try to hide the shit-eating grin that comes to my face. Is that jealousy I detect? My little detective might as well turn green as she lets that monster show.

This woman does my head in.

Danita

Are you kidding me?

I chide myself as soon as the words are out of my mouth. I have absolutely no right to be jealous, but the feeling rises in me as I watch this woman with her hand on Kevin. She's pretty. Very attractive, in that Instagram model type of way.

Pecan-colored skin, hips and ass for days, a snatched waist. She's killing that pixie cut. One thing becomes apparent to me. Kevin has a sweet tooth; he seems to like him some brown women.

I don't know why knowing this puts something within me at ease. The thought of not being a product of curiosity causes me to look more closely at the night I spent getting to know Kevin.

I quickly shut that door. I'm here to get information, not start a relationship. However, I can't take my eyes off the hand this woman still has on his chest.

He takes a step back until her hand falls away. "This is an old friend, Evelyn. Evelyn, this is Danita," he introduces.

My heart jerks. Hearing him use a name that's not mine brings reality home. No matter if this woman is from his present or his past, I'll never be either. I can't be. He doesn't even know who I am.

She gives a fake laugh. "Old friend? I think we were well past friends."

"That was a long time ago," Kevin says pointedly.

I don't miss the pout that comes to Evelyn's face. I shouldn't be so glad he has made their status clear, but I'd be lying if I said it doesn't give me a bit of satisfaction. Despite knowing things between us will never go anywhere, it brings a smile to my lips. Dismissing this woman and the past she may have had with Kevin, I turn my focus to the kids.

I squat and look between the two little girls at his sides. "Well, who do we have here?"

The younger-looking one steps forward with a wave. "I'm Kasey," she says.

I hold out my hand for hers. "Nice to meet you, Kasey. Such a pretty name for a pretty girl."

Her face lights up instantly. Taking my hand with her little one, she gives a good shake. I then turn to her sister. This one looks like Cal a bit more than the others.

"And what's your name?" I ask the shy-looking girl as she hides halfway behind her uncle's leg.

She looks up at Kevin before she turns back to me with a bright little smile. "I'm Molly." Instead of taking my hand, she moves forward and wraps her arms around my neck.

I'm a little surprised by the gesture, but I wrap my arms around her and give a good squeeze. When I look up at Kevin, he has a shocked look on his face. I lift a brow in question.

He smiles and mouths, *She's super shy.* I nod as I give her another squeeze.

These poor babies have been through a lot. I'm sure she needs a hug. I'm glad to be able to give it.

"It's nice to meet you, Molly," I say when she takes a step back.

The Evelyn chick squats beside me. "Wow, that looked like a great hug. Can I have one?"

I stand and turn to look away to keep from laughing as Molly races back behind Kevin's leg. I guess there's a reason she and Kevin aren't together anymore. They say kids know things.

"She's a bit shy," Kevin says in explanation to Evelyn.

"Oh, that's okay," she says and stands.

When I turn to look back at Kevin, he has mirth dancing in his eyes as he locks gazes with me. He reaches out for my hand and tugs me closer to lean into my ear. That same energy that always passes between us hums through my hand and straight to my belly.

"Molly never hugs strangers. I'm not the only one drawn to you at first sight," he whispers.

I'm not a butterflies kind of girl, but I suddenly have a stomach full. When Kevin backs away, his eyes drop to my lips. It takes everything in me to ignore the heated stare he gives me.

"So, you're a cop too?" Evelyn asks. "Did you guys used to work together or something?"

"She's a detective. No, we never worked together," Kevin responds.

"Uncle Kevin, I'm still hungry," Kasey says.

"Hey, I have some French fries. You want to share them?"

Her little face lights up. "Yeah," she says excitedly.

I go to reach for her hand, but my phone rings. I groan and slump my shoulders. I won't be getting to eat this food or getting the answers I came for.

Excusing myself, I answer the call, and sure enough, I have to go in. I finish the call quickly as agitation builds. I'm already exhausted and stressed as it is.

Frustration covers Kevin's face as I turn back to him. "Duty calls," he says.

"Yup, you've got it. Tomorrow is my official day off. We'll hook up then?"

He nods. "I need to be in the office in the morning, but once I have my work covered, I'll be ready to hear all you have to say," he says.

I return his nod and bend to hand my bag of food over to Kasey. She smiles as she places it down before her to look inside. I look over her shoulder.

"Maybe you can share the burger with Conroy," I say as I look him in the eyes.

The kid looks between me and his uncle, no doubt trying to figure out if he can trust me. I'm willing to earn his trust if that's the only way I'm going to get the answers I need. Kevin reaches to mess Conroy's hair as if to show him it's okay to trust me.

"Thanks," Conroy says.

"Thank you," Molly says around a fry.

"Anytime."

CHAPTER 10

WE NEED TO TALK

Kevin

Looking down at my watch, I snarl at the time. It's after six o'clock and I'm finally getting back to the office after my rounds. I would have been done much sooner if it hadn't been for Quinn being so distracted this morning.

Quinn needs to get it together, but he's not the only one. I toss my key on the desk and plop down in my chair. I stare at the computer screen unseeingly while ignoring the few people that are still here at this hour.

I wanted answers yesterday when Danita showed up at the restaurant. Conroy had this look in his eyes all night after she left. I still remember the look he had when I picked him up after he was arrested.

When I asked him about it last night, he shrugged it off and said it was nothing. I let it slide at the time because I know my nephew. If I push him too far, he'll shut down or start to butt heads with me.

Danita says she needs his help. I'm not going to cause Con to clam up before I know facts. However, patience has never been my strong suit. I've been waiting to hear from her all day.

"Ah, fuck this," I say and grab my keys.

It's never been in my character to let things slide once I know something's not right. Moralez was watching my nephew for a reason. I want to know why now, not later.

I wave Scott off as he heads toward me with papers in his hand.

I know he's coming for me to sign off on his expense reports. I'll get to all of that tomorrow. I'm headed out the door when my phone vibrates in my pocket. I pull it and answer without checking who the caller is.

"Blackhart," I grunt into the device.

"It's me. I'll be getting out of a cab in front of your office in about five minutes."

"Go straight to the black Viper in the lot. I'll be waiting," I say and pick up my pace.

Once outside, I lean up against the passenger side of my car. I take a look at my watch as I stand with my arms folded over my chest. I'm not waiting long before a car pulls up and Moralez steps out in black slacks, Converse, a white T-shirt, and a New York Yankees cap pulled down over her eyes. She has a messenger bag tossed across her torso.

She moves to me quickly, and I open the door for her to get into my car. After she's inside, I round the car, get in, and start out of the lot. I shift in my seat as her scent fills the space.

Silence surrounds us as I wait for her to start explaining. We're almost halfway to my rental apartment when I decide to break the silence. I want answers.

"What's going on, and what does my nephew have to do with it?"

She releases a heavy sigh and turns toward me. I give her a quick glance before turning back to the road. I can't see her eyes underneath the cap, which frustrates me.

"I'm going to tell you as much as I can. Which might not be much."

"The more I know, the more I can help," I say.

"The more you know, the more danger you'll be in. Listen, I need you to trust me. I know I'm asking for a hell of a lot, but it's safer for everyone if I tell you what you need to know and only what you need to know," she says with a hint of a plea in her voice.

I work my jaw. This goes against every fiber of my being. However,

I can feel the desperation coming off her. I bite back the words I want to say and nod for her to continue.

"I have something to show you. Can we go somewhere to talk more?"

"We'll be at my place in a few. Have you eaten?"

"No." She chuckles. "I haven't had a thing since yesterday afternoon. I really had planned to eat and talk to you yesterday."

I frown. I know all too well how the job can cause you to forget to eat. I don't like the fact that she hasn't had something in over twenty-four hours.

I pull into the parking lot at my place and turn off the car to get out. I make a face when I round the car and Danita is already outside closing her own door. Placing a hand on the small of her back, I lead her up to my apartment.

"This is a nice community," she says, bringing me from thoughts of how right my hand feels on her. "I thought that was your place I was outside of the other day."

I grin, knowing she's fishing for information. "I got this place to be able to help with the kids. My house is still under construction. It'll be done soon."

She turns her head up at me. I can finally see her eyes. "You're a good uncle. I can see how much you care about those kids. They're lucky to have you. Especially..." Her eyes turn sad. "I'm glad your sister is awake. How's Cal doing?"

I release a heavy breath, stopping in front of my door to unlock it. "There hasn't been much change. It's not looking good, but we're hopeful for the kids, if nothing else."

"Sounds like you're not a fan of Cal's," she says as I wave her into the apartment ahead of me.

"It's not that I'm not a fan. I've known him since we were little. Cal has always gotten himself into shit. Not that my brothers and I were saints, but we never got caught, not like Cal."

"I wish I would have known this," she says somberly.

I pause and stare at her as she takes her bag from across her body. I tense as realization hits. It never dawned on me that my fuck-up brother-in-law could have gotten Con involved in his shit. I don't know why I'm surprised.

My head is ready to explode. I narrow my eyes at Danita. My anger grows as it dawns on me that she might have information that could have helped us weeks ago.

"Okay, now this has changed to something else," I seethe. "You know something about my sister's shooting, don't you?"

"Yes, but before you fly off the handle, you need to listen to what I have to say. You'll understand why I didn't come to you sooner. Why I couldn't."

"Start talking." I point to the couch for her to sit.

She moves over to take a seat and opens her bag, pulling a file out. I sit beside her, and she hands it over. I scowl as I start to flip through the contents.

"Are you kidding me? What is this?"

"Cal and I were working together to get these guys. He stumbled into my case. I couldn't allow him to keep picking at the thread he was after, because he was going to blow all my hard work. When I figured out how deep he had gotten into the ring with his investigation, it made sense to work alongside of each other. He'd get his case and I'd get what I needed."

She blows out a breath. "For reasons I can't explain, I need to land this case. If you look close enough, you'll see I don't have shit with what's there. Cal was supposed to give me the rest of the pieces I needed on my end. He said he was almost there, and I needed to be patient. We were going to meet the day after the shooting. He thought he had my ace."

She pauses and rubs her forehead. "I'm running out of time to be patient. I can't sit on this case much longer without connecting the dots. Something has to give, and I think your nephew may have the answers I need."

"And what is it you think my nephew has?"

She chews on the inside of her mouth for a moment. "Cal was onto something. He had connected himself to a situation that would lead to the big fish. I need to know who or what that was, so I can finish this."

"And you think my nephew has that information?" I look at her in confusion.

"Yes. My instincts tell me he may know more than that, but I'm willing to start there."

"How do I know we can trust you? How do I know you're not behind the shooting?"

Her eyes tear up. She quickly swipes at the corners of her eyes. I watch her closely. I've never been fooled by tears or emotions. Comes with the job. I look deeper to the core of the person sitting before me.

"I haven't been able to sleep since I heard what happened. Keeping my distance and not saying a word has been the hardest thing I've ever had to do. I wanted to come to you and your brothers to tell you about these bastards, but I didn't know if Cal had led them to me too.

"The last thing I wanted was to bring this shit to the rest of your family's door, and let's face it, I'm not trying to get myself riddled with holes. I went looking for Con because I wanted to get answers, but I also knew it would bring you guys closer so I could give you information as well as find out anything you guys might know," she says.

"Ya don't know me and my brothers. We're not going to just take yer word and be done with it. Especially when yer admitting that yer still hiding details from us."

"Kevin, I have nothing else to lose. This mess I'm in, I'm in it alone. The one person I trusted is fighting for his life and his wife has been caught in the middle. I'm pleading with you to leave what I don't tell you out of this. I'd rather lose my life than drag another soul into this.

"I need to know what your nephew knows, and then I'll stay away from you and your family. That's all I'm asking of you." She points to the file. "When I can complete that, I can get out of all of your hair."

"Again, what makes you think Con can help?" I say, homing in on her to watch for any lie she may tell.

She pulls her cap off her head and tosses it on the coffee table, then runs a hand through her hair. She shakes her head then throws it back. I can see the sorrow that crosses her face.

"I should have called it off that day. Cal was growing sloppy. Too anxious to get whatever he thought was going to be the nail in the coffin.

"He arrived at one of our meetings with the kid in the car. I was so angry with him. He compromised everything. My safety—" She cuts off and clamps her mouth shut.

"Your safety?" I tilt my head to the side.

"He never should have had the kid with him."

"What the fuck was he thinking?" I drag a hand through my hair.

She sighs. "I don't think he was. That's what I'm trying to say. He got reckless. Honestly, I thought this was going to blow back on *me*. I never thought it would hit your sister's door. I now see he was in way over his head."

I sit and stare at her. I can feel her truth. I trust that she's being honest. However, I know she's holding back a lot more.

With my eyes narrowed on her, I tell her why this isn't going to work this way. "I want to help ya, love, but my brothers are not going to help ya without all the details. As is, they're going to want to know what the hell is going on and what Cal got our baby sister into."

She groans. "It's safest this way. If you want to know the truth, one thing sort of doesn't have anything to do with the other. Yeah, this case is huge, and Cal got himself into the middle of some shit, but where

I come in is something entirely different. Something bigger. That's a danger to me, not your sister or your family. At least, I'm trying to keep it so it's not."

I shake my head. "Let me explain this another way. I trust that yer being truthful and that ya want us to stay out of whatever trouble ya have yerself in. However, what ya don't understand is my brother Quinn has this gift. He would say it's OCD, but I think it's a gift. He makes these lists; he's organized about everything. That allows him to see things others don't.

"He's been torn up about things with Erin, and he has something else distracting him at the moment, but when he gets focused, whatever yer hiding, he's going to home in on it and yer going to have to come clean. It's a Quinn thing, and I can promise ya he's going to lock in on ya sooner or later," I say and frown.

"Then I need to get your nephew talking before your brother becomes undistracted."

"Then there's Trenton's six sense."

"Right, avoid Trenton."

I pull a face and look her in the eyes. I don't know what makes me go along with this. It's a gut feeling, not to mention the urge to protect her. An urge that grows stronger the more she talks.

"I'll order something to eat, and then we'll figure out how to bring my brothers into this without them becoming suspicious. We're going to have to have your story together if we're going to pull this off."

"Thank you," she says, her shoulders sagging.

"Don't thank me yet. I'm only going along with this as long as I don't see a threat toward my family or *anyone's* safety. The moment this starts to go sideways, I want the whole truth and nothing but."

CHAPTER 11
GROUND RULES

Danita

"Seriously, this is your great idea? Pretending to be my boyfriend? Really," I seethe once Kevin's brothers have gone after a nightlong interrogation by Quinn and a morning of going over it all again for Trent and Shane.

"I think it's the best idea. Everyone at the precinct saw the chemistry between us. Some know that we have history—"

"Wait, you showing up to pick your nephew up and almost kicking Harris's ass *does not* show chemistry. It shows that you're a hothead. A hothead that was already pissed at *me* for collaring your nephew. How does that in any way lead to us dating?"

"Danita, Danita, Danita. See this with me. It's been two years since our one night together. A night those that were at the bar will assume turned out hot and steamy. You happened to arrest my knucklehead nephew, which brings me back into your life and the sparks are still there. After seeing me ready to defend your honor and seeing that I'm still hot as fuck, we decided to give it another shot," he says with a smug grin.

I bark out a laugh. "Bullshit. I did not sign up for you to become my babysitter. If I didn't think your brother Trenton was going to blow everything up, I would have nipped that shit in the bud."

I'm still not sure Trenton trusts me, and if I'm being honest, I think Quinn is a little wary as well. He spent the entire night watching me. I repeated everything to him almost a million times before he was willing to call Shane and Trenton in to help.

I flop back on Kevin's couch, exhausted and ready to sleep for at least two days. Quinn alone can be intense. Add Kevin and his two younger brothers to the mix and you have a recipe for a stress-induced panic attack.

Kevin winks at me. "It comes with the deal. You want Con to trust you enough to talk to you, you're going to have to be around to earn that trust."

I blow out a breath and toss my head back. "I thought we were going to sit the kid down and...you know, tell him to cough up what I need to know."

He snorts. "You've met my nephew, haven't you? That's not going to work, love. You're going to need to do this my way or find what you need on your own."

"So, this is *only* about me getting your nephew to trust me enough to talk to me," I say, not believing a word.

He shrugs. "I can't help what happens when the two of us get together. Our connection is undeniable. Even if you try to deny it."

I roll my eyes. "Kevin, I told you things are complicated. The last thing you should want is to get involved with me."

"I hear you, love. I hear you. How about for now I make you some lunch?"

"You cook?"

"Ach, you say that as if you're surprised."

I smile. "I think you're avoiding the question."

He gives a boyish grin that does all kinds of things to my belly. It's adorable and endearing all at once. I have to look away. Staring into my lap as if I've found a new case, I busy myself with rubbing my hands on my pants. I really should be leaving to go shower and get ready for work tonight.

"I'm not the world's greatest cook, but I do all right. I can feed myself."

"I think I'll pass," I say teasingly.

"You know how to wound a man," he grumbles as he goes to the refrigerator.

I get up and move closer, sitting at the kitchen island. I laugh a little as he murmurs to himself with his hands on his hips. He runs a hand through his red locks.

"It would seem I may need to go grocery shopping," he says.

I burst into a full belly laugh. He ordered pizza last night. I was so grateful to be filling my stomach with something, I didn't much care.

"I'll order some Chinese. You have anything you want?"

"I'll take whatever. I have to leave soon," I reply.

He rounds the island and comes to stand before me. I'm not ready when he brushes his fingers against my cheek. A shiver runs through me and my nipples harden against my bra.

"I was hoping we could spend a little more time together."

"Kevin," I say in warning. "If we're going to do this, since your brothers think I can't handle myself and you think this is the only way to get your nephew to talk to me, maybe we should set a few ground rules."

He gives me that sexy grin of his. "Ground rules? What do you have in mind?"

"First, I don't think we need to have any type of PDA. Being that we haven't been together long, this is a new relationship. We can say we haven't reached that stage."

"No one is going to believe that. For your safety, this should be as believable as possible," he says with a smile. He leans in to kiss the tip of my nose. "With a lass as beautiful as you, there's no way, as your boyfriend, I'd be able to keep my hands off of you."

"Kevin."

"Aye, that's my name, and I love the way you say it. It reminds me that you make it sound so good in the throes of passion. What's your next rule?"

"This…whatever you think we're doing, doesn't interfere with my job. I can handle myself."

"You asked for my help, love. I only know one way to protect you. I'll be integrating myself into your life in any way I can to make sure I'm doing my job right. Next."

I twist my lips and frown at him. His eyes twinkle as he looks back at me. He's enjoying this.

"This is a bad idea," I mutter.

"So you say." He nods. "Listen, my main goal is to protect you. You don't have to worry about anything else. You're not alone anymore. You have me. I'll be your protector, a friend, a sounding board, or whatever you need me to be. I'm all of that before anything else."

Those words shouldn't hit me in my heart, but they do. It makes me ache to have something real with the gorgeous man standing before me. Kevin will make some woman a great boyfriend someday. For now, I have to keep reminding myself that he's only my pretend boyfriend until I get the information I need.

Then, I'm out. I can finally reclaim my life. Now, to survive this with my heart and my life intact.

Kevin

I've been thinking about Danita and her rules since she left. No PDA. She has no idea how much I wanted to kiss her while she was here, and we were alone.

I'm bound to break that rule the first chance I get, when I have a reason to. Just the thought of her plush, soft lips brings a smile to my face. It's not like her gaze didn't drop to my lips a few times either.

No, I'm not the only one feeling this connection. I rub my chin as I try to think of what else she could be hiding. I don't like the fear

I see in her depths. It's going to be hard to fight back my instincts to do things my way for her protection, but I'll do it until I fix this first issue. Then, I'll get to the bottom of it all.

My phone rings and I groan into my mattress. I've been face-planted here since Danita's departure. I haven't slept and thought I'd get some rest before heading into the office to work late.

"Hello," I breathe into the phone when I finally reluctantly answer.

"Uncle Kevin, you have a minute?" Con's voice greets my ear.

I roll onto my back. "Sure, kid. What's up?"

"You know that cop, the one who arrested me?"

"Yeah, Detective Moralez. What about her?"

There's silence on the other end for a few beats. I pull the phone from my ear to make sure the call is still connected. When I place it back to my ear, Conroy releases a heavy sigh.

"Do you know her well?"

I'm not going to lie to the kid, but I know I need to help Danita gain his trust, so my brothers and I can sink our teeth into what Cal got himself into. The gears grind in my head for a way to earn his trust for her and not break the trust he has in me. Con is a good kid despite his hard head.

"She and I are getting to know each other more. We've shared things about ourselves with each other," I reply.

This is not a lie. In one night, Danita and I told each other a lot of things about ourselves. I still remember a lot of the stuff she told me back then.

"Are you like, dating her or something?"

"Yeah, you can say that. She'll be around more."

He pauses again. "Cool, but…at the precinct. You seemed pretty mad at her. Does that mean you don't trust her?"

I shake my head as if he can see me and run a hand through my hair. "That was a complicated situation for us. Danita and I have some things we need to work on. Con, I've known a ton of bad cops. Guys and women that never should have a badge. I know them when I see them before they open their mouths. Detective Moralez has never given me a reason to question which kind of cop she is."

"So, you think she's one of the good ones? You think my dad could trust her?"

"I think she is, and I think he did."

Silence falls once again. I wait him out, hoping he'll open up and tell me what's going on. However, I don't push. This is Con. I know what pushing can do, and the two of us can and will lock horns fast.

"Okay, I just wanted to know. Seeing as Molly took to her and all. It's my job to protect my sisters," he says after a while.

"Con, you know that you can come to me if you ever need, right?"

"Yeah, I know. I… Everything's fine. Like I said, Molly and Kasey seemed to like her. I wanted to make sure she's cool. If you're dating her, then she must be. You never make mistakes."

This time I take a pause. Does this kid really think that? Hell, I make plenty of mistakes.

Letting Danita get away from me has been one of those. I can't help wondering if things would be different for her now if I would have pursued her then. I shake the thought off and focus back on my nephew.

"How about we play some hoops this weekend?"

"Yeah," he says with the most excitement I've heard in his voice in weeks.

"You're on. I'm going to get some sleep, kid. We'll talk later."

"Okay, thanks, Uncle Kevin. Later."

"Con?"

"Yeah?"

"I love ya. Ya call anytime and come to me whenever ya need," I say as emotions try to take over my voice.

"I love you too, Uncle Kevin. Even when I'm a pain in your ass."

I chuckle. "Later, kid."

CHAPTER 12

SLIP UP

Kevin

"Look alive, Con," I say as I release a jumper.

Con frowns and turns to watch the ball sink into the basket. The hoop at my house is already up and the driveway has been set with new asphalt. Perfect for me to kick Con's ass on the court.

"Oh, man. Come on," he groans. "Aren't you supposed to let me win?"

"Aye, in yer dreams." I chuckle.

"I like when you guys do that."

I tilt my head to the side and study my nephew as his cheeks pink. "Do what?"

"With Uncle Quinn, you're never going to get anything other than an accent, but with you and Uncle Shane, even Uncle Trent sometimes, you guys slip in and out. It's like our family's thing. It's always made me feel… I don't know. Like we have something special about us. Not everyone can always understand it, but I get it and that makes me feel…" His cheeks turn a deeper shade of red. "Safe."

"Safe," I repeat.

I'm hearing that as a need from those around me a lot lately. It makes me both angry and concerned that they feel anything but safe on my watch. It especially guts me when I see the fear in my baby sister's eyes.

This has taken a toll on Erin, and now I can see more clearly that it's having a big effect on my nephew and nieces. I squash my anger to address Con's needs as his words settle in. I want nothing more than for him to be safe and happy.

"Never mind. Forget I said anything. It's stupid," he mutters.

"It's not stupid," I say, allowing my accent to show through. "I think I know what ya mean. In school, when we first started in elementary, it was hard. Mum and Da have such thick Norn Iron accents, it was all we knew.

"I didn't think I'd ever be able to speak like everyone else. I got picked on and teased for at least the first two years, but when I got home around family, it didn't matter. We all sounded the same, and it did feel safe.

"I think that may be why we cling to the comfort now when we get around one another. I get ya, Con. It's not stupid. It makes a lot of sense," I say, reaching to place a hand on his shoulder and giving it a gentle squeeze.

"I remember Mom used to sing me to sleep in Gaelic," he says with a small smile. "Dad tried a few times, but his singing is terrible and so is his Gaelic."

I give a good laugh. Cal is third generation Irish. His Gaelic does suck, and he has always had trouble following our dialect in my family's home. Sometimes my brothers and I make it so he can't keep up. It's funny as hell and pisses him off.

"No one told me we were going to be playing hoops." I turn to find Danita in my driveway in a pair of jeans and heels. My favorite on her. She points over her shoulder. "I have sneakers in my car."

I don't think twice. I saunter over to her and grab a fist full of her black button-down blouse. Without a word, I capture her lips and devour her.

She moans into my mouth and locks her fingers into my sweaty hair, bringing a smile to my face. I let go of her shirt and cup her ass, drawing her closer to me. When I start to grow hard, I release her and take a step back.

She looks at me in a daze for a few seconds. "What was that about?"

I step in closer and place my forehead to hers. "One, my nephew is watching. Two, we don't know who is watching you. Either way, we want this to look real."

"I think number one should have been that you just wanted to," she breathes.

"There's that." I laugh.

"Hey, Detective Moralez." Con walks over. I turn to see a cheeky smile on his face.

"Call me Danita, kid," she replies. "Were you out here giving your uncle the business?"

"No," Con murmurs and looks down at his feet. "He's kicking my butt."

"Is that right? Well, I'm going to go get my kicks. I'll show you how to handle giants like this guy," she says with a saucy smile on her lips.

"Oh really?"

"Yeah, really. I think I have my gym bag with me. Can I change inside?"

I lift a brow. "You're serious?"

She gives me this gorgeous smile that takes over her face. "Yeah, I grew up with three brothers. I can—"

The color drains from her face. I search her eyes to figure out what happened that fast. One minute, she was all smiles and playful. The next, she's so ashen, my heart starts to race as I wonder if she's okay.

She ducks her head and frustration covers her features as I duck my head and try to read her. I reach to lift her chin with my fingertips. I use my other arm to wrap around her and tug her closer to me.

"What is it, love?"

She shakes her head. "Maybe this isn't a good idea. I'll come back some other time."

I grind my teeth. I had asked her to come over and spend time with me and Conroy. I thought this weekend would be a great time to bond with him and get him to bond with her.

I kiss the tip of her nose. "There's no time like the present. Get your bag. You can use one of the rooms in the house to change. You have to beware of the windows is all. No drapes up yet. Don't want to be giving my neighbors a show, you don't."

"I'm so here for this," Con says.

"See, you can't disappoint the kid. You just made some big promises."

She gives a small forced smile. Something is still lurking in her eyes as her gaze takes on a distant look. Con's attention is focused on us, so I let it go and don't press to find out what the heck happened.

"I'll get my things," she says.

"I'll come with you. I can show you inside after."

Con goes back to dribbling the basketball as I walk side by side with Danita to her car. She pops the trunk and retrieves a gym bag. She's lost in her thoughts as we walk back to the house.

"What happened back there?"

"I think I need to get some sleep. That's all," she murmurs.

Okay, she's not going to give me any answers. I run the conversation back and try to figure it out on my own. I stop outside of one of the guestrooms right as it hits me.

"When I first met you, you said you were an only child," I say.

She freezes. "What?"

"You were saying that you grew up with three brothers. However, that night we spent together when I told you I had four siblings, you told me you had none."

"That was two years ago. You're probably mixing me up with someone else," she says.

I scoff. "I haven't been dating. I also have a steel-trap memory. I know what you told me."

She turns to look up at me. "Let this one go."

I crowd her space, backing her into the guest room door. Placing both arms on either side of her head, I look down into her eyes. I search her face closely.

"I'll let this go if you have dinner with me," I say.

Danita

"Dinner with you?" I repeat back to him. My anger with myself rises. "Seriously? I just made a huge mistake. A mistake that's so not like me. The last thing I need to do is go out to dinner with you."

He reaches to trace his fingertips along my hairline. "I don't think anything between us is a mistake. I think your spirit knows mine and you're as drawn to me as I'm drawn to you. You can't help showing me who *you* are."

"I need to keep my head. I have to finish what I started. I don't need anything to distract me from that."

He lifts my chin with his pointer finger. "Distraction. I don't see any distractions," he says before crushing his mouth to mine.

One minute we're in the hallway, the next he has pushed our way into the room at my back. I drop my bag once inside and wrap my arms around his neck. Swift as a cat, he closes the door behind us and slams my back against it.

I moan and claw my fingers into his hair. He groans into my mouth. I've never been silly over a man, but this one has me doing some stupid shit.

Knowing I need to gain control of the situation, I break the kiss and push at his chest. The heat in his eyes as he stares at my lips almost causes me to change my mind. I cup his handsome face.

"What I don't think you understand is that we wouldn't be a one-night thing," I say.

"Never said we would, love. I know we wouldn't."

"Exactly. I can't give you more than one night. It wouldn't work."

He shakes his head. "It's a lie ya tell. My soul burns whenever yer near. It's like it's calling for me to get close to ya. Ya want to tell me that's something that can't work. I call bullshit, love."

"There's so much you don't know about me."

"That's why I want to take ya to dinner. I want to get to know ya."

I sigh and place my forehead against his chest. "What if you don't like what you learn? I'm telling you that you're going to pull yourself into a mess."

He lifts my head. Those green eyes pierce right through me. It's like they reach inside and tug something from me.

"I remember I told ya I'm willing to take ya as ya are," he says and nips at my bottom lip. "Ya don't have to be anything ya don't want to be with me."

"Dinner?" I whisper.

He smiles against my lips. "Aye, love. Dinner."

"Okay, but first I'm going to kick your ass in basketball."

He makes a noise in the back of his throat. "We'll see about that. The bathroom is that way." He points. "I'll see ya outside."

CHAPTER 13

WHAT DO YOU KNOW?

Kevin

"OH, YOU SEE THAT," CON HOOTS AS DANITA SINKS ANOTHER BASKET.

I wish I could blame it on her round ass backing into me. Yes, that has been a distraction, but she's actually a great player. She's been handing me my face for the last hour.

"You ready for some more?" she says as she bounces the ball to me to check it.

I roll my shoulders. "I'm no quitter. Ya can save the trash talking."

"I think he's getting mad, Con," she says and laughs.

"Yeah, he is." He joins in on her laughter. "Man, I can't wait to tell Uncle Trent about this."

Danita dribbles the ball as she blocks me. "Where's your phone? I'm sure he'll love to see video," she taunts.

"Oh, why didn't I think of that?" He rushes to grab his phone and aims it at us.

I roll my eyes and focus on the woman before me. She crosses me up and goes for another layup. I curse as she stands with her head back, laughing.

The sight causes me to stop and stare. She's so beautiful. Even with sweat soaking her face and her hair piled into a ponytail, she's sexy and stunning. The tank top and leggings she has on show off her curvy body.

Danita is a ripe, full lass. She's toned and thick in all the right places. Danita isn't slim, not at all. She has the type of body that causes you to marvel at God's creation.

"Hey, Uncle Kev. Can we still grill some food? I'm starting to get hungry," Con calls, pulling me from my ogling of the beauty in front of me.

"Yeah, sure. I have steaks marinating inside and a few burgers."

"Cool," he says. "I can get the grill started. Uncle Quinn showed me how. It's the same one he has, right?"

"Yeah, you sure you got this?" I give him a smile.

He puffs out his chest. "I got it. I can have it up in no time."

"Careful. I'll go inside for the meat."

I go inside to grab the food. I'll be so glad when this place is officially done. I miss things like being able to grill in my own backyard after work. My place before this was small, but I had that option.

When I return, Con has the grill going and he's having an animated conversation with Danita about basketball. I grin and place the tray of meat down before I go back inside to get us some drinks. I come back with a cooler filled with bottled water and a few beers, glad I had the foresight to plan all this out.

"I'll take over from here," I say as I go to get the meat on the grill.

"I was wondering if you would answer a few of those questions for me," I hear Danita saying as I place the burgers down.

I turn and Conroy looks between me and her. Indecision wars in his eyes. He fidgets around in his seat.

"I don't think I can help you," he says cautiously.

"Maybe, maybe not. I'm only asking you to answer a few things."

"Like what?" he asks.

"Do you remember me?"

Con chews on his lip. He looks at me again, and I give him a nod. When he cracks his knuckles, I know he's nervous. It's his thing. Whenever he's about to get in trouble, he starts cracking those knuckles.

"Sort of. I think so. You know my dad," he mumbles low.

Danita's face lights up with hope. "Yeah, I do. You came with him one time when he came to meet up with me. You remember that?"

"Yeah," Con says into his lap.

"I was wondering if you can tell me about where you guys went that day before you came to meet me?" she pushes.

Con clams up right before our eyes. I bite back the curse that wants to come out of my mouth. The kid is hiding something, and I get this feeling it's more than the answers to the questions Danita is asking.

"I don't remember much about that day. I remember you because you were pretty and I wasn't sure why my father was meeting up with you," Con says.

The kid is smart. That's a nice cover, but as we lock eyes, Danita and I both know it's a lie. We're going to have to keep at it. My stubborn nephew plans to keep his lips tight, which makes me wonder even more what his father was up to.

Danita

"Am I pushing him too hard, too fast?" I say to Kevin as we stand outside my car.

Kevin places a hand on my hip. "You got more out of him than I thought you would. I get the feeling he's still trying to figure out if he can trust you. He'll be sleeping over at my place tonight. I'm going to see if I can loosen his lips a bit."

The night is crisp, and the stars are twinkling in the sky. There's a comfort in the air that I can't afford to get sucked into. And yet, here I stand.

I had fun spending the day with him and Conroy. After eating the food from the grill, we moved inside the house, where Kevin worked on installing a TV mount in the living room. Con and I sat on the floor talking and joking around.

The kid is cute and funny. Not at all the hard punk he tried to portray that first day I met him. He's even sweet.

"I appreciate that. Thank you."

I do. I saw him try to get Conroy to open up to me. I know I'm asking so much of Kevin. It means a lot that he has been so willing to give me his trust. I know from two years ago how much his family means to him.

"When are you free for dinner?"

I grin up at him. "I don't know. I have a few cases I'm working. I'll be keeping late hours this week."

I still need to close that case Graves tossed at me out of the blue. Those rich folks have him breathing down my neck. I'd probably get it done faster if he'd back the hell off. Home intrusions aren't my damn job anyway.

"Then maybe I need to bring dinner to you."

I side-glance him. "I don't know. You already admitted your culinary skills are limited," I tease.

"Ach, you always mean to wound me." He tugs me into his warmth and wraps his arms around me. "Tomorrow. I'll come to yours. We'll have dinner and watch a movie or something. I'll bring a bone for Sunny too."

"Oh, you know how to play dirty." I smile. Thinking of my dog definitely gets him a few brownie points.

He takes my lips in a searing kiss. I cling to his T-shirt as he consumes me. He's still in his basketball shorts and T-shirt from earlier.

I would have never thought I'd find a sweat-soaked guy so damn sexy. I didn't mind when he pulled me in to consume me when I arrived because he looked amazing as I walked up and found him playing ball with his nephew.

Now, hours later—with no shower and the light musk of playing hard beneath his cologne and natural scent—I still find him alluring in ways I should ignore. My brain warns me to pull away, but my lips want more. The more he gives, the more I want.

"You have no idea how dirty I like to play," he breathes when he breaks the kiss. "Drive safely, love. If anything looks strange, you call me. I'll be there."

I'm still stuck on the dirty comment as he kisses my forehead and then my nose. I don't know why the gesture makes me feel so cherished. I haven't known him long enough to be cherished by him.

My phone rings, breaking me from his trance. I look at the time on my watch, causing me to wrinkle my brows. When I pull my phone from my bag and see it's Harris, I suck my teeth, but answer the call.

"Moralez." Even I can hear how less than thrilled I am to answer this call.

"Where are you? I have something I want you to take a look at. I found something interesting connected with that break-in," he says.

Gah. Dáme un respiro. *Seriously, I want a break from this shit.*

This case is a pain in my ass. First Sergeant Graves, now Harris. I'll be glad when I nail these bastards, so I can put this one to rest.

"Remind me again why we're on a robbery? No drugs were found, and it wasn't gang-related," I grumble.

"Actually, you might be wrong. That's what I want you to see. I can come to your place," he offers.

Is that hope in his voice? His words send a chill through me, and not the good kind. He's definitely not coming to my place. I roll my eyes. It's better to get this over with.

"Meet me at the bar by the precinct. We can talk there," I say.

"I'll be there."

No sooner than I hang up, Kevin has my neck cupped in his palm as he kisses me passionately. I'm surprised, but thoroughly turned on. I'm not sure what to think of the kiss.

It's both possessive and filled with want. My toes curl in my sneakers, and it dawns on me that I'm still in my sweaty leggings and tank top. I must look a mess, but you would never be able to tell that from the way Kevin stares at me.

"I'm calling Shane. He can come get Con. I'll come with you."

He pulls his phone from his pocket even as I shake my head. I meant it when I said all of this can't get in the way of me doing my job. I get that Kevin and his brothers are worried about my safety, but my job is my job.

"No, nope, nope, nope," I say, shaking my head. "This is work. I'll be fine. I'm going to see what's up and then I can head home."

He works his jaw as he looks down at me. I think he's probably more handsome when he's pissed off. I know he doesn't like this, but he'll have to get over it. I have work to do, and my fake boyfriend can't get in the way of that.

I lift on my toes and press my lips to his. "I'll call you and let you know when I get home."

A pang in my heart tells me this feels too much like a real relationship. I ignore the feeling as I smile up at him.

"No matter the time," he replies.

"You got it."

He narrows his eyes, but I widen my smile and wink at him. Quickly, I get in my vehicle before he changes his mind and tries to protest. Once in the car, it dawns on me how much I'm smiling.

I wipe it off my face and start the car. I chide myself for getting lost in this charade. This isn't real, nor can it ever be.

The goal is to get the information I need to get out. This…all of this is a recipe for disaster if I don't reel it in. I can't keep slipping.

"Keep your head, Dem. You have to keep your head."

CHAPTER 14

WARNING BELLS

Danita

I GET TO THE BAR AND LOOK AROUND FOR DETECTIVE HARRIS. I don't see him at first and start to get pissed. I want a long, hot bath and a nice cold beer. I don't have time for this shit.

I turn, ready to walk back out and go home, when my name is called across the semi-crowded bar. I turn back around and find Harris waving from a booth in the back corner. I growl as I realize the position this is about to put me in.

"*Carajo*. This motherfu—" I stifle my words and my temper.

Starting for the back of the bar, I tell myself this will be quick. I nod at a few officers I know. Their faces are lit with curious gazes. With each step, I feel like someone has tied weights to my feet.

In this moment, I'd rather be anywhere but here. I'm suddenly glad I'm still in my sweaty workout clothes. I didn't bother to stop home to change or shower.

"I ordered some wings and those pretzel bites you always get," Harris says as I sit.

I scrunch up my face, not sure how I feel about him knowing what I always order. However, I brush it off and reach for the file on the table. He covers my hand.

"We have time to get to that," he says with a smile. "It's not often I get to have you to myself."

"Okay, first, I'm here for this case and this case only. Second, I've had a long day. After I see what you have to show me, I'm going home and climbing in my bed."

"You don't have to do that alone," he says and gives me that smile that he truly thinks is sexy.

"Oh, yes, I do," I say and snatch my hand and the file from his grasp.

I start to look through it angrily. I'm not surprised by the sexual harassment behind the blue wall. It's something women officers face daily. However, I am disgusted that it's so effortless and blatant. Almost like a sense of entitlement.

"What's the deal? Are you seeing someone?"

I look up from the file and glare at him. He has the audacity to have disdain in his voice as if my dating offends him somehow. I think of Kevin, and I've never wanted to say I have a boyfriend more.

"Actually, I am," I bite out.

He sits back in his seat, a sour look on his face. I close the file and pick it up to leave. We don't need to continue whatever this is.

"I'm calling it a night. I'll see you in the morning. We can follow up on this lead then," I say and head for the door.

I'm officially done here.

Kevin

My phone rings and I grin. I wasn't sure she would call. I saw the change in her body language after she got into her car.

She's still fighting us. Before today, I might have been fine with that. However, after spending the day with her and Con, I know I'm not okay with it at all.

We fit.

"Are you home?"

"Hello to you too." She laughs. "Yes, I just walked in. I'm kicking off my shoes and heading for a bath."

Her dog barks in the background. I'm sure he's happy to see her. A smile spreads across my face.

"Next time you should bring Sunny along. He can run in the back-yard and stretch his legs," I say.

"He gets to stretch his legs here. I have a yard."

"Don't sound so offended. I'm not calling you a bad mum. My yard is probably bigger than yours. He'll have more room to spread out and enjoy."

"So now you're saying my yard is too small."

I chuckle, hearing the humor in her voice. "That's not what I meant, but okay. Whatever you say, love."

Sunny is now barking somewhere in the distance. The sound of running water greets me this time. I close my eyes, calling up the memory of her naked body.

I should probably end this call. I'm only torturing myself, but I can't let go. Today was too real to me. The subtle touches she allowed, the heated kisses I stole, the look in her eyes after every kiss.

"Are you a bubble bath kind of girl?"

She doesn't answer right away. I smile as I hear the splash of water as if she's gotten into the tub. What I'd give to be there with her, to have her in my arms.

"Honestly, I love bubble bath, but I can't remember the last time I got to go buy some. I know I can order online, but there are some things you want the experience of, you know?"

"Yeah, like buying a book," I reply.

"Exactly," she exclaims. "I love having access to my Kindle. Still, there's something about walking into the store and the sight of all the books on the shelves. The smell of the pages and the quiet that prom-ises to tell you so many stories.

"It's the same with the experience of buying bubble bath. I want to go through the scents and explore my options. See the state of mind they'll put me in."

"You know you've made me want to take you to a bookstore and some type of bath and body shop all at once."

She releases an adorable snicker. I love that she has this tough side, but I've seen a softer side of her on a few occasions. I don't think that's something she allows with just anyone.

"I loved bookstores and shopping when I was younger. I don't much think about stuff like that now," she says.

The sound of the water splashing as she moves about has helped me to form a full picture of her. Wet breasts, those gorgeous thighs glistening from the water, her small foot lifting out of the tub to tease me with her painted toes. I shake my head clear.

"Danita?"

"Yes?"

"I'm going to go, love. My thoughts have gone far from the bookstore."

There's a momentary pause. "Yeah, okay. That's for the best."

"I'll be around tomorrow. You won't see me, but I'll be there. Good night, love. Enjoy your bath."

"Good night."

CHAPTER 15

JUST FRIENDS

Danita

I DRAG MY TIRED BONES INTO MY APARTMENT AND START TO PEEL out of my clothes. It's been a long day. I don't know what's worse: all the paperwork from closing two cases or all the work that went into the two arrests?

The squad wanted to go out and celebrate, but I dipped out before they could corner me. Between the awkward meeting with Harris last night and plain exhaustion, I knew I wouldn't make it through a single beer, much less through the lengthy celebration I know the guys are capable of.

"Hey, boy. Cut all that noise," I say to Sunny as he runs for the door barking.

He wags his tail excitedly. The doorbell rings seconds after Sunny reaches the door. It's then I remember the man I've forced myself not to think about all day.

There was something last night about the way he told me he'd be there although I wouldn't see him. His words were like a blanket that covered me. It was a reassurance I didn't know I needed.

Tugging my shirt back over my head, I move to the door to answer. When I open it, Kevin is on my doorstep in all his glory. God, this man is gorgeous. The smile on his face says he knows it too.

His black T-shirt molds to his body perfectly. I swear I can see his abs right through it. The blue jeans he has on wrap his long legs lovingly, showing off strong thighs and a nice package.

Yup, I'm tired. My thoughts are proving it. I step back and allow him to walk in.

He moves inside, stopping to dip his head and drop a kiss on my lips. It feels so right, but with no one here to put a show on for, I know it's wrong. Or at least that's what I try to tell myself.

I close the door as Kevin steps into my kitchen. "I'll get dinner heated. You can shower and relax," he says as he busies himself, getting to know my place.

I smile and cross my arms over my chest. "I just walked in. How do you have dinner already? Weren't you keeping an eye on me?"

He looks up with a smile. "I had Shane pick it up from the Golden Clover and drop it off to me."

I tilt my head. "How did you know when I'd be done?"

"Ah, you're asking for my secrets. I can't give them away," he says and winks.

I shake my head. "I'll be back in a few."

Sunny plops down at Kevin's feet like he's an old friend. I roll my eyes. Traitor. When Kevin pulls a bone from one of the bags, I can't help the face-splitting smile that comes to my lips.

I have to force myself away from the sight. He kept his word. I try not to smile so hard as I make my way into my room to shower.

As I strip down, I think of how I used to want to be in a relationship where I could come home to someone. That was before, before I took on this assignment, before I got trapped with no way out. Now, I know that will never happen, not as long as I'm stuck living a lie.

Lies I'm starting to believe for myself. It's getting harder to maintain the differences between Danita and Demaris. I'm starting to feel as though with each day, I'm at risk of never getting out, never getting to live the life I want.

Hold on, Dem. Eric promised you he'd get you out. You have to keep hope that he had a plan.

Tears start to build, but I fight them back. I have to stay strong. If Eric isn't out there, I'll figure this out. One way or another, I'll get out. Then I can cross that bridge of finding myself again once this is all over.

With my thoughts still jumbled, I climb into the shower. I haven't been this overwhelmed and emotional in such a long time. I haven't had the time to be. I've had to look out for myself and try to figure things out.

"Pull it together," I chide and rein it in while washing the day away. I can't fall apart at this stage in the game. I have to keep hope.

Once out of the shower, I tug on a pair of sweat shorts and a T-shirt. Sunny barks from the kitchen and I remember that I should put a bra on. I'm not home alone tonight.

It feels strange, but brings a smile to my face as I walk out of my bedroom and I'm hit with the aromas of something delicious-smelling. My mouth waters and I remember that I only had a banana and smoothie for lunch. The closer I get to the kitchen, the more my stomach starts to growl.

"That smells so good," I say as I stop at the kitchen counter. "What is it?"

"Irish stew and potato cakes," he says.

"They're called boxty, right?"

A huge smile covers his face as curiosity fills his eyes. I shrug and take the bowl and plate he offers me. We both move toward my small dining table.

"Aye, that would be right. Where'd you learn that?"

"When I was younger, I wanted to travel. I'd look up random facts and things to try when I got there. Ireland was on my list."

"I'll have to take you someday," he says and winks at me.

I actually flush. I'm surprised at myself as I feel the heat in my cheeks. He chuckles, but doesn't say anything as he begins to dig into his food. I tell myself he doesn't pick up on the change in hue of my skin. That might be me hoping so more than anything.

"Mmm, this is so good," I exclaim as I take my first bite.

"It's Ma's recipe. My mum has always been a great cook."

I nod and take another bite, this time trying the boxty with the stew. I can't hold back the moans and groans. Kevin smiles across the table at me, a heated look right beneath the surface.

I clear my throat. "You mentioned the Golden Clover. That's your family's business, right?"

"Aye, my father started the pub and expanded when my mum wanted a restaurant of her own."

I smile. "I remember the sweet stories you told me about them. Man, you would think that night was a week. I can't believe the things I still remember." I chuckle.

"I remember everything from the night. I've thought about it from time to time."

I drop my eyes back to the bowl before me and fidget in my seat. Heated memories of that night assault me. It's as if I still can feel his strong hands grasping my thighs.

"Any progress with Conroy?"

He releases a heavy sigh. "Not yet. We were all at Quinn's this morning. I wasn't able to get much from him. Things took a turn, and we had to mobilize."

"Anything I should know about?"

"No, we're taking care of it."

I get a little frustrated. "Taking care of what?"

He's silent for a few beats. "Alicia Rhodes, the woman my brother is seeing, is a friend of Erin's. Until we settle all of this, we want to keep an eye on everyone close to the family. I'm watching over you and now Alicia has someone looking after her."

He goes back to eating, and I know it's the end of this

conversation. My heart twists. I've gotten yet another person involved in my mess. How did I go from Eric telling me to tell no one because it could be life or death, to sharing information with Cal and putting everyone's life in danger?

I try to think of something to distract my thoughts and to lighten the mood. I swallow another bite as my mind races. I settle on something I believe to be safe.

"It looks like the firm has been sustaining. You were concerned about that. You guys have been doing really well from what Cal said." He lifts a questioning brow. "We spent a lot of time together. I've always gotten the impression that you guys mean a lot to him. Almost like he looks up to you and the other two, and Shane is his best friend, right?"

Kevin nods. "We give him shit, but he's family. I think he gets himself into this crap because he's always trying to prove something or please others. I get it. He grew up tough. I think my family was a saving grace for him. He can be a stook, but he means well."

I place my spoon down and smooth my hands across the top of the table, beside my bowl and plate. It's as if a knife twists inside me. I've been blaming myself for what happened to Cal since I heard.

It's all piling up, and I'm feeling the weight press down on me. First Cal and his wife. Now this is affecting others. My chest grows tight.

"I was so desperate for help. You know? I never should have let him get involved. Now, in hindsight, I can see all the times he was unfocused and prone to making mistakes," I say in almost a whisper. "He was a good cop when he was on the force. He was one of the nice ones."

"Hey, Cal would have found his way into trouble no matter what, love. It's his MO. I don't know the depth of what you have going on, but if he was willing to get involved, I know it was for something worth it.

"Cal is always willing to help the underdog. That's what blinds him. He forgets to be cautious because he wants to help the person so much," he tries to reassure me.

This time, the tears do spill over. I swipe at them quickly. Kevin stands and rounds the small table.

He pulls me into his arms, and I sag into his embrace. For the first time in years, I allow myself to break down. I allow myself to feel.

Kevin

"Shh, baby. Shh," I coo in her ear. "None of this is your fault."

"Bullshit." She sniffles. "It's all because of me."

I pull back. "What aren't you telling me?"

She pulls away, shaking her head. "This was a bad idea. Thanks for the food. I'll see you tomorrow."

"Oh, no you don't. You're not getting rid of me that easily. Let's finish our dinner, and we'll watch some TV." I reach to tug her back into my arms. "I think you need a friend more than anything. That's what I'm here for."

It's the truth. I've been watching Danita, and I think she could use a friend or two. For now, I'll be that for her.

It's clear she's barely holding it together. This isn't the same woman I met two years ago. I've noticed the changes. What caused them, I still don't know, but I think this shit with Cal has something to do with it.

She looks up at me, chewing the inside of her jaw. I begin to rub a soothing hand on her back, trying to show her that I'm here to help. She closes her eyes and nods.

We return to our seats, and I watch her closely. She starts on her food again. This time, she's lost in her thoughts. This is not how I wanted this night to go.

I start to wonder if this is the time for me to pursue a relationship with her. I know she's warned me off a few times, but I had planned to ease my way into her heart. You know, show her that she can trust me and the connection we have.

Mind made up, I do what's best for the woman I'm growing feelings for.

"What kind of shows do you like?" I say.

Her eyes clear as if she's coming back to me and the room. "Huh?"

"TV. What kind of shows do you like? Are you into Netflix?"

She gives a small smile. "I like books, remember? When I have free time, I like to read. I'll take a book before I turn on the television."

I put my spoon down and rub my hands together. "Oh, I get to corrupt you," I croon. "Netflix it is. We'll start with *Castlevania*. I should not be the only one in misery waiting for more episodes. We'll hit *The Magicians* after that."

She gives that beautiful laugh. "That's the kind of stuff you watch?"

I tilt my head to the side. "So, you know of them?"

"Yeah, Stevens has two little boys now and his oldest son is like a grown man. I've had to peek over their shoulders to see what they watch. Malcolm, the oldest, likes *Castlevania*. I watched a little with him."

"Stevens." I nod. "He still one of the good guys?"

The light leaves her eyes a bit. She gives a small shake of her head. "Barely," she says softly. "He's skirting the edge as best he can. Enough to survive and stay on the force, I guess you could say."

I tighten my jaw. Quinn and I offered him a job with us in the beginning. His wife was against him leaving the force, guaranteed paychecks, and a pension behind.

I'm sure she's regretting that now. We treat our teams well. Everyone makes a great living at Blackhart Securities and Investigations.

Quinn is a genius. He knew exactly how to position us, and we've been thriving with no problem. There was never any drop-off like I'd feared. We've actually grown.

"We all have choices," I say. "Anyway, I'll clean the dishes. You can log into my account. We'll watch from it."

"Nope, you set up what we're watching, and I'll take care of the dishes. I haven't eaten this well in I don't know how long. It's the least I can do."

I shake my head. "You look exhausted. I'll handle it. You sit and kick back."

She looks like she's about to protest, but she pauses and smiles. "Okay. Thanks."

I give her my login info and head to the kitchen with our dishes. It doesn't take me long to clean up. When I get to the couch, she has the first episode lined up.

I reach for her legs and bring them into my lap. She gives me a shy smile as I start to massage her foot. I take the remote and start the show, placing my focus on the screen.

I can feel her eyes on me at first, but I continue with the massage as if we're two friends watching TV. Soon, she fully relaxes, and we're totally engrossed in the series.

"Oh my God. That's it? I don't think I like you anymore," she pouts six hours later. "I've stayed up all this time for it to end like that. Where's the rest?"

I laugh and shrug. "Told you I needed someone to suffer with."

"So dirty." She yawns. "I'm going to be worth crap to the world today. The birds are chirping, but so worth it. It was so good."

"If I would have known you would binge-watch the entire thing in one night, I wouldn't have started there." I laugh.

She gives me a soft, tired smile. "Thanks. It was exactly what I needed."

I drop my gaze to her lips, but remind myself I'm here to be a friend. Instead of leaning over to kiss her, I stand and stretch. My bones crack and creak.

"I'll see you later. Your shift is in the evening, yeah?"

"Yup. I can sleep a bit," she says and stands. She searches my face as she looks up at me. As much as I want to kiss her, I don't. "So, I'll see you later?"

"Aye, love. I'll make myself known before I float into the shadows," I reply with a grin.

I turn and start for the door. I try to ignore the tugging in my chest. As if I'm walking away from a vital part of me.

When I step out of the front door, I turn and look down into her eyes. "Later," I murmur and lean in to kiss her forehead.

"Later," she says. If I'm not mistaken, she has a hint of disappointment in her eyes.

Telling myself again that a friendship is what she needs most, I give her a smile and turn to leave. It's one of the hardest things I've ever done. Her sweet lips call to me even as I make my way to my car.

CHAPTER 16

GOING PUBLIC

Kevin

IT'S BEEN A WEEK, AND INSTEAD OF MY FEELINGS DYING DOWN, I'M falling for the friend I've gained in Danita. She's funny, smart, and beautiful. I've been enjoying our moments at her place, but I think it's time I insert myself deeper into her life.

Especially after what happened yesterday. I'm glad I demanded she let me drive her to the scene of Erin's shooting. I figured if she rode with me to the house, it would look as if she were there with me, not going to check the place out on her own.

She'd had a gut feeling to go by the place. She was right. We found that asshole Duffy sitting on Erin's place and watched him for an hour.

To be honest, finding that guy outside of Erin's drove all this bull-shit home. Watching from the shadows is one way to do things, but it's not the safest. I need to be a part of Danita's life. It's time I step it up a bit.

Which is why I stroll into the same bar we met in two years ago. Instead of heading home after work, she came here with a few of the female officers. When she sent me a text to take the night off, she'd be fine, I was a little pissed.

She ought to know better. I'm not leaving her uncovered, no matter what she says. So tonight, I'll be introducing the world to her new boyfriend.

When she and a few other cops come into view, I saunter over to their table. A grin breaks across my face the moment she turns to me and her eyes widen. I stop right in front of her and take her lush lips in a searing kiss.

I know this is breaking my friend zone rule, but I need to establish to all these people that she's my woman. Danita doesn't seem to mind. She whimpers and grasps the front of my shirt, pulling me into her.

I break the kiss and place my forehead to hers. "It would seem ya miss me, love," I say, and I'm not talking about since I left her place this morning after we had breakfast together.

That kiss said she's been missing our stolen kisses as much as I have. We're friends, but that connection still lurks beneath the surface. I capture her lips once more because they're too irresistible not to.

"Whoa," someone sings. "Is that Blackhart?"

I look up to find Maureen Reed. She has a huge grin on her face as she looks between the two of us. I wrap an arm around Danita and tug her into my side.

"How are you, Reed? How's life been treating you?"

"Better now that I'm seeing your face. It's Detective Reed now. Go on, turn that accent up. I miss your ass around here," she replies.

I laugh and kiss the top of Danita's head. Reed's gaze continues to bounce between us, a sparkle in her eyes.

"Ya couldn't miss me that much. I never get invited out the way I used to."

Reed's face sobers, and she looks down into her beer mug. The atmosphere around the table seems to change. I home in on everyone's reaction.

"How's Cal? I was hurt to hear what happened. He was a good cop. We miss him too," she murmurs, still not looking up at me.

"He's hanging in there. No change either way," I say and narrow my eyes.

Something flashes across her face. Sensing that I want to give my attention to this lass a bit more, I pull Danita from her seat and bring her into my lap. When I turn to her, it's clear she's fighting off the shock. I give her a gentle squeeze, then turn back to Reed.

She's watching us closely. "When did you guys start hooking up?" she asks.

"I busted Kelley's kid for cutting school. We sort of reconnected from there," Danita says.

It's the story we agreed on. It made the most sense and could be verified by every cop that saw me get into Harris's face that day. It's also the closest thing to the truth.

"Yeah, I heard about that," Reed says and sips her beer. "Heard Graves's head almost exploded."

"How was I supposed to know who the kid was?" Danita says and shrugs.

"Must be destiny," says Officer Carson, one of the other women at the table. "The kid brought you two together."

"I keep telling her that," I say and turn to Danita.

"Always said you're a lucky one, Moralez," Reed says.

"I think I'm the lucky one," I say.

"It's nice you have a bright spot during all of this," Reed says; her tone causes me to turn back to her.

I nod as I take her in. "It's been a lot on the family. It's good to be able to spend time with someone that can take my mind off it all."

"I'm sure when Cal is all better, he'll be happy to see you two together."

Danita shrugs. "I don't know if he remembers me. It's been, what? Like two years since he left the force." She turns to me for confirmation.

I lift my shoulders. "He didn't know we hooked up that night. So, I don't see it making a difference either way."

I want to tighten my jaw, but I don't. I can tell Reed is fishing, and her name was in that file Danita handed over. I'll be looking into her a bit more. Shane will have to see if he can link her to the shooting. I don't like the vibe I'm getting from her.

Danita pushes a hand through my hair, bringing me out of my thoughts. "Come dance with me," she says with a smile.

I grin and lift from my seat, bring her to her feet with me. I will never turn down a chance to have this woman in my arms. I nod toward the dance floor.

"Country music, are you willing to doubt me this time?"

Her laugh illuminates her entire face, drawing me into the orb of light that always surrounds her, even when it's a little dim. I brush her cheek with my fingertips, needing to have that connection with her. I would love to spend all my days bringing that smile to her face.

We leave the others behind and move to the dance floor. The song changes to a slow one and I smile. I pull her into my embrace and start to sway us to the music.

"What was that?" she hisses at me, but the smile is still on her face.

"Doing my job," I say.

"No, I'll get at you about all that later. I meant, did you pick up on that vibe?"

I nod and twirl her around. "Sure did. We'll look into it."

"Did your brother come up with anything else useful on Brunson?"

"Nothing. He's a shit bag, but nothing stands out of the ordinary. We're keeping an eye on him. He sent that other prick to Erin's for a reason." I try not to show my frustration. "It's like bumping our heads against glass."

"You can say that again."

The last thing I want to do is talk about how we're failing at finding Cal and Erin's shooters, or getting Danita any new leads for her case. All we know is that someone's running the ring from within the department, and there are cartel and other big wigs connected. Trafficking of drugs, humans, and guns are involved, but I still don't understand how or why Cal has wrapped himself in the middle of it all.

It's apparent Cal must have stumbled across the bigger players in the matter—the real shot callers—and that's the part that's still missing. I need a moment to recharge and regroup. I plan to do that with the woman in my arms.

I slide my hand down her back, holding her closer. Her eyes soften and her smile turns to the genuine one I know her for. I nuzzle the tip of her nose with mine. Danita ducks her head shyly.

"Kevin," she says in warning.

"We're having fun, love. Let it be."

"Maybe we should leave so we can talk," she murmurs.

"And give up this chance to have you in my arms? I think not. Good music, good company—I think I like it here."

She glares at me, but I ignore it and dance us across the floor. I can feel all eyes on us, but I don't care. The only thing that matters at the moment is the woman in my arms.

Danita

"We shouldn't get things confused."

"No one should be confused, love. We're having a good time. I'll buy you a few beers and we'll have a few laughs. Then we can go back to your place and binge-watch one of our shows," he replies.

Our shows.

This man is dangerous for my heart. I've had so much fun with him in the last week. However, I wasn't expecting him to show up tonight.

I especially wasn't expecting the suspicious questions from Reed. She was definitely digging. Which is why I allowed Kevin to put on this scene. At least that's the lie I sell myself.

The truth is, my trust and respect for this man have gone through the roof in this last week as he's been the friend I need. I had won-dered if he's known how much I needed him, or if he has decided to move on and put me in the friend zone. I'll admit the latter has stung a bit, but when he walked in here with all that sexy swag and devoured my mouth, I lost all thoughts of being in the friend zone.

You don't kiss friends that way. Nor should I have butterflies swarming for a friend. Yet here I stand in his arms, as he sways us to the music, trying my best not to melt into him.

He shakes his head at me. "You do know I can feel you holding back from me, right?" he says.

"It's what's best." I try to convince us both with the words.

"Best for who, love?" I don't reply. He kisses my forehead. "Just dance with me. We don't have to do more than be in the moment. Be in the moment with me."

I lose my fight as the song changes again. This time it's "I Hope You Dance" by Lee Ann Womack. I smile because I know the song well.

Kevin returns the smile as he wraps his arms around me and holds me tighter. It's like a deeper connection begins as we look at each other. No words are spoken or need to be spoken.

I'm entranced by those green eyes. While that nagging voice in the back of my head tells me to shut this down right now, the part of me that's been lonely and needing a connection to the real world latches on to this moment with everything I am.

As if having a mind of their own, my hands find their way into his hair. I play with the silky strands at his nape. My fingertips tingle and my belly drops.

He leans into my ear and whispers, "I don't know what you're hiding or what you're afraid of, but in this moment, I vow to slay it all. I'm willing to take it a step at a time, but I'm going to make you mine, Danita."

I close my eyes as my heart twists. Hearing that name is a dose of reality. "You don't even know who I am," I say.

"That's why I'm here. My father once told me that he earned my mother's heart by having faith in love being a teacher. He learned patience and, in the end, he was rewarded with a best friend and the love of his life. I want that lesson, and I think I'll find it with you," he says softly next to my ear. "Take a chance."

When our eyes connect this time, I'm breathless. His words have punched right through me. Why did I have to meet him now?

If this were another time in my life, I'd be more than willing to pursue things with this man. He's everything I would want and more. I've never felt this connected to anyone.

"Kevin, I—"

I don't get to say the words as he captures my lips. I swear it's like I'm lifted from my feet simply from the kiss alone. Wrapping my arms around his neck, I get lost in the kiss and forget everything else.

That is until my name is bellowed from across the bar. I pull from Kevin's hold and blink away my daze. I turn to see the table we left has filled with most of my squad, including Harris, who had called my name.

He's holding up two beers with a forced smile on his lips. "Get your ass over here. We never got to celebrate your skills last week," he says.

I don't miss the scathing look he gives Kevin. At my side, Kevin mutters something in his thickened accent. It's so thick, I haven't a clue what he says.

I look up at him. His face is clouded over, but he quickly clears his expression and leans to kiss my forehead. He tightens his hold around my waist and leads us over to the bar, where he orders two fresh beers, handing me one.

When we arrive at the table, Harris stares at the beer in my hand like it's shit. I grin and take a sip from it. It hadn't dawned on me what Kevin was doing by ordering the beers at the bar. I was too wrapped up in thoughts of that dance.

Damn, this dude is petty. I like it. Harris picks up one of the beers in front of him with a salty look on his face.

"I like you two together," Stevens says.

I give him a genuine smile. Stevens truly is a good guy. I hope to get him as much leniency as I can when this is all said and done.

Trafficking of any kind is serious. Couple that with all the corruption, and yup, these guys are into some heavy shit. A lot of heads will roll when I finally nail them. That's if I can get to what Cal was holding back.

"Good to see you, Stevens," Kevin says.

"Likewise. This place really did go to shit once you and Quinn left. Don't get that type of dedication and honesty anymore," Stevens says before he cuts off and looks down as if he's said too much.

Yeah, he's had a few. This isn't the first time I've heard him talk like this, but that's usually between us. His cheeks are red, and his face is a mask of frustration and anger, maybe even a bit of disappointment or shame.

"You guys still planning the baseball game for the picnic this year?" I ask, trying to lighten the mood.

Harris's face brightens. "You planning on playing this year?"

I shrug. "Not sure, maybe."

"I've been trying to get you to play for the last two years. Come on, you're an ace in our pocket. Have you seen her play?" He directs the last part to Kevin with a smug grin on his face.

"Not baseball, but she's a champ with a basketball," Kevin replies. "We'll have to play with the whole family next time. I think my brothers would like that, baby."

Burn.

The look on Harris's face says it all. I ignore the pissing match between these two and join a conversation that starts at the other end of the table. They'll be at it all night, I can already tell.

CHAPTER 17

OUR MAGIC

Kevin

I PAT THE TOP OF MY CAR THAT SHANE IS DRIVING. I HAD TO CALL him to come pick us up after a few too many drinks. Dipping my head, I nod at him.

"Thanks," I say as I look into the driver's window. "Don't fuck up my car and don't get any tickets."

"Wait, yer staying?" he says with a grin.

"Mind yer business," I say and turn to look at Danita digging in her purse to find her keys. I shake my head and pluck the bag from her hands. Turning back to Shane, I nod and straighten. "See ya later."

"See ya." He chuckles back as he revs the engine of my car.

I'm going to kick his ass tomorrow. Rolling my eyes, I reach for Danita's hand and start for her front door. She leans into me as we go.

"I've exceeded my limit," she says. "How is it you get me to do things I'd never do?" she says and hiccups.

I snort. "It must be the Irish charm. It will get you every time," I tease.

When we reach the door, I release her hand to dig into her purse and pull out the keys that are right on top. I smile to myself and shake my head. She has definitely had too much to drink, but we had a good time.

At least, I did. It was the first time I've seen her let her guard down since that night we first spent together. Tonight felt real. I have to remind myself that it's not, no matter how much I want it to be.

As I unlock the door, she reaches to push my hair from my forehead. I turn my gaze to her and find those pretty brown eyes on me. The tender look she gives me is like a caress.

I push the door open and wrap my fingers around hers, bringing them to my lips. I kiss the tips before leading her inside. Sunny runs up and I squat to greet him with a good back rub.

"Hush, Sunny. It's late," Danita says.

The dog gives a little whimper, but quiets down as he nuzzles into my hand. I stand and shrug out of my jacket. The night cooled down. I was grateful to have it in the car.

I watch as Danita shrugs out of her own jacket. She looks good tonight. I love seeing her in heels and jeans. It seems to be her after-work uniform.

I nod toward the couch. "Movie night?"

She shakes her head. "Not tonight. How about we chill? No TV, no distractions."

I lift a brow and allow my eyes to roam over her. I should probably call Shane and tell him to come back and get me. All those kisses from the bar have me feeling a certain way.

However, I know I'm not going to pull away tonight. I want to spend this time with her. I reach for her hand and start for the couch, but she tugs, bringing me to a halt. I turn to look over my shoulder.

"Come on, we'll hang in my room."

Wordlessly, I allow her to guide me to the bedroom as Sunny follows us. Danita kicks her heels off once we're inside. I look around. It's not like her other bedroom in the old apartment. This one is bigger with a large bed in the center. Yet, it still feels the same... like her.

I kick off my shoes as well, freezing when she begins to shimmy out of her jeans and tugs off her T-shirt. I lick my lips as memories flood my brain. Her taste and touch come back to me so easily.

"I'm going to jump in the shower," she says and blinks a few times as if to sober up. "You can chill in my bed, but not in your street clothes." She frowns. "I think I have some old sweats. Hang on."

Still in her panties and bra, she moves to one of the dressers and bends over to open one of the drawers to dig around inside. She makes a cute little cheering sound when she finds what she's looking for. With a smile on her face, she moves back over to me, holding out the sweatpants.

"And whose are these?" I say.

She smiles wider. "The accent is out. Are you jealous, baby?"

I can't help the grin that comes to my face as she calls me that. I grab for the sweats, pulling her to me with them. Placing a hand on her ass, I look into her eyes.

"I don't make it a habit of wearing another man's clothes," I reply.

"They're mine. I ordered them, and the wrong size was sent. I never returned them. So, you are the first that will ever wear them."

I trace her hairline, then brush my fingers across her cheek. I like her like this. Playful and open.

She takes a step back. "I'll be back," she says.

I nod and watch her as she grabs a few items and disappears into the bathroom. Once she's out of sight, I start to strip from my clothes and tug on the sweats she gave me. I take another look around the room and observe—like I did in her other apartment—that she doesn't have any family pictures.

Not a single one. There are a few black-and-whites of Sunny on the wall in the living room, but nothing with humans. I look around for things that will tell me more about the woman I'm falling for, and realize there's nothing.

Sunny comes over and leans against my leg. I bend down and pet his head. "What can you tell me about your mum?" He looks at me, but doesn't make a sound. "Tight-lipped just like her. I see ya."

I chuckle to myself and stand to move over to the bed. Remembering that she likes to sleep on the right side away from the door, I climb in on the left. The memory brings a smile to my lips.

She had actually refused to switch places that night. I understood the need and had no problem with it. It's one of the many things that have stuck with me about her.

I'm lost in my thoughts when she exits the bathroom in shorts and a tank top. Those thick, toned legs on display. I can't take my eyes off her as she climbs into the bed. She looks a little more steady after her shower.

I'm a little surprised when she moves in close and snuggles against my chest. Surprised, but I welcome her soft body as I wrap an arm around her. I kiss the top of her head, and she releases a sigh and relaxes.

"You know there's something I always wanted to ask you," she murmurs.

"What's that?"

"That night we met. Everyone seemed to be in on your dance skills before we made it to the dance floor. What was that about?"

I laugh. "Before I retired, I'd get involved with the fundraisers. A couple of years we teamed up with a local dance school and did like a *Dancing with the Stars* event. I took to the lessons and the events better than everyone thought. I was the winner two years in a row and raised a shit ton of money for the kids."

She turns her face up to look at me. There is a smile in her eyes. It makes her gorgeous face light up.

"I would have loved to see that," she says.

"Not in the beginning. The blisters and the aching bones almost made me quit."

"Funny, I don't see you as a quitter."

I drop my gaze to her lips. "I'm not, which is why I stuck with it. I'm glad I did. It proved to come in handy some years later."

She sits up and puts some space between us as she leans her back to the headboard while looking down at me. I place my arms behind my head and enjoy the comfort of her bed. The thought of having her in my bed every night circles the edge of my thoughts.

Reaching out, Danita starts to run a finger down my ribs. I don't move, but I grow harder from her touch. Closing my eyes, I revel in her skin caressing mine.

"You used to be leaner," she whispers, causing me to open my eyes.

"Changed my diet a little. Wanted to put on more bulk."

"It's perfect. Not too much, but right for your frame."

I smile. "Are you saying you like my body, love?"

She goes to pull back and ducks her head. I grab her hand before she can retreat. Lacing our fingers together, I wait for her gaze to meet mine.

"You're a beautiful man," she murmurs.

"Aye, maybe, but you're the stunning one in the room. I could look at you all night," I say as I make circles in her palm with my thumb.

"What's the story with Evelyn? Was that her name?"

I smile. I know she remembers her name. The fact that she does says I was right when I picked up on her jealousy at the restaurant.

"What does that matter?"

Danita

He's right. It shouldn't matter to me. However, I couldn't keep the words from coming out of my mouth.

Remembering the woman makes so many questions pop into my head. Besides, focusing on her will help me ignore the stirring happening in my belly as he makes those circles in my palm. His touch has everything tingling, yet I can't force myself to pull away.

"I don't know. I'm curious," I breathe when I finally find my voice again.

"Aye, but curiosity killed the cat. If you don't mind, that's a road I don't want to return to. We were wrong for each other. It was toxic and I walked away."

I lick my lips and nod.

"Tell me, love, how long have you been waiting to ask that?"

I shrug. "You do know women can be petty? We'll hold something in for years to wait for the right moment. I'm Afro-Latina. Trust me, it's ten times worse."

He barks out a laugh. I grin, but another question comes to mind. I bite my lip as I contemplate asking.

"Is she the only woman of color you've ever dated?"

He unlinks our fingers and starts to drag his long digits up the inside of my arm. I shiver at his touch. At first, I think he's not going to answer the question.

"No, she isn't. I've never thought about it, but I've dated a few women of color. I don't know if I can say I have a preference. I like women in all shapes, colors, and sizes."

"Interesting," I murmur.

"Why is that?"

"No reason."

He grins, but lets it go as he moves on. "You said you're Afro-Latina. Your last name is Moralez, so where are your parents from?"

With the alcohol coursing through my system and the buzzing of his touch, I almost tell him that Moralez isn't my real name. Instead, I bite my lip and watch as he moves to run his fingers along my thigh.

Am I panting? I think I'm panting. His touch is light, but goose bumps rise across my skin anyway. I watch as his paler skin glides against mine and can't help wondering what his body would feel like against mine.

"My mother is African American, born and raised in Brooklyn," I push out as another shiver runs through me. I close my eyes, knowing I have said too much. It's not the cover story. Still, I tell him more of the truth. "My dad is Puerto Rican."

"Have you ever dated outside of your race?"

"Once, maybe twice." I shrug.

He sits up and leans in until we're nose to nose. I think he's going to kiss me at first, but he speaks instead. His breath fans against my lips.

"Is my heritage a problem, love?"

I shake my head. "Not if you don't make it one."

Placing a hand around my neck, he brushes his thumb across my bottom lip. My nipples tighten to the point of pain. I want to kiss him, but I fight not to close the connection as a voice wars in the back of my head.

"What does that mean?"

"One guy I dated mentioned the color of our skin all the time. During intimate moments, as compliments, it started to come off as a fetish. I'm not into that. I don't want to hear how good you think your white dick looks in my black pussy every time we're going at it." I frown in disgust. "It's not my thing. If you're dating me, you're dating me, not my color."

"While I love the color of your skin and I would love to see it against mine, it's not the only thing that attracts me to you. I don't think we'll have a problem there."

I smile at him and tilt my head. "I thought you placed me in the friend zone. How did we undo that in one night?"

His laugh bursts against my lips, causing me to crave his kiss more. I lean in, almost closing the distance fully. However, he doesn't complete the passionate kiss I desire. Instead, he brushes his lips softly against the corner of my mouth.

"I'm whatever you need, love. I'm taking you as you are, remember?"

My heart swells. I don't know why, but those simple words hold so much weight in this moment. I kiss his cheek.

"Let's get some sleep. I want to go out for breakfast in the morning."

CHAPTER 18

BREAKFAST FOR TWO

Kevin

"YOU ARE SO FULL OF IT." DANITA GIGGLES AROUND A MOUTHFUL of bacon.

Her eyes are lit up as she laughs. Not for the first time, I note how beautiful she is with her hair loose, framing her face. She also looks happy and relaxed, something that makes me happy.

This quaint diner is the perfect tucked-away place to have breakfast and kick back. The old-fashioned decor and friendly staff place us at ease. It reminds me of some of the older movie diners.

The food isn't bad either. I'm glad I remembered it. It seems like Danita has let her guard down a little more since we've been here.

I can't help it. I reach over and brush a curly wave from her face. Then tuck another lock behind her ear. She gives me a sweet smile as she covers her mouth and looks into my eyes.

"I promise ya, love. It's true," I say.

Her eyes sparkle as she tilts her head to the side. "You've met the entire band?" A girlish charm takes over her face. It's cute and endearing.

"Aye, we've done security for them." I nod and cut into my waffles, taking another bite.

Metal Guns is a band that my brothers and I have done some work for. Danita seems to be a big fan. I like them; they remind me of a new-aged Aerosmith.

"I love their sound. They remind me of Aerosmith, only younger," she says.

"I was just thinking the same thing."

I find we have a lot more in common than I thought. The more time I spend with her, the more that fact is clear. We like most of the same foods, we have similar taste in movies and music, and we even want to travel to a lot of the same places.

"Great minds think alike," she says when she finishes chewing.

"They do. I'll see if I can get you some tickets to a show."

"You don't have to do that." She says the words, but I can see the excitement in her eyes.

"It's no big deal. They have offered plenty of times to hook us up. Shane is a big fan too. They get him tickets and backstage passes all the time."

We actually saved the drummer's life and managed to keep the entire thing from hitting the news. I think we earned free passes for life. I don't tell Danita this, though.

"It seems like you guys have a sweet thing going on," she says while pouring more syrup on her pancakes.

I love watching her eat. That sensual mouth taunts me with each bite and every chew. Then again, everything about her turns me on. I shake the thought away.

"We do well. I can't complain."

Something changes right before my eyes. I noticed as she got dressed this morning that she was a little melancholy. I had thought it was about me sleeping over, but I dismissed that as I watched her stare off into space a few times as she twisted the ring she put on her thumb.

I've seen her wear the ring once before, but today, it seems to hold some meaning. A part of me wanted to point it out, but the wiser part of me decided against it. Now, her eyes take on that same distant look.

She's somewhere else even as she speaks to me. "It must be nice to have your family around so much," she says.

None of the laughter and mirth from moments ago are in her voice. I study her as I try to figure out where her mind has gone. Suddenly, thoughts of her slip that day at my house come to mind.

There is a deeper story there. Again, I decide not to pry. I don't want to lose the light banter we've had while here. Although, the PI within me screams for me to dig deeper and find all her secrets. I watch as she looks at her plate and starts to push the food around on it.

"It has its ups and downs, honestly," I say after a few beats.

"Huh?" She looks up from her plate, confusion lighting her eyes.

I shrug. "Working with family has its up and its downs. Sometimes I want to throttle them. Other times, I wouldn't do it with anyone but them. If I'm going to have to trust someone to have my back, it would be my brothers."

She nods and swallows. "I know what you mean. I think I'm finished here."

She reaches for her wallet. When she pulls out a few bills, I stretch my hand out across the table and cover hers. Her eyes meet mine.

I shake my head. "This is on me."

That sweet smile returns. "Not this time, but thanks."

"Danita—"

"I want to treat a friend to breakfast. Let me."

Her words sting a little. She woke in my arms this morning. We slept all night with her wrapped around me. We felt like more than two friends. However, she wields that word like a shield.

I nod and release her hand. I'm officially done with my food as well. I pull out my phone to text my brother for a ride.

I shouldn't be bitter. I know she's not ready for a relationship beyond our friendship, but it doesn't bite any less. I'm growing feelings for her and I can't stop them.

It's like we take two steps forward and a million back. Last night was something different; I felt it and I know she did too. For now, I'm done pushing the limits of our "friendship." I'm ready to go lick my wounds in private.

"Where can I drop you? Is your house finished?"

Hearing her mention my home makes this burn more. My empty home. The one I want to share with a wife and kids someday.

The home I see her in when I think about it. Aye, I need to go. "Don't worry about me, love. I'll be fine," I reply.

Danita

I can't stop thinking about the hard edge to Kevin's words at the end of our breakfast. Today is my oldest brother's birthday. I know my mind had been elsewhere as I thought about what my family is probably up to. Forty, that's a big one. Five years away, and I've missed so much.

Yet the constant fear that if I contact my family or walk away from my assignment, I could be putting everyone's life in danger lurks over my head. So much anxiety builds when I think of calling on my brothers for help. I'd never be able to live through knowing I've brought the same fate as Cal to my family's door. I'm barely holding it together as it is.

I was so lost in feeling sorry for myself and longing to be with my family, I don't know what I said to make Kevin angry. Although it was clear that he was pissed. I expected at least a kiss to my forehead or cheek when we separated.

I only received a curt nod and a "see you later." It left me feeling cold and wondering what I'd said wrong. Again, I hate the position I'm in.

My phone rings, pulling me from my thoughts. I look to see it's Harris. I purse my lips and release a breath through my nose. I'm not in the mood, but I know I need to answer in case it's important.

"Hello."

"Hey, I wanted to see if you put any more thought into playing in the baseball game. Ordering the jerseys and I wanted to know if I should get you one."

I scrunch my face up and move the phone to look at it. Sunny lifts his head from his bed and starts to bark. I guess his BS meter is swinging as well.

"Quiet, boy," I say to Sunny first, then I reply to Harris. "No, I don't think I'm going to join. I have some personal things I need to focus on."

"Trouble in paradise already? Does that mean you're free for dinner?"

"No and no."

There's a pause and I swear, I'm tempted to hang up. Harris has to be delusional. I've never given him the idea that I'm interested in his arrogant ass.

"Yeah, all right. Let me know if you change your mind. About the date and the game. I'll be waiting." With that, he hangs up.

He'll be waiting a hell of a long time. I suck my teeth and toss the phone. I think about sending Kevin a text to check in, but it feels like something a girlfriend would do.

Suddenly, it hits me. I called him a friend. After that, his attitude changed. I huff and let my shoulders slump.

Damn it. This is my fault. I keep allowing the lines to blur. I know I can't have a normal relationship with Kevin, but that doesn't keep me from craving one the more time I spend with him.

Last night, I fell asleep in his arms so easily. His warmth and strong embrace felt so natural around me. Especially after his simple touch had my entire body on fire.

A part of me felt like Kevin made love to my soul. His touch and sweet words are everything and more. They spoke to the longing growing inside me.

Kevin would be perfect for the fun-loving, free-spirited, family-missing Demaris. Danita, on the other hand, can't afford to fall in love. At the moment, the two are warring within me. I know the difference between right and wrong, but I've been under for so long, I'm starting to question if maybe I should start to settle into this life I'm trapped in.

"Too dangerous," I say to myself.

My doorbell rings, causing me to jump. Rubbing at my forehead and muttering to myself, I get up to answer the door. Sunny beats me there, his tail wagging. I know from his reaction exactly who's on the other side. Not that I get any visitors as it is.

I think I'm as excited as Sunny when I open the door. My heart leaps into my throat as I take Kevin in. His hair is damp, causing it to curl and the strands to look a darker red.

He has on gray slacks and a white dress shirt that's open at the collar. I feel like I've opened the pages of a magazine as I look at him. His green eyes are so intense as he stares back at me.

He holds up a bag. "I have ice cream," he says without a smile or any indication of his mood.

I step back and allow him in. Locking the door after closing it, I try to gather myself before I turn to face him. When I do turn, I groan out loud.

His tight ass looks amazing in his slacks. It's already bad enough that his cologne has permeated the space, causing my mouth to water and my heart to race. Come on, how am I supposed to fight this attraction when he walks in here like this?

I wish things could be different. My thoughts jumble as I move into the living room once again. My mind goes back to my brother and his birthday as I twist the ring he gave me around my thumb.

Kevin sighs, pulling my attention to him standing in front of me with two pints and two spoons. He hands me my favorite—salted caramel truffle—bringing a smile to my face. I question how this man has come to know me so well.

He takes a seat beside me. "Are you going to tell me what's been eating at you today?"

My smile falls. I want to talk about this with him, but I can't. It's for the best if I don't. I open the ice cream slowly as if it's the most important task in the world.

I lift my shoulders as I look down into the container. When I do look at him, those penetrating eyes search for answers. It aches that this can't be simpler.

I give him a pleading look. He releases another heavy sigh and reaches out to wrap an arm around my shoulders. Tugging me into his warmth, he encases me in a cocoon of comfort I've been needing more than I know.

"Whenever you're ready to talk, I'm here. I'm a vault; it will be safe with me."

I close my eyes. I know this. I'm just not ready to bury him in my world.

CHAPTER 19

IN THE DETAILS

Danita

"Come on, boy," I say as I grab my keys and Sunny's leash after my stretch.

I scroll through my phone to find a playlist as I head for the door. Sunny starts to bark and a smile comes to my face. We have a visitor, and I know exactly who it is.

I wasn't expecting Kevin until later. He said something about spending time with the kids. I hope he was able to finally get something out of Conroy this time.

Looking at my watch, I've let this day get away from me. After binge-watching more Netflix with Kevin all night, I decided to sleep in. Things between us have been interesting, to say the least.

We've sort of eased back into the friend zone, but the sexual tension has almost doubled as has the connection I shouldn't be allowing to form. When I open the door to find him in sweats and a T-shirt, I have no doubts why the attraction has increased.

He makes the simplest outfits look like fine tailoring. His hair is a little messy as if he didn't take the time to style it after his shower. However, I know he's showered because I can smell his fresh body wash and cologne.

"Going somewhere?"

I clear my throat and hold up the leash. "Taking Sunny for a walk, might get in a run while I'm at it," I reply.

"Sounds like I'm right on time." He nods toward the street. "Come on, they're talking about rain. We should get a move on."

I look up, but the skies are still clear. I shrug it off and head out of the door and lock it. Kevin takes the leash from me and hooks it to Sunny's collar. We start for the dog park in silence.

I get lost in my thoughts for a bit, until Kevin bumps me with his shoulder. I look up into his green eyes, and I'm entranced for a second, causing me to trip over my own feet.

Ay, just great, Demaris.

Kevin reaches out an arm and catches me before I face-plant, tugging me into him. My breasts squish up against his hard chest, and I melt into his hold. My lips part and I stick my tongue out to wet them. Kevin's gaze drops to my mouth and follows the movement.

This time, he's the one to clear his throat as he releases me. I take a step back, and we both begin to walk again. My palms start to sweat as if I'm a teenager on my first date.

"I talked to Con today."

"Did he say anything?"

"No, I think you should spend some time with him again. You're the one we need him to trust. I think seeing you around the family will loosen him up," he says as we stroll.

I nod. "Sounds good. I'm ready to give anything a try."

His eyes are on me, but I don't turn to face him. I can feel the questions on the tip of his tongue. I know it's getting harder for him not to ask them. They haven't gotten any new leads, not even with the file I gave them.

Not able to help myself, I chance a peek at him. He's examining me closely. He tilts his head and squints a bit.

"You're not a natural brunette," he says, almost as if saying it to himself.

Shit, I meant to dye my roots this weekend. I noticed them show- ing a few days ago, but between work and the time I've been spending with Kevin on the case and as friends, I haven't had the time yet. I lift a shoulder and squat to release Sunny from the leash.

When I stand, Kevin searches my face and hair closely. "You're a redhead," he says as if he's in awe.

"Not really red. A reddish sandy brown. In the summers, it tends to look more red."

He bobs his head, lifting his hand to brush my temple. "What else don't I know about you?" he murmurs.

"Kevin," I warn.

He opens his mouth as if to protest, but he clamps it shut just as quickly and shakes it off. We begin to walk again. I'm startled when he reaches to lace his fingers with mine.

Looking down at our joined hands, I smile, only to frown at myself. This feels too real. Not like we're putting on a show for whoever could be watching.

"I forgot the popcorn in the car," he says randomly.

"Huh?"

"The popcorn. We ate the last of it last night. I told you I'd pick some up. It's in my car."

"Oh, okay. Were you planning to hang out late again tonight?"

I hate the hope that I hear in my voice. Although what I hate more is my reaction to the breathtaking smile he turns on me. God, this man is so gorgeous.

With the fading sun at his back, all his features are on display. The light causes the reds and golds in his hair to stand out. The wrinkles around his green eyes say he laughs a lot and smiles plenty.

I want to reach out and brush his cheek—like he often does mine—to feel the light stubble that has started to grow. I have to demand my body not to move closer to him. He's like a magnet all in himself.

"I had planned to stick around. If you have something going on, I can head back to my place to change or something," he says.

"Oh, no, you don't have to change or anything. I was only asking," I say, tearing my eyes away from him.

He releases my hand and wraps an arm around my shoulders to tug me into his side. With a gentle squeeze and a kiss to the top of my head, he leads me closer to where Sunny is chasing a butterfly. Again, that feeling of this being right slams into me.

"So, you plan to cook for your man tonight?"

The question jars me a little as it speaks to so many of my thoughts. I know he's only teasing, but the title feels way too accurate. Especially when he shifts my body in front of his to embrace me from behind as he buries his face in my neck.

"You promised me some of your famous chicken egg rolls. Wait, no, I think I'm more in the mood for spaghetti. You were talking big junk about your spaghetti," he teases.

"I'm making you neither. You'll have empanadillas tonight. I've been craving them, and I have everything at the apartment."

"Sounds good," he breathes against my skin.

I fight not to squirm as his breath fans my neck and causes butterflies to build. I immediately feel the loss of him as he releases me and whistles for Sunny to come over. I watch him as he stands and waits for my dog to run to him.

I take in every gesture, every move. He runs a hand through his messy red locks as a genuine smile lights his face. He squats to play with Sunny, only turning to look up at me as I've been watching them for a while.

"I think your mum has a lot on her mind today," Kevin says to Sunny.

Sunny barks his agreement, bringing a smile to my face. I shake my head clear. "Maybe," I reply.

"You can talk to us, love. We're listening."

"I'm good. I won't be needing a seat on Dr. Sunny or Dr. Blackhart's couch, thank you."

Kevin puts his fingers to his chin thoughtfully. "Dr. Blackhart. You know, I never thought about it, but that would have had a nice ring to it."

I laugh. "It's never too late to start over," I joke.

He looks me in the eyes. "Aye, love. Ya speak a truth there."

I look away, checking my watch. "Want to get in that run with me?"

He lifts to his full height and starts to stretch. "Sure, why not?"

While he stretches, I make myself busy with finding my playlist and getting my buds in. Not that I'll use either. Kevin has the stamina to run and talk. The first time we jogged together, he challenged me and showed me that there are levels of fitness, and I wasn't on the level I thought I was.

"Okay, ready?" he asks as he pats my ass, snapping me out of my thoughts again.

I blink at him as he jogs backwards away from me, Sunny following after him. I growl at Kevin and start after him. "I'm going to kick your ass for that."

"You have to catch me first, baby," he taunts before turning and taking off.

I give chase, but not without taking notice of the pang in my chest. If he were any other man, I would have slammed him to the ground and tried to break his damn arm. Instead, I can't stop thinking of his touch.

Crap, I've fallen for him.

Kevin

"This is so good," I say as I eat my mint chocolate chip ice-cream cone.

"It sure is. Look at how fast you're devouring it." Danita laughs. "Come here, you have some on the corner of your mouth."

We pause so she can reach up and wipe away the sweet treat from my face with her fingertips. I remind myself this is one of those moments when we're in the friend zone, and I don't turn to suck her fingers into my mouth to clean them. Instead, I smile and we begin to walk again.

"You know we're defeating the whole purpose of that run, right?" she says beside me as she licks at her ice cream.

I wink at her. "Live your life, lass. You only get one."

A look crosses her face, but it's gone as soon as it appears. Again, I remind myself that in time, I will be able to learn everything about her. For now, I'll take what she gives.

I wasn't expecting her to admit that her hair isn't naturally black. I'd been taken by surprise when I saw it. You'd have to look closely to see the reddish-brown color trying to pop through. It's the first time I've noticed it in all the time I've known her.

"It turned out to be a perfect day after all," she says.

I nod at the horizon before us. "I don't know. Looks like some clouds are rolling in. I won't count us lucky just yet."

"A girl can dream."

"Tell me one."

She glances at me. "One what?"

"Dream. It only has to be one. Tell me something no one else knows."

She seems hesitant as she thinks it over. I watch as she sucks her lip into her mouth. Suddenly, a bright smile takes over her face.

"I wanted to be a chef when I was a little girl. I had planned to open my own restaurant."

"Yeah?"

"Yup, I had this little kitchen set and I'd cook up imaginary meals and make my own menus. Then, when I was old enough to get in the actual kitchen, I fell in love. I'd spend hours in there, cooking up new recipes."

"Aye, so I'm in for a treat, then."

"Maybe." She smiles. "I'll definitely need some extra time on the treadmill at work tomorrow."

I squeeze her fingers and point my cone at her. "Yer perfect the way ya are."

She giggles. "You remind me of my dad. He has that whole Spanglish thing going on. One minute he's speaking in English and the next he's in a full-blown Spanish conversation, and it doesn't matter who you are or if you comprehend."

She beams up at me, and it's clear she hasn't noticed the slip yet. The first time we met, she told me her father wasn't in her life when she was younger.

"You slip in and out just like he does. I miss that." She turns to look forward and gets lost in her thoughts again.

I don't point it out as I finish my ice cream and slip into my own thoughts. The one thing I know for a fact is that Danita is undercover. How deep and what agency is what I'm trying to figure out. There are some other things out of protocol, but I'm positive she's not an ordinary Suffolk detective.

I'm no fool. I've known something was up from the beginning. One day it clicked. Now, I fear these slipups. I don't know if they've become exclusive to me or if she's been under too long.

I war with saying something. As her safety blares in warning, I decide that I should. It's only right she knows that she's been making the little slips around me.

I tighten my hold on the hand that has hers and the leash. She turns to look up at me, brushing her now-empty hand against her leg. "I'm going to say something, and I want you to listen." She nods. "I get that you're undercover."

She stiffens and pulls away from me. I turn to face her, reaching for her waist to pull her into me. I lock my eyes on hers.

"I figured it out a while ago. I'm not going to press you for the details now. Although, I want you to remember my warning about Quinn. It's only a matter of time before he sees it too.

"However, that's not my biggest concern at the moment. This thing between us is growing, and I want to think the connection is what's making your tongue so loose, but if it's not, and you're making mistakes with others—"

"Fuck," she exclaims as her eyes widen. She tugs at her ponytail and tears well in her eyes. "Kev, I'm exhausted. Mentally and physically, but, no, I don't make these mistakes with anyone else. With you, it's just… I…"

I cup the back of her neck and bring her closer. Placing a kiss to her forehead, I breathe her in. Sweat mixed with her fruity scent fills my nostrils. I relish that smell.

"It's hard to fight something so strong," I say.

She pulls away slightly to look me in the eyes. "But you understand, don't you? Everything you know about me is a half-truth." She lowers her voice. "I don't remember who's who sometimes. Me, the real me, she's lost. How can I build more with you?"

I swipe away the single tear that has slipped free with my thumb. "I told you before, I'll take you as you are. I've always known there was more. That you've been hiding something."

"If I could tell you more, I would. I can't. God, what I'd give to be normal and live a normal life again. I'm asking you to trust me, but I'm also telling you that all the lies between us have more weight than you can imagine.

"When this is over, if it's ever over, I have a lot of shit in my head I need to handle," she says. "I don't want to hurt you at the end of this, Kev."

"That's the second time you've called me that, love. I like it." I give her a teasing smile to try to ease some of her anxiety. "My gut has told me that it's a hell of a lot more than you're letting on, but I'm trusting you. I won't ruin your case. Although, I've been trying to figure out why they haven't pulled you out."

"Kevin," she pleads.

"I'm giving you time. We'll figure out what my nephew knows and take it from there, but I'm not going to ignore this any longer," I say before covering her lips with mine.

I kiss her with all the pent-up shit I've been carrying for weeks. When she moans in my mouth, I deepen the kiss. Plunging my tongue into her warmth. Sunny barks and moves around us until his leash locks us together.

Danita links her fingers into my hair and tugs tightly. I groan, holding her closer still as my arms band around her. We're lost in the kiss even as Sunny barks at us. That is, until the sky opens up and it begins to pour.

We're not that far from Danita's place. I release her and untangle us from Sunny's leash, allowing us all to take off for the apartment. We're completely soaked as we get to the front door.

Our gazes fix on each other and no words are needed. I can see what I'm feeling reflected within the depths of her eyes.

CHAPTER 20

AFTER THE STORM

Danita

I fumble with the keys to get us inside. Kevin is wrapped around me, kissing the side of my neck. I do my best to focus on the task at hand as he distracts me. We both laugh as we rush into the apartment once the door is open.

"Go to your room," I tell Sunny.

The poor dog doesn't bother to whimper or argue. He rushes off to the guest bedroom he calls his own. Clearly even the dog knows what's about to happen.

"Come here," Kevin says huskily, his voice raising goose bumps across my skin.

Grasping my hips, he looks into my eyes as he draws me in. I cling to his shirt as he starts to devour my lips again. This time, I hold nothing back at all as I return the kiss with as much vigor as he does. Lifting me onto his waist, he doesn't break the connection as he starts for my bedroom.

He cups my face in one hand and deepens the kiss, pulling a whimper from me. Dragging his mouth from mine, he moves across the skin of my chin to my neck.

"Kevin," I pant.

"Aye, love." I shiver as his voice caresses me, gentle and wanting. Like an old lover that has been graced with a second chance and doesn't want to make the wrong move. Something about it turns me on in a way I can't explain. The timbre and the silky tone are enchanting.

"Do you have protection?"

I'm going to freaking scream if this man doesn't have at least one condom this time. I will jump in the car and go to the nearest store myself if I have to. I can't ignore this need for him a second longer.

He grins against my skin. "Baby, I'm glad you're not pulling the brakes." He breathes in relief and chuckles. Sucking my flesh into his mouth, he rolls it against his tongue until a moan and whimper leave me. His hair is wet and plastered to his skin from the rain, yet I claw my fingernails against his scalp anyhow, and he nearly growls.

"You like that?"

"You have no idea," he says and nips my lip before looking me in the eyes. "I placed a box in your nightstand about a week ago."

I give him a side-glance. "A box of what?"

"Condoms."

"Really? You're kidding, right?"

"Not at all." He slips his hands into the waistband of the back of my spandex. "This has been building for weeks now. I wanted to make sure if we ever decided to go there, we'd be ready this time."

I scoff and shake my head at him. "I should send you home with blue balls."

He releases a loud laugh before taking my lips again. I slide down his body to my feet, noting the impressive erection I rub against. I reach for the hem of his soaked shirt, but he tugs it off for me and tosses it to the floor.

He wastes no time peeling off my tank top and sports bra. My breasts jiggle free from their confines, bringing a heated look to his eyes. I feel so exposed as he sets his gaze on me, appraising.

He shoves his sweats down as I shimmy out of my pants. My panties are the only thing between us when he closes the distance and palms my ass with one hand. Grasping my face hard, he tugs me to him.

His kiss is demanding and sets a feverish pace to our pawing hands and the sipping from each other's lips. He groans long and deep when I reach between us to grab his pulsing length. He's so hard, but he feels silky soft in my palm.

"Danita," he grinds out in warning.

I close my eyes. The truth slamming into me like a brick wall. "Please, don't call me that. Dem is fine."

The room is so silent, a pin could drop in the next room and we'd hear it. I open my eyes and those greens are focused on me so intensely. Slowly, he moves his grasp from my face to my neck.

"I hate seeing you in this pain. We'll figure it out, baby. I promise we will, and the first thing you will tell me is the name of the woman who has stolen my heart," he says.

With that, he has his lips on mine again. I don't have time to process his words or their depth as he lifts me around his waist once again and carries me over to the bed. I had other plans. I wanted to return the favor from last time, but Kevin has a plan of his own.

He kisses, licks, and sucks at my skin as he moves down my body. The tight grip he has on my sides is so possessive and demanding. As if he's commanding my body to yield to the pleasure he's offering.

"Kev," I whimper when he goes to settle between my legs. "I don't think I can take that right now. Please."

His breath fans my weeping sex as he laughs. He turns his head and licks my inner thigh. Then he turns back to my mound and covers my center with his mouth over the fabric of my panties.

"Ya will thank me later, love."

His accent is in full force, his voice has dropped low. I gush from the rumbling sound alone. When he snakes his tongue beneath my panties and drags it over my skin, I release a soundless cry.

All I can do is open my mouth and roll my eyes in the back of my head. The tearing sound that fills the room replaces my voice. I look down in time to see him tossing what used to be my panties over his shoulders.

"Hold on tight, love," he says before he buries his face between my legs.

I do exactly that. I cling to the sheets and arch my back. It's better than I remember. Probably because I'm completely sober this time. I lift my arms over my head and plant my palms against the headboard.

I gain enough leverage to ride his face as I balance on my tiptoes. Kevin groans and invests himself in the task all the more. The sound of him slurping and moaning eggs me on as I reach out with one hand and guide his head.

He links his fingers with mine, holding on tightly as he lifts my hips off the bed and feasts on me in an all-consuming way. I hold on for dear life. I don't know what's sending me over more, the sound of his pleasure or the feel of him taking all of mine for his own.

"Kev," I scream out as my first climax hits.

He finally releases my hand and lowers my hips to the bed. He locks that intense gaze on me and wipes his palm down his face before dragging his tongue against it. I promise, I think I almost come again from the gesture and look he gives me.

The bed dips as he moves over to the nightstand. Somewhere in the back of my mind, I note that it's the side of the bed I don't sleep on. It's the side he has used every time he spent the night with me.

His side.

I shake the thought away as it tries to take root. I watch as he pulls out the box and rips it open. With a foil packet between his lips, he tosses the rest of the box on top of the side table.

I'm breathless as he rolls the condom onto his thick, long length. I give an appreciative smirk. Sucking my lip into my mouth once he's fully sheathed, I force my eyes up to his.

He leans in and seizes my lips. Immediately, I taste myself on his mouth. A sense of remorse hits as I note that I haven't gotten to taste him.

He goes to move between my legs, but I find my second wind and push him onto his back. He smiles up at me as I straddle him and palm his dick. He's so heavy with need.

Slowly, I begin to slide down onto him. Oh God, he was right. I need all the help I can get to take him. It's been so long and he's super thick. As slick as I am, I still have to take my time, breathing through my nose.

"Take yer time, baby. We don't have to rush," he says tightly.

I nod with my mouth open. As much as I want him, I do pace myself. It takes a few short passes before I can fully seat myself.

Kevin is still at first. However, the first time I take him to the hilt, he begins to move. He palms my breasts and starts to thrust up into me.

I bite my lip and stare down at him. His face contorts with need and desire. It matches the feeling building on the inside of me.

"You feel so good," I gasp.

"Aye, love. Yer killing me. Yer so tight." He drops his eyes to our connection. "I've wanted ya for so long, I don't want this to end."

He lifts and grasps my throat, taking my lips with his. I tighten around him, and shiver, causing him to smile into the kiss. He nips my upper lip, then the lower.

"Come for me. I feel ya ready. Come for me, love. Give me all ya got," he breathes, reaching with his free hand to palm my ass and squeeze.

He guides me up and down his shift, groaning and grunting as he moves me to his pace. Not too fast, not too slow, but perfect. I throw my head back and let go. I cry his name and claw at his shoulders.

The feelings I have for Kevin will never be able to remain in the neat little box I've tried to hide them away in. I knew this would happen. He's shattered all my resolve. In this moment, I'd give him all my secrets. My secrets and my heart.

The look in his eyes says he's after the latter. I should be afraid. I should probably be more cautious, but I want what I see in his green depths: the care, that reverence, the passion. Those are things I've longed for. Someone to look at me the way Papi looks at my mom.

Kevin gives a silent nod as if giving me permission to take all he has. Or maybe it's his signal for me to allow myself this one thing, this trip into the unknown and overwhelming. A trip to bliss that promises the finer things.

Whatever it means, I accept. I crest and crash, trembling in his hold. I've never come like this for anyone. I'm so wet, I'd think he came with me if not for the barrier between us.

"That's my girl," he breathes next to my ear. "Now, let me take you for a real ride."

Kevin

Before she can catch her breath, I flip her onto her back. She yelps as she hits the mattress with a little bounce. I'm still pulsing deep inside her. She feels incredible.

I reach to release her wet waves. Her hair spills across the pillow in a thick black mass. I can't help wondering what it would look like with its natural color.

Digging a hand into her locks, I tug her head back and go for her neck as I drive inside of her. I can't get enough of how good she smells despite our run and her sweat. Flattening my tongue against her skin, I lick her neck and hum. She tastes salty and sweet.

"Kevin," she cries. "Please."

Her pleas rock me to my core. I know my feelings for her have grown, but there's something about being inside her. Having my hands on her soft, silky smooth skin.

Each time she says my name, I feel like she's weaving magic around my heart. Although I know the magic intends to pull the organ from my being in the end, I can't find the strength to stop it. In fact, I welcome it.

"Yes, baby," I say through my teeth as she works her hips into me.

We move in sync. Her body stretching and yielding to take me easier with each stroke. Her body was made to accept me. The perfect fit.

A tingling starts at the base of my spine. I'm not ready to explode inside her. I grind my teeth and close my eyes, calling on all my strength.

When she digs her nails into my back, I almost lose the battle. I tighten my hand in her hair and pound harder as she begs for me. My toes curl into the mattress as I dig in deep and still my love for her coiling within.

Warring with how deep my emotions are this first time, I latch my lips to hers and say all the things I know she's not ready to hear. I've fallen for her. I'm in love with a woman I only know pieces of, but I *am* in love with her.

Breathless, I break the kiss and look into her eyes. Alternating my strokes, long and deep, short and swift, I work her next orgasm to the surface. She releases a keening sound that pierces the air and has me panting to hear it once more. My cock swells and I know I'm not going to be able to fight it much longer.

With her big brown eyes, she looks down our bodies at our connection. "Dem," I call the name she asked me to use. She snaps her gaze to mine, and it softens. That look, it's one I want to see in her eyes repeatedly. I nuzzle her nose with mine. "I'm going to come. I need you with me this time."

"Okay," she puffs out and nods.

I reach to throw her right leg over my shoulder, opening her sweet pussy for me. Oh, Christ have mercy. She feels even better.

"I'm going to ruin this pussy before the day is over. Don't plan on walking much tomorrow," I say and grind my hips.

"Oh shit," she breathes, pressing a hand to my abs, trying to hold me off.

I knock her hand away and reach between us for her clit. She places her hands on the headboard and starts to scream, none of her words making sense.

Sunny's growls can be heard through the door. "Quiet, boy," she sobs. "Mommy's only getting her brains fucked out."

I smile and peck her lips. "You may want to put him outside for the next few rounds."

She doesn't get to answer as her eyes roll back and her entire body convulses. I start to see stars as the most powerful orgasm of my life slams into me. It's like a punch to my soul that starts in my toes and rises, exploding first in my loins, spreading to my chest, and setting fire to my scalp, leaving me breathless.

"Fuck," I bellow when I can finally get the word out, and collapse.

I knew things would be amazing between us, but I had no idea it would be like this. I tighten my arms around her and roll onto my back with her in my embrace. I kiss her cheek before nuzzling it.

"That was amazing."

"Aye, love, well worth the wait."

"Yeah, that it was."

CHAPTER 21

WATCH YOUR BACK

Kevin

"Good morning," I murmur as Dem stirs from her sleep.

I enter the room with a tray in my hands, Sunny following behind me. It's not much—toast and eggs with some sausage. I figured she'd be hungry since we didn't eat much last night. She never made it into the kitchen to make the empanadillas she promised.

Instead, we spent the night getting to know each other inch by inch. I smile as I think of the many ways I now know her. I can't say I regret the way I woke this morning.

Dem in my arms and her leg wrapped around mine. It's the way I feel I should be waking every morning. It felt right, like we've been doing it for years. I no longer feel like something is missing.

"Good morning," she says, covering her mouth. "Please give me a minute to become human."

I purse my lips to keep from laughing and nod, placing the tray down on the nightstand as she gets up and goes into the bathroom to freshen up. I watch her go, growing hard as her lush curves come into view. I'm tempted to follow her, but I want to get some food in her system. If I go in that bathroom, we'll be eating anything but food.

"Kev, you're going to stop using my toothbrush. I bought you one, damn it. I'm placing it in the holder. It's the blue one."

"Okay, baby. I'm sorry," I say as I try not to laugh.

She's told me this before. The last time I slept over on the couch.

It truly ticks her off. When she peeks her head out of the bathroom to glance at me, her little nose is turned up and her lips are pulled tight.

I hold my hands up. "I've got it. The blue one is mine. I won't use yours."

She rolls her eyes, but a smile teases the corners of her lips before she disappears again. I reach for my phone to check my messages. I grunt; it's all the same. We still have nothing. Frustration builds, causing me to toss the phone back down.

"What's the matter?" Dem purrs as she straddles my lap with a piece of toast in her hand.

I hadn't noticed her come from the bathroom. Placing my hands on her hips, I take in the fact that she's in my T-shirt. I slip my hand underneath and palm her breast. She wiggles in my lap and smiles back at me as she munches on the toast.

"Nothing now," I say and kiss her lips.

"Then what's that look for?" She tilts her head and studies me.

"What look?"

She rolls her eyes and tries to climb out of my lap. I'm not having it. I wrap my arms around her and hold her in place. I drop my gaze to her lips.

How did I get so lucky? Not only is this woman gorgeous, she makes my heart race with one single look. I can't remember ever feeling this way about anyone. I can see having a future with her. Whatever's out there threatening her safety, I'm ready to tackle it head-on.

"I have to head in today. Serg mentioned I might actually be assigned a partner," she says.

I frown. I've been secretly fuming about that. It's not right and it's gone on for too long. I've been grinding my gears to keep from calling Dugan on that shit. He should be aware of it and put a stop to the bullshit.

Danita kisses my lips. "I see that look," she says as I silently stew.

"I can handle myself. I don't want to find out you've stuck your nose in this."

"I don't know what you're talking about."

"Uh-huh." She twists her lips up as she looks at me. I knead her breast beneath her shirt and soon lust and desire fill her eyes. I bite my lip as her amber eyes speak to me. "Kev."

The sweetly spoken word is trapped between our lips as I claim her mouth for a kiss. I can't get enough of her. I want to kiss and touch her all day and night.

"Let me take you out to dinner tonight," I say against her mouth.

She shakes her head. "I need to get focused. I can still feel my time running out. By the way, did your brother find anything on Detective Reed?"

I frown, hating the change in subject. I especially hate it because I have nothing new to give her. At least nothing useful.

"He found out that she and Harris were fucking for a few months and that she's heavy into the ring at this point—"

"Ew. Wait, you're kidding, right?"

"Nope."

"Ugh, she could do so much better. He's such an asshole," she says and frowns.

That reminds me. "I've been meaning to ask you: What's the deal with him and you?"

Orin and I already have a dodgy history. I trust Dem, but that doesn't change things between me and Orin. I'd hate to have to beat the shit out of him again.

"There is no deal. He's asked me out and I've told him no. Over and over and over. He doesn't seem to get the point. I'm not interested."

I bob my head, mostly to myself. I'll be having a talk with him sooner than later. We've never liked each other. He's been a dick from day one.

I'm going to make sure we have an understanding about my

woman this time around. She's off-limits, period. If he doesn't get the point, I can make it clear for him. Like I said, it wouldn't be the first time I've had to knock him on his ass to make my point.

"Anyway. You were saying. Could Shane connect Reed?"

"No connection to Cal and the shooting as of yet. There's no connection to anyone in that file. I'll give them that. They cover their tracks well."

"But not well enough. I've caught them slipping and so had Cal. All I need is a big enough slip."

I grunt. "That's what we're all hoping for."

Before I can stew in my thoughts, she pushes a hand through the front of my hair. I love when she does that. I kiss her softly and smile at her.

"It's one night. One date. We can still focus and enjoy each other," I say, hoping I can coax her into a date.

She looks at me cautiously. A mix of emotions cross her face. I'm not able to place them before she shuts them down.

"Last night was amazing. More amazing than I imagined, but I think we are playing with fire. I care about you. You've become a really good friend. I don't want to see you hurt," she says.

Good friend.

I smirk and tap her nose. "Yer so cute."

She scrunches up her face. "What?"

Nuzzling my nose against hers, I rub soothing circles against her back. Slowly, I kiss her lips. A mere brush at first, applying more pressure gradually. Flicking my tongue against her lips, she opens for me and I dive into her mouth, turning up the passion and intensity.

When I fully devour her mouth, I pull away to make my point. "Ya were mine the moment I pushed inside ya, love, but I'll let ya figure that out."

"You're mad," she says, searching my face.

"No."

"You are." She runs her fingers across my brow. "You have to know how much you mean to me as a friend, Kev. Last night doesn't change that. I will always cherish the friend you've become, and as a friend, I want to protect you."

"And as yer man, I'll be doing the protecting."

She rolls her eyes and places her forehead to mine. "You're going to be difficult about this, aren't you?"

"Explain to me what I'm being difficult about. What do you think is going on here?"

This time when she goes to pull away, I allow it. She reaches for another piece of toast and sausage before she sits on my thighs. I remain silent as I watch her chew thoughtfully.

Once she swallows the last bite, she covers her mouth and clears her throat. "I'm not going to lie to you. I feel like I do enough of that as it is. I have feelings for you. Feelings that I can't allow myself to get invested in.

"For now, can we maybe keep this to ourselves and take it slow? I know we're doing the whole fake relationship thing, but perhaps we can dial it down in public now that things have turned up in private," she says and starts to chew on her lip.

I grab the front of her T-shirt and drag her to me until we are nose to nose. "Again…you are adorable."

"Kevin," she chides.

"*Ba mhaith liom tú go deo. Ní dhéanfaidh aon ní níos lú.*"

"Huh?"

I let my breath fan her lips as I debate on whether or not to tell her I want her forever and I will take nothing less. Lifting my hand not grasping the T-shirt, I brush my thumb across her bottom lip. The shy look in her eyes tells me not to push.

Instead, I seal my lips to hers and distract her from wanting an answer. Reaching for the nightstand, I grab a foil packet. Then lean into her until she falls back and I'm hovering above her.

"You were able to walk to the bathroom a little too easily for me. Only a slight wobble won't do. Let's get you ready for work." I breathe against her lips as I suit up to be inside her once more before we start our day.

———————————

Danita

Sex with Kevin is amazing. Last night was off the charts, but there was something different this morning. I felt more like he took his time to make love to me.

I've been trying all afternoon to avoid thinking about it. However, every time I go to walk or sit, I have a constant reminder. I've gotten strange looks from a few people as I hobble around the station.

"Moralez," Sergeant Graves calls as he moves to my desk. He looks perplexed as he hovers over me and folds his arms over his chest. He glances around, then nods toward his office. "Let's take this in my office."

I follow after him as best I can. I'm going to kill Kevin. While he made love to me for most of the morning, he did pull me onto all fours and pound into me like a mad man at the end.

I swear, I thought the man lost something inside the walls he was trying to knock down. This morning if anyone asked me what Kevin did for a living, I'd tell them construction. Demolition specifically.

"Close the door," Serg says as he takes a seat behind his desk. I close the door, then amble over to the chair in front of his desk and ease into it. "Are you all right?"

His brows are pinched as he looks at me while I try to sit gingerly. My face is on fire as embarrassment sieges me. I shrug, trying to play it off.

"Overdid it in the gym," I lie.

"Hmm, anyway. I had intended to assign you a partner today." He pauses and steeples his fingers in front of his lips. The silence becomes thick. "I give you shit, but you're one of the best on the squad. I'll admit that. Who the hell have you pissed off? I can't afford to lose the one detective I have that can close a damn case without me questioning every damn detail. Yet, someone is hell-bent on blocking me from giving you a new partner," he says the last part as if he's speaking to himself.

"I just do my job," I say.

He scoffs. "Sweetheart. This shit is coming from way up. Some part of you doing your job has ruffled feathers. I want you to be careful out there. I'm making Harris and Dawson available to you as much as possible. I'm also moving a few of your cases around."

I bite back my response. I have a ton of shit I want to hurl at him. This is bullshit, and we both know it. However, what rings loudest in my ear is that I need to get the hell out of here. My time has run out. The clock has reached the final hours, and if I don't make a move, I'm going to be left holding my head in a bag after these pricks blow it off.

I narrow my eyes and take in Sergeant Graves. He has his flaws, but the jury is still out on if I can trust him in all of this. I've yet to weed him out of all the filth.

He leans into his desk and lowers his voice. "I've watched you. You haven't gotten involved with the bullshit. This precinct has gone to the dogs. They assigned me this shit to have a scapegoat when it all blows up. Black sergeant that let his squad run amok. I can see the headlines now. Don't take it personal when I ride your ass. I'm one of many puppets around here. I've accepted my fate, but what I don't like are the strings I'm starting to see pulled around you. Be careful, Moralez."

I nod and stand. "I hear you, Serg. I'll watch my back."

He looks at me for a moment. "Are you sure it's wise to be dating Kelley's brother-in-law? Have you thought of how that can blow back on your door?"

My eyes widen. I had no idea he knew about Kevin. I shouldn't be surprised. Gossip moves like wind around this place.

"Blackhart is a great guy. What happened to Kelley is shit, but what happened to him and who I'm dating have nothing to do with each other. Besides, I don't see why my dating life is anyone's damn business."

He holds up his hands. "I'm only pointing out where your problem may be coming from."

"Honestly, Serg, I didn't have a partner before I started dating Blackhart. So forgive me if I don't see the connection."

He makes a face. After a beat, he nods. "Fair enough, you're right." With a sigh, he runs a hand over his bald head. "This place—" He cuts off and shakes his head. "You lose yourself. One way or another, it changes you and everything you thought you were getting into. The politics, the corruption. You don't change it; it changes you."

His words hit too close to home. I haven't changed a thing here in the last five years, but I've changed. So much so, I don't remember the carefree agent I once was. I was so young and hopeful.

"I guess we have to hope that we'll change for the better one of these days," I say and turn to leave.

CHAPTER 22

I'M NOT YOUR GIRLFRIEND

Kevin

SHE'S DYED HER HAIR. I NOTICED IT YESTERDAY. I'M STILL CURIOUS as to what it looks like naturally. I never knew I wanted red-haired little girls until I learned that her hair isn't truly black.

Her hair isn't the only thing I noticed. "What's going on?" I ask for the millionth time.

Dem has been more distant than usual for the last few days. I know it's not about us. From the time I walked into her place the other night with my key she gave me, she pounced. I took her all over her place. Against the front door, the coffee table, kitchen countertop, the shower, her bed.

It's been like that since the first night. When she's too sore to take me, I feast on her and she feasts on me, but we can't keep our hands off each other. When we're not all over each other, we've been building on the foundation we started with.

She turns from the beer on the table in front of her to look at me. Not for the first time, I note how right it feels to have her here at the Golden Clover to meet all my family. I know this is more about Quinn bringing Alicia to meet everyone, but I'm glad I could talk Dem into coming along.

At least that was before… Something is bothering her. I don't like it, and I need her to talk to me so I can fix it. I reach to brush a loose strand of hair behind her ear. It's the strand that always pops out when she doesn't gel it back.

She's searching my eyes as if she's looking to find something. "Serg called me into his office to tell me to watch my back. Someone has been blocking the assignment of my partner. I'm running out of time," she says.

I move in close and cup the side of her face. "We're going to get Con to talk. We'll work on him tonight. I'll give Quinn a nudge as well. It could mean him turning his focus to you sooner."

"At this point, it's a chance I'm willing to take. I'll deal with that when it comes."

I narrow my eyes. "What else aren't you telling me? Something else is going on."

She runs a hand over her hair. Her brows dip. "When I took Sunny for a walk this morning, it felt like someone was watching me. I tried to shake it off, but I know I'm not crazy. When I got back to the apartment, Sunny was... I don't know, a little anxious or something. It wasn't like him. Something was off."

I clench my jaw. I had to take the kids to school and Dem had to go to work. It was the first morning we couldn't all maneuver our schedules to make sure everyone was covered. I took care of the kids and made it to Dem in time to follow her to work. That was an entire hour she was without me.

"You should move in with me," I say without thinking.

"What? Come on, I can't move in with you. We've just started this thing between us. I'm not moving in with you. Besides, you keep the kids sometimes. If someone has started watching me and this shit is about to blow up in my face, I don't want your nieces and nephew anywhere around me."

I rock back on my heels. When she puts it that way, she has a point. However, she's important to me, and so is her safety. I'll do whatever I have to, to make sure everyone is safe.

"You let me worry about that."

"Aren't you about to move back into your place? You should be settling into your home. Not worrying about me."

"You still don't get it, do you?"

"Get what?"

"You're not some random—"

"Kev," Trent booms from across the room.

I turn and frown at my brother. He holds up a beer and waves me over to the bar. I release a sigh. I told him and Shane I'd be over there about twenty minutes ago.

"Go on. I'm going to head to the restroom, and your mother invited me to sit with her and Erin," she says, placing a hand on my chest.

I tug her to me and kiss her passionately. I place a kiss on her nose then press my lips to her forehead gently, lending her my strength as I feel her sag into me.

"We'll figure it out. We will have enough time to get to the bottom of this if I have to create it myself," I breathe.

"Is it crazy that I believe you?"

"Not at all, love. Not at all."

Danita

I hadn't planned to tell Kevin about that weird crap that happened this morning, but something about it has been nagging at me. I roll it over in my mind again as I wash my hands and finish up in the restroom. My thoughts turn to what I'm doing here in the first place.

I still don't know why I said yes. When Kevin asked me to come to this dinner, I had planned to say no. I've already crossed so many lines, and I'm growing attached to him. He's stayed over in my bed since that first day we slept together.

Trust me, I'm not complaining at all. Not when it comes to being satisfied. However, these feelings and all I have on my plate need to be handled with care.

"What are you doing, Dem?" I say to the mirror.

I wish I could give myself an answer. The level of guilt I had when Kevin introduced me to his parents as Danita, his girlfriend, was so intense, it felt like it would crush my windpipe. This all feels so wrong.

I shake my hands out and head back out into the bar. When I look for Kevin and his two brothers at the bar, they're gone. I start for the back room in the restaurant where we were when we first arrived. Kevin is right outside the doorway, with his head bent over his phone as I make my way to him.

He lifts his head and his eyes light up as they fix on me. He places a hand on the small of my back and draws me into him. I don't have time to protest the kiss he places on my lips.

"What happened to dialing it down in public?"

He snorts. "That was your naff idea. I never agreed to it."

"Naff?"

He gives me a pointed look. "Stupid," he says, his accent in place, showing his annoyance.

"It's not a stupid idea. I don't want people to get the wrong idea."

He gives me that look again. "The point is for everyone to get that idea, love."

Okay, he's right, but I'm trying to keep a grasp on my sanity here. I don't know what the future holds for me. I need to put the brakes on what's happening between us somehow.

He brushes my cheek and butterflies take off in my stomach. I have no idea why that simple gesture always gets to me, and I swear he does it because he knows. I close my eyes and bask in his touch.

"Do me a favor. Stop overthinking things with me. Use your gut, follow what it tells you about us."

"Are you so sure my gut will lead me to what you want?" I say.

"I'm positive." He says the words with so much conviction, I open my eyes and look up at him.

He gives me a sexy smile and lifts my hand to his lips. "Come on, Quinn and Alicia are here. We should join everyone else."

"Tea will be served now that everyone is here," Renny, Kevin's mother, calls as we enter the room.

Kevin leads me over to Quinn and his cute little girlfriend. She's pretty and curvy—a few shades lighter than me and a bit shorter. I lift a brow as I realize she's African American as well. It brings to mind a friend once telling me that she had no shortage of interest when she took a tour of Ireland and Scotland.

Okay now.

"Alicia, meet my girlfriend, Danita," Kevin says. I don't miss the taunting in his voice.

I scowl up at him. We just had this conversation. I want to strangle him. For one, it stings to hear him introduce me as Danita. A part of me gets angry that he can't introduce me as Demaris—and doesn't have a clue that it's my name in the first place.

Then there's the fact that I don't know what it is about him calling me his girlfriend, but it makes my heart skip a beat. Trying to keep anyone else from seeing it, I elbow him for being an ass.

He keeps that smile on his face as if I haven't touched him. Alicia holds her hand out to me, drawing my attention away from Kevin. It's a good thing because I might lose my temper with him, and I know he doesn't deserve it. It's not his fault that I'm warring with my shitty life.

"Hi, I'm Alicia," she says as we shake.

"Nice to meet you," I say, then turn to Kevin. "Boyfriend, can we talk?"

"After dinner, love," Kevin says, turning to walk away.

Oh no, he doesn't. I meant it when I said we should dial it down. I follow after him, grumbling under my breath. Catching him by his arm, I halt him before he can get close to anyone else.

"I meant what I said," I say.

"You've said a lot. So, you'll have to tell me what you're talking about."

I purse my lips and frown up at him. Releasing his arm, I throw my hands up in the air. He folds his arms over his chest.

"I'm not your girlfriend. Stop introducing me to people as such," I say.

He makes a sound in the back of his throat and glares at me. "Are you serious?"

"Do I look serious?"

He looks around, there are quite a few eyes are on us. Grabbing my hand, he quickly leads us to a little alcove out of sight. "First, let's get this straight. I"—he points to his chest—"belong to you. I'm your man." He points to my chest. "Which makes you mine. Since I haven't put a ring on your finger yet, that would make you my girlfriend.

"It's a pretty easy concept, love. You share your bed with me. I'm yours and you're mine. Second, the entire point is to make everyone believe we are dating, for your safety." He steps up to me, cups my neck, and leans in, his breath fanning my lips. "I plan to keep this same energy because this is what it looks like to be mine."

With that, he kisses me. I swallow my argument. Not because of the kiss, but because I'm not making sense. Not to me and not to our cause. The only reason I'm truly upset is because I want to be his, I want this to be real with everything that I am.

"Oh, come on, Uncle Kev. Get a room."

Kevin chuckles as he breaks the kiss. "Ya wait until ya get ya a little girlfriend, Con. I'm going to make ya pay for that one."

"The ladies love me. I can't just pick one," Con says cockily.

I snicker and turn to find the teen looking at us in our hiding place. "He's so much like you." Kevin wraps an arm around my shoulder and kisses the top of my head. "And by the way, keep this same energy? Really?"

He shrugs. Yup, Kevin would totally be my type if I had the freedom to date and fall in love. However, with Graves's words of caution and the incident this morning, I know I don't have this luxury. Eric's warning rings in my ears.

I shouldn't get involved with anyone. The knowledge of Cal being in a hospital bed because I didn't heed Eric's words sends an ache through me. I look over at Erin, and I know I need to cut this off and soon.

Too bad you're already in love and he's not going to make this easy.

I watch Kevin with his brothers and smile. I'm not going to head over there. I'm only observing. This is one tight-knit family. It reminds me of my own.

My brothers are overprotective and loving. While all in law enforcement, they were pissed as hell to learn I'd entered the training academy for the FBI.

Diego, my middle brother, warned me about this life. I look down at my feet. It's the one time I should have listened.

"Hey, Detective Moralez," Conroy says, drawing my attention.

I had gone to the bathroom and was heading back to the room we all had dinner in until the guys caught my attention. As I turn to Con, I notice Alicia sitting with Renny and Teagon, Renny and Kevin's dad. A pang hits my chest.

They've taken us both in tonight. However, it doesn't feel right because I'm not being true to who I am. They don't know me. I don't belong here.

"What's up, kid?"

"I was thinking about asking Uncle Kevin if we can hang out again once he moves back into the house. He said it's ready."

"Sure, I'd like that. We can get more footage of me kicking his butt on the court."

The smile that takes over his handsome face almost makes me laugh. He nods. "Yeah, or we can invite my other uncles this time and they can see it for themselves," he says excitedly.

"I'm there."

His eyes grow distant for a moment. I hold my breath and say a prayer that he's ready to talk. He's been opening up to my presence more and more all night.

"Did you know my dad when he was a cop?"

"I did. Not well, but I did know him. We became close after," I reply. "I know he was a good cop."

He beams, his chest seeming to swell with pride. He opens his mouth as if he's going to say more, but stops as his eyes lock on something behind me. I turn to see Mckenna talking to one of the younger staff members who's clearing a table. He's a tall lanky blond.

I don't blame her for the dreamy-eyed look she's giving the boy. He's cute and looks like he knows it. She flips her hair and giggles at whatever the boy has said.

"She's so boy crazy. None of them are good enough for her," Conroy says angrily.

I turn back to him. Remembering the time when my brothers were just like him, I smile. I can't help wondering what they would think of Kevin. My oldest brother Emilio is a lot like Kevin; I think they would get along.

He would probably butt heads a little with Diego, but I still think they would vibe. Joaquin is the most easy-going of the three, but he's the most protective. I can't say how he would respond to Kevin. In Jo-jo's eyes, I should never date or marry. I should remain his virgin baby sister. I have news for him.

"She's a pretty girl. I'm sure the boys are into her as much as she's into them," I reply to Conroy.

"Yeah, that's the problem. Hey, I'll catch you later."

Before I can caution him to allow his sister to be a teenage girl, he's headed over to her and the guy that has a piece of her hair wrapped around his finger. I smile and shake my head.

Glancing at my watch, I see it's getting late. I think it's time I call it a night. Instead of starting for the back room, I walk over to let Kevin know I'm going home.

I didn't ride with him, so he'll probably insist on following me out to ensure I make it home safely. When I stop at his side, he reaches for my waist and pulls me into him. I almost lose myself and lean in to kiss him.

"I'm going to head home," I say.

He leans into my ear. "Come stay the night with me." He searches my eyes when he pulls back.

"I don't think that's a good idea. I'm going to take a night to think to myself."

He frowns and turns to his brothers to excuse himself, then leads me away from their table. Once in a corner by ourselves, he cups my cheek. Again, he takes his time appraising my face as if he can find all the answers there.

"You're pulling away." It's a statement not a question.

"I'm going home to get some sleep and sort out my thoughts. You and I know that's not going to happen if we're together."

He's silent for a moment. Reaching into his pocket, he pulls out a set of keys. I eye them with curiosity.

"I have a key to your place. I thought it only fair that I make you copies for mine. The smaller ring is for the apartment. The larger one is for the house. I'll give you your space tonight, but if you change your mind…my door is always open to you," he finishes.

My phone rings as he says his last word. I pull it out and groan when I see it's Harris. His timing is complete shit.

I connect the call. "Hello."

"Serg wants you in on this one. Where are you? I'll pick you up," Harris replies.

"Text me the address. I'll meet you there."

There's a pause for a few seconds. "Yeah, all right."

He ends the call, leaving me grumbling to myself. I look up at

Kevin, and he's watching me closely. I reach to brush his hair off his forehead.

"I'll call you when I get home."

"I'm coming with you."

I shake my head. "Enjoy your family. It's work. I'll text you when I'm headed home and call once I'm there. We'll talk then. I think we have a few things to sort out."

He thins his lips, but he doesn't protest, which lets me know he's pretty upset. I remind myself that I need to start putting this space between us. Kissing my forehead, he hands me the keys.

"Be safe, love."

CHAPTER 23

THE ONES WE LOVE

Danita

THINGS LIKE THIS MAKE ME SO SAD. LOOK AT HER. SHE'S SO YOUNG and had her entire future ahead of her. Now, her life is gone, and she has a needle sticking out of her arm.

"Why, Mommy?" I whisper as I squat beside her. "You had a whole life to live."

The party stopped here for her. Inside an abandoned warehouse at a rave. She's so pretty with her strawberry-blond hair and tanned skin. With her eyes closed, she could be Mckenna.

This girl is only a few years older than the twins. I'm guessing she's no older than twenty, maybe twenty-two. We've been getting a lot of these calls. It's pissing me off. The gangs are selling some new shit that's too pure.

What boils my blood is that I know for a fact the supposed good guys have a hand in this somehow. I glance down at the girl's hand and find an engagement ring on her finger. My jaw clenches.

She has someone who loves her, someone waiting for her to come home, and she made the choice to be here. To lose it all like this. I can't help but wonder if I've hurt my family with my choices the way she has tonight.

"What's with the attitude? Blackhart not getting the job done?" Harris says over my shoulder.

I turn my head to glare at him. He's been getting on my nerves since I've arrived. This isn't his first comment about Kevin. Honestly, I'm on the verge of losing it.

Between the look on Kevin's face when I left, this young girl lying before me, and the crap coming out of this asshole's mouth every five seconds, I swear I'm about to hit the roof. Standing, I turn around fully. I place my hands on my hips and glare at Harris.

"This would work so much better if you would do your part instead of hovering over me," I say.

"View's better over here. Besides, you smell nice. How about we forget all this bullshit and head back to my place?" he says with that smug grin of his.

I press my hands to my temples. My head feels like it's ready to explode. I drop my hands and look up at him, tilting my head to the side to see if maybe I'm the one with the comprehension problem. I've been a straight-A student all my life, but I tend to have my dunce moments in the practical world.

Okay, lies.

I don't do stupid, so stupidity goes over my head. Therefore, this shit right here has missed me on so many levels, I might be the one who's confused. I narrow my eyes.

Harris is not a slow man. He's actually not a half-bad detective when he does his freaking job. This is purely his lack of give-a-fuck when it comes to rules, other people's feelings, and the fact that some-one might not be attracted to him.

"I'm going to break this down for you real slow. I. Don't. Want. You. Not today, not tomorrow, and no time in the future. It's never going to happen. We will never be a thing. I'm not dropping my drawers for you. I'm not getting on my knees for you or any of the other things you've suggested repeatedly that I've turned down," I hiss.

"You act as if I haven't offered to take you to dinner first," he says smugly.

I growl. Seriously growl in frustration. This motherfu—

Calm down, Demaris. Do not lose your cool on this nut.

My emotions are already all over the place. Kevin handing me those keys was a big deal. I haven't had time to process that. I don't know why I gave him a key to mine. I was in a rush to get to work after we'd spent the morning in bed together. I hadn't had time to feed or walk Sunny. Kevin offered to do both and catch up with me.

I was in a cloud from our first night together and relishing the lingering soreness of our love making. Okay, I was dickmatized. I handed over the spare key without a second thought.

Not like my heavy thoughts tonight. Kevin asked me to move in with him before giving me his keys. I said no, but the metal in my pocket is weighing down my entire being. With all of that riding my thoughts, I don't think I have it in me to hold on to my sanity for too long.

Then there's this girl. Her lifeless body has placed a spotlight on my life. My decisions always hurt the people I love.

Yes, there is a dealer who sold drugs to the partygoers who packed this place earlier, but this girl made choices that led to this path. Ultimately, she sealed her fate. I'm doing the same every day. Making choices, hurting people—it doesn't matter that there are bad guys I want and need to put away.

How many people who love me have to suffer along the way? I think of Kevin. Can he love me the way I've fallen in love with him? I'll never know as long as I continue to choose to push him away.

"Fuck off, Harris," I grumble and turn back to doing my job.

"What…you too good for me? Is that why you'll spread your legs for him and not for me? Or is it the money? I'm not a million-dollar Sherlock Holmes so I'm shit on your shoe?"

I whirl back around on him. "What business is it of yours who I sleep with? Furthermore, what the hell are you talking about?"

"Kevin and his brother thought they were something special when they were on the force. Then they went and started that fancy investigation and security firm with their high-profile clients, and now we're all supposed to kiss their asses. Bite me."

I squint at Harris. That green-eyed monster is seething as it shows its head. I know that Kevin has high-profile clients, but I've never thought about the kind of money he makes. Actually, when I think about it, his home is in a very nice neighborhood, and it's a really nice house on at least a half an acre from what I can tell.

If I'm honest, Cal's house is pretty nice too. I know for a fact his neighborhood can be very pricey. Cal has told me that they do well. However, it never dawned on me how well.

"If it bothers you that much, I think they're hiring," I tease, just to be a bitch.

"Yeah, we'll see who gets the last laugh."

Like a toddler having a tantrum, he turns and storms off. I'm grateful to be left with my thoughts. Oh, and I have plenty.

If Kevin does make that kind of money, what has watching over me cost him and his brothers? My Jane Doe's ring grabs my attention again. It's a nice rock.

Some poor guy is going to be devastated to find out that the girl he loves is gone. Maybe she wasn't who he thought she was. Or maybe, just maybe, he knew her enough to take her as she was.

Kevin

"No, I'll look into it in the morning," I say tiredly into the phone as I step out of my car.

"All right, wanted you to know. Bridget was pretty pissed, and since Quinn left here snuggling with his bird, I thought you should know," Trent replies.

"When isn't the lass pissed off?"

"Don't let her hear you say that." He chuckles.

"I'll give them both a bonus for this job. We knew he would be difficult." I sigh.

I knew that baseball player, Knox, was going to be a problem when he requested two of our females. High-profile clients like him tend to be a pain in the ass. Don't get me wrong, Bridget and Q are two of our best. Heck, all the women who work for us are professional and at the top of their game.

I get the feeling there's a whole lot more going on with that case. If I can get things to settle here, I'll pop in myself to see what the issue is. At the moment, my tired brain can't comprehend why my agent and the baseball player she's assigned to are having problems.

"Yeah, but I get the feeling it's more than him," Trent repeats my thoughts.

"Shane check in yet? Has he started to rattle those cages like Quinn asked?"

My brother Quinn is starting to put the pieces into place. I totally agree with him that we've been chasing our tails, and it's time to regroup. When we talked at the Golden Clover, I'd been a little distracted, but I'm totally in favor of calling the noise to us.

Shane is the best at poking the bear and getting attention. He left not long after Dem to get started on his new task. I'm sure we'll start to hear something soon enough.

"Not yet, but I'm sure it won't take him long to have something for us. I think Quinn is on to something," Trent replies.

"I was thinking the same thing."

"Anyway, it's been a long night. The rest of us are all headed out soon. I'll talk to you in the morning."

"Aye, later," I say.

I drag my feet as I walk to my apartment. I don't want to go into that lonely place. I'm not sure what brings me here. I'll be letting this place go soon. Normally if I don't have the kids, I'll sleep at the house.

Well, lately I've been at Dem's place more than my own. Running a hand through my hair, I chide myself for pushing too hard. It's the look in her eyes. I can read her better than she knows.

She's thinking about pulling away, but there's a part of her that doesn't want to. That's the part I've been getting to hold in my arms. I'm so in love with her, and I don't know what to do if this shit blows up in my face.

There are so many variables not in my control. I'm not used to not knowing everything to control the narrative and my environment. I'm the operations and tactical manager at the firm.

Quinn sees the holes, and I create the strategies to plug them up. We've been this way since we were little. It's how I can sense that I don't have much time before he figures out what's going on with Dem.

Dem… Danita. It doesn't matter either way to me. All I know is I've fallen for a woman whose name I don't know. I'm twisted in knots over her, and walking into this empty apartment is going to feel like death tonight.

Or so I thought.

I lift my head to find a distracted-looking Dem trying to get into my place with the keys I gave her. When she turns to me, tears are soaking her face.

I don't think. I rush to her side and look her over to make sure she's okay. She throws her arms around my neck and holds on tightly, burying her face there as well. I look around for any signs of danger. Once I've assessed there's no immediate danger, I push my key into the lock and let us in.

"Are you all right, love?" I ask, cupping her face so I can look down into it.

Instead of replying, she shrugs from her jacket and then out of her holster. She lifts onto her toes and grasps a hold of my ears to bring my lips to hers. Her feverish kiss pulls a groan from me. I palm her full globes, but I don't deepen the kiss. I pull away and kiss her forehead.

"Don't," she whispers.

"Don't what?"

She brushes her fingers through the front of my hair. "I don't need you to be my friend. I need my man. Don't cuddle me."

Her words are like the match that lights a firestorm. I lift her onto my waist and kiss her hard and deep. I don't think we're going to make it to my bedroom.

Not the way she's clawing at my face and the back of my head. There's a voice in my head telling me I should ask questions. She hadn't planned to come here earlier. Something had to have happened.

Yet, the taste of her kisses and the feel of her pressed against me completely silence that voice. I walk her over to the back of the couch and perch her on it. Her button-down is the first thing I reach for.

Frustrated with the first two buttons, I grab the shirt and tug it open. The buttons fly every which way. Dem looks up at me with a cheeky grin and raises her brow. I stare at her with hooded lids, making sure she can see my desire for her.

I believe she catches the point. She shrugs out of the shirt and tosses it. I reach for the tank top she has on beneath and tug it from her jeans.

"So sexy," I breathe when her gorgeous breasts come into view.

Needing to do more than look, I tug the right cup of her bra down and palm her breast as I dip my head to capture her peak between my lips. Dem arches her back and cries out. I've learned exactly what my girl likes.

I swirl and flick my tongue against the hardened tip. That wins me the prize I'm after. She squeezes her thighs together and begs for more.

Grasping her legs, I part them and step between their warmth. When I lift my head, the mix of want, need, and vulnerability that I see on her face is enough to fold me. Of all the looks she's given me, this one tells me something has changed.

I open my mouth to tell her I love her, and that's when her phone rings. I have never begrudged her job or the late-night calls, but this…tonight, in this very moment, I loathe that phone and the fact that she's a detective.

Annoyed, I double back for her jacket where the phone is ringing. Dem covers her breasts with one hand and reaches for the device in the pocket of the jacket with the other. Tossing the jacket over the back of the couch, I can't help but reach for her waist, if for no other reason than to have my hands on her.

"Hello," she answers the phone and pauses. "Sure, the password is scathingly brilliant. What's this about?"

I watch as her face becomes confused. Something is wrong. I gather her clothing and start to help her get dressed as she listens.

"No, I'm on my way. Thank you." She hangs that call up and accepts a call right after. "Hello, Ms. Pearl."

She's shaking as she tugs her tank top back over her head. I'm getting frustrated with not knowing what's going on. When she lifts tear-filled eyes toward me, I think I'm going to explode.

"I'm on my way," she says into the phone once again.

"What's going on?"

"I have to get to my place. I need to get to Sunny."

"What happened?" I say and lead her toward the door, grabbing her gun to hand to her.

"My place is on fire," she says in the most haunted voice I've ever heard.

CHAPTER 24

BURNING

Danita

I CAN'T BELIEVE THIS. I ALMOST LOST SUNNY. I CRADLE HIM AWK-wardly in my arms in a tight embrace as I pace. He's heavy, but I manage to hold him up, not wanting to let him go.

"*My home, my fucking home?*" I sob, my blood boiling.

It hasn't sunk in where this has come from. Only the fact that they tried to take Sunny from me. My dog. Who the fuck goes after a help-less dog? When Eric warned no one around me would be safe, I never thought that would include Sunny.

I'm at a complete loss as I watch my place burn down and the fire-fighters move about as they get the fire under control. Kevin wrap his arms around me as I rock back and forth with Sunny pressed against my chest.

"Shh," I coo as Sunny whimpers. I kiss his head, unable to stop the tears from rolling down my cheeks.

Sunny was a gift from my grandmother right before I went under-cover. She passed away not long after. I've cherished Sunny as if I've had a part of her with me. Eric fought me on bringing Sunny with me, but it was a battle I won.

"Are you okay?" Kevin whispers in my ear.

All I can do is nod. I'm too choked up to speak. I have so many emotions running through me. My anger has won out over my fears in this moment.

"A warning," Shane says.

"Aye, but who the fuck are they to warn *me* of anything?" Kevin seethes. "I'm going to rain hell on their heads."

I'm seething too. Kevin told me on the way over that he and his brothers decided to turn the tables tonight. They mean to draw these cowards out. Kevin believes this is a result of Shane tapping at the right door. I'm not too sure of that.

I think this is the ring's way of telling me I'm next to meet with the same fate as Cal. Eric was right. I should have kept my mouth shut and held this assignment tight to my chest.

"We have to figure out who *they* are," Trent grunts.

I zone out as I run through all the bastards on that list. I may not have the big guys, but I have enough names to rock a few heads to sleep. My anger has me envisioning my hands around a few throats.

If they want to come after me, I can return the favor. For the first time, I want to go with my gut and say fuck caution. What has it gotten me? I want these guys to pay.

I look up and lock eyes with Quinn. My wandering rage-filled thoughts must shine through my eyes from the look on his face. I quickly shut down all my emotions before his prying gaze claws in.

I have to remind myself I'm nothing like the monsters in the ring. They traffic drugs, humans, and guns. They are willing to gun down a man and his wife in front of their home. Yet my anger is so fierce… in this moment, I can't say what I'll do.

"Sunny is the last piece of my *abuela* I have left; if he had gotten trapped in there…if I had lost him," I sob. "I'm going to fucking gut them. Do you hear me?"

"Aye, love. We hear ya," Kevin says, kissing the top of my head.

I space out again as Quinn and Kevin talk about where I'll be staying. All I can think about is how this changes things. Kevin catches a set of keys Quinn tosses to him, bringing my attention back to the present.

"I'll take ya up on that one," Kevin says and starts to lead me away from the scene.

Kevin

I want to get Dem out of here, and the cabin is the perfect place for her to be able to regroup. I can only imagine what's going on in her head. I go to pull her closer when Sergeant Graves and Detective Harris come into view.

"Moralez, are you all right?" Sergeant Graves asks with true concern etched into his face.

"I will be."

"I don't like this. I don't like it one damn bit," he grinds out. "I want answers."

Dem leans into me. "I'm going to find out who did this," she snarls.

"Maybe you should focus on getting away from here for a while instead. It's obvious you've gotten in over your head," Harris says.

In the blink of an eye, I release Dem and get into Orin's face. "Only one in over their head is you," I hiss.

"You better get the hell out of my face," he says.

"Or what?"

"Why are you even here?" Dem says. I turn to see her narrowing her eyes at Harris.

"I heard the call. I came to see if you were okay."

"She doesn't need your ass to come checking on her."

"Right, because you're doing such a bang-up job of keeping her safe."

I grab him by the collar, ready to knock his ass out. I need somewhere to aim this frustration, and his stupid face looks more and more like the perfect place to land it.

"Gentlemen." Sergeant Graves sighs, grabbing everyone's attention.

He shakes his head at us, causing me to reel it in and release Harris. Rubbing a hand over his bald head, Graves places the other on his hip. His assessing eyes are on Dem.

"Listen up, Moralez. I think you should take some time off. Get out of town for a bit, maybe. Someone has it out for you. I'm convinced now. It's not a question. If they're behind this… Look, I can call in some—"

"Serg, with all due respect, I'll be fine," Dem cuts him off.

"All right, but you're taking the time. I'll get in touch if anything comes up."

I pull a card from my pocket. "You can get in touch with me if you need to contact her."

Harris snorts. "Typical."

I turn back to him slowly. "You got something you want to say to me? Spit it out now while you still have teeth in your mouth."

Dem places a hand on my arm. "Kevin, let's just go. I'm tired."

I clench my jaw, not turning from Harris's glare. It's the gentle flex of her fingers against my arm that causes me to take a step back. I swear I can't stand this guy.

"Take care of yourself, Detective. I'll be in touch," Graves says to Dem as I wrap an arm around her shoulders and start for my car.

She nods. "Thanks."

CHAPTER 25

LOVE AND COMFORT

Kevin

"ARE YOU ALL RIGHT?" I ASK AS I RUN MY FINGERS THROUGH THE front of Dem's hair.

We've been at Quinn's cabin since last night and have yet to get out of bed, but I'm not rushing her. I think she's needed this time to process. I'll figure out breakfast in a bit, but first, I want to see where her head is at.

We'll have to go out at some point to get her some clothes and pick a few things up for Sunny. The two have been clinging to each other all night. I don't mind.

I've wrapped them both in my arms, which seems to have kept them happy. I know it's grounding me from leaving them up here where they're safe, while I go find who did this and rip them to pieces. Dem has never broken down in front of anyone other than me. Seeing her fall apart in front of my brothers spoke volumes.

Dugan better start coughing up some answers. First Cal and Erin, now this. I'm not going to play nice for too much longer. I can get as dirty as the bastards that have started all of this.

"I'll be fine."

Her words are so soft and unlike her. I reach for her chin and lift her face to meet my gaze. There's that vulnerability again.

I release a heavy breath. "Something was already bothering you when you arrived at my place. We never got to talk about that, and now all of this has happened. Talk to me, baby. What's going on in that head?"

"A few of the gangs have been running a new batch that's uncut. They've also been hosting these raves. Last night…something about seeing this young girl with her life…everything gone. It brought so much home for me," she says.

I wrinkle my brows. "Like what?"

She tightens her hold on Sunny in between us. At first, I don't think she's going to answer me. I fully expect her to shut down. However, after a few moments, she starts to speak.

"I made choices that led me here. Those choices continue to affect people I love and care about. I don't want a toe tag to be how my family—" She cuts off as her voice fills with emotions, choking her words. She kisses the top of Sunny's head. "I'm sorry. I can't."

"You hear that, boy. I think your mum has admitted she loves me," I tease when I see this is too much for her to talk about. Especially without being able to give me all the details.

Dem looks me in the eyes, but I don't see the reaction I was looking for. I wanted to make her smile or laugh. Nonetheless, this look will do.

"I do love you," she says. "I wasn't supposed to fall for you. It's stupid and dangerous—"

She doesn't get to finish as I kiss her and cut her words off. Sunny squirms out of the way and plops across both of our legs. I lock my hands in Dem's hair and hold her face to mine. I'm so gone for her, she could tell me that she's an assassin and I'm her next target that she's struggling to kill, and I'd still be in love with her.

"I've been in love with you for longer than you could know," I say in between nipping at her lips. "Every time I look at you, I have to tell myself to be patient. One day you will see the way I feel about you."

"I think I've seen it all along. I've been denying it because I know this could fall apart."

"You like waiting for the other shoe to drop, love. No matter what, my feelings aren't going to change. I want you, and I'm willing to fight to have you. If that means I'll be slaying your demons and Cal's, so be it."

"Kevin—"

"Baby," I say, and give her a pointed look. "Listen, you've been through a lot. Last night was emotional for you. I know you've been overwhelmed with everything you're dealing with on your own. If you can't share that with me, then I'll help you to forget it for now."

She gives me a wobbly smile and reaches to place a hand on my ribs. Her touch is electrifying. However, as much as I would love to make love to her, I know she needs food and some fresh air more.

I caress her cheek. "Come on, let's get showered and we can head out for supplies and breakfast."

Grasping my hand, she gives it a squeeze. "Thank you for understanding. I know with all my heart this isn't easy for you. Especially since it involves your family and I'm a total stranger."

"You are not a total stranger," I say as I lace our fingers together. "You know me better than most, and I have this feeling I know a lot more about you than you think."

I lift her hand to my lips and kiss her fingers. "For now, it's me and you for a few days. Graves gave you the time. Let's take advantage of it."

"Oh God, I thought he was going to put me in the Witness Protection Program. I've never seen him so concerned about me. You know, at one point, I thought I was going to nail him with the rest. I'm starting to question that."

I work my jaw as I think about how she's a real-life sitting duck. She has snakes all around her and she's trying to weed them out. It takes a moment for me to remind myself she's good at her job.

Although, last night could mean that her job is compromised. I don't want to think about that now. I shove it to the back of my mind.

My brothers will help me to figure out if this is about her case or our shit with Cal. Hopefully, the two haven't met in between.

My instinct is telling me to be cautious for now. I don't think we should fly off the handle and show our hand. Last night, in the heat of the moment, I was ready to knock down everyone's door. Now that I have Dem here where I know she's safe, I'm starting to think clearly.

"Babe," Dem calls me out of my thoughts.

"Yeah?"

"I meant what I said."

I draw my brows as I watch the dark look that comes over her face. "What's that, love?"

"I'm going to gut whoever was responsible for that fire. Whether I take them down in this case or nail their balls to the wall some other way, they're going to pay."

I smile and give a small chuckle. "I know, babe. I know."

Danita

"This is nice," I sigh to myself as I settle into the bathtub.

Kevin took me to a brewery, a cute little bath works shop, and a bookstore. It felt good to let my guard down and be. Things between us are so easy when I'm not fighting it.

Kevin can be so affectionate and attentive. There was never a moment when he wasn't at my side or didn't have a hand on me in some way. If it wasn't his hands, it was his lips.

My face hurts from smiling up at him. Not to mention how much he has made me laugh. Today, I've felt more like myself than I have in five years.

"Try this. You have to try this," Kevin says as he comes rushing into the bathroom.

I look up from the book I'm reading. I almost scowl at him. When I get to read a Tiya Rayne book, I get invested. She's on my top five list with Blue Saffire, Ivy Harper, KT Adler, and Verleiz. I'm deep in this book and it's getting good.

However, when I see the wide-eyed expression on his face, my heart melts. He's holding a piece of one of the papas rellenas I made. I roll my eyes and laugh.

"I know what they taste like, babe. I made them."

He still comes to hold it to my lips. I take the bite and hum. Damn, it is good. I haven't made them in a while. I was feeling homesick when we were in the grocery store and I saw the ground beef. The potato balls came to mind.

"These are so good," he says.

"I'm glad you like it. Now, are you going to let me finish my book?"

He gives me a sheepish smile that makes me fall for him all over again. This big strong man has a way of tapping at my heart in all the right ways. Kevin isn't afraid to show his feelings. In moments like this, it's cute and makes me wonder what a little boy with him would look like.

I allow myself the thought this once. In the perfect world, I'd want to have as many babies as this man asks for. In reality, I know that can't be.

However, for these few seconds, I look at Kevin and see a little brown boy with red locks and his father's smile. I have no doubt we'll have a kid with some type of red hair. My natural reddish-brown waves probably wouldn't fight Kevin's red locks too much.

"What's that look?" he says, bringing me from my musing as he leans over to place a kiss on my lips.

"Nothing." I smile and shake the image away.

"Want some company?"

I'm about to beg off because I seriously do want to find out what's going to happen next in this book. However, he does it again. Takes a chunk out of my armor.

"You can read to me or I'll read to you. As long as you're in my arms, I don't care."

Oh my God. How do I say no to that? I smile wider and scoot forward.

"Come on in."

He peels out of his sweatpants and climbs in behind me. Once I settle against his chest, he kisses my shoulder and plucks the book from my hands. I was going to read to him, but once his soothing voice starts to bring the words to life off the page, I'm glad to sit back and listen.

We sit through a few chapters. Each time the water cools, I release some and add more warm water. Although the bubble bath he purchased for me has faded, the bath is still soothing. His arm that he has banded across my shoulders doesn't hurt in making me feel secure.

"We should get out and eat dinner," I say when he goes to start another chapter.

When he hesitates, I turn to look at him. He's frowning. I scrunch up my face.

"What?"

"It was getting good."

I burst into laughter as I watch the pout that comes to his face. I love this man. With every moment, I learn something else about him that makes me love him more.

"We can finish while we eat. I'll read this time. I want to try that beer you had to have."

His eyes light up. "You're going to love it. I get it whenever I come up here with Quinn. I found that place by accident."

"It absolutely does not look like a brewery. I thought it was a cute place."

He nuzzles behind my ear. "They have great burgers on Thursdays. I'll take you there for dinner this week."

I can't help the smile on my face. I've always wanted to be able to plan dates with someone and know they'd be there for me to spend time with. This is a bit surreal. I try my hardest not to think of why we're here.

However, in the back of my mind, I'm terrified that my cover has been blown. Sergeant Graves was concerned that whoever has it out for me decided to send a message. I don't know.

After some thought, something's not adding up. I've been after this ring for years. This isn't their style. Nothing I've seen from them fits this MO. Besides, if they linked me to Cal, why haven't they come for me sooner? Why burn my place down while I wasn't home? When these guys target someone, they target them.

It's all off. Shane is the only piece that changed recently, and despite Kevin and his brothers thinking that was the trigger for the attack, I don't think so. It was too fast, too soon.

After all this time…I know something else is going on here. While I'm not completely sure that my cover hasn't been blown, I have this feeling I should be focused on the bigger picture. I need to know what Cal was hiding from me. Maybe that will provide some answers.

"Come here, baby," Kevin says, and I focus back on the bathroom we're in.

I stand from the water as he holds up a towel for me. He already has one around his waist as he stands outside the tub. Stepping into the fluffy fabric, I look up at him with adoration. He wraps me up and tugs me into his warm body.

"You take such good care of me," I say teasingly.

"*Is tú mo thief croí beag*. I will always take care of you."

I narrow my eyes at him playfully as he smiles back at me. "What did you just say?" I ask cautiously.

"I called you my little heart thief."

All my tough girl flies out the window. Not that she ever remains when he's around. I lift up on my toes and wrap my arms around his neck. He meets me halfway and kisses me before I can take the initiative.

My knees grow weak as he reaches into my soul with this kiss. I tighten my hold on him and give myself over to all that is Kevin. He groans into my mouth and grasps ahold of my ass.

Right when I think he's going to take this further, he breaks the kiss and places his forehead to mine. "Let me feed you, love. Then we can get lost in each other for a wee bit."

"What do you consider a wee bit?"

He gives me that breathtaking smile as he laughs. "The rest of the night, love. I'll be lost in your pussy for the rest of the night if you can handle it."

"Ready to be served, *papi*. So ready to be served."

CHAPTER 26

A DAY WITHOUT WORRY

Danita

KEVIN WALKS UP BEHIND ME AS I LOOK OUT AT THE MOUNTAINS. He palms my forehead and tugs my head back, placing a kiss on my nose then my lips. The playful and tender gesture brings a smile to my face as I snuggle into his chest.

"What's on your mind?"

"Nothing and everything." I give a small snort.

He wraps his arms around my waist and buries his face into my neck. Closing my eyes, I savor his embrace. I don't want to bring the mood down, but it's time to face reality once again.

"It's only been a few days and we need to go back," I say.

He sighs. "Aye, I know. I have some meetings and new clients to tend to. I've been putting things off enough."

I turn to face him. "I'm sorry. I've taken over your entire life. First, you've been watching over me, now this."

He grasps me around the throat and pulls me in for a deep kiss. I never thought I'd be into breath play, but Kevin makes it sexy and affectionate. I've found myself enjoying a lot of things I never thought I would since we've been exploring each other.

I can't help clinging to his thermal T-shirt as he takes the kiss further. I don't think he's ever kissed me without passion, but this has reached yet another level. It's been like that…one level after the next. I'm falling so hard and don't know how to stop it.

"You are never a burden to me. Never. We have staff coming back in from their assignments. I'll have more hands on deck. You are not disturbing anything. Okay, love?"

"Okay." I nod. I rub my forehead. "I need to spend time with Con, but I don't want to put him in danger."

He kisses my forehead. "Let me worry about that. You'll be staying with me. You'll have plenty of opportunity to talk to the lad."

"About that." I look down and rub my hands on my leggings. "I was thinking that I should find a place. Or maybe I can sublet your apartment since you're moving back into your house. That way I'm not bringing any danger to your family."

He taps his knuckles against my temple lightly. "Are ya hearing me? Has anything I've said gotten through to ya?"

"Kevin, we don't know what I'm up against. I don't think it's wise for me to move in with you."

"Whatever *we* are up against, we'll be facing it together. The safest place you can be is with me. You and Sunny will be safe in my home."

I pinch the bridge of my nose. I knew he wouldn't agree to this or see things my way. Eric's words still haunt me from two years ago; if Kevin only knew how dangerous connecting himself to me could be, he'd think twice about wanting me around him and his family. If only I could be sure where Cal's attack came from, and if it was because of me.

There has to be a way out without involving people I care about or putting them in danger. I've officially given up on Eric coming through for me like he promised. I don't even want to think of what might have happened to him.

"Talk to me," Kevin murmurs, pulling me from my thoughts.

I chew on my lip as I decide on what I want to share. To hell with it, I bite the bullet. "Something about that fire is nagging at me."

"Like what?"

I pause to gather my thoughts. Shifting through the ones I can share. Serg is right, someone has it out for me within the department. Although I can't ignore that's a factor, what if I'm right and the fire isn't related to that?

"I'm not so sure it's connected to the ring or the case. It doesn't fit the profile. Unless someone's writing their own playbook, this one is off. Shooting Cal? That's the type of shit they would do. This fire, my not being there at the time? It's not them."

However, if it's not the ring, then who? And how much longer do I have before these bastards do figure out who I am? Fuck, Eric has left me holding a bag full of crap.

"Okay, when we get back, I'll start digging. I want my own look at the surveillance around your place."

I sigh. How much more can I take?

When Kevin wraps his arms around me and places his chin on top of my head, I swear I can feel his protectiveness course through my body. I hold on to that security, only to get angry with myself.

I've become dependent on Kevin. That was never supposed to happen. I can't afford for that to happen. As the baby sister to three domineering brothers and a strict dad, I've been a fighter and handled myself fine for years.

"I feel ya pulling away," he says and releases a heavy breath. "Let's get home, and we'll take it a step at a time. We have so much stacked against us as it is. Let's not be our own worst enemy, aye?"

I give a little smile he can't see. He's becoming more comfortable around me. His accent slips out more and more lately without annoyance or frustration.

I've found myself slipping into Spanish around him as well. Only little things, like I would at home with my family. However, I was pleasantly surprised when he was able to not only understand me, but reply as well.

"Can you promise me something?"

"What's that, love?"

I turn my face up to look into his eyes. "Don't make me fall for you any more than I already have. I need to be able to survive when I have to walk away."

This time when he wraps his hand around my throat, he brushes his thumb over my lips. "I'll never tell ya a lie. So that's not a promise I can make. I intend to keep falling, and I'm taking ya with me every step of the way."

With those softly spoken words, he kisses me tenderly. Even after the words are said, I feel them rumble through me. They're the true promise made.

I know he's going to take me with him, that is if I don't fall faster and deeper than he does. When he breaks the kiss and I look into his eyes, I see the same thing I feel. I don't think I ever stood a chance.

"If this is our last night in this bubble, how about we go dancing?"

He beams at me. "I love how that sounds."

I've been having a blast tonight. The little bar in town has live music and the people are friendly. Spending a night dancing in Kevin's arms isn't the worst thing to be doing.

I can think of a hundred of those, and they all start when we get back. I know I need to get to the bottom of what's going on. Which is why curiosity has me excuse myself from our light banter at our table to go to the restroom to freshen up and check my phone.

I haven't given it much attention while we've been away. Most of the time Kevin has had it, refusing to let me do anything but relax. It's why I don't check it in front of him.

The first thing I notice is a ton of missed calls from Harris. I find that to be odd. He knows I took a few days' leave; he was standing there when Serg told me to disappear. There are also a few calls from an unknown number.

My finger hovers over the number debating on whether or not I should call it. The phone rings right as I decide against it because I don't want to ruin the night, but also I want to have Shane around when I do. He handles all the tech for Blackhart Security and Investigations.

I answer the call with a roll of my eyes. "Hello."

"Damn it," Harris breathes into the line. He sounds a little drunk. "Why haven't you been answering your phone?"

"Why have you been calling?"

There is a long moment of silence on the other end. My temper starts to flare with each second. It's not lost on me that he could be involved with the fire at my home. I still don't know why he was there afterwards. I'm not buying that scanner shit.

"I wanted to make sure you were okay. Where are you? Where are you staying?"

"How is any of that any of your business?"

He huffs into the line. "Listen, I want to make sure you're okay. I have—"

"I'm with Kevin. He's taking care of me, but thanks."

"Yeah, okay," he says bitterly. "Figured. Be careful—"

"Are you threatening me?"

He takes another pause. "If I were threatening you, sweetheart, you would know, but I can tell you this: you're going to want to watch your ba—"

I hang up on him. Game on. Harris has moved to the top of my list. I'm going to finally find something on him and nail him with all the rest.

"Asshole," I grumble as I turn to walk out of the bathroom.

I run right into a solid chest when I step out. His cologne grabs my attention without me having to see his face. When Kevin places his big hands on my waist, I look up to lock eyes with him.

"Are you ready to head back to the cabin?"

The hooded look in his eyes tells me that he's ready to end our night out. If that weren't enough, his voice is thick with desire, causing his words to come out like smooth honey. I place a hand on his chest and nod.

"Yes, I'm ready," I reply.

CHAPTER 27

EVENLY MATCHED

Kevin

"That was fun," Dem says as she finishes a glass of water and places it in the sink.

"Aye, it was. I enjoyed all of our time here."

She tips her head to the side as she looks back at me. I stand across from her with my butt against the kitchen island and my legs crossed at the ankles. We stare at each other as her thoughts race across her face.

"Yeah, I did too. Thanks. This was what I needed to clear my head."

She looks down as if thinking over her words. In this moment, the wavy bun she's stacked up on the top of her head makes her look younger, more vulnerable. I narrow my eyes as something dawns on me.

I know what the background check says, but I also know most of that is bullshit. I have no idea how old Dem truly is. I take a second to decide if I want to push for an answer. I've been trying my best not to ask her questions.

Fuck it.

"Can I ask ya a question?"

"Uh-oh, must be a serious one," she teases. "Okay, shoot."

"How old are ya, love?"

Her eyes round for only a moment before she recovers. She looks away and chews on her lip. I feel a little uneasy for a moment.

"I'm younger than you," she replies when she looks back at me. "Is that a problem?"

I fold my arms across my chest. It can't be that much of an age gap. I'm thirty-four.

"How much younger?"

"Five years."

My brows shoot up. "You're twenty-nine? Your background check said thirty-three."

She comes to stand beside me, mirroring my stance. When she meets my eyes, I see a sadness there. I want to kick myself.

"I've told you. There's a lot you don't know about me. If it's a problem, I'll understand. I've always liked older guys, but that may not be your thing."

"No, it's not." I smile at her. "I've never been into older guys. See, love, we keep learning new things about each other."

She laughs and swats at my shoulder. My attention is drawn to how gorgeous she is when she laughs. I can't take my gaze off her.

"What?" She stares at me with that pretty smile and a twinkle in her eyes.

Pushing off the counter, I move to stand in front of her. I place my hands flat on either side of her on the kitchen countertop. I'm silent as I take her in. Her makeup has placed a glow on her face, highlighting her gorgeous features.

She looks like a precious baby doll. Her amber, almond-shaped eyes pop against her darker skin. It's a contrast that draws attention to her entire face. Her cute nose, those full lips, the dimple in her right cheek.

"If I hadn't seen you purchase it, I wouldn't think you had on any makeup other than the glow it's placed on your face. You're already flawless without it." I reach to run a thumb across her bottom lip.

Twenty-nine. I'm a little blown away. She's so mature for her age. I would have never pegged her for her twenties. Now, looking at her face, I can see it. Heck, thinking she's twenty-five is generous to be honest. I don't know why it never occurred to me to ask.

My gaze dances across her face. "You're perfect, love. Twenty-nine isn't as old as I thought you were, but I'm too far gone to care now."

"So, it would have been an issue before?"

"No. I don't think there's anything that can keep me from you."

I let those words hang between us. She searches my eyes, then drops her head to break the connection. Placing two fingers beneath her chin, I lift her gaze back to mine.

"I just want to look at ya for a bit."

When she suggested we go to town for her to pick up some things for tonight, I didn't know this would be the result. I've been semi-hard all night. When she slipped off to check her phone—which I know is what she went to do—I had reached my breaking point.

I wasn't the only one that had their eyes on her all night. She may have been oblivious to the stares, but I wasn't. She had the attention of everyone, male and female.

This dress. I bite my lip to keep from groaning as I let my gaze pass over her. She reaches to palm my jaw.

"You're not so bad yourself. I love you in a pair of slacks," she says with a smile.

I've wanted to get her out of this dress since she walked out of the bedroom in it before we left for the bar. I hadn't seen it when she tried it on in the store. She wanted to surprise me tonight.

Aye, I was surprised. I'd never seen her in a dress before. I love that it falls right below her knees. I never knew a dress that covers so much could be so alluring. Her sexy calves and curvy body beneath the fabric have taunted me all night.

Leaning both hands back on the counter, I place my forehead to hers. I close my eyes as I feel her energy course through the connection. I can't name a time in my life that I've felt this way with anyone else.

A grin comes to my lips when she slides her hands across my stomach to my back. Going lower, she squeezes my ass and draws me closer.

Unable to wait a moment longer, I cover her plush lips with mine. I mimic her gesture, palming her full globes. This woman does my head in.

Everything about her entices me to want more. I have to have her. Without a second thought, I band an arm around her waist and lift her from her feet.

We're moving for the bedroom still connected as we sip from and consume each other. As I cross the threshold into the bedroom, I slap her ass, causing her to yelp. I release a laugh as I place her down onto her feet and steady her.

With a naughty smile, she reaches for my belt. I shake my head and block her reach as I begin to back her toward the four-poster bed. I stop a few steps away from the foot of it.

"What are you up to?" she coos with an amused smile.

"Turn around for me. You will see."

Her eyes light with anticipation. I note the heave of her full breasts. Without question, she turns before me.

"Good, baby. I'm going to undress you, but you're not going to move. Nod if you understand me."

She nods, much to my pleasure. While eyeing the back of her dress for the hidden zipper, I move close and rest my hands on her hips. I frown when I can't find the fastening.

"Where's the zipper?"

She laughs sweetly. "It's pull-over. There's no zipper."

No wonder it fits like a glove. I run my hands down her sides, the soft fabric allowing a smooth passage. Sucking my bottom lip into my mouth, I watch her stand before me waiting.

My first thought tells me to lift her and toss her onto bed before us. Then there's another voice in my head whispering that this will be the last time I have her like this. Open, ready to give her all to me with no questions.

Once we leave here in the morning, everything changes. I know her guard is going to go back up. So I'm going to take advantage of this time we have and savor every single moment.

"You're so beautiful," I say against her neck.

As I place soft kisses across her skin, I reach to release her hair from its bun. The dark waves fall around her shoulders. For the millionth time since I realized this isn't her natural color, I wonder what she would look like with her birth-given locks.

With a hand splayed against her belly, I bring her flush to my growing erection. The moan that slips from her lips brings a smile to mine. I slide my hand lower, bending my knees to reach for the hem of her dress.

I tug it up to her waist, making sure to thrust into her as I straighten once again. With my free arm, I wrap her waist to keep her from tipping over in her sexy heels. Her gasp fills the air. It's a sound I plan to hear plenty of tonight.

"Don't move, I've got you," I whisper in her ear. "That's my girl."

"Kevin," she whimpers.

"Aye, love," I reply as I slip my fingers inside the side of her panties. "Do you want me as bad as I want you?"

"Yes," she says breathlessly.

"No, no, you don't. Not yet." I grasp her chin and tilt her head back. My lips are inches from hers as I speak again. "But you will."

Her next whimper is captured by my lips. I go from circling her clit to slipping my fingers inside her warmth. The feel of her tight sheath around my fingers causes me to ache to be inside her with my cock.

"Please," she breathes into my mouth.

"Are you going to come for me, baby? You're soaking my fingers."

"I'm so close, babe."

I chuckle. "So soon? I don't think so."

Her legs are shaking, but I have no intention of letting her finish. I pull my fingers free and lift them to my mouth. Dem looks up at me in confusion. I kiss her cheek.

"What the hell?"

I laugh, reaching to tug her dress the rest of the way off. She lifts her arms over her head, allowing me to free her. Tossing the dress, I take in her full breasts. I test their weight in my palms, loving the way they feel in my hold.

"I need you to want me as bad as I want you. I don't think you're there yet."

"Um, I think I was almost there before you stopped."

I shake my head as I knead her mounds. "Too easy. I want ya begging for me. I need ya dripping wet. When I put my cock inside ya, ya'll be blind with need for me."

She places a hand behind my neck and tugs me toward her. "You really want to play this game with me? Oh, Kev, you have no idea who you're dealing with. I haven't begun to fuck with your head the way I'm capable of."

Her words set my blood on fire. I take her chin in my grasp and nip her bottom lip, tugging it a bit before setting it free. Holding her gaze, I lick her lips.

"Show me."

It's more of a command than a request. I step back and widen my stance while I start to release my cuffs. I hungrily take in the sight of her in her bra, panties, and heels.

I'm ready to burst from my pants. However, I don't show how unhinged I feel. Instead, I continue to release the buttons of my shirt.

Dem saunters over to me with her hips swaying. Those sexy heels are lethal. I can't wait to have them wrapped around my neck.

"You sure you're ready for this?" she says with mirth in her voice.

"As long as you know I'll return whatever you throw my way." I lift a brow. "If you are ready for me, I'm more than ready for you, love. But…be sure you're ready."

She throws her head back and laughs. When she locks her eyes back on me, I shiver for a moment. Perhaps I'm the one that needs the warning. The look she gives me speaks volumes.

"As you wish," she purrs.

With that same little evil look on her face, she reaches into the pocket of my black slacks. I give her a curious look as she pulls out my phone. She knows my password because she's been using it to connect to the sound system in the cabin.

I watch as she swipes at the screen and pulls up the song she's looking for. My lips curl up as she turns on Chris Brown's "To My Bed." She's played this back at her place before.

When she's done with my phone, she tosses it on the bed and turns back to me. Sticking one hand in my half-buttoned shirt, she uses the other to run the backs of her knuckles against my length. My cock twitches in response to her taunting.

Her seduction continues as she glides her warm hand across my chest and down my ribs. I stand rigid, waiting for her next move. Leaning forward, she places a kiss on my chest. As she starts to circle her tongue against my skin, she works on the rest of the buttons on my white dress shirt.

Unable to help myself, I run my fingertips down her spine. She shivers and looks up at me through her lashes. I give her a crooked grin as I slide my fingers between the crack of her cheeks.

"Careful, *papi*. Don't start nothing you don't intend to finish."

"I plan to finish everything I start," I say and dig my fingers into her plump flesh.

She bites her lip as she pushes my shirt from my shoulders. The fabric falls to the floor and she moves to work on releasing my belt. I nearly groan when she finally frees me from my confines. My shaft bobs straight at her, thick and heavy with need.

I step out of my pants, grateful I kicked my shoes off when we arrived. One less thing in my way. I bend to take my socks off and straighten to stand before her, naked as the day I was born.

She gives me a cocky smile as she squats before me. From the look in her eyes, you would think this was something new for us. As I take in the look of excitement and pleasure on her face, I think perhaps I don't give her a turn at fair play enough. I'll have to keep in mind to let her have this more often. Who am I to be so selfish?

"You ready, big boy?" she says against my tip.

I give a curt nod, not able to answer. The sight of her so hungry for me, with those plump lips so close but not close enough has pre-come dripping. She flicks her tongue at my essence and hums like it's the greatest things she's had in her life.

My patience is shot. I reach to grab ahold of her hair and guide her to take me into her mouth. My grip tightens as she takes me and starts to slurp. My flesh glistens as she salivates over me. Using her hands to spread the moisture, she has me gritting my teeth.

I release her hair and push both my hands into mine. That's when she makes me eat my words. My eyes grow wide as she gives me a blow job worthy of a gold medal. The sound, the sight, the feel, it all drives me insane.

"Dem," I hiss.

"Mmm," she moans back.

My toes curl, and I throw my head back. I've had women that shy away from my size and cheat the task of sucking me off. Dem holds back from not an inch. Her hands and mouth work me without a break in the dripping wet loving she gives to my cock.

Who is this woman?

CHAPTER 28

NEW TROUBLE

Danita

THE LAST THING I SHOULD BE DOING TODAY IS SMILING FROM EAR to ear, but I haven't been able to stop. We returned yesterday morning, but I didn't have to report for deputy until today. I spent my day on the couch in Kevin's apartment, in his arms, relishing the last moments of the world we created.

It was nice to feel normal and have a simple chat about nothing. Not to mention, I was grateful for a day to recover from the other night—i.e. the reason I still can't stop smiling. My sore body has been a reminder of the savage Kevin is in the bed. The man is perfection in every sense of the word.

"Hey, Moralez," I turn to find Reed moving toward me.

"Hey."

She looks at me curiously. "You look great for someone who had their place burned down."

I shrug. "I'm learning not to let the little things get to me. My dog is safe and I'm alive."

She gives me a grin. "I don't know. I think a certain ex-detective might have something to do with that smile."

"Maybe, maybe not."

I think about what Kevin told me about her sleeping with Harris. She's a pretty woman with her golden-brown hair and tanned complexion. Although I think the tan comes from a bottle. Not for nothing, she has a nice shape too. Being a few inches taller than me, she carries her weight nicely.

She could totally do better than Harris. I decide to keep those snarky thoughts to myself. Besides, I'm not supposed to know about them in the first place.

She laughs and holds her hands up. "Hey, it's none of my business. I wanted to check in and make sure you were okay. Believe it or not, there were a bunch of us worried about you."

I tip my head to the side. "Why wouldn't I believe it?"

"Come on, Moralez. We all know you keep to yourself for the most part. You keep your nose clean and mind your own business. I respect that, but I also see that you're in your own world."

I nod. "Thanks for checking in. I'm fine, though. Things can be replaced."

"Did they find out what started the fire?"

"You mean who? And, no. Not yet."

She narrows her eyes. "So, it was a who. Again, not to be in your business, but do you think it's wise to be dating Blackhart? Between you and me, they're dragging their feet on the Kelley investigation for a reason. Erin and Cal's shooting should have had some answers by now. I don't want to see you get caught up in anything."

I fold my arms over my chest. Instincts. I've survived off them. Right now, they're telling me to take in and take apart every word she says.

"Listen, I've been keeping an ear out. I can't say for sure if that shit was connected to Kelley, but I want you to be careful. Cal didn't have many friends around here before or after he left. The wrong people are getting curious about your relationship."

"One has nothing to do with the other. Everyone should keep their noses in their own business, but thanks."

She places her hands on her hips. "We have to stick together in this place. It will eat you alive if not. You've been lucky, Moralez. Know that much. There are a lot of us that wish we still had your freedom," she says and gives me a tight smile.

She pats me on the shoulder and turns to walk away, leaving me to analyze her words. My phone buzzes in my pocket, pulling me from my musing. I sigh as I read the text. Dawson, Harris's partner, is waiting on me across town. Graves assigned him to help me on a case.

When I turn for my car, I spot Harris in gym shorts with his workout bag. He's standing by his Mazda, glaring at me. Ignoring him, I move on about my business.

I'm headed for my unmarked car for the day when out of the corner of my eye something catches my attention on my car's windshield. My squad car forgotten, I move toward my Nissan. Plucking the paper from the windshield, I unfold it.

"Who has your back? Let's see what happens now with your protection gone," I repeat the words on the page.

A chill runs through me. I crumble the paper in my hand and look around the lot. Harris's taillights flash as his car exits the parking lot.

Him showing up after the fire pops into my head. Suddenly, I start to think of all the other times he's been hostile or aggressive toward me. This note has a hint of his voice to it. That fire wasn't organized like the jobs of the ring I'm after, but it was sloppy as fuck like some shit Harris would do.

"Okay, asshole. You want to play."

I shove the note in my pocket and march to my patrol car. My blood is boiling. I've never been more motivated to take these assholes down in all five years I've been here.

If Harris wants to make this personal, we can get personal. It's time for me to sweet talk his blabbermouth partner and see what I can get.

No risk, no reward. I'm tired of playing it safe. I want my life back and I want these guys to pay.

Kevin

"What's going on?" I ask as I work the knots out of Dem's shoulders.

She sits on the floor in front of the couch I'm on, lost in her thoughts. She's been stewing since she got home from her shift. I had one of the guys watching out for her today since so much needed my attention at the office. I had a ton of catching up to do, so I don't know what her day was like.

"Nothing. Work stuff. First day back, and it's like everything waited for me to return," she replies.

I call bullshit, but I bite my tongue. Instead, I kiss the top of her head and wrap her in my embrace. Some of the tension releases from her body.

"You in the mood for some binge-watching?"

"Not really. This is nice. I want to stay like this."

Burying my face in her neck, I inhale deeply. It's times like this that I wish I could take it all away. The things she's not telling me, the job, all of it.

If I could, I'd make it so she never has to worry again, but I'll be honest with myself. From the time I first met her, I knew the job meant something to her. I don't know if she'd be happy without it.

"Have you ever thought about having kids?" I blurt the words out, not thinking.

She stiffens in my hold. I'm frustrated with myself, but it's out there. I can't take it back now.

Instead, I reach to lift her into my lap and sit back on the couch with her in my arms. She stares into her lap while chewing on her lip. I can see the wheels turning.

"Humor me, love."

"Yes, I've wanted a family. At least, it's been something I've thought about in the last few years. I have a long way to go before I can get to something like that, though."

"What does that mean?"

"You somewhat understand my situation. It's been a long time. I've lost pieces of me. I don't know if I can explain it. All I know is this: I'm going to need time to find… I'll need to get back to me."

I totally understand where she's coming from. You can't begin to imagine how hard it is to go deep undercover. If I do the math and I'm right, she's been under for over three or four years. In my opinion, she should have been pulled by now.

I still have so many questions as to why she hasn't been. I've been guessing at which agency or department she's with. None of it makes sense.

"Did you renovate that big house for a wife and kids?" she asks, breaking through my spinning thoughts.

"Aye, well, with the hope of someday having a wife and a few wee 'un, I've been wanting to find the one and settle."

"Kevin, I—"

"We're talking," I say and kiss the side of her face.

"I don't want you to get hurt."

"I'm a big lad. Don't fuss yerself."

She purses her lips. "Have you guys had any new breakthroughs in the shooting? Anything I can look into?"

I accept the change of topic, for now. The last thing I want to do is drag her mood down any further. However, this topic is a mood killer for me. The frustration of returning to pretty much the same status boils my blood.

"Quinn is about to return from following a lead. We're sending Scott, one of our guys, to keep an eye on the situation. It's the most we've got. A guy named Lo Davis, it's an alias, but we've pinned him down and tracked him to Boston. He was the last person Cal called.

"We don't want to play our hand too soon, so Scott is going to sit on him and see what we can learn. We're still flying blind. As much as I hate to, I think we're going to have to put some pressure on Con to find out what he can give you to help speed things along. Trent has tried questioning him, but the kid clams up. It's not just you he's hiding something from," I explain.

"But we don't want to push him too hard. How about we try to loosen him up one more time? If you think pushing him will cause him to shut down, we can't afford to rush things now."

She's right. It's the reason my brothers and I haven't forced the issue and have been trying to work around this. If we can figure this out, we don't have to involve the kid.

I nuzzle her cheek. "You look tired. Come on, let's get you to bed. I have to be at the house for the movers in the morning. Maybe you can come along for a bit and help me figure out how to make the place look like a home. We'll set something up with Con for your next day off."

"Tomorrow. Set something up for tomorrow. I'll make the time."

"Aye, you've got it."

CHAPTER 29

VISION OF US

Danita

I step into the basement of Kevin's house and smile. This wasn't what I was expecting to find down here. He has a fully equipped gym, including a boxing ring, heavy bag, weights, and a wall of mirrors.

That body doesn't work itself into shape. This place screams of his dedication to keeping that six-pack and all the rest of his delicious body in order. Speaking of dedication, I stop at the bottom of the steps and lean against the wall to watch Kevin and Con in the center of the ring.

"Aye, that a boy. Keep your hands up," he says proudly to his nephew.

The affection that oozes off Kevin is heartwarming. Whenever I see him around the kids, I can tell how much they mean to him. I don't think he realizes it, but his entire demeanor changes.

I bet he would make a great father. I think back to our conversation last night. My heart aches. I wanted to be excited about the question, but I know better than to get either of our hopes up. Even if I get out of this, I have a lot of work to do on myself before I can think of a family.

At Kevin's age, he probably wants all of those things way before I'll be ready to give them to him. Yet, a tiny part of me can't help but daydream about what if. That's the part that's bleeding out as I watch Kev with his nephew—seeing our own son sparring with his dad.

"Never going to happen," I huff under my breath.

"Hey, Detective Moralez," Con says as he and Kevin turn their attention on me.

"Hey, Con." I wave and push off the wall. I'm dressed in leggings and a tank. Kevin told me we'd be playing a game of basketball or something along those lines. Although I'm an hour behind the time I was supposed to arrive. "So, do I get to embarrass you in the ring too?"

"I would love to see that," Con says, taking off his gloves.

Kevin laughs and shakes his head as he moves to step out of the ring. I will never get tired of the sight of this man all sweaty and sexy. I bite my lip as I watch the beads of sweat roll down his abs, his tattoo glistening.

"Aye, but it won't be today," he says and stops in front of me to tug me into his sweat-soaked body by the front of my tank top.

His warm lips feel like home. It's been a long day, made longer by annoying suspects and witnesses. People will lie to cover the simplest thing and hinder an investigation from coming to a swift end for nothing.

I place my head against his chest and take in his strength. What I would give to have this all the time. I wrap my arms around his waist and almost forget we're not alone until Con walks over.

"Hey, thanks for getting that bike fixed for me. I thought I was going to have to kick Soren's ass," Con says.

"Next time, don't be cutting school and borrowing bikes," Kevin grumbles and musses Con's hair. "And ya'll be paying her back every cent. Ya hear me?"

The smile falls from Con's face. "Yeah, I hear you."

I pull from Kevin's arms and toss an arm over Con's shoulders. "I think you've gotten taller since the last time I saw you."

This brings that adorable smile back to his face and a blush to his cheeks. He looks up at his uncle with a smirk on his lips and tosses his arm around my waist to taunt his uncle.

"I'm not yer Uncle Trent. Don't test me," Kevin says with mirth in his eyes, but warning in his voice.

"What do you mean?" Con says innocently.

"Aye, playing with fire. A muppet yer mum didn't raise."

Con throws his hands in the air. "All right, all right," he says and takes a step away from me as Kevin moves toward him.

I can't contain my laughter. I cover my mouth as I snicker at them. Kevin rolls his eyes at me.

"Why don't you go hit the shower? I'll get the grill started and you can take over once you're done?"

Con's face lights up with the promise of taking on the responsibility. "Sure, I'll be quick."

He takes off upstairs and Kevin pulls me back into his embrace. I look up at him and smile. However, he has a frown on his face.

"You look racked. I shouldn't have had you come with me this morning," he says with concern.

"I'm fine. It was a long day, but nothing some good food and a beer can't fix."

He seems to get lost in thought for a beat. When his eyes clear, he cups my face and kisses me gently. I draw my brows in. It's the opposite of the Kevin I know. He can be tender, but those moments aren't as frequent as the passionate ones.

"What was that for?"

He looks my face over, then gives me a bright smile. "I've missed you today. Did you get to look through the house on your way in?"

I give him a skeptical glance, but answer anyway. "Yeah, it looks great. You did better than you thought you would. I like it. It has a homey feel to it."

"You say that as if you didn't help out a ton before you left for work. I got the hang of it after watching you direct the first few rooms. It's not like Erin didn't do most of the work already. I only had to figure out where it all went," he says.

"Well, you did a fine job, Mr. Blackhart. I would totally feel at home if it were my place."

He gives me a little squeeze. "It is your home. Did you not see Sunny up there in his new room?" I give him a warning look. "It's home. At least for now. We'll be staying here tonight. Con has already claimed his room."

"Speaking of which, I know you. You sent him to shower for a reason. Let's get the grill going so I can hang with him while you disappear for a bit."

"Ach, she thinks she knows me, she does."

I laugh and step out of his arms, giving him a shove toward the stairs. "I'm going to kick your ass in that ring one of these days."

"Maybe I'll give you a chance."

Kevin

I take my time in the shower to give Dem a chance to bond with Con some more. When I step out, I dress in sweats and a T-shirt. My mind hasn't stopped wondering about her words down in the gym.

She could feel at home here. I've never wanted to make that happen more. It felt right having her here this morning, helping me to get this place set up.

I let her take over. Something about her putting her personal touch on my home struck a chord in me. A few times her face lit up as if she were thinking the same thing I was.

This could be ours.

My phone rings, bringing me back to the present. I go to answer and find that it's Trent. Taking a deep breath, I answer the phone.

It never used to be this tense when one of my siblings would call. Now, each call holds a heavy weight. I never know what I'm going to hear when I answer.

"Trent, what about ye?"

"What's up, bro? I need your thoughts on something," he returns.

He has my attention. Something in his voice intrigues me. Trent is always sure of himself, but there's a little hesitance tonight.

"Shoot, you have my ear."

He takes a pause before he breathes deeply into the phone. "Fuck, I should be focused on the case, but…the lass has corrupted my noodle."

Now he has my full attention. I move over to my new bed and sit at the foot. This may take a while.

"Who exactly are we talking about?"

"Molly's dance instructor."

"Ah, okay, this is new."

He sighs. "Not really. I've been flirting, but I… She's different. Sweet, but sassy. Gentle, but tough. I get this feeling she's hiding from something, though."

I rub my forehead. "At least she's not hiding something."

"What?"

"Nothing." I purse my lips. "So, what's the problem?"

"Like I said, she's hiding from something, and I think that's why she's reluctant to take me seriously."

"Trent, no one takes you seriously. You make that impossible."

"Screw you, Kev. I know how to be serious."

I chuckle. It feels good to rib my little brother. We haven't had a one-on-one talk like this in a while.

"Aye, ya do, but I've never seen it."

"Why did I call you?" he groans. "I would be better off talking to Molly."

"Okay, okay, I'm sorry," I say through my laughter. I think about my own situation and my heart pangs for my brother. "Sometimes you have to wait it out. If this is what you want and it's worth having, take your time. Let her get comfortable enough to trust you to know her and what she's hiding from. Be there."

"Is it crazy that I think she's the one?"

I pause. I think I knew Dem was the one from the first time I saw her. I may not have known what that feeling was, but I felt it.

"Not at all. When you know, you know." The words leave my mouth, and I know I'm talking to myself as well.

I know Dem is it. She's the piece I've been looking for all along.

"Kev?"

"Yeah."

"I don't have a good feeling about whatever she's hiding." He allows his words to hang in the air.

I know my brother. When he gets a gut feeling, it's right 100 percent of the time. I clench my jaw.

"Then, when ya find out what it is, we'll be ready to have yer back. Ya know this."

"Aye, I do. Thanks, Kev. I needed to get that off my chest."

"Not a problem. Anytime."

I get ready to hang up, but he's not done. I should have known better. He turns the table on me.

"So, you're gone for her?"

"Aye, I am."

He snorts. "You do know she's keeping something from us."

I scoff. Trent has been onto Dem from the beginning. I've tried to warn him off, but he's been like a dog with a bone. It's that damn intuition.

"You let me worry about that," I reply.

He gives a hearty laugh. "Oh, you are going to have something to worry about. I give Quinn another week before he zones in on it. He's been distracted with Alicia. As soon as he pulls his head out of her pussy, you two better be ready," he warns.

"We'll be fine."

"Hmm. Okay, don't say I didn't warn you. Anyway, I have that job in the morning. I'm going to get some sleep."

"Good night," I say.

"Night, bro. Talk to you later."

Danita

"I make a great burger, don't I?" Con says with his chest poked out.

"You did a good job. You have skills," I say as I wipe my mouth and stand to take our plates to the sink.

Kevin joined us for dinner, but excused himself in the middle. Again, he's giving me the time I need to bond with Conroy. So far, so good.

"Can I ask you something?" Conroy says, his voice full of apprehension.

I look up from the sink and over at him. He has moved to sit at the island across from me. His green eyes are fixed on me.

"Sure."

"Do you think my dad's going to pull through?"

Oh wow, I wasn't expecting that. I school my features and straighten my spine. This is going to take all I have, to get through.

I still feel like this is all my fault. I'm the reason this young man and his sisters are in limbo, hoping their father pulls through and that their mother will make a full recovery. I don't want to think about the way Erin looked the last time I saw her. That was not Cal's wife.

"I'm hoping he does. He's a great friend. It hurts that something like this has happened to him. I wish there were more I could do," I say.

"You seemed angry with him that day…" He trails off and looks down at the countertop. "I watched you guys talk. You were mad at him."

"Yeah, I was. He put you in danger. You shouldn't have been there," I say.

"Is that the only reason?"

"Yeah, kiddo. Your father was working on a dangerous case. It was a risk that we were meeting up in the first place. I was concerned about your safety."

"My dad is a good man. Everyone gives him shit for messing things up sometimes, but he means well. I think...I think he's smarter than people give him credit for.

"I know what that's like, you know? Being smarter than people think. They underestimate you and don't listen because they think you don't know better or that they know more than you.

"Dad said I should let them talk. Allow them to think they know whatever. I'll always be able to show them better than I can tell them," he says, giving me the most trusting look he's ever given me.

"He's right. I know exactly what he means. I think that's why we get along so well. Your dad gets me," I say and smile.

He's silent as he stares back at me. I hold my breath, hoping this is it. He's finally going to open up and give me what I need.

"Well, I'm glad he has a friend like you. Thanks for the talk. I'll see you in the morning."

I breathe in disappointment but force a smile to my face. "I'll see you in the morning."

I watch as he gets up and heads to his room, Sunny at his side. I don't know what's with this family and my dog. He seems to cling to them instantly.

I guess he knows good people.

CHAPTER 30

HIDDEN MESSAGES

Danita

I LOOK AROUND THIS PLACE AND MY BLOOD IGNITES INTO FLAMES of fury. The bust I made yesterday had $1.2 million in cash and drugs that was supposed to go into the evidence locker. Half of the money is gone, and four kilos of coke have evaporated into thin air.

Today everyone moves about this precinct as if nothing has happened. It's crazy to me how this has become the norm. No one is as pissed as I am about this.

Honestly, I don't know why I'm surprised. Things have changed around here, and not for the better. The ring is recruiting again. We've had three new officers move up to detective, and they were immediately placed on my squad. Yet, I still don't have a partner and I'm pretty sure those assholes have already recruited two of the three.

"Hey, Moralez, you got a minute?" Harris says as he walks over to my desk.

I haven't said much to him lately. I've gotten other notes on my car. The second one was the same morning Alicia was chased down on the highway.

It read along the lines of "He can't protect you like I can." The others that have followed have been more of the same. I get pissed just thinking about them.

I still haven't told Kevin. He's been stressed out, and to be honest, if I tell him, he'll try to wrap me in bubble wrap and hide me away.

I have a job to do. I thought it a bit extreme that we all moved to his parents' and are essentially on lockdown. If it weren't for my job, I don't think he would let me out of the house.

Thank God I don't have to be there around the clock. Alicia and Tari are losing their minds. I'd be too. Four kids, plus Kevin's hilarious and brutally honest parents. Yes, thank God for my job.

When we are at the house, it's tense. Everyone is tense. So I've omitted the fact that I think this asshole has been placing threats on my windshield.

The one thing that has become clear is that my cover hasn't been blown. Not like I thought. I don't think the fire had anything to do with what happened to Cal or the ring I'm after. I was right; the MO doesn't match.

I narrow my eyes on Harris. I'm going to make his ass pay when I can prove he almost killed my dog when he torched my place. Those notes have his voice written all over them.

Jealous, arrogant, and entitled.

I look Harris up and down before I answer him. "What for?" I ask dryly.

"I had a question for you about that bust yesterday..." he starts but trails off as he looks past me.

I turn to see what he's looking at. Two guys are walking in our direction with vases of red roses in each of their hands. Four vases in total. I look on in confusion as it seems they're heading straight for my desk.

"Detective Moralez?" the taller of the two asks.

"Yes, what is this?"

They both place the vases on the desk and the one who spoke hands over a piece of paper for me to sign off on. I eye the vases for a second before I sign. A ball of nerves mixed with butterflies starts in my stomach.

"You have a good day, ma'am," the guy says when he takes the paper back from me.

I nod and fall back in my chair as I turn to look at the flowers on my desk. I'm going to kill Kevin. I can feel everyone's eyes on me.

Harris plucks the card from one of the vases. I stand and place my hands on my hips as I glare at him. He has a lot of damn nerve as he reads the card aloud.

"'Missing you, love. Can't wait to hold you in my arms. I hope every petal brings you a smile,'" Harris reads before turning his eyes on me. "Moralez—"

"Next time I'll send ya flowers of yer own since ya admire them so much."

I turn to find Kevin glaring at Harris. He looks gorgeous. His hair is neatly combed into place, and he's in a black suit.

Oh God, what that suit is doing for this man. It pours over his body like a loving friend. Knowing what the body beneath looks and feels like has my pulse racing and certain body parts pulsing.

Kevin turns those green eyes on me. A slow crooked grin comes to his lips as he takes in my lust-filled ogling. He crowds my space, places a hand at my nape, and tugs me toward his lips.

He does it so fast, I don't have time to protest, and once his soft, firm lips are on mine, I don't want to protest anyway. Harris is completely forgotten. At least he is by me.

When Kevin breaks the kiss and looks down into my eyes, I'm left feeling dazed and a little light-headed. I place my hand over his chest and the beating of his heart brings me so much comfort. I can't believe that I've been growing more and more attached to him.

With each week that passes, I've gotten no closer to what I need, but Kevin has found a way to make me feel like it will all work out in the end. Which is why I feel so guilty about not sharing everything with him. I tamp down the ever-rising feeling and give him a smile.

"What was that for?"

"I told you. I've been missing you," he says and kisses my

forehead. His face clouds over and he looks over my head. "Do ya need something?"

"I work here. Remember? Unlike you. You know what? Never mind," Harris mumbles and turns to walk off.

I roll my eyes and sit back at my desk. "If you give me ten minutes, we can get out of here together. I've had enough of this place for one day," I say and start to finish up the work on my desk.

I had been wrapping things up before I got distracted looking around at the lack of morals surrounding me. I try not to go down that path before I get pissed off all over again. Seeing Kevin and the roses has changed my mood, and I'd like to keep it that way.

I feel more than see him lean over my desk, placing his hands flat on either side of me. He kisses my neck. I look up to see if anyone is watching.

"You do know I have to work here?"

"I don't much care. It's not like we get to be this affectionate at the house. I'm craving you. We'll have to do something about that," he whispers against my skin.

"We could always go back to your place," I suggest.

"Hmm," he murmurs.

I get that the guys want to keep the family together, but the full-house vibe is enough to make a sane person question everything. I'm over it, and I'm over not having solid answers. It's been almost four months.

Nothing has changed with Cal as far as I know, and while Con has become more trusting of me, he hasn't told me a thing that I can use to find out what happened to his dad or how I can get my life back. Not that the kid hasn't looked as if he wants to spill his guts. Lately he's had his head in his computer most the time, looking more stressed than a kid on summer break should.

I had thought maybe he was taking summer courses or something, but Kevin told me both twins opted out of the advanced college courses they were supposed to take this summer. With all that's going on, I can't blame them.

"Just think of the one-on-one time we could have," I purr.

"That sounds like a grand idea, but I need to be at the house tonight. Trent won't be around. I want to at least be there through the night."

"Then we'll only take a few hours." I turn up the seduction in my voice.

He leans into my ear, his breath tickling my skin. I have to squeeze my thighs together beneath my desk. I wonder if he's driving me crazy on purpose.

"You and I both know if we go to my place, I'm going to fuck you into next week and we won't move from my bed for anything but water and to relieve ourselves." He drops his voice lower and the rumble runs right through me with his next words. "I've been wanting to get my hands on you and make you scream for mercy for weeks. Even thought about tearing a page from Quinn's book and hiding out in the laundry room."

My cheeks heat. We walked right past the laundry room that day as Quinn obviously gave Alicia the business. They thought they were being quiet. It was a good thing Shane had the kids occupied with silly stories.

"With my luck, we'd get caught by your mom or something."

"Aye, a lie you don't tell. My mother has caught me giving every girl I dated in high school a snog. It's like she has radar. As soon as I pucker my lips, bam," he says, his accent slightly thicker, making me laugh all the more.

"I would have loved to have seen that. I can only imagine," I say as my shoulders shake.

"You *would* laugh." He nuzzles my neck. "We'll take a raincheck on that trip to my place."

I don't let on my disappointment. We really could stand to have some alone time. I close my eyes and marvel in the scent of his cologne.

"*Ay, papi, ¿Por qué me haces esto?* You smell so good." The words are out of my mouth before I can think better of it.

Kevin chuckles and kisses the top of my head. "What am I doing to you, love?"

"You know."

"Only returning the favor." Lifting his hands from my desk, he gives my shoulders a gentle squeeze and moves to sit in the chair next to my desk.

Thank God. Maybe I can think straight now. Between his body heat and his delicious scent, my brain waves start to skip functions.

"Didn't you have to be on an assignment?"

"A security detail that ended early. You were on my mind, so this is where I needed to be," he replies.

I look at him for a moment. Sometimes he says the sweetest stuff. I still can't believe he sent these flowers. I didn't even know I was that girl until this moment. Like, I've never looked for guys to send me things like that. At least, I've never been hard-pressed for it. Now, it has this warm feeling in my belly that I like way too much.

"Have you eaten?" he says to my silent musing.

I shake my head clear. My stomach growls on cue. No, I haven't eaten. I've been too busy being pissed off.

"No, I was supposed to grab something, but I didn't get around to more than a protein bar," I tell him.

He pulls out his phone and starts to swipe at the screen. He looks so out of place here. Like a supermodel or angel that dropped from heaven into this hellhole.

I sit waiting for these fuckers around here to burst into flames in his presence. I start to snicker at the thought. Kevin lifts his gaze from his phone. "What?"

"Nothing. Me having a silly moment."

His lips lift in the corner as he gives me a once-over. Pinning me with a knowing look before he looks around the precinct, he snorts. With a shake of his head, he turns back to his phone.

"I'll make reservations. I have this place I've been wanting to take you. You'll love the food and there's a Latin club next door."

I look down at my clothes and frown. "I'm not dressed for anywhere fancy." A slow grin takes over his face. "What?" I ask, knowing that look too well.

"You were just saying that you always loved that scene in *Pretty Woman* when he took her shopping." He lifts his arm and flicks his wrist. "We still have plenty of time to get you pampered and dressed."

"You're calling me a prostitute," I say with a straight face.

His mouth falls open, and I burst into laughter. He picks up a paper clip and tosses it at my chest. I knock it away as I continue to laugh.

"You're serious, aren't you?" I say through my laughter.

"Why wouldn't I be? You could use a day to kick back and relax. Come on. Finish up. We'll make an evening of it."

I do my best to contain my excitement. It's not the shopping or the pampering. It's the alone time we'll get. I miss our time at my place, watching Netflix or simply talking.

I finish my paperwork quickly, and we grab two vases each to head out of the precinct. When Chief Dugan passes by, I notice the look he gives me, then Kevin. Kevin doesn't show much of a reaction, but I know this man too well not to see the subtle change.

However, I know better than to ask while around this place. I've never gotten a bad vibe from Dugan before, but today, I won't lie and say I'm not on alert. He's just been added to my list to dig deeper into.

"Did you need to grab anything else?"

"No, I'm straight."

Kevin dropped me off this morning, but I wasn't expecting him to pick me up. Shane was going to swing by. While Shane is a sweetheart, I'm happy Kevin is here.

In the middle of our light banter, we head for the Viper. I stumble to a stop when I see the slip of paper stuck to his windshield. It's like all the other notes.

"What?" Kevin says as he looks down at me.

I shake my head and try to recover. If I can get to the paper and pull it off before he does, I can crumple it and wave it off. However, I'm dating an ex-detective turned PI. His eye is keener than most.

He moves to the car, easily balancing both vases in one arm. He plucks the paper from the windshield and opens it. His face tightens and grows red with anger right before me.

The anger in his green eyes when he looks up at me feels like a punch to the chest. He looks like his head is about to pop right off his shoulders. Without saying a word, he opens the car and places the vases in his hands in the back seat.

I move to the passenger side in silence and place the other two inside as well. Climbing into the front seat, I wait for him to speak once he gets behind the wheel. He sits brooding, not saying a word.

He hands the note over to me, and it's like the others. More threats and harsh words. Something about Kevin having seen this one stings. I know the words aren't true, but this still isn't something I would want him to see.

My vision goes red as I read the words over and over. I don't like being threatened. Especially not by a coward.

You're a slut. He can't protect you like I can. You're going to pay for this.

"From the lack of surprise on your face, I'm going to go with my gut that's telling me this isn't the first time you've seen one of these," he seethes.

"It isn't," I mumble.

"How long?"

I sigh. He's going to be pissed when he gets that answer. It's one of the reasons I've kept this to myself. I know he has a temper. Especially when it comes to protecting me or his family's safety. I have this image in my head of him sitting on the hood of my car with a baseball bat waiting for whoever has been leaving the notes.

"A few weeks. They have been showing up on my cars since we returned from the cabin," I admit.

"Dem, are you shitting me?" he fumes. "Wait a minute. Does this have anything to do with the shit you're keeping from me?"

While I believe Harris is a part of the ring, I don't think these notes have anything to do with the actual case. I think this is him acting on his own. I was hoping to get a match on his prints from one of the other notes, but they were clean, not even a partial, which didn't surprise me.

"No, this is something else."

"If this has nothing to do with yer case, why would ya keep this from me?"

"There has been so much going on. At first, I planned to ignore it, and then I decided to take care of it myself. You already have enough on your shoulders—"

"How is this happening right under my nose?" he says in a mix of pain and frustration. "First Erin and now this. *Fuck*."

I close my eyes and release a deep breath. I knew he would take this there. I open my eyes when he pinches my chin between his fingers and turns my face to his.

"I'm crazy about ya. I'm in love with ya. It's not okay for someone to be leaving ya notes like this. It's not okay for me not to know that it's happening."

"You had to turn your focus on work and Erin's case. I've actually been getting them at random times and places. You can't always be there. It's not fair for me to weigh you down with this on top of everything else. I can handle myself."

He closes his eyes this time, and I can feel him vibrating with anger through his simple touch. I reach to cup his face. He opens his eyes and the vulnerability glaring back at me floors me. This big strong man looks lost for a brief moment.

"I'll take care of this. I'll figure out what the hell is going on," he says.

He leans to kiss my lips and runs his fingers across my temple. I go to protest, but my phone goes off. Kevin's face hardens.

My job has the shittiest timing in the world. I answer the call, knowing there will be no date or pampering for me. Duty calls.

"I'm sorry," I whisper when I hang up. "I need to head to a scene."

"I'll follow you." No sooner than the words are out of his mouth, his phone buzzes.

He looks down at the text, and his face tightens more. I don't believe he'll be following me anywhere. I place my hand on his chest and lean in to kiss him on the cheek.

"I'll text you when I'm headed home. You don't have to come for me."

"I changed my mind," he says, and my heart comes to a halt.

A million thoughts race through my head. Has he changed his mind about me? Is he over me and my secrets?

"We'll be spending the night at my place," he continues, and the tightness in my chest loosens.

"Oh, okay. I'll meet you there."

Kevin

I haven't been able to settle my mind since Dem stepped out of my car. I wanted to follow after her, but Shane needed to see me. He thinks he may finally be onto something.

I sent one of the guys to shadow Dem, for me to have peace of fucking mind. Someone has been leaving those notes for damn near three weeks. It's not like I forgot about her feeling like she was being watched right before the fire. In my line of work, something like this isn't swept under the rug so lightly.

Dem knows this. She knows better. The investigation over the fire at her place sucks ass. Again, I don't think those asshats are doing their damn jobs. Which has led me back to the surveillance footage.

I run a hand through my hair to reel my temper in. I'm following my instincts and protecting what's mine. I lean forward and squint at the screen.

"Would you look at this," I say to the image before me.

"Hey, I think I was right about Cal," Shane says as he walks over to my desk with his laptop bag slung over his shoulder.

We agreed to work in the office to be able to have some quiet time without distraction. I pause the video on my screen and try to focus on him. *Try* being the operative word. This nagging feeling demands I keep watching these videos before me.

"So, you think Cal took one of your programs to… What did you call it? Daisy-chain?"

"It's something like daisy-chaining. He's linked one system to another. If that's the case, it would explain the reason why I can't get into the laptop. You see, it's designed to transfer files from one system to another without leaving a trace. I never thought of it before because I haven't told anyone other than Cal about it. I didn't think he understood it enough to do something like this. Fuck, I still don't believe it, but it's the only thing that makes sense. It's my fucking program. I know it is. I just can't believe he figured out how to use it. I swear, I hope he wakes so I can kick his ass. What the hell was he thinking and what the fuck is he hiding?" he says the last part more to himself, hurt lacing his voice.

I've been wondering the same thing. It's clear Cal was in over his head, but he was determined as hell to see this through. Whatever is the root of Dem's problem, Cal was riding it out to help her.

"So, you believe there's another laptop?"

"I know there is. There has to be. You know me. I should have been into that laptop weeks ago. It's like someone is fighting me, but this would make sense. At least, it would make it begin to make sense," he replies, rubbing his chin thoughtfully.

"Okay, I'm with you. Follow this, and we'll make sure it's solid before we bring it to Quinn. Can you have concrete facts for me by the morning?"

"Aye. I'm working on something."

I nod. "Good." I turn my attention back to the screen in front of me. "Have you ever taken a look at the security footage at Danita's apartment the night of the fire?"

His face crumbles. "Aye, I did. It was trash." He takes a pause and thinks for a moment. "You know something, I watched it few times. Something nagged me about it. I still don't know what it is."

"Do you think it could be the fact that it's a loop?"

His eyes grow large. "Shit, aye, that could very well be it."

"Yeah, the footage from that night is bullshit. I hacked my way into a few of the other cams in the neighborhood."

"Wait, I'm sorry. Excuse me," he mocks.

"Listen, I may not be a convention-going, tech-spewing, computer geek like you, but I know how to use these things for when I need to get the job done," I grumble and fold my arms over my chest. "Anyway, this is a loop from the night before. It's not the real thing."

"So, someone made sure to cover their tracks."

"Aye, one of her neighbors is a young college student. He's a cocky little fucker. He has these two girlfriends. One drives a red car and the other a silver one. He keeps them on a schedule. They never show up on a night that's not theirs. The kid has been consistent for over two months. Come look at this."

He places his bag down on a nearby chair and rounds my desk. I start the footage for him and watch the cam from Dem's neighbor's home. On the neighbor's cam, the red car is in the neighbor's driveway. On the footage from Dem's, the silver car is in the kid's driveway at the exact same time stamp.

"The transition is so smooth. It's why it got by me the first time," I say.

"Aye, I was thinking the same thing. I don't know if we're dealing with the same fuckers that shot up Erin's. They weren't savvy with the cameras. They disabled them. Less effort, less skill."

"Exactly."

"I'm not liking this," he mutters.

"That makes two of us." I clamp my mouth shut before I say anything else.

I'm pissed, and I might say the wrong thing. This is something I need to handle, but first, I need to talk to my woman. She's keeping secrets we haven't agreed upon. If things between us are going to continue to work, she has to be honest with me when it counts.

"Do ya want me to jump on this tonight as well?"

"No, you stick to verifying that Cal used your program. I'll handle this."

"All right."

CHAPTER 31

TELL ME THE TRUTH

Danita

I was so tired when I arrived at Kevin's, I could barely keep my eyes open. He waited up for me. I could see the frustration in his face when I walked in worn out. Once again, I was assigned to work with Harris and Dawson on a case.

Keeping my distance from Harris took most of my energy, because all I wanted to do was kick him right in the balls. His audacity to glare at me made my blood boil. Not wanting to look like a mad woman who has lost her mind, I clamped down on my anger and did my job.

However, this morning, my job is the last thing on my mind. Kevin is angry and rightfully so. I've been keeping secrets from him as it is. I should have told him about the notes.

I sit up in bed and press the side of my face to his back. He's been sitting like this since I opened my eyes. His bare back straight, tension rolling off him, his knees bent with his arms draped over them, and his head facing forward—although I know he's aware that I'm awake and watching him.

"Talk to me," I whisper.

"You should've talked to me a long time ago," he replies.

"And I'm sorry about that."

I reach for his ribs and start to lightly drag my fingers up and down his side. He doesn't release the tension. If anything, I think it gets worse. I turn to kiss his smooth back.

"I did some digging, and I think you're right. Those letters don't have anything to do with Cal's shooting. I thought confirming that would make me feel better or something. It doesn't. I'm even more angry. I want ya to take some time off. I'll talk to Dugan if I have to," he says, his accent thick.

"You know it's not that simple, and I can't do that."

"No, I don't. I don't know that because I don't know what's going on. This isn't going to fly much longer. I feel it in my blood. Time is up. Quinn is going to put the pieces together soon," he says tightly.

I move away from his warmth, causing him to turn his angry eyes on me. There's more than anger reflected in his depths. I see hurt and something else I can't quite put my finger on.

"I'm no closer to getting any of the answers I need," I say in defeat, my voice raising louder than I mean for it to. "I can't tell you anything more than I already have."

"Then how am I supposed to help you? How can I protect you?"

I push a hand in my hair and tug. Why did I think this wouldn't happen? It's been brewing for months. Yet, I thought I could avoid it.

"Look, maybe it's time I start to look at other ways to get out of this mess."

"What mess? Tell me what the mess is, and I can help you figure a way out." He reaches to cup my face, forcing me to keep eye contact with him. "I love you. I want to make this right. I want you to trust me."

"I do trust you."

"Then tell me what the hell is really going on. What does all this have to do with Cal? What are you hiding from me? What is it you think Con can tell you? I can't sit back and wait any longer. Not only because my brother is bound to blow this wide open and find out that I've been hiding things from him, but I can't have your life in danger from shit that you're keeping from me," he fumes.

"I shouldn't have kept the notes from you, but I'm doing the right thing not telling you the rest. I won't put you and your family in that type of danger. I'm already too close to you all. I think I need to back off of Con and find another way," I say and start to get out of the bed.

"Dem," he barks.

I stop and stand stock-still. The emotions in his voice crack like a whip. I close my eyes, but don't turn to face him.

"Take me as I am."

"You don't get to do that. Not when I can feel in my bones that this is about to go left."

"It's all I have."

He scoffs, and I turn to open my eyes and look at him. He looks more hurt than angry this time. He's rubbing his thumb in the center of the palm of his other hand.

"I want ya to understand that all this time, I've been going against my instincts to respect yer wishes. I've given ya trust that surpasses who I am to my core. Blind faith, I've given ya." He lifts his gaze to mine. "If you can't give that back to me, I don't know how to protect ya. I'm at my wits' end."

"Maybe it's time we take a break."

He snorts. "Unbelievable. Ya know, I didn't think I could be more disappointed than I was last night when Shane told me he thinks Cal stole one of his computer programs to do some bullshit to his laptop. Ya've just proven that a lie."

Suddenly, it's like the air is sucked out of the room. I palm my forehead and start to pace. I don't know why I didn't think of this sooner. I was so focused on Conroy. How could I be so stupid?

"What does this program do?"

"What?"

"The program. What is it supposed to do?"

He looks at me in confusion. "It chains one system to another. Why?"

I stop my pacing and look at Kevin. I start to bounce on my toes as I think this through. How much should I give away?

Kevin climbs from the bed and stands before me. He reaches for my waist and pulls me to him as he narrows his eyes at me. I look up at him, biting my lip.

Before I can give him an answer, his phone rings. He curses, but releases me and rushes to his phone while keeping his eyes on me.

"Aye, Shane, what about ye?"

He listens to his brother on the other end while nodding. That look of anger clouds his handsome features once again. I need time to think.

Before he can get off the line, I head into his bathroom to take a shower. Hopefully, he'll give me enough time to clear my head and wrap my mind around my thoughts. Cal may have left me a clue all along.

Kevin

"Are you going to talk to me?" Dem says from the passenger seat of my car.

I haven't had a clear enough mind to say words, and I still don't know why she decided to come with me to the office. I want to trust her, but that's going out the window with all the secrets. I have to think about my family, and now that Shane has stumbled upon something new, I can't wrap my mind around anything or lock my temper down enough to string two words together that she'll actually understand.

"I don't have anything to say." The words come out thick and heavily accented.

"What are you thinking?"

I pull a face. What am I thinking? I've been stewing since I woke up this morning. Not that I got much sleep. I kept playing those surveillance videos over in my head, feeling like I was missing something. Not only in the videos, but with everything.

That call from Shane this morning pushed me over the edge.

At first, Shane was hurt and confused. Cal has been his best friend for years. My brother has never hidden a thing from Cal and never thought he had to protect his side projects from him.

Shane is a bit of a computer savant and has enhanced a lot of our work gear and computer technology at the office. From time to time, he geeks out, and Cal is the only one that will listen even though he hasn't a clue what Shane is talking about.

Which is where the confusion came from. Cal doesn't get it. Shane has shared ideas with him and never thought twice about Cal stealing them. That's where the nugget of truth lies.

Shane and I both know Cal wasn't capable of pulling off duplicating that program. However, there's one little fucker who is. I've texted Trent to bring Con into the office.

This is the part I'm not telling Dem. My nephew is more involved than any of us thought. Shane remembers Con being around when he demoed the program for Cal. The little runt actually asked Shane about it.

Con is smart. Too damn smart for his own good. He thinks this is something we don't know, but we're all well aware of it. It shouldn't have taken us this long to figure out he knew something about that laptop. Which might make the little fucker smarter than us all.

"Kevin." Dem sighs, breaking into my rambling thoughts.

"Answer me this. What exactly is it you think my nephew knows?"

She shifts her weight in her seat uncomfortably. Bingo. Just as I thought. Nope, I'm done. No more secrets, especially when they are tied to my little lying nephew that I love to pieces and will protect from whatever the hell his father has gotten him into.

"I'm not sure I need him anymore," she says slowly. "You mentioned that program. Cal asked me a few questions once. They were hypothetical. He…he knew about my training and background. I was able to answer the questions, but I didn't know what they were for."

"So, you think you helped him gain access to use Shane's program?" I say as my wheels begin to turn.

If this weren't Cal, I'd believe this were possible. I'm not saying she's lying, I'm saying I don't believe my nephew is innocent. Cal could very well have asked the questions, but he relayed the answers to Con, I guarantee it.

"I think I helped him, but I also think he wanted me to know about the laptops. There were two. He mentioned them a few times that day. It totally slipped my mind. I need to get my hands on those laptops. They have to be the key."

I grind my teeth, but I don't tell her what I know. All morning I've been questioning myself and wondering if I let my dick and my heart guide all my decisions. Even now, I can't look at her.

I need to detach myself until I figure out how this all involves Con and affects my family. This is not a case of harmless questions. If Con has that laptop, there's no telling what he knows.

Cal had him in that car when he went to meet Dem for that meeting. We don't know how deep Con is in. I swear, I want to ring Cal's neck.

"Kevin, what aren't you telling me?"

"That's a grand question. Why don't you go ahead and answer it for me?" I say as I pull into my parking spot at the office.

I stare ahead at the brick wall. My grip on the steering wheel so tight, my knuckles turn white. I don't know where to place this anger, frustration, and hurt.

Cal isn't around to be accountable. Con is a kid. That leaves the woman sitting next to me, and I'm not totally sure that she deserves to bear the weight of any of what I'm feeling.

Is she the enemy or the victim? If she's the victim, I'm failing all around, aren't I?

"Look at me," she demands.

I don't respond right away. I work my jaw as I pull it together. Mum has taught me never to lose my shit on women. She'd collar me for reaming Dem out the way I want to.

When I turn to face her, her eyes turn sad. My heart squeezes.

This is why I wanted to avoid looking at her. It's like having a gorgeous doll break within your palms.

Yet I have to steel my resolve. Once she shows me I can trust her again, I can make the rest right. For now, I need more answers.

Her lips tremble a little before she lifts her chin and her eyes harden. I want to kiss that defiance right out of her. I have to ball my fists in my lap to keep from reaching for her and doing just that.

"I've been as straight with you as I can be. I've told you that I mean you and your family no harm. I want this mess over with, and I'll be out of your hair for good," she says.

I'm not expecting her words to punch me in the gut so hard. I don't know what's worse, her throwing verbal daggers or watching her pull away. It's like I've started a collision course and I'm helpless to stop it. So, I do my best to change course and not address the knife she's thrown at my heart.

"We need to be prepared for when Quinn figures this out. I know my brother well, and we've run out of time."

"You let me worry about that," she says and turns to get out of the car.

I grunt in frustration, climbing out at the same time. "It's not that easy," I call across the roof of the car, placing my elbows on top.

"Nothing around us ever is. I told you, I've got it."

"Why?"

"Why what?"

I shove a hand into my hair. "Why do ya have to make things more complicated? Talk to me. I'm here to help. I don't want to fight with ya, I want to protect ya, I want to be there for ya. If yer not the villain here, show me. Give me something."

"I need that laptop. The sooner I have it, the sooner you can have answers."

"That's not good enough," I snap.

"It's going to have to be."

I storm around the car until we are standing mere inches from each other. I place my hands on top of the car on either side of her. She looks up at me with that same defiance.

"Ya treat me like an enemy."

"You're looking at me like you don't trust me."

"Yer not giving me a reason to," I challenge.

"*Mi vida está loca.* You think I don't want to let you in? I want to so bad it hurts, but my life is complete and utter crazy shit. I don't know whether I'm coming or going, and I live with the fear that I'll never get back what I've lost. All I'm asking is that you trust me a little longer. I promise, when I can tell you more, I will. You are the last person in the world I want to hurt," she says as she swipes at a tear.

I place my forehead to hers. That connection is there. It's always there.

Dem grabs the sides of my T-shirt as if she's holding on for dear life. I know I'm not wrong about her. My true problem is that I can't see pass my anger, and I needed somewhere to place the blame.

Placing a kiss on her forehead, I release a heavy breath. "Let's get inside. I think there's something you need to know."

CHAPTER 32

CHILLING FACTS

Danita

WE HAVEN'T BEEN IN THE OFFICE FOR TWO MINUTES WHEN EVERY-thing comes to a shrieking halt. One minute Shane is heading for Kevin as I spot Conroy looking nervous and unsure. The next, Quinn is roaring through the office as he glares at me.

"*Fuck.*"

I stand frozen, much like everyone else in the room. Isn't this what Kevin warned me about? Quinn looks like an angry bull in a china shop. His gaze is locked on me and his eyes are clear and focused.

It's like he can see all of my secrets, and I don't believe that's a good thing. The hairs on the back of my neck stand up. When he speaks his next words, I know he has figured me out.

"Ya've been right under our noses," he says. "How many lies have ya fed us? I want the truth and I want it now."

I nearly flinch from the whip-like tone of his voice. I know he's pissed. The flaring of his nostrils is only one giveaway.

"Shit," I mutter, reaching to rub my forehead.

"Quinn, it's not what you think." Kevin jumps in and my heart swells. There's no question that he's pissed at me. He's been warning me this was coming, but for him to still stand up for me… I know how close these brothers are.

When he turns to me, I can see the anger in his eyes. He has every right to be. I've dragged him into my mess. His words sting more than the look on Quinn's face. "And this is the shit I warned you about."

I push through the pain. The cat is out of the bag now. I know what I need to do.

"And I told you, the less you know, the safer everyone is. I need the files on that laptop—"

"It's my fault," Conroy says before I can finish getting the words out of my mouth.

I pause and turn to look at him. He has sweat on his forehead and upper lip. The kid looks so confused and nervous.

"What?" Kevin and Quinn say in unison.

"Dad told me to keep scrambling the computer if anything happened to him. I have a laptop that I'm frying the other one from. Every time you try to get in, the scrambled files come to me." His words make it all click into place.

Cal wasn't asking me those questions so he could link those computers. He was asking to help his son do it. Which means this kid is a little genius. I only confirmed the things Cal had asked me and gave one or two suggestions.

Wow. Just freaking wow.

I half listen to the rest of his story. He's not telling the complete truth. I plan to get to the bottom of that once I get the laptop he's been hiding.

However, when he speaks his next words, I do think he believes them. This is what breaks my heart and forces the truth from my lips. I'm done hurting Cal and his family.

"Dad was freaked. He kept saying he had to fix it. I think they came for him because of me."

I can't allow fear to keep me trapped any longer.

"Shit, kid." I blow out and tug at my hair. "It's a little bigger than that. None of this is your fault."

"Explain," Quinn snaps at me.

"Go on. We trust everyone in this room with our lives," Kevin says, folding his arms across his chest. "I'm more than ready to hear this."

This is it. My moment of truth. This will either bury me or finally get me the help I need. Either way, I'm doing this not for me, but because I'm tired of hurting the people I care about even when I think I'm protecting them. Ignoring Eric's warning, I spill the one secret Kevin hasn't figured out on his own.

"Nothing is as it seems. I'm FBI. I was planted on the force. I've been on this case for years. I'm so deep undercover, I don't exist anymore. Which is how this whole mess started. Cal stumbled into my case around the same time my handler went missing.

"I had no one to pull me out of this mess, and I was desperate. I have a few of the low-level guys dead to rights, but Cal was so damn close to getting me the guys calling all the shots. Cops, judges, cartel, this case is my resurrection.

"If anyone in that precinct figures out who I am, I'm dead, and no one will ever know the difference. Danita Moralez doesn't even have family to mourn her. My family is in Puerto Rico, probably already visiting a grave with my real name on it. A year turned into two, and two turned into three and now... I need that laptop, Con," I say, feeling breathless.

It's the truth. Well, most of it. My mother and father have returned to Puerto Rico. At least that's what I was told last by Eric. My oldest brother is still in NYC and the other two were in Miami, last I heard. I haven't been able to risk looking further into any of them because of the fear I would be opening a can of worms around us all.

However, there's no telling how much has changed in their lives in the last two years. My heart aches at the thought of them believing I'm gone forever. Quickly, I try to push down on the lid that all those emotions have been loosely contained beneath.

"This is what you've been hiding from me?" Kevin says. My gaze bounces to him, and he looks like he's about to lose it.

I plead with my eyes for him to understand. "Look at what happened the last time I told someone," I say, my throat tightening with my emotions. "I've caused your family enough trouble."

"And the fire?" Quinn asks.

"Unrelated," I reply.

"You sure?"

I didn't think Kevin's face could show any more rage. Yet if looks could kill, we wouldn't need to find the person responsible for setting the fire. Kevin's face alone would cause them to drop dead wherever they are.

"Yeah, she's been getting notes on her car," Kevin says tightly. "Different problem. I'll be handling that one."

"Hmm," Quinn grunts.

Suddenly, Quinn becomes distracted and sits back at his desk, hacking away at his computer. Kevin closes the distance between us, reaching for my hand to tug me into him. I look up into his eyes, and the anger has lowered to a simmer. He looks more hurt and concerned than anything.

"This, you could've told me. I was so close to the truth... You could have said something. You *should* have said something," he says low enough for me to hear as the office starts to buzz around us again.

"No, I really couldn't. I was warned not to. However, I don't think that matters now. Eric, my handler, told me to wait him out, that he'd take care of things if anything happened. Two years is a long time to wait. I'd been working with Cal at first in hopes that when Eric popped up, I'd be good to go. Then as time went on, I changed courses, and I've just been trying to figure out how to fix this without Eric. I need that laptop from Con."

He nods. "We'll be getting that. I had Trent bring him in. Shane figured out that he was involved and had to have the other laptop this morning," he says.

I can still hear the frustration in his voice. This isn't over. I've dropped a colossal bomb, and I know he's going to want more details once he has a chance to wrap his head around it.

"He's had what I needed all this time."

"Aye, he did. He's bullshitting, though. He knows something else."

I scoff. "Yeah, I picked up on that."

"Let's grab him and head back to the—"

We both turn to Quinn as he roars another curse. This time, he has the phone to his ear, already moving for the door. I can tell from his body language this isn't good.

"Go. Someone should stay behind with Con," I say as I look at the indecision in Kevin's face as he looks between me and his nephew.

He palms the back of my neck and kisses my forehead hard. "We'll talk when I get back. This isn't over."

I nod and reach to give his wrist a squeeze. He hesitates only a moment longer before releasing me and rushing off behind Quinn and the others, leaving me, Con, and the office admin, Debbie, behind. Con moves over to me with big, wide eyes.

"I'm sorry. I didn't know what to do. I did what Dad told me to. I… I'm sorry."

"Con, believe it or not, you did the right thing. This is all dangerous and your father trusted you. That was a lot to have on your shoulders." I reach to squeeze his shoulder. "Have you eaten breakfast?"

"Yeah, I had something."

"Okay, well, I haven't. You want to come with me to get something?"

He wipes his hands on his jean shorts. "Honestly, I want to get you that laptop. You said it's important and that you're FBI. Maybe you can help find who did this to my mom and dad."

"Kid, I love you so much right now," I say and sigh in relief.

Conroy starts to blush. I reach to ruffle his hair, causing him to redden more. He's not a bad kid at all. I can see he was only doing what he felt was right.

We sit at the outdoor dining table at Renny and Teagon's home. I stare at the blue and silver laptop I've seen Conroy with almost every day. I, like everyone else, assumed he was on social media or playing around on the simple device.

I had no idea he was monitoring the files to the biggest case of my life. My life, my future, my freedom have been sitting in this child's lap, and we were all so oblivious to this fact.

Knowing that Con has had this laptop here at Kevin's parents' home all this time causes an ache so deep, I have to breathe through my nose. We've been on lockdown for over three weeks, and this laptop has been this close. Tears fill my eyes, but I hold them back.

"Hey," Con says, placing a hand on my shoulder. I look at him. "I'm so sorry. I wanted to tell you. I really did. First, I needed to be sure that Uncle Kevin trusted you. Then, I didn't know how to say something. I tried a few times. My uncles are going to be so pissed at my dad." He cuts off and starts to chew on his lip.

I give him a warm smile, doing my best to suck in my tears. This kid has had enough on his back.

"Con, you can trust me. I want to find out what happened to your parents."

"And get back to your family, right?"

I nod. He's silent for a moment. After a few beats, he releases a long breath.

"I sort of lied." He starts to fidget and runs a hand through his hair. "I've been trying to solve my dad's case on my own. I'm receiving the files, but I can't get into them. The day you picked me up, I was on my way to the place Dad went to before coming to meet you. I thought I could find something out to tell my uncles or find some clue on how to get the files open."

"Oh, Con. That was so dangerous."

He looks down in his lap. "Yeah, I know, but I was trying to tell them that I knew something then, and they were treating me like a baby. I thought if…if I could figure this out, they'd see I'm smart. I don't mess things up like my dad does sometimes.

"I wanted them to see me. Dad had asked me if I understood what Uncle Shane had shown him that one time and I tried to explain it to him. There were a few things I wasn't sure about, but he asked a friend for me and I was able to duplicate everything and create the add-ons.

"I...I did sneak into Dad's car that day, but it was because I figured out how to recreate Uncle Shane's program and I added on the enhancement to destroy the original files as they moved to the new computer. He was mad, but once I told him what I was able to do, he was so proud and said I had helped him and his friend out," he says proudly.

"You were struggling with the encryption and firewalls. You needed to cloak the files while they transferred. I was so vague in the information I gave your dad. You're so smart, Con. You still figured it out."

His eyes light up. "It was you? You were the friend he asked?"

"Yeah."

"Cool. Here, let me show you," he says, all apprehension gone.

It's clear that he now trusts me without a doubt. He scoots his chair closer and opens the laptop. He's adorable as he excitedly shows me the program he cloned from his uncle. I don't have the heart to rush him.

I think I actually hold my breath until the screen lights with the files that hold my life in their hands. My mind moves a mile a minute as I take the laptop from Con. I click on the first file, but as he said, it's password protected.

"Dad said the right person would know how to get into the files," he says, his green eyes expectant.

I turn back to the computer and stare. Anxiety claws at my throat. What the hell could the password be?

Come on, Cal. What were you thinking?

For two years, the man had become the only friend I had. We

talked a lot. Erin and the kids came up often. Cal is a proud father. It's so clear he loves his family.

He spoke of his brothers-in-law as well. There was a sense of longing and admiration there. I, on the other hand, was never honest with him about the real me. Cal always got Danita. With one exception. He knew my handler went missing, and he knew his name was Eric.

Suddenly, a memory comes back to me. Cal and I were in an old office building in Binghamton. We'd taken the long drive to meet up there because we were worried things were getting too hot.

"Erin lost her shit this morning. I told her I wanted to try for another boy," Cal had said.

I laughed. "Four kids. She has her hands full. And it seems like you're in the business of making pretty little girls."

He shook his head and looked me in my eyes. "I feel it in my blood. Con is my pride and joy. I'd have another boy in a heartbeat if I could. September 25. It was the greatest day of my life. I got to hold my son for the first time."

"I bet that was a great moment."

"Yeah, I'd thought April 20 would be the greatest day of my life until the day I died."

I wrinkled my brows. "What's April 20?"

He gave me a huge smile that took over his face. "It's the day I married Erin. There are just some days you never forget."

At the time, I didn't understand why he put so much emphasis on the word *you*. Now as it plays back in my head, it stands out. What he said next reinforces that I'm on the right track.

"I bet you remember the last day you saw Eric. You probably know the date by heart," he said.

"February 25," I replied, without thinking.

I come back to the present with a gasp. My fingers fly over the keys as I enter all three dates. I cry out when the file unlocks, turning to Con to pull him into a hug.

"My dad really did trust you," he says. "I hope this helps us get the guys that hurt him and my mom. Detective—"

"Call me Dem, kid. You just saved my life."

"Yeah, about that." He starts to blush again. "I like having you around and my uncle...he loves you. Uncle Kevin is crazy about you. I've never seen him this happy. Can you promise me something, please?"

I hesitate a bit. I don't want to make a promise I can't keep. "What's that?"

"Don't leave. If you can get your life back and still be in ours, please stay."

I can't help the smile that comes to my lips. I ruffle his hair and kiss his cheek. The shy look that comes to his face makes me laugh.

"I'm going to do the best I can and what's best for everyone."

His smile falters a little. "Yeah, I get it. It's not a promise you can make, but think about it, okay?"

Little does he know, it's all I can think about. I have this laptop, but what does that mean and what will I do next? I don't want to think about losing Kevin, but it's a strong possibility.

Pushing those thoughts aside, I start to scroll through the file. Opening the folders to see what Cal had been up to. A folder named *Read Me* catches my attention.

I click on it, and it's all here. All of the holes. Names, documents, pictures, recordings, everything that I could imagine, to create the perfect case. I open the document flagged in green.

"It's the freaking infrastructure. He created a tree of the organization," I say in awe.

My heart stutters to a stop when I see that the brackets at the top are blank. There are three of them that sit empty. I push a hand in my hair.

Sure, there are plenty of names and their positions within the organization as well as their occupations in the real world. However, it's not enough. Without the head to this serpent, I'll never be safe or free. Especially as I notice one of the brackets at the top has a single piece of information under it. FBI is listed in the occupation section. Eric was right.

I return to the other files. This time, something else sticks out. It's a folder with my name on it.

I open the folder, and I think I'm going to be sick. I find pictures of my funeral and my grieving family. I have to stifle the soul-searing sob that creeps to my lips. Wrapping my middle with my arms, I rock in my seat.

"Dem, you okay?" Con asks softly.

I nod jerkily as I swipe at my tears with the back of one hand. I move to the other documents in the file, and my confusion and anger only grows. These photos and the documents are from two years ago.

It says I was killed in the line of duty. My chest is so tight, I'm barely breathing. I always feared my family thought I was dead. Now I have proof.

However, what rips me to shreds is the next document that states that Eric Myerson was also murdered. His case is listed as unsolved, the same as mine. I cover my mouth with my hand and release the sob I've been trapping in.

"Should I call Uncle Kevin?"

"No," I say and shake my head.

I drag my hand under my nose and continue to look through the documents in the folder with my name on it. It's in here for a reason. I know Cal is leading me to something. I have this feeling in my bones.

I concentrate on each file I open, looking for the string to pull. Most of these files are confidential. I have no idea how Cal was able to get his hands on them.

I know when I find it—the one thing Cal wanted me to see—and my breath *whooshes* through my lips. I'm trembling as I read the page over and over.

"What is it?"

I shake my head in confusion and disbelief. "It has here that Vivian Demarco was my handler. It also has me on some bogus case when I supposedly was killed in the line of duty. None of this is adding up," I say more to myself.

"Do you know that Vivian lady? Have you ever worked with her?"

I turn to Con. "She's my godsister." I frown as that old pain returns. "She disappeared before I took this assignment. She's the reason I took this case."

I think it's time I reach out to the people I trust the most in this world. The same ones I've been thinking it's too dangerous to contact. This is starting to feel too personal. Something is wrong, very wrong.

CHAPTER 33

DEMARIS

Kevin

"Are you sure?" I grumble into the phone.

"Aye, seventh floor. That's the room," Shane replies.

"Thanks."

I end the call and place my phone in my back pocket. With my eyes narrowed at the building standing across the lot from me, I frown as if something bitter sits in my mouth. I should be smiling.

This day didn't go as wrong as it could have. Alicia is safe. My brother has found out that he's going to be a father. Finally Ma will get those grands she's been harassing him for.

However, at the moment, a frown mars my face because when I arrived at my parents' home, my woman wasn't there. I sit here against the hood of my car as I stare at the hotel she's inside of, feeling like I have lead in my boots. The wind has picked up, blowing my hair around my face. Still my hands remain in my pockets, clenched in tight fists.

I don't know what she's doing here, only that she told Conroy that she needed to handle some business. He said something on the computer seemed to upset her, and she told him she needed to go.

"What are you doing now, love?" I mumble into the night.

My brother was able to track her car and that led me here. I've told myself to leave. Turn around, get in my car, and let her live her life. She's found what she was looking for.

However, it's my heart that makes me get up and start for the front of the hotel. Something tells me the woman in there needs me, and no matter how much I want to fight it, I need her. That is a fact I can't deny or run from.

"Excuse me," a guy says as he runs right into me, bumping my shoulder.

He doesn't stop long enough for me to accept his apology as he rushes toward the parking lot. I grunt and keep going. That is, until a loud roar of pain comes from behind me. I turn to find the guy that bumped me crouched in the middle of the parking lot.

He looks like he's in anguish as he wraps his arms around his middle. When he releases another cry, it's more like a sob of agony. He claws at his head as his body trembles.

I go to ask him if he's okay, but he stands and storms toward a black car and jumps inside, speeding out of the lot. I watch after him for a few beats before I turn and head inside. I don't stop at the counter. Instead, I head right for the elevator.

As I'm walking, two tall guys head toward me. I slow my stride as one of them catches my attention. He looks like a male version of Dem. Only taller and a shade or two lighter. His dark brown hair has the same wave pattern as it's pulled back into a low ponytail.

I look to the one with him and notice traits of Dem in his face as well. His hair is not as dark as the one next to him. His reddish brown waves are cut low and pop against his brown skin. His eyes—although red-rimmed—are the same amber-whiskey color as Dem's.

"Should we go after Jo-jo?" the one with waves says in a hushed tone, but I still hear him as I approach the two.

"No, I think he's gone, anyway. We'll catch up to him. Hell, I think we all need a minute to breathe, Diego. Jo-jo especially."

"He looked like he was going to be sick. I don't blame him. I feel like we were talking to a ghost. I can't believe this shit," Diego says with a lost look on his face. "Why are we leaving? We should go back up there and make her come home."

"She needs our help."

"God, Emil, what are the chances she would call us when we're all here? Bro, I almost didn't come down. I don't think we should leave." The one named Diego goes to turn back for the elevators.

Emil—I'm assuming—places a hand on the other's shoulder to stop him. "Listen, our baby sister needs us. We have to keep level heads. As level as we can in this situation. It's best if we go about our usual routines until we answer some questions and figure out what the hell happened."

Diego sighs and turns back to start out of the hotel again. "This still doesn't feel right."

Emil nods. "But at the moment, I don't think exposing her will be the best thing to do. She's a smart girl. She survived this long because she's brilliant and strong," he says with mixed emotions in his voice.

"She's been alive all this time. Papi is going to lose it."

"First, let's get to the bottom of this. Then we can get Papi and Mommy to come home. Or we take her to them. A trip to PR is probably what she'll need after all of this."

I clench my fist at my sides with his words. The reality of Dem's other existence roars to life and waves in my face. If I didn't understand her reluctance before, it's clear to me now.

A cloud covers both of their faces as they head toward the exit of the lobby. In that moment, Emil locks eyes with me. He's silent as the three of us cross paths.

I would know they are both in law enforcement even if I didn't see the gun and badge on Emil's hip. It seems Dem comes from a family of public servants. Which makes me question how she ended up in this situation. There are still dots I need to connect, and I plan to do so tonight.

I get to the elevator and ride up to the seventh floor with an elderly couple. I can't help grinning at their banter. When he reaches to tuck her hair behind her ear and kiss her forehead, my heart squeezes.

Those are the simple things I want to be able to do with Dem in our future. Talk about our grands and our children and make her

flush with little gestures. The lift chimes on the seventh floor, bringing me from my vision of a future I'm not sure I'll ever see.

I push off the wall I've been propped against and exit. "He reminds
me so much of you when you were his age," I hear the woman say as
I walk off.

"I don't remember being that strapping."

"Yes, you were. I remember it well," she says lovingly.

I smile as I head for the room Dem should be in. When I stop in
front of it, I place an arm over my head on the doorframe and lean my
forehead against the door as if I can feel her through it. Lifting my other
hand, I tap against the barrier.

It only takes a few seconds for the door to open. She takes my
breath away from the moment I see her tear-stained face. Like a
broken doll that needs healing.

Our eyes connect, and that's all it takes. Her need for me blazes
behind all of the pain. I cup her neck in one hand and push my way
into the room. She moves with me, taking a few steps back before I
reach for her with my free arm and lift her onto my waist.

"Name," I command against her lips.

It's all I have to say. She understands what I want and need. She
runs her hands through the back of my hair as she presses her nose
to mine.

"Demaris Mercado, but my family calls me Dem," she breathes softly.

I nod and nip at her chin. "Tonight, Demaris may be the name I
call, but I'm not making love to a word. When I'm done, you'll know
I've fallen in love with the woman, not the name. Everything else
we'll get to after I'm done proving my point."

She responds with a bob of her head. I squeeze the hand I have
around her neck and lust fills her eyes. I understand this woman so
completely. She's one step closer to her real life. A life she doesn't
think I can be a part of because she's been in so deep and has lost
pieces of herself. I've comprehended this for longer than she knows.

As a former detective, I understand it more than most. There is who you are and who you become while doing your job. The longer you are that other person, the more you disconnect with the truth. However, I've fallen for the core of her. I want her no matter what persona she's offering.

As many questions as I have, as many holes as I want her to fill in—in this moment, none of that matters. It's her and me. My love doesn't end with whatever she's learned from that laptop.

I take her lips and kiss her deeply. I don't have time to figure this place out, so I turn and press her back to the nearest wall. She already has my T-shirt halfway up my torso.

Reaching for the hem, I tug it the rest of the way off. A shiver runs through me as she drags her small hands up my sides. Biting my lip, I reach for her open button-down shirt and push it from her shoulders.

In impatience, I pull her tank top from her high-waisted jeans and tear it down the middle. A small gasp leaves her lips as fabric gives beneath my strength. Pushing the ruined shirt from her shoulders, I let it fall to the floor. I seal our mouths again and savor the flavor of her and her tears.

She whimpers into my mouth as I work the buttons of her jeans. I wasn't this nervous the first time I was with a girl in my teens. My hands are trembling, and my thoughts have turned into a mosh pit of anxiety.

However, my determination kicks in. If I can't find the words after all is said and done, she will at least have felt me and every single emotion I have for her. That's what I can guarantee.

Danita

I need this. I need Kevin to erase the last two hours of my life. My brothers yelled, they cried, they freaked the hell out. I can't blame them.

However, the hurt in their faces will forever haunt me. That's why I need Kevin. I know he can make me forget it all.

"Kevin," I whimper when he starts to kiss his way down my neck.

I'm used to his aggression during sex, but this is something different. Once again, he's showing me another side of himself. It's a mix of tenderness and almost as if he's subjecting me to a slow seduction.

Each touch, every kiss feels like he's luring me deeper into his web. If touch could speak, I truly believe Kevin has created a language for us. A speech that's slowly soothing my hurts and intriguing my senses to crave more.

I place my hand on his cheek as he moves down to my collarbone. He turns his head slightly and his gaze links with mine. Again, unspoken words pass between us.

He continues his descent until he gets to my lace-covered nipple. I don't realize how hard I'm breathing until he pauses, only allowing his breath to fan the hardened peak. I buck my hips against him as he keeps me pinned to the wall at my back.

"Patience. That's what it's taken to have you and that's what it'll take to keep you," he murmurs against the tight bud. The slight brush of his lips is enough to make my core clench and weep with desire and all-consuming need.

Instead of taking my nipple into his mouth, he straightens and hooks his hands into my jeans. Torturously slow, he peels them off. I release my legs from his hips and plant my feet on the floor as he gets the pants from my limbs.

I can't help but run my hand through his fiery locks as he bends his head to kiss my thigh. Could this be the last time I feel him, look at him, hear him this way? I should walk away and let him live his life.

I thought this was out of control when Eric disappeared. Now that I know he's dead and someone has been trying to erase me completely from this earth, I know it's time to let Kevin go.

"Demaris," he says as he kisses his way to my inner thigh. He flicks out his tongue against my skin and lifts his eyes to mine. "I'm not giving up on you. I'm not allowing you to walk out of my life so easily. You can stop thinking about it because it's not happening."

I go to open my mouth to challenge him, but he tosses my leg over his shoulder and buries this face at the apex of my thighs. All coherent speech is lost to my cries of pleasure. Kevin eats my pussy like he owns it.

Honestly, he does. I can't see myself with anyone else but him. Leaving wouldn't mean I'd be finding someone new. It would mean I'd be giving up on love and intimacy because I don't want it from anyone else. He has ruined me for life, and in this very moment, I'm not complaining one bit.

I rock my hips against his face, causing him to growl into my center. He tosses my other leg over his shoulder and lifts me higher up the wall. I drop my head back and roll it from side to side.

I've never felt this much pleasure in my life, and Kevin has never disappointed in the past. This is undeniably next level. He's a man with a mission.

"Kevin, I can't take any more," I pant as he works his way through my third orgasm.

Time and space have ceased to make any sense. My legs are trembling as I squeeze them against his ears. Yet he doesn't let up. My body is already tightening again, but he powers through, taking me right to the brink before he backs off, leaving me gasping for release.

"Babe," I groan. "I was almost there."

He kisses me hard on the lips, then softly on the forehead. The sound of his belt jiggling greets my ears as he lowers me to his waist, coaxing my legs around him. I have no idea where he pulls the condom from or how he gets it on so quickly. I cup his face with one hand and push the other into the side of his hair.

"I love you, Demaris," he says as he thrusts into me hard.

My back hits the wall and I tighten my legs around him, crossing

my ankles. My teeth chatter as he continues with the punishing pace.
Yet his hands caress my skin tenderly as if I'm the most precious thing
in the world to him.

"I love you too."

My tears spill over. This time, they are because I'm so confused.
I do love him and I want to see where things could go with us in the
long run, but I still don't know if that's possible. Seeing my family has
driven that fact home.

My brothers were ready to take me and run. I would have been in PR
before the night is over if I didn't put a stop to the plan Jo-jo started to
spit out. I couldn't leave, not after Conroy's request and not after sitting
in this hotel room waiting for my brothers to arrive. All I could think
about was Kevin.

I cling to his back as if I can cling to him forever. I want to melt
into him and become one with his soul. The way he looks into my
eyes and breathes against my lips as if stealing my essence from me,
leaves me entranced in a world that is all Kevin.

Each time he enters me, it's like he's filling me up with his love. I
close the distance between our lips, but he commands the kiss once
we make the connection. Our tongues dance and lock together. It's to
the point I don't know where I stop and he begins, but I don't want to
figure that out because I never want him to let go.

I savor the bite of pain that comes from his deep thrusts. They are
a reminder that this is all real. This can be a reality if I allow it. Not
everything in the last five years has been contrived and fleeting.

Breaking the kiss, he places his lips to my temple and says, "I'm
sorry for your loss."

"What?"

"You already know I own this pussy, but tonight I'm taking your
voice, your heart, and your soul. Hang tight, love. I'm about to ruin
ya."

He pulls me from the wall and turns to find the bedroom. It's not long before my back hits the cool sheets. Still inside me, his eyes riveted to mine, he pushes my thighs back and lifts to his knees.

When he starts to thrust in a downward motion, I dig my nails into his forearms and release a cry that leaves my throat raw. It's right then that I know he's going to make good on his words. This is going to be one of those nights, but it's exactly what my heart and mind need. Time to get lost and forget. The only thing on my mind for the next few hours becomes Kevin Blackhart, the man that has stolen my heart right from under my nose.

Kevin

"Talk to me," I mumble into her hair as I trace her hip with my fingertips.

She shifts the thigh she has thrown over my stomach, but I reach to trap it in place. I want to feel the weight of her body on mine. It's keeping me sane.

"I saw my brothers for the first time in five years. I knew it would be hard, but not as hard as it was," she replies.

"I'm sure that wasn't easy for any of you."

"They thought I was dead. The files on the laptop say that I've been dead to them for two years," she chokes out.

It takes her a few minutes to gather her thoughts before she starts to tell me everything she found on the laptop. I listen quietly, squeezing her in my embrace to comfort her as she makes the picture clearer for me.

"We've always had a code," she says when she starts to tell me how she ended up here. "If one of us was undercover and needed help, we'd text our nicknames and a location. Emilio, or Emil as we call him, my oldest brother, has been on the force for a long time. He's seen a lot of things go down. Especially when it comes to African American and Afro-Latino officers. He has always drilled us on watching our backs. Our father was in law enforcement. We all wanted to be like him." She snorts.

"He was so pissed to find out that I was going to follow him too." She pauses to sigh and kiss my chest. "The burner phone I used to text my brothers went crazy when I finally sent the text I should've sent two years ago."

"I have a question. Why didn't you call on them sooner?"

"On top of the threat to their lives, I put it off for so long because I didn't want to feel like a failure. All three of my brothers are decorated in their fields. All through Quantico, I had to live in Diego's shadow," she says, then shakes her head before she continues. "Although I know calling them now was the right thing to do, I still feel like a failure."

I palm her face and turn her head up until our eyes meet. "Where have you failed? You survived for two years and built a case with Cal to bring this all to a head. I know Cal. He was holding that file on you for a reason. We'll figure that out, and then you can move on with your life, but you're not a failure."

Lifting up, she presses her lips to mine. "How did I get so lucky?"

She looks down at me with a sparkle in her eyes. I can still see the sadness in her depths, but she's happier than she was when she opened the door for me. I brush my finger across her lower lip before sitting up to taste her sweet mouth.

It doesn't take long for the kiss to heat up. I haven't been able to keep my hands off her since I arrived. Reaching for her ass, I seat her in my lap.

"I'm the lucky one." I drag my thumb from her temple to her chin. "I've talked with my brothers. Now that we know that Alicia's situation wasn't connected to Cal, we're letting up on the lockdown. We can move back into our place permanently."

Her shoulders sag. I already know what's coming. I've been

preparing myself for this. She's going to try to place that wedge between us, but I won't allow it.

"Once Emil and Diego can clear me, I'm going to need to go home." She furrows her brows and murmurs, "Wherever that is."

"Have you stopped to think that maybe home is wherever I am?"

She blinks those long lashes as her amber eyes fix on me. I rub soothing circles on her back, already starting to grow hard beneath her. I ignore my growing desire, placing my forehead to hers.

"Kevin." Her voice comes out as almost a whisper.

I pull back to meet her gaze again. Her word sounds too heavy for me not to read her face. There is a war going on and a storm brewing.

"Say it, love. What's on your mind?"

"I have to find my way back to me. I'm so confused on what or who that is. My mind is telling me to let you go so I can do that, but my heart's telling me I can do it with you. That I might actually *need you* to do it with me." She frowns and puffs out her cheeks and lips.

"I'm going to need you to tell me to stay. Not Danita. I need you to tell Demaris to stay because my old life will tug at me, and I need a reason not to go back to what I know."

"Stay," I say and nip her lip. I grasp her throat and tug her into me. "Stay. Demaris, stay."

This time when I make love to her, I make it clear that I can't live without her.

CHAPTER 34

SHOW YOUR HAND

Kevin

IT'S BEEN A MONTH AND THIS MEETING IS LONG OVERDUE. DUGAN stands with his hands in his pockets looking as if this is the last place he wants to be. I can't unclench my jaw as Quinn and I walk over to him.

As Quinn's godfather and our dad's long-time friend, we thought we could count on him. We've always been there for him. As the police chief, we thought he would come through for us. The fact that this is the first time we're hearing from him since he gave Quinn that useless file on Cal is beyond me.

"This place smells like horse shit," I grumble.

"Aye, it would. They've been using the place to auction black market horses," Quinn replies. "Drugs and horses. Nice bust."

Dugan frowns and rolls his shoulders. I narrow my eyes at him, taking him in once again. This time, I note how tired he looks, the bags under his eyes aren't normal for him. His eyes are red as well. He hasn't slept in days.

"I'd like to know how you can find a ring of horse traders in Queens, but you can't find my sister and brother-in-law's shooters right in your own backyard."

"Kevin," Quinn grunts.

I fold my arms over my chest and glare at a man I once had respect for. It's waning with every passing day. I'm still trying to figure out why Dugan thought it was a good idea to take off for a month without saying a word. I thought we were closer than that.

"You know as well as I do this was Danita's case. I had nothing to do with the groundwork or the bust," Dugan says. "Listen, I know you guys have been trying to get answers from me."

"You think?" I say and step toward him.

Quinn places a hand on my chest. I take a breath and move back. Cracking my knuckles, I try to reel it in.

"You boys know I see you as my own. Erin is like a daughter to me. I've been doing all I can. You have no idea how far this shit reaches," Dugan says.

"That's funny. You can't be too worried. It's seems you took off for a vacation out of the blue," I growl.

"It seems," he barks back. "*Seems* is the word you need to pay attention to. I need to make things look a certain way. Do you understand the pile of shit we've all landed in the middle of?"

"We've been waiting for ya to tell us," Quinn says, folding his arms cross his chest. "That little file you gave me felt more like a distraction than any help."

"It was supposed to be a distraction. There's an FBI agent hiding in my department." I stiffen at his words. He still doesn't know who Dem is. "Someone blew the whistle and an agent was dropped into the precinct. I don't know who they are or if they're still here. If there is a chance that someone can clean up this shit show without getting killed, I want it done. I couldn't chance you boys getting in the way of that. I'm sorry about what happened to Erin and Cal. Cal's a good kid. He's trying to do the right thing, but he's gotten us all in a bind with this, and I'm covering as many tracks as I can," Dugan grits out.

"How do you fit into all of this?" I ask.

"I'm trying to keep my fucking job and my life. You think I don't know how corrupt that place is? I told you boys not to join the force in the first place. Whoever blew the whistle isn't the first. I've tried to have that place cleaned out my damn self, and I was told to shut up and do my job or I'd find myself without one and behind bars or worse.

This goes higher up than me or the commissioner. Pockets deeper than the Atlantic. I'm no match for that. I do what I can, but I know my limits," he says and pulls a tired, sour face.

"So how do ya know that there's an agent lurking?" Quinn asks the same thing that's on my mind.

"I told you. I've put in calls to have the place cleaned up myself. It was blocked at every turn, but I bent the ear of a friend or two before I got shut down. They couldn't give me details, but the word was that someone was being sent in. A few rookies and transfers showed up around then. No one that stood out, but I was pretty sure that they arrived. Then about a year and a half ago, Cal started to pop up on my radar. I didn't know what he was up to. I thought maybe you guys had a case he was working on. Perhaps one of the boys was helping him out with it. He started popping up at the bar and around some of my questionable guys. That's when I started to pay more attention. He was onto something."

"How do you know that?" I say.

"I cornered him. If he wanted to keep working my precinct, I wanted to know what he was working on. He wouldn't tell me who his person was. Only that he was working with an FBI agent, and he planned to blow the whole thing open with him," he replies and drags a hand down his face.

"I should have stopped him, then. The kid just had this look in his eyes. I know what they did to him. He deserved justice. Cal was a good cop. Now, I'm covering his ass, mine, and whoever he was helping," Dugan huffs and rubs the back of his neck.

"All right, I'll bite. What do you have for us now?" I say.

"While on vacation, I did some fishing, if you know what I mean," Dugan says. "No one seems to know shit, nothing useful anyway. I'm getting mixed stories. I was told a task force was created, then there was a small secret team, and the last I heard was that it died before it could get started. Now none of that adds up.

"My buddy that was trying to push through all the red tape had a mysterious seizure and…I owe his wife some flowers. I don't think Cal was lying to me. He may not have wanted to give up a name, but there was an agent working with him. My gut tells me to believe that much."

I turn to look at Quinn. He nods slightly. There has been something foul about this case from the time Danita took it. Her brother has told her the same thing. All the names she was able to give him that initially knew about the case are dead or have moved up and won't say a word about it.

Someone wants Demaris Mercado to stay buried. From the names in Cal's files, it could be any one of the wealthy scumbags on that list calling in favors to make it happen. However, I don't think that's the case.

"Cal was on to something," Quinn says. "However, he didn't complete it or at least he never got to document the last pieces. We need to fill in the blanks."

Three blanks to be exact. There are three major players Cal didn't get to list. Something tells me those three names are our keys to who shot Erin and Cal as well as the person behind all that has been going on with Demaris as far as the files on that laptop are concerned.

I think if we want to find out what happened to Cal and Erin, we have to go back a little further into Demaris's case. One doesn't exist without the other.

"Whatever you boys think you have, you better make sure you can make it stick. These are not little petty criminals. If this blows up, it's going to blow up big," he warns. He draws in a deep breath. "Tell me how I can help. I'll give you everything I've got."

Danita

"Dem." It feels so good to hear my real name.

Molly's sweet giggle fills the room as I tickle her. The kids have been staying with us for the week. Tonight, us girls are making a girls' night of it while Conroy spends time up in the new room Kevin gave him. Mckenna called Alicia and invited her over too.

"This is so much fun," Molly says as I return to painting her toenails.

"It is. This is such a pretty color on you."

"Thank you," she says and wiggles her toes.

I look up at her pretty little smile. It's good to see her smiling. It's something that's missing all too often with these children, and I totally get why.

Which brings my attention to Kasey. She's sitting off by herself with her knees tugged into her chest and her cheek resting against them as she faces away from us.

"Kasey, are you okay?" Alicia asks as she lifts her head from Mckenna painting her fingernails.

When Kasey lifts her head and turns to us, her face is covered in sadness. My heart aches before she has a chance to express what's the matter. However, when she speaks, it shatters into a million pieces.

"I wish Mommy were here to have fun with us," she says softly.

"Oh, honey. I'm sure she wants to be here too, but she's getting strong so that she can hang out and do stuff with all of us," I reply.

"Right, she's getting strong for your birthday party," Mckenna adds.

This seems to tip Kasey over the edge. Her little lips start to tremble, and tears fall down her cheeks. As fast as she tries to wipe them away, more roll down her face.

"I don't want that stupid party," she sobs.

I turn to Molly and nod to let her know I'm finished with her toes and excuse myself. She returns the nod and scoots back on the couch, drawing her knees into her chest. Her smile from moments ago is now gone as she looks at her crying sister.

Standing, I go over to where Kasey has been sitting. I take a seat on the floor next to her and she throws herself into my lap, holding onto my neck tightly. I wrap my arms around her and give her a good squeeze.

"You were so excited. What happened? Uncle Kevin went to get the dress you picked out last week. Your mom and Auntie Ali have been working on all the cool stuff you wanted."

She sniffles and pulls back to look at me. "I've been waiting. I thought Daddy would be back by now. He's not. He's going to miss it. I don't want to have it without him," she says then gets up to cross the room, retrieving her tablet.

When she returns, she sits back in my lap with her back to my chest and snuggles in. Tapping the screen, she brings the device to life and starts to play a video. The YouTube video is of a little girl dressed as Belle from *Beauty and the Beast* and a man—I'm assuming to be the girl's father—dressed as the Beast.

It's the cutest, sweetest thing I've ever seen. They dance together while in the costumes. Everyone cheers them on. Tears come to my eyes as I begin to understand Kasey's point. Despite the fact that every single one of her uncles would fall over themselves to do this for her, she wants it to be her father.

I palm her forehead and kiss the top of her curls. I understand this so much. Although my brothers have asked about Kevin and my relationship, I want my father to meet him first and to get to know him.

I can only image how this little one feels. Her father is her hero, and he's not going to be there for one of the biggest moments she's been dreaming of. My throat clogs with emotion, causing me to have to clear it before I speak.

"Sweetie, if you don't want to have the party, we can talk to your mom and tell her. I'm sure she'll understand," I say and look to Alicia to make sure I'm saying the right thing.

"I know she will," Alicia reassures her.

"I want to wait for Daddy. I'm not having it without him," Kasey says.

My heart twists, shattered pieces and all. I don't have it in me to tell her that could mean she will never have a party at all. Even if he does wake, there's no telling if he'll ever be able to dress up and dance with her. Keeping that all to myself, I say a silent prayer that Cal recovers.

"Who wants hot fudge brownie sundaes?" I look up to find Kevin with his eyes on me.

I didn't hear him come in. I'd been anticipating his return. He gives me a nod and mouths, *Thank you.*

All drama is forgotten by the girls as they jump up and run into the kitchen. Still lost in my feelings, I get up to follow them. Alicia touches my hand to halt me.

"You said all the right things. You'll make a great mom someday," she whispers and winks at me.

I reach to touch her new little bump. It's so funny how fast it has popped. She gives me a gentle smile.

"I'll leave that to you for now."

She laughs and heads into the kitchen where Con and Sunny have shown up, and the girls are now giggling and laughing in the middle of a lively conversation. Kevin tugs me into his arms and plants a kiss on my lips. I smile up at him. He looks tired and annoyed.

"Meeting didn't go well?"

He kisses my lips again. "You let me worry about that. Tonight, we talk about anything but that meeting or anything that has anything to do with it."

Seeing how frustrated he looks, I don't argue. Things have been quiet for the most part. Strange things have happened, like finding one of my tires flat and that one time Sunny wouldn't stop barking while Kevin and I were having sex in the shower.

After, when I let Sunny out, it looked like the flower beds were disturbed on the side of the house. I shrugged both incidents off. Especially since the notes stopped and Harris has been keeping his distance.

I had been to the car wash before the flat; it wouldn't be the first time I've gotten a nail in a tire after that. As for the flower beds, although he hates the idea, Kevin may need to fence the front of his property. His neighbors have an annoying dog that they allow to roam the neighborhood freely. I swear, if he jumps his little ass at Sunny one more time, I'm slipping his owners in cuffs. They've been warned.

So honestly, I don't want to seem paranoid. If anything, the fact that I've been closing more cases and making more busts would piss Harris off and make him more jealous, which would have escalated the stalking behavior. It hasn't. Something has changed, but I'm still keeping an eye on him.

"Auntie Dem, can you help me make my sundae?" Kasey calls as she comes running over to us.

My mouth drops open. All the kids call Alicia, Auntie Ali. They have never referred to me as such. Kasey takes my hand and looks up at me expectantly.

Kevin chuckles then slaps my ass and kisses my temple. "Get to it, Auntie Dem. We can't keep the wee ones waiting."

"But for that, *you* will be waiting," I warn in Spanish so only he understands.

"You sound funny." Kasey giggles and squeezes my hand.

"Come, I'll teach you how to sound funny with me while we make your sundae."

"*Te amo y esperaré por siempre si es necesario,*" Kevin calls after me.

I look over my shoulder. "Yeah, babe, I love you too. We'll see about the rest."

I hope he has that kind of patience, because some days it feels like it might take forever for my life to get back in order. However, when he smiles at me the way he is now, I know I'm willing to try my hardest. Besides, Kevin speaking Spanish with a hint of his Irish accent showing is straight fire.

I know what I'm looking forward to tonight.

CHAPTER 35

TUTUS AND POINTS

Kevin

I'D BE A LIAR IF I SAID I WASN'T GRUMPY THIS MORNING. I WAS RIGHT in the middle of making Dem scream the walls down as she clawed at my back when Trent called to say Molly left her dance bag at the house when he came to pick everyone up.

Finally an empty house, and I couldn't enjoy it in peace. I can still hear Dem whispering dirty shit in my ear in Spanish. The best part was watching her eyes light up when I responded back in fluent Spanish. If I would have known how much that turns her on during sex, I would have been doing it a long time ago.

"Show him again, Ms. Shayla. You can do it, Uncle Trent." Molly giggles as she's wrapped around my brother's leg, looking up at him.

I lean into the doorjamb as the soft classical music floats toward me. I have to see this. Trent has two left feet. He couldn't dance his way out of a pop quiz and the kid is a pure genius—although I'll never tell his smart ass that.

"I thought I had it this time," Trent replies, beaming down at Molly.

"No," the pretty lass in the room says, shaking her head. "You aren't remotely close."

"Come on," Trent groans.

This causes Ms. Shayla to smile, elevating her from gorgeous to stunning. I can see why my brother is taken with her. Her brown skin isn't as dark as Dem's or Alicia's. Her complexion is much lighter. I'd say she looks like Ciara, the singer, when it comes to her shape and skin tone.

Quinn and I tend to lean toward thicker, curvier women. Trenton loves them tall and lithe on top; he'll give or take on the bottom. This time, it looks like he's taking.

Aye, she's my brother's type of bird to a tee. Smallish breasts and curvy hips, beautiful face. Her posture and frame scream dancer.

"You have to relax. You can get it," Molly coos. She moves to wrap herself around her dance instructor's leg. I notice the small stumble and wince, but the woman recovers quickly. *Interesting.* "Please, show him again, Ms. Shayla."

Ms. Shayla laughs. "Oh, all right, but I don't think it's going to help."

"You're breaking my heart. No faith in me at all."

"I'm still not convinced you're this bad. I think you're trying to get extra attention from the teacher or something," she says with that pretty smile.

"Shit, I might suck at this, but if you let me show you some of my other moves, you'll be begging for more," Trent says in that teasing tone he's known so well for.

"Oh no," Molly gasps. "Swear jar, Uncle Trent."

Trent groans and rolls his eyes. "How about we pretend that didn't happen and we cut me some slack this time? I almost went broke last week alone."

"A pact is a pact. You have to put in one dollar," Molly says firmly.

Trent sighs. "Fine, kid."

"Swear jar?" Ms. Shayla says and lifts a brow.

"I'll tell you all about it over dinner."

"Trent," she says in warning.

My brother reaches to wrap an arm around her waist to pull her closer. He splays his other hand over her belly. Leaning in to rub his nose against hers, he breathes.

"Progress. You're calling me Trent. Now we're getting somewhere. I'm wearing you down, baby. It's only a matter of time before you're dancing to my beat."

Smooth, little brother. I stifle a laugh. Trent is taking it easy on her. I know he is. I've heard some of the shit that has come out of his mouth to ensure him one night without question. This one means more to him than that and it shows.

She takes a step back. "When did you say your brother would be here?"

I push off the wall and step out of the shadow of the doorway, holding up Molly's dance bag. "I'm here."

Shayla's eyes grow wide as her gaze bounces between Trent and me. Aye, my brothers and I look a lot alike. Trenton would be my twin if not for his dark brown hair and freckles.

Again, I watch her recover, tucking away her shock quickly. She's prettier up close. Her full lips are a perfect match for her small but wide nose. Her soft features are welcoming and almost cause a man to want to be protective of her.

I can't explain that part. It's like I know she's hiding from something. I get what Trent meant that night he called me.

"Thank you, Uncle Kev," Molly sings as she hugs my legs before she takes her bag and runs off to change.

"I was expecting a class full of little ones," I say to the two before me, trying to hide my mirth.

"Molly has two private lessons a week," Trent replies.

"Is that right? When did those start?"

"Molly has great potential. I thought it would be a good idea to work some more with her. She'll take on a solo for the recital."

"Ms. Shayla, is it?"

"Yes." She sticks her hand out to shake mine.

"Nice to meet you. I've heard so much about you."

She blushes, and it's so cute. I look to Trent, and he looks like he wants to clobber me. I bite my lip to keep from laughing.

I go to continue teasing him, but my phone buzzes. When I pull it out and see it's a pic of Dem in a red panties and bra set, I forget about anything other than getting back to the house. I turn and head for the door without another word.

"Rude much," Trent calls after me.

"Aye, today I am."

CHAPTER 36

FAMILY CIRCLES

Danita

"WHAT'S ON YOUR MIND?" EMIL ASKS AS HE STARES AT ME ACROSS the table.

We're in the back room of the restaurant one of his best friends owns in New Jersey. We agreed it would be the best place to meet. Leana has been one of Emil's best friends since they were little. We trust her like family. Although, I did slip in without anyone becoming the wiser.

"A lot," I reply and massage my temples.

It's been two months since I found those files and contacted my brothers. Diego and Jo-jo had to go back to Miami, but promised they would be returning as soon as possible. Diego has also been doing some digging from his Miami office.

Kevin is salty with me because I wanted to come to this meeting with my brother without him. As I told him, I'm not ready to introduce him to my family. I want my father to meet him first, and at this point, my father still doesn't know I'm alive.

I need that time for him and my mother to adjust before I drag Kevin into the mix. First things first, we need to find out what happened. Why is someone hell-bent on making me disappear?

"I wish I had more answers. This shit has us going in circles. I don't like it. I think you should go stay with Papi in Puerto Rico while we figure this out," Emil says.

I'm already shaking my head. "I can't. I'm not running."

His eyes become near slits. I look so much like my brother, especially now that I dye my hair darker. It used to be hard to take him seriously because it was like looking in a mirror. However, in this moment, from the look he's giving me, I can't help but take him seriously.

"Why won't you allow us to pull you out? Is this about this guy you're with?"

"Emil—"

"Don't *Emil* me." He leans into the table. "This is your life. We all thought you were dead. Do you know how that felt? Me, Diego, and Jo-jo are going to do whatever we have to, to make sure you're safe and if that means sending you to Papi, that's what we'll have to do."

"I get it, but you guys have to understand that I have another life I can't just walk away from."

"Why not? If it means your safety, he should understand."

I snort. "You haven't met Kevin." The words are spoken more so under my breath.

"What's that supposed to mean?"

"It means that the man loves me enough to throw himself in front of a speeding train for me. My safety is always his first concern. I drive him crazier than I'm driving you. If he could keep me in the house in bubble wrap, he would.

"I love him too, Emil. I can't walk away and act like his feelings don't matter. It would hurt him not to be the one protecting me. He's an ex-cop that's now in private security and investigations. You, of all people, should understand how protective he can be and why leaving isn't an option," I say pleadingly.

"So, what do you plan to do when this is over?"

I look down at my hands before me. I know what my heart is telling me. Then there's my head.

"I don't know. I'm messed up in the head. Kev has started to call me

Demaris. He called my name five times the other day before I answered him. I was sitting right there, watching TV with him, and I didn't answer to my own name. I'm conflicted about a lot. Kevin wants to get married and start a family. I want those things too, but I need to search for who I am first," I say.

"I told you this life wouldn't be easy." He releases a long breath and sits back in his seat.

"Is that why you never got married?"

Something crosses his face before he looks away. "Something like that." He clears his throat. "Okay, you love old boy and you're not trying to leave him. Well, are you still feeling secure in your cover?"

I nod. "I'm handling myself, and my crazy boyfriend has someone on my ass when he's not around. I'm never uncovered."

"Okay," he says and rubs his jaw. "We're going to keep at this. Jo-jo took a leave from his job. He'll be in town soon. Diego wants to stay in Miami for now, so he can use his resources. We're going to figure this shit out, Dem."

"Anything on Vivian and how she's involved in this?"

He gets this look. "No. I didn't think Diego could focus on that. I took over, but I'm not getting anywhere there either."

"Yeah, about that. How is he holding up?"

"I don't know. He was seeing someone before your text. I think she broke things off. No telling what prompted that."

"God, why is all of this happening?"

"I don't know, *linda*."

I smile at the term of endearment. My father used to use it all the time. I look at my brother and note that he has aged a little. I wouldn't believe he's forty, but I can see he's older than when I started this case five years ago. So much time has passed, I wonder what my parents look like.

"Did…did they move to PR because of me?"

"Yes and no. Papi was ready to go home and retire. You know

Mommy. She's down for whatever Papi wants. Once they told us you were gone, the trips back and forth stopped. He couldn't take walking by your old room," he says and shrugs.

"We have to fix this. Emil?"

"Yeah."

"Eric may be gone, but his caution still resonates in my head." I lick my dry lips. "We'll give it about another month or so. If we're not any closer, I'll at least go see Papi and let this burden off his chest. He and Mommy don't deserve this."

"Good. That sounds good."

CHAPTER 37

THE HAPPIEST OF MOMENTS

Danita

"No," I cry out as I laugh and run through the house.

Kevin is hot on my heels. I slide across the foyer floor before taking off up the stairs. His heavy footfalls echo behind me.

"Demaris, I'm going to kick yer little arse."

I bark out more laughter as I race into the bedroom. I jump on the bed and run across it. Kevin skids to a stop to run over to the side I'm on. Seeing him heading for me, I roll back onto the bed to get to the other side.

An actual squeal leaves my lips when he pounces the bed, trapping me onto my back. His wet hair dripping into my face, he looks down at me. He growls at me before starting to drop rough kisses all over my face.

I can't stop laughing. This is a much-needed stress reliever. I leave for Puerto Rico in the morning. It's been a little over a month since I made Emil that promise. The trail has run cold, and we know nothing more than we did three months ago. We're still spinning in circles. As of yet, I don't feel safe enough to take this into the Bureau blindly. After all, someone has been trying to erase me.

Cal is the only one that seems to know what we're missing, and although we thought he was going to wake a few times, he still hasn't. At this point, I don't think we'll ever find the truth.

"Ya think it's funny to pour water all over me," Kevin pants against my neck.

"So…so…sorry," I stutter through my laughter.

"Ach, you're not sorry at all."

I bite my lip as I look at that sexy grin on his lips. Reaching up, I push my hand through his wet hair, and I pout. "You made me do it."

"*I* made you pour a pot of water over my head?" He gives me a pointed look.

I shrug, running my hand all the way through his hair, down the back of his neck. He searches my face, amusement still on his lips. I lift to kiss his chin.

"I asked you what you wanted to do tonight. It's not my fault you answered wrong," I taunt.

"Your response to me saying I want to fuck all night because I'm not going to see you for a week was to pour water over my head."

"Someone needed to cool you off," I say as I burst into laughter again.

The way he jumped up and over the couch was priceless. I can still see the shock on his face when he whipped his head in my direction as the water soaked him. I wish I had gotten that one on video. Con would have had a good laugh.

Kevin's eyes soften as he homes in on my face. "I love seeing you like this. I'm going to miss you."

"Aw, babe. I'm going to miss you too. It's only a week. I'll be back before you know it."

The words coming out of my mouth are true, but the fact that I've been building up a wall as this trip gets closer is also a fact. It's been the elephant in the room for the last two weeks. I have every intention of returning; it's the reality that I'll be returning to that's scary for me.

Kevin has been hinting more and more about marriage and a family. I've yet to process that I may never be able to resurrect my real life. I feel like I'm in limbo, and I don't know how to handle all of that.

He opens his mouth, but closes it again quickly. I know he wants to protest this trip for the millionth time. Well, not so much the trip, but the fact that I'm going without him.

It's the last night we'll be together for a week. I don't want to weigh it down with all of the crap we have going on. I wiggle beneath him until I can free my legs to wrap around his waist.

Closing his eyes, he places his forehead to mine. "Have you thought about what we talked about?"

I release a long breath. "Yes. I thought about it. I hear what you're saying."

"I don't have to be there for the week. I can come the last few days. You will have plenty of time for you and your family. I only want to know you're safe."

"I'm a trained FBI agent, babe. I'll be fine. Besides, you said yourself that you should be here helping Quinn figure out the case."

"Which is why if I come in at the end of the trip, it works out for everyone."

"Are you challenging my skills to protect myself?"

"Not at all, love," he breathes against my lips.

In a swift move, I flip him onto his back and straddle him. I laugh at the startled look on his face. He rolls his eyes and sits up on his elbows.

"You were saying?" I lift a brow pointedly, folding my arms across my chest.

He reaches to run a finger along my jaw. Feeling playful, I turn my head and suck his finger into my mouth. His eyes darken with lust.

"You made it clear that's not what you want tonight. Don't start something you're not in the mood to finish," he says huskily.

Pulling his finger from my mouth, I leave my lips parted as I lower his hand over my chin, down my neck, between my breasts, and into the waistband of my shorts and panties. I tilt my head to the side and bite my lip.

"Does it feel like I'm not in the mood?"

It takes only a second for him to push his fingers inside me while tugging me forward to capture my lips. He groans as I start to drip down his fingers. I was turned on when he made his earlier comment. I only poured the water on him because I thought it was funny. His words were hot but crass, and he deserved it.

I reach to place my hand over his heart to steady myself as I rock my hips. The heat from his bare skin soothes me. It would be a bold-faced lie if I said I hadn't been drooling over him as he walked about the house shirtless in a pair of sweats.

"Damn it," he hisses as both our phones ring at the same time.

I feel his frustration as I pull my phone from my bra. Climbing from his lap, I allow him to pull his phone from his pocket to answer. I watch his back longingly as he stands and walks out of the room to take his call.

"Hello," I finally answer my phone.

"Hey, you all set?" Jo-jo calls into the phone excitedly.

"My bags are packed and at the front door. Kevin is taking me to the airport in the morning."

"That's the boyfriend? Why isn't he coming?"

My brother's question stings. Why won't I let Kevin come? Because that means merging my worlds, something I'm not ready to do.

"I think I need to make this trip with family first. He can come next time."

"So what, dude ugly or something? Why you trying to hide him?"

I laugh. "Shut up, Jo-jo. He's not ugly. You're so stupid. I just don't want to add too much to the mix. Mommy and Papi are already going to be overwhelmed with me coming back from the dead."

"Okay, I can understand that, I guess. We still want to meet him, though."

"You guys will."

"Bet. Your flight is actually a connecting flight to mine and Diego's. When you land in Miami, we board."

"Awesome. I thought I was going to have to run through the airport when Diego said you guys wanted to fly with me," I reply.

"You know I had you. Emil was the only one that couldn't leave on our schedule, but he'll fly out tomorrow night. Papi is going to lose his shit. Yo, I'm so glad you're alive. It's been so hard. I think we all blamed ourselves. Seeing your face…that was… I'm glad you're okay. I love you, Demaris. Whatever you need, I'm here. You know that, right?"

"Yeah, Joaquin. I know."

"A'ight, I'm going to get my things ready. Oh, by the way, I sent something over for Emil to look at before I called. I don't want to get your hopes up, but I think I found something useful. I'll have my laptop so you can take a look tomorrow."

"That's great. I hope it's something. Do you mind if I give you Kev's brother's email? Maybe he can link it to what he's working on," I say and chew on my lip.

Once again, I've been keeping my two worlds apart. Rationally, I know they could probably work better together as one, but my brain has me convinced the two worlds shouldn't touch until I'm ready to deal with the fact that I'm feeling split in two.

"Yeah, okay. Text it to me. I'll send it over as soon as I can. I'll see you tomorrow."

"Love you, Jo-jo. See you tomorrow."

I end the call and my thoughts swirl. This trip is going to be a big deal. I'm a ghost coming back to my parents. I can't shake the eerie feeling I have about tomorrow.

Instead of dwelling on it, I get up and head for the bathroom. Tossing my phone on the counter, I look into the mirror. *What are you doing, Dem? Why won't you let him go with you?*

I quickly shut the questions down. I don't want to open that Pandora's box with everything I have going on. I push off the counter and turn from the mirror.

Stripping from my clothes, I step into the shower to wash away my wandering thoughts. I turn on the spray and let the water cascade down on me as I place my forehead against the tiles. My chest feels so tight.

I've never questioned myself more in my life. Kevin checks all the boxes. He didn't run when he found out the mess that my life has become. He has loved me through it all, and yet, I don't know what tomorrow brings and that limits how much I can freely give.

"While you're away, I need you to remember how much I love you."

A chill runs through me as he speaks the words against the back of my hair. His arms are on either side of my head as he cages me in. His presence always makes it harder to think.

When he surrounds me like this, he's all I feel, and it feels right. So, when he places a kiss on my shoulder, I know that I may keep this wall up, but I'm not going to deny him anything tonight. Not because I'm weak, but because I want to be wrapped in his comfort and that's something I need above anything else.

Kevin

I drag my hands down the tiles, not touching her, yet surrounding her. When my hands are level with her hips, I move to rest my palms against her wet, soft skin. Inhaling her hair, I remind myself that she can take care of herself and this is something that's long overdue. She needs to go see her parents.

"I know you do," she says.

There it is. That wall she's been building between us. It started slowly, but has increased over the last few days.

It's been painful to watch, but I've allowed it because I know she's struggling. She's so close to her freedom, yet so far away. It's changing her.

Sometimes I don't know whether to say the changes are because she's allowed her true self to come through or if it's the stress of it all. All I can do is observe and continue to love the woman I know, as I have this entire time. Losing her is not an option.

"Do you?" I lick her neck and slide my palm up her belly, pausing over where she would carry our child.

I want Dem swollen with my baby so much, it hurts. I want the ring I've had in my top drawer for over a month on her finger. I want her name tatted on my arm, announcing to the world the day we get married.

"Yes, you tell me all the time."

"Sometimes words are too much and sometimes they're not enough," I reply.

Kissing the back of her soaked waves, I reach for her shampoo and pour some into the palm of my hand. Once I start to massage the shampoo into her hair, she releases a moan and relaxes her shoulders.

I let my fingers do the talking, running through her strands and across her scalp. Once done, I guide her under the spray to rinse it out before putting in her conditioner and covering it with her cap. I turn her to face me, lifting her chin with my fingertips.

"Kevin—"

I shake my head to silence her and kiss her on the lips. If we talk, this uneasy feeling I have is going to cause me to say more than I know I should. She's a grown woman. I need to let her do this without coming off as an insecure asshole. She's right; she can take care of herself and her brothers will be there with her.

I duck my head to take her nipple into my mouth. This is the only language we need to use tonight. I'm going to miss her while she's gone. Like having a limb cut off.

Her soft moans spur me on. I tighten my grip on her hips. When she locks her hands in my hair, I suck harder.

Releasing the peak with a pop, I lift to my full height and push my hair out of my face. Dem places her hand in the center of my chest and pushes me against the wall outside of the spray. Gliding her hand up my chest, she keeps her eyes on me until she cups my jaw.

With her eyes still on me, she turns her back to my front. I look down at her, wondering what did I do so right that this angel walked into my life. While she leans her head back and reaches over her shoulder to caress my face, I run my fingertips from her wrist down the length of her arm, down her side, until I place my hand across her belly.

Dem lifts on her toes and our lips connect. I grasp under her chin with my free hand and devour her lips. Sucking her tongue into my mouth, I groan.

Sliding my palm down over her wet stomach, I reach for her mound and find her nub. She spreads her legs for me, and I start to bring her sweet pussy the pleasure it deserves. Breaking the kiss, I place my forehead to hers and continue to stroke her center.

I move my other hand to her breast and begin to roll her nipple between my fingers. In no time, I have her panting and coming for me. The beautiful expression on her face begs me to do it all over again.

Although, she ends up having other plans. Dem reaches for the glass jar of condoms we keep in here and plucks a foil packet out. I shake my head at her and grin, but I cover her hand with mine and bring it to my lips to bite into the pack. Her amber eyes light with lust and amusement.

I take the condom from the foil wrapper and slip it on. With a slow caress of her sides and hips, I watch her pant for me. I kiss her lips and caress her cheek.

She wraps her hand around my shaft, and I hold my breath as she backs up onto me. I can't help clenching my teeth as I enter her. It's like entering heaven every time.

We set an easy pace. Not too fast, but right for the depth of emotions surging between us. Our eyes say all that we don't. Her lips part as she looks up at me. I band my arms around her, rocking my body into her gently.

I imagine this will be what it is like to make love to her as my wife one of these days. In this moment, I make a vow that I'll die before I live on this earth without her. A week apart will feel like an eternity. I miss her already, and she hasn't left yet.

"Ah," the sound leaves her lips as she bathes my balls in her essence.

Widening my stance and leaning back against the wall, I release her to push her forward. That arch in her back is a gorgeous sight. I can't stop watching my hands dance across her skin. She throws her hips back as I thrust deep inside her.

Not able to hold back any longer, I grasp her hips and start to pound into her. The chatter of her teeth makes me grin. I bite my lip and bend my knees. The shift in angle tears a cry from her lips.

Her legs start to shake. I can feel my own release tingling in the base of my spine. My eyes cross as I release into the barrier between us.

I pull her back to my front and wrap my arms around her once more. Burying my face in the cap on her head, I smile. One of these days, there will be no barriers between us. I will be bare to her, and she'll be bare to me. No walls, no secrets, nothing that can hold us apart.

"I love you, Kev."

"I love you too."

CHAPTER 38

BREAKTHROUGH

Kevin

"The flight has been delayed," she says into the phone.

The noisy background makes me close my eyes to picture her in the airport. Her face had been glowing when I'd dropped her off for her flight. Those amber-brown eyes had sparkled up at me as I'd held her for one last embrace.

When I open my eyes, frustration fills me as I find myself standing in my bedroom alone. "I wish you would have allowed me to come with you."

She sighs. "We covered all this last night. I've been missing in action for five years. I think I should let them see me first before I introduce you. It's only fair."

"Fair to who? You can only make so many excuses, Dem. Commit. It's not that hard."

"Wait, where's this coming from?"

"You knew how I felt before you left. I wanted to go with you. If for no other reason than to make sure you're safe," I grumble.

"I'll be fine. I can take care of myself."

I roll my eyes and clench my fist. "It's not about if you can take care of yourself. I wanted—Why are you so stubborn?"

She laughs. "What happened to accepting me as I am?"

I snort. "I've accepted you as ya are. I've accepted a lot. All I want to know is what exactly are ya asking me to accept this time?"

I grind my teeth, knowing I've shifted the tone of the call. It's like I've turned on a vacuum and sucked the air out of the atmosphere. Too late to take it back. I brace for her response.

"What's that supposed to mean?"

"Exactly what I said. What am I to ya? Where do ya see this going?"

"Kevin, don't do this now."

I grunt, doing my best to reel in my frustration. Knowing that Quinn planned to propose to Alicia today has me in my emotions. My brother is moving forward with his life, something I'd like to do as well. I'm not getting any younger at thirty-four, going on thirty-five soon.

I know all the reasons why we're standing still in this relationship, but for some reason, I can't keep my mouth shut and call on the patience I've built to be with her. It's like the switch has been flipped and I can't turn it back. The anxiety that has been riding me gets the best of me.

"Why is yer guard always up with me? Why can't ya answer the questions?"

"Because I'm not ready," she yells back.

I rock back on my heels as I stand in my bedroom, staring at the bed we shared last night. The same bed I held her in as her laughter filled the air. I close my eyes.

"Will ya ever be ready? Or am I wasting my time?" The words are harsh, and I want to take them back the moment I set them free.

"Fuck you, Kevin."

My eyes fly open. I should have kept my mouth shut. I know I should end the call, but I can't put the brakes on the train wreck coming out of my lips.

"No, I've had enough of ya doing that. I want more. I'm not going to allow this wall ya keep trying to place between us.

"One minute I know yer with me, and the next I feel like I'm on the outside looking in. What would have been so bad about yer family meeting me? Ya've met mine.

"Damn it, baby. They've taken ya in as one of their own. If we can't get through simple shit like this, how are we supposed to move any further?" I say in frustration.

"Your family took in a lie. Everything they know about me, everything you know about me, lies."

"That's a fib and ya know it. I know ya. I know ya better than ya know yerself sometimes."

"What do you want from me?" she snarls. "You have me in the middle of a crowded airport looking like a crazy person. If you have to have this conversation now, tell me what you want."

"I want *you*."

"You have me."

I shake my head as a sorrow—so unfathomable I feel it in my bones—takes over me. I'm not sure where all this is coming from, but the feelings run deep. They cut deep and have already started to fester. I inhale, trying to ground myself.

"No, no, I don't. I want you to dig past all the bullshit to us. From the first time we met, there was something there, something more than the lies you had to tell. We have never been a part of the lies—"

"Oh, yes. Yes, we have. That's what you don't see. We have."

"No, we haven't. I know we haven't. Think back to the beginning. Back to us."

"I'm doing the best I can, Kevin," she murmurs. "This isn't easy for me. I'm trying to find my truth again. You fall somewhere in the center of all that. You know how I feel about you. I don't know what to say."

"From the beginning ya asked me to trust ya, and I have." I fall into my accent once again—this time much thicker—as my emotions get the best of me. "Ya took my heart, love. I'm not asking for it back. I'm asking ya to take care with it."

"You're asking me to rush something that I can't," she protests.

"No, I'm not. I'm asking ya to try. Stop waiting for a conclusion before we start our future. I'm telling ya that I'm here to help you find what's missing. Even if that means I have to find ya in all that ya've wrapped yerself in. Yer not alone. Ya don't have to go this alone."

There's a pause on the other end. Her stubbornness is one of the things I love about her, but it's also what keeps me outside looking in so often. I get it. She's had to be guarded to stay alive, but this is different. This is us.

"They're boarding the plane," she says.

I shake my head. The conversation wasn't what I intended. Too much on my mind and the frustration of her being away from me with so many unknowns still lingering over us, I pushed things too far. "Look, enjoy your trip. Check in when you get settled."

Danita

"Yeah, right," I say into the phone and hang up.

Last night was so perfect. Only a few hours ago he held me in his arms for one last embrace. Looking up into his green eyes, I had no questions as to whether or not I would be returning to him.

My phone rings and hope blooms. I don't want to get on this flight leaving things the way they are. There's so much more I need to say to Kevin.

However, the name on the screen isn't his. I bite back the tears and answer before my brother hangs up. I lied to Kevin; that wasn't my flight that was being called. I just couldn't fight with him a second more.

"Hey," I say into the phone as chipper as I can.

"*Los tenemos ya*! We got it, *Cariño*! Jo-jo is brilliant. I'm going to kiss him when I see him."

I gasp and grasp at my stomach. "Are you sure?"

"Yeah, this is it. I know it in my bones. I'm sending over the file to the email you gave him last night."

I roll my eyes. I should have known Jo-jo would send Quinn's email through to Emilio first. It doesn't matter. All that matters is that I'm going to get my life back.

Emil continues when I can't find the words to say. "This is only a lead, but this is the right lead. I'm shoring it up as we speak."

"Can you get me the other three names?"

He releases a breath. "Ay, mama. That part we may need to let go. I can get you home, but I can't promise that case."

I close my eyes. That's good enough. There's a chance I'll end up with a target on my back, but for now, I'm going to take it. It's time for this phoenix to rise. Maybe I can cover more ground once I'm brought back to life.

"Emil. Can you call Diego and Jo-jo? Tell them I'm not getting on this flight. I have to finish this. I'll meet you at the spot, how soon can you get there?"

"It'll have to be a few hours. I'll make that call."

"Thanks."

I cut the call and make quick work of getting to the baggage claim desk to try to reclaim my bag. Luck is on my side, the girl behind the desk tells me she will have it retrieved and brought to the desk. Usually they will tell you they don't have enough staff to get your bags right away.

"Excuse me."

"Yes, ma'am?" the clerk responds.

"I'm going to run to the restroom. I'll be right back."

"No problem. I'll be on the lookout for your luggage. If it gets here before you get back, I'll hold onto it."

"Thank you," I say and give her a smile.

I make my way to the bathroom, debating calling Kevin. I know he's pissed. I chew on my lip, staring at my phone.

When I go to hit the call button, movement out the corner of my eye catches my attention. I look up to see a guy with a TSA uniform on, not the airport's usual maintenance and service crew uniform, and a black mask over his face, standing in the restroom with me. It's pretty early and the airport hasn't starting buzzing with a lot of traffic yet, so there's no one in the bathroom but us as far as I can tell.

No matter. I slip my phone in my pocket and take my bag off my shoulder to grasp it in my hand as a weapon. I'm not going down without a fight. He has height and weight on me, but I'm not going to make this easy.

"I don't know who you are, but you walked into the wrong bathroom today."

He snorts and charges me. I swing my bag at his head. The e-reader and all my snacks add enough weight to pack a punch, and it does.

His head snaps to the side and he stumbles. I give a vicious grin and dance back away from him. "Ow, that's going to leave a mark," I taunt.

"Bitch," he snarls as he covers his face and spits out blood.

"Oh, your mother didn't teach you any manners. Let me help you with that."

I jump up and toss a kick, catching him right under the chin. His head jerks back and he loses his footing. Seeing that the strap on my bag has broken, I drop it and ball my fist.

He gets to his feet and rushes me, causing me to move quickly to dodge him, switching positions with him. I go on full attack. Throwing a three-punch combination, I end it with an upper cut.

Not giving him time to recover, I lunge at him and grasp the back of his head. Pivoting slightly, I use my momentum to turn and slam his head down on the countertop. He flails an arm to his side to reach for me as he cries out in pain.

"Who's the bitch now, asshole?"

He turns to me slowly, seeming to shake off his daze. Despite the mask, I note the smile that comes to his face. I know then and there, I've made a mistake. I turn my gaze to the mirror, he was only a diversion. As the realization hits, strong arms wrap around my shoulders, and something pricks me in the neck.

I struggle against the hold even as my vision turns blurry and I start to fade. I'm fighting, but I don't think my limbs are moving any-more. It's a battle I'm having in my head.

At least, it is until it all goes black.

Kevin

"Tell me everything ya know," Quinn says gruffly.

I'm pacing the living room as he walks into my home. My head hurts from tugging at my hair. Still no word from Dem.

"Her flight to Miami should have landed in Puerto Rico by now. Last I checked, the delay wasn't long enough to prevent the connec-tion flight. Her brothers should have been on the plane with her, and they should have made it to their final destination," I reply.

Quinn nods and takes his phone out. I watch as he frowns down at the device. He lifts his green eyes to mine.

"Do you know an Emilio Mercado?"

"That's one of Dem's brothers. The oldest one, I think," I reply.

He turns his attention back to his phone at the same time the doorbell rings. My brows wrinkle. I only called Quinn; I'm not expecting anyone else.

I rush to the front door. Maybe Dem decided to come back. When I open the door, Detective Reed is standing on the other side. Her face is panicked, and she has blood on the front of her shirt.

"You have to help me. I didn't know where else to take him," she says in a rush.

"Take who?"

"Harris. He was beaten so badly when I found him. He's breathing so shallow now. Please, you have to help me."

Tears start to fall from her eyes. I'm confused as fuck as to why she'd bring him here of all places. However, Quinn and I follow her out to her car. Sure enough, Harris is in the back seat of her vehicle, looking like someone tried to beat the life out of him.

"What the fuck?" I say as I open the door and check his vitals.

"I know you guys know people. He needs a doc."

"Why didn't you take him to a hospital?" Quinn asks.

Reed runs a hand through her hair. She looks around nervously. It only takes a second before she makes a decision.

"If I take him to a hospital, they'll make sure he dies. They won't help him. The Knights of Justice will finish him. He's a traitor to them now," she says.

I rock back on my heels. "What exactly are you saying?"

"We should get him inside. I promise to tell you everything you need to know if you get him inside and help us."

"Maureen," Harris groans.

"I have to do this, Orin. Enough is enough. They'll probably come after me next anyway," Reed says, her eyes wide and fearful.

"Ach, let's get him inside. I want to hear what the lass has to say," Quinn says, reaching to pull Harris out of the car.

We work together to get Harris into the house. He's no help at all. From a once-over, I'd say his arm is broken and maybe even a leg.

We get him onto my couch, and Quinn puts in the call to get him some help. I may not like Orin, but this is hard to see. The entire left side of his face is nearly black and blue. His lip is busted, and his right eye is sealed shut.

He licks his chapped lips. "You have to get to Danita. She's not safe," he pushes out hoarsely.

From his labored speech and the way he's cradling his side with his good arm, I believe he may have a broken rib or two. However, I can't focus much on anything else once Dem's name leaves his mouth. I ball my fists and glare at Reed.

"Ya said ya can explain. Ya best get to talking."

"Orin figured out she was the FBI agent sent after he blew the whistle on the ring. The Knights of Justice serve no justice. They take and they ruin great cops. They bully us into doing what they want, even if we don't want any part of it.

"Orin was tired of it. He thought moving up the ranks would get him in close enough to bring them down. He made a call to the FBI. It took some time, but he figured out that Detective Moralez was the one. He's been trying to protect her since—"

"You're shitting me, right?" I scoff.

"Orin isn't the dick everyone thinks he is. It's an act for the most part. He knew no one would suspect him as the whistleblower if he maintained his role in the ring, and the bigger ass he was to Moralez, the less anyone would suspect.

"They wanted to recruit her, but he put a stop to it. We couldn't figure out what changed, why she hadn't shut them down. Not until after Cal was shot and she started seeing you…then Orin stumbled onto something.

"There's this guy. We've been answering to him for years. Suddenly, he's gone and this new dude shows up. He had Orin doing some crazy shit, like he wanted him to prove his loyalty. Then, we found out they were trying to frame Orin for the entire ring," she explains.

"Well, what happened to him?" I ask, nodding at Harris.

"Today, I went to his place because I hadn't heard from him and he didn't answer any of my texts." She covers her mouth as a sob escapes. "I found him in his garage, beaten like this. Those bastards meant to kill him. I'll name every single one of them. Moralez can have anything she needs," she says heatedly.

"The doc is on the way. You hang in there, Harris," Quinn says.

Harris groans, letting us know he's still breathing. I think back to how Harris was always up Dem's ass. I glare at Reed to see if she's telling the truth.

"Listen, I know what you're thinking. Orin gave Moralez a lot of shit, but it was an act. He was trying to get close to her to keep an eye on her. We've been dating secretly for the last three years. They hate for recruiters to sleep with the recruits," Reed explains.

"Which makes ya the recruit?" Quinn asks.

"Yes. Orin has been a recruiter for a long time. It's a long story; he can tell you better than I can. He shuts down about it," she says.

I go to ask another question that's been rolling through my head, but the doorbell rings again. I look at Quinn, then at Reed and Harris. These two may have brought this shit to my door.

With a grunt, I turn to get my gun before I head to answer my front door. When I look out of the glass panel, I find three very angry-looking versions of Dem. Tucking my gun in the back of my waist-band, I open the door.

"You Kevin Blackhart?" the tallest one says. If I remember right, he's Jo-jo.

"Aye, that would be me."

The one I remember to be Diego from the conversation in the lobby of the hotel snorts as he travels his eyes over me appraisingly, then looks at the flag hanging on my porch. "Only Dem. Some Irish cat. Is she serious?"

"Right now, he could be a purple panther from Mars, and I wouldn't give a fuck. All I want to know is have you seen our sister? Is she here, bro?"

My heart sinks to my feet. Just as I feared, she's missing. I knew it in my bones.

"I haven't seen her since I dropped her off at the airport. I thought she would be in Puerto Rico by now."

"I've called Shane and Trent. Now it all makes sense. I didn't see this file ya sent me until now. Kevin, you're not going to believe this," Quinn says from behind me.

"Just tell me you know how to find her."

"No, but we will."

CHAPTER 39

RUNNING OUT OF TIME

Danita

I LOOK AROUND ME AS MY HEART POUNDS. ELECTRIC WIRES ARE woven above my head like a ceiling that sparks in an evil threat as the rising water beneath me slowly soaks through the bottom of my jeans. It hasn't risen high enough for me to fear yet, but I face another evil as I sit in this darkened space.

I move away from the wall I've been propped against. The hissing of the live wires causes me to jump. My breathing increases as I take in the small vault-like space and the restraints that keep me from moving too far, not that there's much space for me to.

My wrists and ankles are chained. There's about twelve feet between me and the wired ceiling. Taking another look around, my eyes begin to adjust to the dim lighting. I turn left and come face-to-face with a glass panel. Almost like a long picture window. There's a chair on the other side as if someone plans to sit and watch me in here.

"Hello," I call out. "Somebody."

I'm greeted by nothing but the hollow echo of my own voice. Sweat beads down the side of my temple. I don't know how long I've been in here.

Suddenly, as if my thoughts are heard, the sound of a clock ticking fills the air. I squint my eyes to look through the glass. There's a clock on the wall outside with red numbers ticking down as if to taunt me.

Pushing through the fog in my brain, I try my best to remember how I got here. Nothing comes to me. All I can remember is the fight I had with Kevin.

Kevin.

My heart aches and tears burn my eyes and nostrils. That can't be the last time I ever get to speak to him. I said things I didn't mean. I understand his frustration. I can't blame him. I know the part I play in it.

He wants to get married and have a family. No matter how hard I fight him on it all, I want that too. However, it's not that easy.

His questions weren't unreasonable, even if his timing sucked. I was wrong. I know I was. I knew how much he wanted to make the trip with me, but I couldn't do it. Now, I don't think I'll ever get to tell him I was wrong.

The irony is I'm finally getting my life back. No…I have more than my old life. I've found something I never thought was for me. I thought I was the one that would destroy it all with the walls I started to build, but someone else is out to take it from me.

Who?

"Hello. Anyone out there?"

The wires stop hissing as if someone has shut them off. My teeth start to chatter as the chill in the tight space permeates through me. I close my eyes and tighten my fists at my sides. Fury builds inside me as I tug at the chains. More than five years undercover. I lost my entire identity, but I survived.

I'm not giving up now. This can't be the end. I have unfinished business outside of these walls.

"Kevin, if I ever needed you to find me, it's now," I whisper. "Keep your promise."

Kevin's words play in my head. *Think back to the beginning. Back to us.*

Suddenly, memories flood my brain, it all starts to come back to me. Emil's call, baggage claim, going to the bathroom, and that guy. I should have torn his mask off.

I have to stay calm, not an easy task as the water seems to be rising more rapidly in this tiny space. I try to stand to gauge how deep the water is. Sitting isn't going to help as the water is now at my waist in a seated position.

As I thought, it's at my lower calf. Spinning in a circle, I search for an exit or something to help me break through the glass. Of course, I find nothing.

Nevertheless, I walk up to the glass and start to pound on it. It's thick. The sound of the chains clinking against it confirm what my eyes and hands can tell. Not that I expected anything less.

As if to taunt me, the water seems to slow once again. I start to wonder if it's on a timer or if I'm being watched and the watcher is controlling both the flow of water and the wires above my head. As that thought enters my mind, I start to look around for signs of cameras.

I find nothing. Right when I go to turn to feel across the walls for a hidden exit, a figure appears from out of the shadows. Pressing closer to the glass, I squint my eyes. I want to see the face of the bastard I plan to destroy when I find my way out of here.

"Who are you?" I snarl and bang on the glass when they stop right outside of my sight.

The lights come on in the other room, blinding me for a moment. I blink, waiting for my eyes to adjust. When they finally do, I take a step back.

My mouth runs dry, and the small room seems to get smaller. My brain is twisted and confused, tripping over itself for a logical answer. If I can be seen through this glass, I'm sure the shock and surprise are written all over my face.

"Hello, Demaris," he snorts. "Or should I say Detective Moralez? Being as I made sure Demaris Mercado will never see the light of day again."

"Eric?" I breathe when my brain snaps back into action. "What the fuck is this bullshit about? Let me out of here."

He tips his head to the side, looking like a deranged lunatic. "You know, this is how it's always been. Me looking in on you." He drops his gaze to my heaving breasts. "Wanting, desiring, but you don't see me until extreme measures are taken.

"Hell. You didn't give a single thought to my warnings. Or was it that you couldn't care less? No, no, I know exactly what it was. You didn't see it was me. You thought it was that idiot snitch that was chasing behind you like a puppy," he grits out.

The aggression rolling off him is strong. It takes me a few seconds to follow him. When it clicks, ice runs through my veins.

"The notes were you?"

"Ding dong, sweetheart. You know, I had such high hopes for you. That is before you became a whore. Dangle a little dick in your face, and you become a complete nitwit."

"Fuck you, Eric."

He licks his lips. "I wish. It was the plan until you started letting that live Ken doll put his hands all over what's mine. Do you know I was still going to let you live? I love you that much, baby.

"I was going to walk away and leave you to think about your actions while stuck in a life I knew you didn't want. That was going to be your punishment, but no, you and that rent-a-cop started getting too close," he seethes.

"Rent-a-cop?"

"That idiot Kelley. He turned out to be a real problem. The boss wanted him dead, but I had covered you. Always doing my part. I've been covering your ass for five years, and this is how you repay me. So disloyal.

"I should've killed Blackhart when he first entered the picture. I had planned to, but someone in the Bureau stumbled across our trail. I had to make us disappear. I went through so much work so we could be together. You couldn't wait for me though, could you?"

"What the hell are you talking about?"

"I've been in love with you from day one. You smiled at me your first day in the elevator and I knew. You were the one. Smart, gorgeous, so damn talented. I risked it all. Everything I did was for you. *Everything*," he bellows.

He pushes his hands in his hair and starts to pace. I've never seen him like this. Eric has always been sweet to me. Mostly mild-mannered. Although, now that I think of it, he was kind of high strung when he moved me to the new apartment right before he disappeared.

This time, I tilt my head as I peer at him through the glass. He seems to have bulked up since I last saw him. He isn't wearing his glasses either.

Stress lines his face, and he looks like he hasn't been sleeping much on top of the crazed look in his eyes. It's clear the hinges have come loose. This isn't the Eric I knew. Which leads me to wonder, did I know him at all?

That clock is still ticking on the wall. The water is steadily rising around me. I try to think fast to get myself out of this.

"What exactly do you mean by everything?"

He turns and narrows his eyes on me. "Do you know how long I waited to find a case I could get you on? A case that I could use to get closer to you. Then the call came in trying to topple over the Knights. I was going to squash it like all the others, but it got past me, and they mentioned sending you in."

He licks his bottom lip as he snarls. "That bitch almost ruined everything. Always in your fucking business, blocking your assignments to *keep you safe*." He makes air quotes. "She called herself, looking out for you. Whore just wanted your brother's attention if you ask me."

I compress my face until it dawns on me who he's talking about. My stomach churns with grief. Vivian… Could he have been behind her disappearance?

Things never made sense with the way she vanished. We were all in shock when we were told there was no foul play. As if Viv would just up and leave.

I didn't believe it until her diary appeared in my mailbox. It was her writing. We verified that. In her last entry, she said not to look for her. She wanted a new life. Her last message was to me.

Be strong, Dem. The world needs more agents like you. Some people are made for this life and you are one of them. Take them by storm.

I remember reading her words with tears in my eyes. The next morning, I was assigned to this case. I took it in honor of her. I wanted to make her proud.

"What did you do?"

"I did what was necessary for us to be together. You're the one that ruined that," he bellows. "I've been a part of the Knights for years. I was trusted, I had respect. I never should've risked that to chase after an ungrateful whore like you. I let you get too close. You were better than I thought. I never thought you'd start to figure things out as fast as you were," he seethes.

"What?"

"You weren't supposed to figure the ring out. Once I realized you were onto it, I tried to turn your attention to Harris. I knew in my soul he was a trader. I didn't know he was the whistleblower then, but I knew I couldn't trust him," he replies. "I was going to let him take the fall back then."

"Unbelievable."

He frowns as if he's perplexed. "You know, I still haven't figured out who was on to us. I buried your case as soon as I got you onto the force. Killing us both was my plan B. It was the beginning of the end, you know. I never should have gone that route."

He turns to me, and his face fills with hurt and rage. I don't know how I missed this. I would never have pegged Eric for being this crazy.

"You let him touch you, baby. Why? Why would you do that to us? I was on my way back as soon as things calmed down. Viv meant nothing. I used her to—"

"Let me out." I bang at the window. "Let me out of here."

I'm going to kill him with my bare hands. I keep hitting the glass, ignoring the burn in my hands and arms. Vivian was my best friend growing up. We did everything together. She was like a big sister to me.

"I can't do that. I have to erase you all. The Knights need to come first this time. I need to get their trust back. It's bigger than us. You know too much. I have to fix this mess I allowed to happen."

"When I get out of here, because I promise you I am, I'm going to rip you apart and I'll do my time with a smile on my face. They can throw me under the jail as long as I make you pay," I hiss.

He walks over to the wall and hits a button on the panel I can now see with the lights on. The water starts to rush into the tight space faster and the wires come back to life. In no time, the water is up to my chest.

"Big threats from a trapped slut. I told you, he would never be able to save you."

"Don't worry about who will save me, Eric. You worry about who will save your soul, you sick bastard."

CHAPTER 40

FOUND HER

Kevin

"WE'RE ALL HERE," TRENT SAYS AS THE LAST CAR ARRIVES.

Shane located Dem's phone pinging off a cellphone tower in Farmingdale, around the area of Republic Airport, a small private airport. It seems they dumped her bag and her phone, but weren't smart enough to do it before getting near their final location. I'm thanking God for that one.

It was the start we needed, even though we were at a dead end. At least, we were until Reed offered up a lead. Stevens. He fucking hates the Knights of Justice.

They've been forcing him into their ranks all this time. A few calls, and Stevens was able to get us to a location. He has led us straight to this place. There are tons of these old lab/office buildings around here.

If not for Stevens and Reed, we never would have found Dem this fast. What's disappointing is finding one of my old squad members banged up like he met with a Mack truck, standing watch outside this place. Jennings was one of the good guys before I left. I get the feeling that whatever happened to his face is going to piss me off—and not in his favor.

"It's a small crew, but they're armed," Emil says.

"So are we," I say tightly.

"Yeah, but we're not all in our jurisdiction," Jo-jo says.

"You leave the red tape to me," Dugan replies. "Let's get that girl out of there."

The moment Quinn called Dugan for a few favors in case we have to get down and dirty, Dugan insisted he wanted to be here himself. I think he understood from Quinn's voice how important Dem is to me. That, and he's been waiting to find closure for his precinct, and this might just be it.

"Guys," Shane calls from his perch in the back seat of the SUV with his laptop in his lap. "I think you're going to want to see this."

I walk over to Shane along with Dem's brothers. I know something is wrong when I see the three stiffen as soon as they peer at the scene. When I get a glance, my brows shoot into my hairline.

A fragile figure comes up lying on a cot. She's too thin to be Dem. This woman looks emaciated. Her clothing too big for her frame. She stares at the camera as if she knows she's being watched.

"You guys know her?"

"That's Viv," Diego chokes out. "That's fucking Vivian. I'm going to kill those sons of bitches."

"Calm down, Dee. We need to get her and Dem out of there," Emilio says with a more level voice than his expression belies.

Shane turns the laptop back to himself and hits a few keys. "Fuck. Let's go. We need to move in now," he exclaims, then turns the screen toward us again.

Rage moves through me as Dem comes onto the screen in a room rapidly filling with water. Some type of sparks are going off around her. She's moving closer to the sparks as the water rises.

"Let's move," I bark.

Danita

I'm running out of give on the chains around my ankles, and I'm getting too close to the wires to keep my head above water. I try not to panic. I don't feel like dying today, so I'm going to figure a way out.

"God help me," I say before I draw in a deep breath and dive under water.

I swim toward the glass and bang at it. Eric stands there with his arms folded over his chest as he watches me. Something over his shoulder catches his attention, and he leaves the viewing room.

This is a waste of time. I push up and cautiously break through the surface to take a gulp of air. It looks like this will be the last one I'll be able to take. The wires are now too close.

Diving down once again, I look for a way out. I feel at the walls, hoping to find some latch or something. I refuse to lose hope. This is not how I die.

Kevin

Diego and I find the hallway Shane directs us to. Both Demaris and Vivian are in the same corridor. I nod Diego right and take the left. Gunfire can be heard in the distance behind us.

"Third door down on yer left, Kev," Shane says in my ear.

I keep moving, needing to get to that room before she drowns. I'm a few steps away from the door when it opens and a guy steps out. He looks somewhat familiar.

I squint and it clicks. He was the new tenant that took over Dem's apartment when I returned from my trip two years ago. His glasses are missing. I remember him being talkative. He had said he'd moved in a few days before after moving here from Boston.

"Good, I can kill two birds with one stone," he says with a sinister smile on his lips.

"Move before I put a bullet between yer eyes."

Before I have a chance to react, he charges me, knocks my gun from my hands. I don't let it faze me. I want to beat the shit out of him as it is.

I throw a right hook at his face. His head snaps to the side, but he's quick to recover. He returns the punch, but I block it. He's fast to counter, catching me in the ribs.

I grind my teeth against the sharp pain, but throw a combination, hitting him in the jaw, his right side and then his temple. He stumbles back and shakes it off. I don't give him time to recover. I plant my boot in the center of his chest.

He flies back and lands on the floor. I go to stomp him, but he rolls out of the way. Instead, I wrap my arms around his neck and put him in a choke hold. Flipping onto my back, I wrap my legs around him and initiate a sleeper hold.

He claws at my arms. "Let…me…go," he gasps out.

"Fuck you," I snarl.

"She's…going to…die." I turn my head and I have a full view of the room and the glass Dem is behind. We lock eyes as she bangs at the glass.

"Fuck," I roar. My hold loosens slightly.

"You want to save her or waste time with me," he taunts.

I bring an elbow down on his head, knocking him out. Tossing him out of my hold, I get to my feet and grab my gun. Rushing to the room, I look for a way to get her out.

Dem's eyes widen as she points to the wall behind me. I turn to see the panel there. Not wasting another moment, I move to the panel and find the cutoff for the water. I shut it down and try to figure out how to get the water to rescind or a way to get into that room she's locked in.

I start to press buttons, looking over my shoulder to see what they trigger. The first one releases the chains at her ankles, allowing her to kick more freely. I press the one next to that and her wrists are free. Next, I find the shut off for the wires above her, but that's about it.

There are no other buttons on the panel that are useful. I growl in annoyance. Pulling my gun from its hustler, I turn back to the glass. I start to wave her from the barrier.

"Baby, move. Get back," I yell.

Understanding what I intend to do, she nods and swims away from the glass and up toward the surface above her. I aim low and fire. I shoot two more rounds, making a triangle.

Water leaks forward in little streams. I holster my gun and grab the metal chair that's sitting in the middle of the room. With all my might, I swing at the glass. The spiderweb cracks from my shots spread a bit, but not enough.

I swing again, and this time the entire glass panel shatters. Water rushes forward, knocking me on my ass. The feeling of pieces of glass cutting into my skin registers in the back of my mind, but my focus is the body that floats through the opening.

I get to my feet and run toward her as fast as I can, scooping her into my arms. Her body shivers as I hold her close. It's never felt so good to have her in my embrace.

"Are you okay? Are you hurt?"

"I'm okay. Where's that bastard?"

"Outside. We'll take care of him." I stand back to look her over. "You're cut."

She looks down at her arm. "It's a little gash. I'll survive."

I frown, but take her hand and lead her out of the room. I freeze when we step out, and he's gone. Diego and Jo-jo are at the other end of the hall. Diego has the frail woman in his arms.

Dem gasps and covers her mouth with her hand. "Is that Viv?" she says with a sob in her throat.

"Come on," I say tightly. "We need to get you both seen."

"Where is he?" she hisses.

"I don't know, baby. Hopefully, one of the others cut him off before he got away. I care more about getting you to a doctor for that cut."

"Damn it!"

I turn and cup her face, placing a kiss to her lips. "We know who we're looking for. We'll find him if he got away. We know a hell of a lot more. Let's get you patched up so we can set you free and start to plan our future."

She melts into my arms, wrapping hers around my waist. I bury my face into her wet hair. Dem places her cheek against my soaked shirt and locks her fingers in the back.

"I'm sorry. For everything I said and for putting up a wall. I love you, Kevin. I'm committed. I want to do this with you. When I go to see my parents, I want you with me," she says in a whisper.

"I'll be wherever you need me, love. I'm so sorry for pressuring you. We can move on your time."

She lifts her head and looks into my eyes. "No one knows me better than you. You know when to push, and you're never wrong to. I'm with you, Kev. Never be afraid to give me a shove when I need it," she says.

I lean in and kiss her soft lips. For today, I only want to hold her. Tomorrow, we can think about the rest.

"I love you," I say against her mouth.

CHAPTER 41

LIFE'S FULL OF SURPRISES

Kevin

"Babe, you want a beer?" Dem calls from the kitchen.

"Aye. Thanks, love."

I wipe my sweaty palms on my lap for the millionth time. I've never been this nervous in my life. Shane better have done this right. I sit on the couch waiting for Dem to join me with the popcorn.

We're supposed to be binge-watching our shows, but I have a surprise for her. Things have settled as much as we could have expected in the last few weeks. Eric Myerson was able to get away, but we haven't given up.

"Ugh, I'm coming. Mommy keeps texting me." She laughs happily.

"Take your time."

This has been the norm lately. It's a long time coming. I don't mind it at all.

Demaris was debriefed, her identity was reinstated, and she is still active as an agent. Quinn and Diego made sure of that after pulling some strings. Although the case she was supposed to be on was sealed and tucked away almost immediately.

As far as the FBI is concerned, Dem was on a case that didn't exist, and Myerson misled her the entire time. We know it's bullshit, but Dem hasn't let on that she knows. My woman is smart; she never turned over that laptop or Cal's files. They don't know any of it exists. We plan to find the other three names that complete Cal's bracket of filth, and we'll shut down the Knights of Justice once and for all.

However, what has been the greatest outcome was watching Demaris reunite with her parents. It was emotional for everyone. I was there for her, and her family welcomed me with open arms.

Instead of going to Puerto Rico, her parents came to New York after learning that Vivian was found. Dem's brothers held off telling them that Demaris was alive and well. I will remember that day for the rest of my life.

The relief on my woman's face nearly brought me to my knees. She's happy now. Does she struggle sometimes? Yes, but I'm always here to comfort her through it and remind her that she's loved no matter who she is or what she does.

"What are we watching?" Dem asks as she comes over and places the beers on the coffee table and takes a seat beside me.

"It's something new I want to start," I reply.

"Cool. Hey, I meant to ask, did you hear any more from Reed? How's Harris doing?"

I shrug. "He's healing. It will take some time before he can walk on that leg, but he'll be fine."

She chuckles. "Are you ever going to tell me why you hate him so much? I mean, I had my reasons, but what are yours?"

"He's an asshole." I shrug. "Remember Evelyn?"

She pulls a sour face. "Yeah."

"She and Orin almost had a thing behind my back when I was on the force. He claims he didn't know, and I know that was her way to get attention from me, but I wasn't having it either way."

"Seriously?" she says with wide eyes.

"Harris is arrogant with an ego. Evelyn knows how to stroke that type of thing to get what she wants. He may not have known she was with me in the beginning, but he knew at some point. That made it more exciting for him."

"I can see that." She laughs, placing the popcorn in my lap and snuggling into my side. "Okay, I'm ready. Let the watching begin," she sings, digging into the bowl to pop some of the popcorn into her mouth.

I reach for her face and turn it up so I can kiss her lips. "I love you."

"I love you too, but we're watching this show. We can get naughty later."

I laugh and rub my nose against hers. She has no idea. Nothing can keep me from watching this. Nothing.

Danita

Kevin has been acting a little weird all day. I look into his green eyes and search for what could be going on in his head. He schools his expression and reaches for the remote beside him to start our show.

"I hope this one is good. You picked duds the last couple of shows we watched," I tease.

He tickles my side, causing me to squeal with laughter. I never knew I was so ticklish until we started dating. I kiss his cheek when he stops tickling me and snuggle back into his side.

"I like this," I murmur and sigh.

"I'm hoping you do."

I frown in confusion at his tone, but shrug it off and focus on the screen. The opening scene looks so familiar to me, and then the credits come up. I sit up.

The setting would look familiar. It's the beach house his family owns. We spent almost a week there with my family. My father and brothers got to know Kev, while my mother spoiled me with her cooking and kisses.

I read the words on TV and tears come to my eyes. *When a Man Loves a Woman* is written across the screen.

"How…? I watched you start this from the Nexflix menu," I choke out.

"Shane and Con," he says simply.

My lips begin to tremble as my family and his come on the screen. Each one telling me how they figured out Kevin loves me. Kasey and Molly are adorable as they do their part, but it's Con that takes the cake.

"I knew Uncle Kev loved you because he allowed you into our family. From that first day, he didn't take my head off for getting arrested because he couldn't take his eyes off you. That day, I thought he was more mad at you than me. Then I figured out that he was just batshi—"

"Con," Kevin growls somewhere off camera.

Con hold his hands up and laughs. "All right, all right. My uncle lost his noodle over you. That's not like him. So I know you're the real deal."

"I love that kid," I say and sniffle, wiping at my eyes.

Kevin is next to appear on screen, and he looks nervous as hell. I turn to look at him in real life, and he has pretty much the same look. He places a hand on my back and nods for me to focus back on the TV.

"Demaris. Love, I think I've been in love with you since the first time I laid eyes on you. Your smart mouth only sealed the deal for me. You told me to give you a push when I felt you needed one. Baby, this is me pushing. I don't want to spend another day not knowing you're going to be my wife. I want to fill our home with little adorable babes that are as smart and tenacious as you are. Dem, what I'm trying to say is…" Before he can say the words, they appear on the screen: *Will you marry me?*

I turn and stare at him. Kevin has always shown me so many sides of him. I know he can be romantic, but this has taken it to another level for me.

He puts the popcorn on the coffee table and shoves his hand into the cushions and pulls out a ring box. Opening it up, I see a brilliant ring winking back at me. It's a solitaire diamond, but boy is it jaw dropping.

I look into Kev's eyes. I'm sure I look bewildered. He hasn't really mentioned our future in the last few weeks.

And still, I know my answer. It's the look in his eyes that reminds me why I love him so much. There has never been a time when I have questioned his love. So, there is no question in what's about to come out of my mouth.

"Yes."

"Christ, were ya trying to kill me?" he mutters and pulls me into his embrace.

"Nope, was testing that patience of yours. You're going to need it."

We both laugh, and it's the best feeling in the world. For the first time in a very long time, I finally feel whole. He found me when I needed him the most. I can totally live a life with love this deep.

EPILOGUE

CELEBRATION

Danita

"You're glowing," Alicia says as she walks over to me, holding one of the twins.

"I've never been this happy," I say, looking around at all of our family. "Thanks for letting us share this all with you guys."

"Oh, please. I didn't see the point in wasting money on two engagement parties. I was more than happy to share."

"Still, you guys were engaged first."

"Dem, please." She waves me off. "Besides, I love your mom. I knew she would make this amazing."

I laugh. It's been so great having my parents back here in New York. We've all become one big happy family. Diego and Jo-jo are in New York more than they're at home. Well, Diego has practically moved back. He's waiting for his transfer to go through while he's on leave.

There isn't a weekend that you can't find a Blackhart with a Mercado. Papi loves Kevin. Jo-jo is warming up to the fact that I have a boyfriend. Wait until he finds out he's going to be an uncle.

I smile at that thought. We decided to start trying after we got engaged. I don't think either of us expected it to happen on what felt like the first try.

I'm happy. I look across the Golden Clover, over at the bar where Kevin stands with his brothers and mine. We lock eyes and my smile grows. Kevin bites his lip as his gaze roams over me.

"You guys are so cute." I turn back to Alicia.

"How are things going with you and Quinn? The boys must be a handful."

"I'm exha—" The blood drains from her face. "Oh my God."

Kevin

"Ya look like yer going to go over there and eat her." Quinn chuckles.

I turn to look at him holding his son. It looks good on him. The wee lad looks tiny in my brother's arms despite his whopping ten pounds. The boys aren't more than three months old, but they are bruisers.

"Look who's talking," I toss back at him. "Don't think I didn't see the two of yous sneak off when Mum took the wee ones from ya."

Quinn's cheeks turn red, but a brilliant smile comes to his face. "Aye, wait until ya have yer own. Ya will see what it's like. Ya'll take it whenever ya can get it."

"Hey, that's still my baby sister," Jo-jo grumbles.

Diego and Emil wince and shake their heads. I snort and try not to blurt out that I'm going to be a father. We said we'd wait a bit before telling everyone.

"I think Kev and Dem think we're all stuttles," Shane says with a smirk on his lips.

"Now why would we think ya foolish, little brother?"

"Because—"

"What the fuck?" Trent jumps up from the stool he was perched on at the bar.

I turn toward the entrance he's looking at. In comes a woman badly battered, she's dragging her left leg behind her. Her hair is 'ed to the blood on her face.

She parts her lips and a single word comes out. "Trent."

It takes me a few beats to recognize her through the swollen eye and busted lip. My heart squeezes as my brother rushes to her. The moment she's in his arms, she collapses as if she's made it to her destination and can finally rest.

I rush over to see if I can help, but not wanting to touch her for fear of causing more damage. Up close, she looks worse. Trent is trembling with rage.

"Shayla? Baby? Who the fuck did this to you?" Trent sobs.

She can't answer. Ms. Shayla, Molly's dance instructor, is unconscious as Trent gingerly lifts her broken body into his arms. I feel helpless as my little brother falls apart in front of my eyes.

"We'll find out who did this," Quinn says as he places a hand on Trenton's shoulder.

"Aye and when we do, I plan to batter them just the same, I will. Trying to hide from me will be biscuits to a bear, because I will find them and I will end them," Trent says with his accent as thick as Quinn's, his anger showing through indeed.

I don't doubt he means every word. Hiding from him will be a waste of time. This has now moved up all our list of priorities.

ACKNOWLEDGMENTS

Hey! Another one! I'm so happy to be done with this book because book three in the series has been screaming so loud, it's been hard to stay focused on completing this one. I promise you I almost stopped writing this book to start and finish book three first. It was that bad. LOL.

I hope you enjoy Kevin and Dem as much as I do. I think they are perfect for each other. He had to learn patience and she had to remember herself. Thank you for taking this journey with them.

Whether new to the world of Blue or old, I want to thank you for being here. If not for you, I'd just be a crazy woman talking to the characters in her head. Thank you for every email, comment, like, share, and post. I appreciate all the support and encouragement.

Thank you to my husband who's there to help me talk out plots and scenes when these books drive me crazy and I'm on the verge of a panic attack because the characters aren't doing what I need. You are my rock, and I wouldn't trade you for another. Team Blue.

A book will never end without me saying thank you, Lord, because it never starts without me calling on your strength, support, and guidance. These books wouldn't be possible without every step being ordered and every word being blessed. So thank you, Lord. All for your Glory.

So we are off to the next! Trenton, good grief. I can let you loose now. I hope you keep that same loud energy for your turn.

ABOUT THE AUTHOR

As a young girl, Blue's mother introduced her to the world of love and creativity through movies. Once she got her hands on books, an authoress was born. A story here, a few songs there, but she actually didn't complete a manuscript until 2009. Blue is now an award-winning, bestselling author of over forty contemporary romance novels and novellas.

The self-proclaimed hermit was born in Far Rockaway, New York, but is now a Long Island resident with her loving and supportive husband. The two work round the clock creating music and characters. There is no shortage of laughter or creativity in their home.

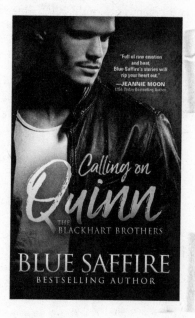